Discretion

usa today bestselling author

jenna hartley

to all the exes
who made us
realize we
deserved more

jenna hartley

CONTENT WARNINGS

This story contains explicit sexual content, profanity, and topics that may be sensitive to some readers.

For more detailed information, visit the QR code below.

NOTE FROM THE AUTHOR

Dear Reader,

Discretion touches on a parent who was diagnosed with Alzheimer's and the complicated decisions and emotions that come along with that. If a friend or loved one has experienced Alzheimer's or memory loss, sections of this book may be difficult to read. I did my best to handle these topics with care, in the hopes that others would feel less alone when navigating such a difficult situation themselves.

If that's a sensitive subject for you, please feel free to reach out for clarification. Or if you need to skip this story for your mental well-being, I totally understand.

With much love and hugs,
Jenna

CHAPTER ONE

JASPER

"You're just in time." Darla grinned, her distinctive Southern twang as prominent as ever. I didn't miss the twinkle in her eye either.

My former chief of staff might be pushing sixty, but her gray hair was the only indication. She was just as feisty as ever.

"Just in time for what?" I asked, wary.

I'd come over to take her out to dinner. To wine and dine her so she'd remember how much she'd loved working with me. And ultimately, to convince her to return to her job.

"Book Club Bitches. They've all been dying to meet you."

So much for wining and dining. But I wasn't easily deterred.

"Darla…" I let out an exaggerated sigh. "What did you tell them about me?" I was teasing.

"Enough." The corner of her mouth was turned up in a mischievous smile. She grabbed my arm and pulled me into her house. "They actually wanted to ask you a few questions."

Really? "About what?"

"You'll see," she said, vague as ever.

Intrigued, I let her guide me out to her back garden,

which was lush and overflowing. It reminded me of Gran's garden from my childhood. It made me miss both her and my brother, Graham, who now lived in France. They had a gift for creating the most magical outdoor spaces. So much so that sometimes it felt as if stepping into another world.

"How's it going with Sumner?" Darla asked.

"Great," I said. "Thanks again for recommending her. She's brilliant."

Darla grinned. "Good. I knew you two would hit it off."

Darla had been right, of course. Sumner was my life coach, and she'd been full of thoughtful advice. She'd helped me gain insight not only into the company but into myself. My motivations. My fears. My goals, especially as I'd transitioned into my new role as CEO.

"And here we are," Darla said as we approached a group of women. "Ladies, this is Jasper Mackenzie."

I felt as if they were sizing me up. Several of them were not at all subtle in checking me out, and I bit back a smile.

"Good evening, ladies," I said to the group.

Darla made the introductions, and I greeted each of them by name. Becky, Beth, and Mary.

"So nice to finally meet LA's *infamous* playboy billionaire, Jasper Mackenzie," Becky said in a cheeky tone as I shook her hand.

Infamous? What had Darla been telling them about me? And why did I get the feeling this was a trap?

"Let's just get this out of the way since I know everyone wants to ask." Darla turned to me. "Are you seeing anyone?"

Jeez. Talk about putting me on the spot. "I'm not sure that's an appropriate question for an employee to ask the boss," I teased, evading the question.

"Former boss," she corrected.

"You're right," I agreed, pretending to be chastened. But then I said, "Still not appropriate."

"When has Darla ever been appropriate?" one of the other women—Beth—asked with a laugh.

I chuckled and took a seat next to Becky. "With me? Never."

Becky patted my thigh. "I have a granddaughter I'd love to set you up with."

"Granddaughter?" I jerked my head back. "I'm sure she's way too young for me."

She gave me a playful swat. "Oh, you are a charmer, aren't you?"

I chuckled and leaned back in my chair. Darla handed me a glass of what looked like sangria, and I took a sip, eager for some liquid fortification. "Damn. This is smooth."

"Hibiscus sangria."

"Delicious." I savored the flavor, analyzing it. "I'd love the recipe for the café."

"Good luck with that," Mary muttered. She leaned over and held a hand up to her mouth. "Secret recipe, so she says."

I laughed. I couldn't remember the last time I'd felt so at ease. Ever since taking over as CEO four months ago for my family's luxury hotel business, my life had become one meeting after another—politics and posturing. But these women were funny and authentic. They didn't hold back. They told it exactly how it was.

"You didn't answer the question." Becky nudged me.

"A gentleman never tells."

"I was under the impression that label didn't apply to you," Mary said.

Their responses were a chorus of "ooh" and "burn." I chuckled, enjoying their good-natured ribbing.

"So why did you really lure me here today?" I asked.

"Well, we've been reading some billionaire romances..." Beth started.

I arched my brow. Billionaire romances? That was a thing?

"And we wanted to know how accurate they were."

"Okay." I was game for just about anything. "Sure."

"So, in this one book," Becky started, "the billionaire had a—"

"Sex club," Beth interrupted. "Do you own a sex club?"

I nearly choked on my sangria. "No. Jesus." I coughed a few more times.

"But you have a private plane."

"And a private helicopter," Darla chimed in.

I furrowed my brow. "What does my family's private plane have to do with a sex club?"

I could envision the horror on the board members' faces if I suggested such a thing. The amusement alone might be worth the mention.

"Nothing," Beth said, interrupting my runaway train of thoughts. "We're just trying to establish the profile of a real-life billionaire."

"So...since the fictional ones have sex clubs," I said, "you're wondering if that holds true in real life?"

"Maybe," Mary said. "Or if they frequent them."

Interesting. Okay. "Why, though? In my experience, women love the idea of dating a rich man. It's not hard to find a willing companion you don't have to pay."

Mary's eyes widened, and Becky laughed into her hand. Darla slapped me on the shoulder.

"What?" I shrugged, turning to her. "You know it's true. Don't tell me you've already forgotten the many women you had to turn away."

"Oh, I didn't forget," Darla sighed. "I merely tried to block it out."

It still wasn't as bad as some of the stuff my cousin Nate had dealt with over the years. Not only was he a billionaire like me, he was also a famous movie star. One time—before he'd met his wife, Emerson—he'd found his daughter's previous nanny naked in his bed.

Fortunately, I hadn't had to deal with finding naked employees in my bed. Well, apart from Halle anyway. But that had been consensual. Magical.

What I wouldn't give to have her in my bed, in my arms, again.

I didn't care that it was reckless. I missed her.

But things had changed a lot since last summer. Back then, I'd been working in London temporarily. Now, I was the head of the company, and since she was relocating to LA, we were going to be working together for the foreseeable future.

I was going to have to see her every day, work with her every day, and pretend nothing had happened. Pretend she hadn't turned my world upside down.

"Nor the parade of women you—"

"Okay. Okay." I held up my hands. "I never claimed to be a saint."

"Well, that tracks," Beth said, not pulling any punches.

"Tracks?" I asked.

"Oh, with a lot of the billionaire romances. Many of them are total manwhores."

"Manwhores." I chuckled, though it sounded hollow.

While I'd once been happy to be labeled as a playboy, it was a moniker I was finding difficult to shed. It didn't matter that I hadn't slept with anyone since Halle. It seemed that my past behavior—even if exaggerated—continued to follow me around.

"What's the most outrageous thing you've ever done for, or on, a date?" Mary asked, eyes gleaming with anticipation.

"Outrageous how?" I asked, arching one eyebrow. They'd already asked about sex clubs. Surely they weren't…

"Up to you," she said, and they all leaned in a little.

I considered it a moment. I'd taken dates on private helicopter rides. Invited them to stay in some of the most luxurious hotel suites in the world. And yet, none of that was what I mentioned.

"I prepared a picnic to share at St Dunstan in the East," I admitted.

"Oh." Mary turned to Beth. "It's this beautiful ruin in London. Very romantic."

I nodded. "That's right. I paid to rent it out so we could have it all to ourselves."

"You…what?" Mary gaped at me. "Seriously? I didn't even think that was possible."

It wasn't. Not really.

"That had to be expensive," Becky chimed in.

"Worth every penny," I said, and I meant it. Besides, the money had gone to a worthy cause.

"Are you sure about this?" Halle asked nervously. What she meant was, are you sure we should be seen together in public?

The driver had stopped at the curb, waiting for us to make up our minds. I had worked so hard to pull this off, to make it special for Halle. I'd never been more sure of anything in my life. But I didn't want her to feel pressured to do something she was uncomfortable with.

She was taking a risk with this fling, with me. If anyone found out…well, she definitely had more to lose. Keeping it secret was in both our best interests, but that didn't make it any easier. Not when I wanted to lavish her with attention. When I wanted to take her to the most amazing spots in the city—as my date, not as my colleague. And that wasn't something I'd wanted in a long time, maybe ever.

But I respected her boundaries. Hell, I knew they were necessary. But that didn't mean I liked them.

"Trust me," I said to Halle. It wasn't a question. It was more of a plea. I wanted her to know that I would take care of her and keep her safe.

She looked to the side, then down, biting back a smile.

"Is that a yes?" I asked.

She hesitated a moment longer, and I thought my heart might lunge out of my chest. Finally, finally, she whispered, "Yes."

"Good." I leaned over to give her a quick peck on the cheek. Then I opened the door and stepped out onto the curb, holding out my hand. She placed hers in mine, and then I led her to the entrance to the garden.

She didn't try to release my hand even now that we were out of the car, and I intended to hold on for as long as she'd let me. I guided her through the ancient archways, and she gasped as we crossed the threshold into the center of the old church. Candles lined the stone walkway, surrounding a picnic blanket where a basket awaited us.

"Jasper." She shook her head, lifting her hand to her mouth.
"Do you like it?" I asked, hating the desperation that crept into my tone. I'd never been so eager to impress a woman. I'd never wanted something more.

And with Halle, I definitely wanted more.

That was why I'd planned this evening. To show her that this wasn't just about sex—at least, not anymore. Not for me. I was falling for her—hard.

I'd thought falling for someone would scare the fuck out of me, but nothing had ever felt more right. I wanted Halle in my life, permanently. And I wasn't ready to say goodbye.

"It's beautiful." She spun slowly, taking it all in. The lanterns that hung from the majestic limbs of the tree. The plaid blanket artfully draped over the ledge where we'd share our meal. The sky up above, a cathedral full of stars.

"You must have really wanted to impress her," Darla said, interrupting the memory. "Who was that for?"

If I knew Darla, and I did, she was mentally cataloguing every interaction, calendar appointment, and detail from that time period. If I weren't careful, she'd put the pieces together.

Shit. I couldn't let her find out that it had been with Halle. She was my sister's chief of staff, for chrissakes.

I mimed zipping my lips shut. Darla narrowed her eyes at me.

"Did this mystery woman love it?" Beth asked, and I latched on to her question, grateful to have a pretext for ignoring Darla's question. "Did you make love beneath the stars?"

I chuckled. *These women.*

"Yes, she loved it. At least until her so—" I tried to regroup. I'd nearly slipped up and mentioned Halle's son, and now Darla and her friends were watching me even more closely. "Her—" I cut myself off again, trying not to mention

Kai. "She had a family emergency."

"So romantic." Beth pretended to swoon, but Darla was still staring at me. Hard.

No joke. It had been the perfect evening until Halle's ex had called. Kai had gotten a stomach bug, and he was throwing up and wanted his mom. I didn't doubt the fact that Kai had wanted his mom, but based on everything Halle had told me about her ex, I also suspected that Craig hadn't wanted to deal with a sick kid.

I gnashed my teeth at the reminder. Yes, I'd been disappointed that our already limited alone time together had been cut short. But I'd been concerned for Kai. And what was Craig thinking, demanding that Halle come pick up Kai? I got that Kai wanted his mom, but what kind of father didn't want to be there for his son?

More than anything, I'd hated the defeated look in Halle's eyes. The resignation. The fact that she'd tried to do something for herself, and it had backfired.

Darla sipped her sangria, her eyes on me the entire time. But it was Becky who spoke next. "Then what happened? Are you still together?"

I shook my head, glancing away. After that, Halle had pulled back from our fling, from me. Even once Kai had recovered, I'd sensed a coolness from her. A distance.

When I'd tried to bring up the idea of a future together, she'd shut me down. It had gutted me—her unwillingness to even discuss it. And then I'd returned to LA, and that had been the end of it. The end of us.

"That was it?" Beth frowned. "It just…ended?"

"It's complicated," I said, hoping they'd leave it at that. "And long-distance is not for the faint of heart." Though, soon, the distance would no longer be a factor.

It was a big reason why I was here—ready to beg Darla to come back if necessary. My life already felt out of control, and with Halle relocating to the LA office, I was going to need stability more than ever. Without Darla, I was adrift.

"Honey, if she's not interested, I am," Beth said.

I chuckled. "Thanks, Beth. I'll keep that in mind."

"No, seriously." Beth shook her head. "What's wrong with her? You're handsome, rich. And from everything Darla tells us, kind and considerate."

"Aw, Darla." I feigned embarrassment. Though, truly, I was blushing.

It wasn't often that people complimented me, let alone for something not related to wealth, family, or fame. When I wasn't lambasted for my bad decisions, I was lauded for things I had zero influence over. For most of my life, I'd been overlooked in favor of my siblings.

Graham was the perfect brother. In control and in charge. He'd been selected by my grandparents to run the family business. Sloan was the baby. The only girl. She could do no wrong.

Knox and Nate were technically my cousins, but they'd always been more like brothers to me. The five of us—Nate, Knox, Graham, Sloan, and I—had been raised by our grandparents after a plane crash had claimed the lives of my parents and my aunt and uncle.

Hell, sometimes I felt closer to Nate and Knox than my actual siblings. Though that was probably only because they weren't as involved in the day-to-day management of the family brand. Nate was busy with his production studio and acting. And Knox owned LA's pro soccer team, the Leatherbacks. As much as I loved Graham and Sloan, running the family luxury hotel empire could put a lot of pressure on our relationship at times.

But Darla had always seen the real me. Which was why I needed her now, more than ever.

"What's it really like to have all that money?" Mary asked,

and I was grateful for the reprieve from the topic of my love life. "Do you just…spend it on whatever you want? Go swimming in the cash like Scrooge McDuck?"

"This might disappoint you," I said, "but most of my assets are tied up in my family's business or investments. I don't go swimming in the cash, though that sounds like fun. And my grandparents taught me to be mindful of my spending. They believed that we had a responsibility to our employees and our communities to give back."

"That's why the CEO's salary is capped at the Huxley brand," Darla said.

"Exactly, but it goes beyond that. We offer some of the most generous paid leave and health insurance in the industry—to all our employees, regardless of where they work or the type of position they hold. And we are passionate about investing in local communities. We don't want to come in and take over. We want to learn from the locals. We want to respect their traditions and their culture. Their land and their priorities."

They all nodded, clearly impressed.

"What about your car collection?" Mary asked.

"Oh, Darla told you about that, huh?" I smirked. When she nodded, I said, "Did she also mention that I inherited most of them from my dad?"

They turned on Darla. "No. No, she didn't mention that," Becky muttered, narrowing her eyes at Darla.

Darla shrugged. "You wanted to believe the fantasy. Who was I to burst your cherry?"

I nearly spewed my drink. "I believe the saying you're looking for is burst your bubble."

She waved a hand through the air. "Same difference." She smirked, knowing damn well it was not the same thing.

"No." Mary wagged her finger at Darla. "We wanted the truth. And that's why we asked you to invite him."

"Invited?" I scoffed. "Feels more like I was lured here under false pretenses and then ambushed."

Mary looked horrified. Becky shot daggers at Darla. "You said you'd told him."

"I did," Darla responded. "When he got here."

The others sighed, and one or more of them said, "Typical Darla."

I nodded my agreement.

"Well, thank you for humoring us," Becky said.

"Absolutely." I lifted my glass to them before taking another sip. "Now, let me ask you ladies something. Your love of reading has inspired me." All evening, an idea had been percolating in my mind. A way to enhance the guest experience and provide an extra perk for our employees. "I'm thinking about creating a lending library for my employees and guests."

"Ooh. That would be amazing," Beth said. "Digital or print?"

"I think print. I like the nostalgia of it. A way to encourage guests to get off their devices, relax, and immerse themselves in the experience."

"Exactly," Becky said. "Would it be two separate libraries or the same one?"

"Probably two separate ones so employees could peruse the shelves on their break."

We discussed the logistics for a while, and then it was time for me to go. I stood, shaking each of their hands and thanking them for a memorable evening.

"Come back any time," Beth called out as Darla led me back down the path to her house. I smiled and winked at her over my shoulder.

"Thanks for coming," Darla said once we were alone. "And for being a good sport to answer their questions."

I chuckled. "Your friends are fun. So…" I nudged her. "I

actually came here to ask you something." I took a deep breath, bracing for the rejection I assumed was coming. But still, if I didn't ask, I wouldn't know. "No one compares to you, and I'm willing to be flexible on hours if you only want to come in part time. You can even keep your same salary."

"So you're going to pay me more to work less?" I saw an unmistakable twinkle in her eye. "That doesn't sound like a savvy business move, Mr. CEO."

Maybe not, but some things just made sense. And not all business decisions were based solely on money.

"I'm willing to do whatever it takes to get you to come back." I took her hand in mine and knelt to the floor, knowing Darla would appreciate a dramatic gesture. "Please say yes."

She paused, looking me dead in the eye. "Will you tell me who your mystery London girl was?"

My stomach dropped. I could never tell anyone about Halle. I would never betray her trust like that. Not even to Darla, the woman who knew almost all my secrets.

I stood slowly, releasing her hand to take a step back. "No."

"Then I'm not coming back," she deadpanned.

"Seriously, Darla?" When I realized she was joking—at least about her reasons for being unwilling to return—I added, "You're a pain in my ass."

"And you're a pain in mine." She hip bumped me.

We laughed. It was said out of love. But I really did need her. She kept my life on track, and now that I was CEO—now that Halle was moving to LA—I needed Darla's calming, assertive presence more than ever.

"How am I supposed to run the company without you?" I asked, feeling adrift. All the temps the agency had sent had been underwhelming, if not outright incompetent.

"I have faith in you," she said with the utmost sincerity. "You just need to have a little more faith in yourself."

"What if I was willing to tell you who London Girl was?" I was almost desperate enough to do it too.

She shook her head. "You're always welcome to tell me." Then she took my hand in hers and placed her other one on top. "Jasper. You know I love you, honey. But I gave that company thirty years of my life. I'll always be here for you, but it's time for my next chapter."

I wasn't above begging, but I sensed that nothing would persuade her to change her mind. It was unfortunate but not surprising.

She pulled me in for a hug. "Take care of yourself. And next time you come to Book Club Bitches, be sure to read the book first."

I scowled. "Maybe I would've if you'd given me a heads-up."

She shrugged. "I told your assistant."

I gnashed my teeth. I really needed to find someone new.

CHAPTER TWO

HALLE

"So...don't hate me," Zara said, unwilling to meet my eyes.

As if I could ever hate her. Zara was my best friend.

"What'd you do now?" I teased.

Zara and I had spent the day visiting all our favorite haunts. It had been fun but bittersweet. After a decade of living in London, I felt more at home in this city than the small town in Oregon where I'd grown up. And while I'd miss everything from the accents to the architecture, I was going to miss Zara the most.

She sipped her sparkling rosé from her perch on my bed. Kai was spending the weekend with his dad, Craig, before we moved to the States. Part of me still couldn't believe Craig had agreed.

I'd been in overdrive the past few weeks, trying to wrap up things at the London office for my boss, Sloan. Coordinating her move as well as preparing for my own. Obsessing over what to take and how my five-year-old son was going to adjust to me uprooting our life.

Kai seemed to alternate between excitement and apprehension, as did I. But I also wondered if I was making a huge mistake. It was exhausting.

"I set up a profile for you on a new dating app," Zara said in a rush.

The dress I'd been holding slipped from the hanger, and I gaped at her. "You did what?"

"You need to get back out there," she continued. "You're hot and young—"

"Pfft. Right." I wasn't sure either description fit me anymore. I was in my late thirties. I was a single mom. I was tired. And it showed.

Besides, I wasn't interested in dating. Even if I had the time or the desire to date—which I didn't. I was done letting a man have any say in my life.

I hadn't gotten divorced only to shackle myself to someone new.

Zara glared at me. "You *are*. You're a knockout. All you need is a good night's sleep. Slap on some concealer and wear your hair down for once, and you'll see that I'm right."

"I appreciate that," I said, and part of me knew she was right. A lot of what I was feeling was anxiety and exhaustion. "But get real, Zar. I'm a single mom who's going to be living in a new city. Not to mention that I'll be crazy busy at work. And helping my parents." My dad had been diagnosed with Alzheimer's last summer, and my mom had been dragging her feet about moving him into a care facility.

I knew a big part of it was money. Alzheimer's care was hella expensive. But I also understood that a lot of her resistance was emotional. She didn't want to have to make that decision for him. She didn't want to live apart—him at a facility and her at their home.

I'd been so relieved when Sloan had asked me to relocate to LA with her. I felt so far away in London. Too far away. My parents were just a few hours' flight from LA. I was looking forward to visiting them more often because our weekly video chats were no longer enough.

"I know," Zara said in a gentle tone. "I know you'll be busy, and you have a lot on your plate. But you're the one who said you wanted to go to LA, not just to be closer to your parents but because you needed a change. You'll be in a new city, and LA is the perfect place to meet someone."

"I get that you own a luxury matchmaking business—"

"A very *successful* luxury matchmaking business," she added with a grin.

"Yes. And I know you just want everyone to be happy and fall in love. But you know I'm not interested."

"In marriage, maybe. Which is why I haven't tried matching you with anyone—" I gave her a look, so she added, "Lately." Her expression might be contrite, but I wasn't buying it. "I have not tried matching you lately. And hey, maybe you're not ready for a relationship, but what about sex?"

"What about it?"

"I hear a good shag can do wonders for stress relief. You've been divorced for almost two years. When's the last time you were well and truly fucked?"

"Not as long ago as you'd think," I muttered.

"Wait. What?" She climbed onto her knees. "*Who?* And please tell me it was not Craig."

"Seriously?" I rolled my eyes. "Give me a little credit, Zar."

"You're right. Sorry. I know you wouldn't get back together with him. I think…" She got up and took my hand in hers with a sigh. "I think that's just my biggest fear."

"I know." I nodded.

And I understood. I did. Before the divorce was finalized, Craig had tried to convince me to give him another shot. And for a brief moment, I'd been tempted to give him that second chance. Mostly for Kai's sake. For the guilt I felt

—the guilt Craig had made me feel—for breaking up our family.

"Yeah. That's never happening." I scoffed, annoyed that Craig had nearly manipulated me yet again. But I was smarter now. Stronger.

I was also happier without Craig. And I had faith that Kai would be okay too. Craig and I might not be in love with each other, but that didn't mean I loved our son any less.

"So…I'm forgiven?" She batted her eyes at me.

Was she kidding? Zara was the one friend who had been there for me. Who had stood by me through the divorce when all my other so-called friends had deserted me.

And she kept showing up for me. Just like I did for her.

"Of course you are."

"So who was it, then?" she asked.

"It doesn't matter. It was…inappropriate." That was putting it mildly. Unprofessional. Unethical. *Wrong.* It was wrong.

"Inappropriate?" She arched an eyebrow. "Now I'm even more intrigued."

Should I tell her?

No. I shouldn't tell her.

Should I?

I trusted Zara not to tell anyone. Honestly, I'd thought about telling her so many times already that I found myself whispering, "Jasper," before I could stop myself.

I tried to suppress the way my body responded to the sound of his name alone. It had been easy to ignore those feelings when we were separated by an ocean. I wasn't sure how I was going to react when he was sitting across a boardroom.

Her eyes widened. "Jasper *Jasper*? As in Jasper Mackenzie, one of the world's most eligible billionaire bachelors and your boss? That Jasper?"

My cheeks heated at the reminder of Jasper and all the reasons I shouldn't have slept with him. Still, I felt compelled to defend myself. "He's not *my* boss. He's my boss's brother. And anyway, it was a one-time thing."

I snapped my mouth shut to stop my continued rambling. Okay, so maybe we'd had sex more than once. But it had been confined to that *one* summer. And that's how it would stay. Zara didn't need to know that. Eight months had passed since, and it was done. Over.

Too bad the thought of ending things with Jasper didn't make me any happier now than it had then. But such was life.

"Mm." Zara crossed her arms over her chest, grinning. "Naughty. Naughty. Does this mean we're finally entering your 'fuck it' era? How delicious." Her eyes gleamed with mischief.

"It was not delicious. It was bad." *I'm bad. I'm a terrible person.* I covered my face with my hands and groaned.

"The sex? Sex with Jasper was bad?" She sounded offended by the mere suggestion.

"No. No." I sighed, lowering my hands. "The fact that I slept with him is bad."

"So the sex was good," she said, leaning forward with a wicked grin. It wasn't a question. Not really.

"Very good." My cheeks heated. Amazing. Out of this world. Even now, all these months later, I still found myself daydreaming about it.

She arched her brow. "Good to know the rumors about him are true."

Ugh. I hated any reminder that I was yet another notch on his bedpost.

"Oh, don't look so disgusted," Zara said. "Anyone would understand why you did it. Even if he weren't rich, the man is hot. No one would blame you for sleeping with him, especially after all the shit Craig put you through."

"Not sure Sloan would be too pleased, let alone the Huxley brand. I could lose my job." My chest tightened. It was the first time I'd admitted that aloud, and it seemed much more real now.

"Do you think that would happen?" she asked. "Because I think Jasper would be in more trouble than you."

I'd spent a lot of time actively trying *not* to think about it. Because when I did…it wasn't good.

It was bad enough that I'd slept with my boss's brother. One of the owners of the family business. Jasper was now head of the entire company. And soon, I'd be working in the same city, the same office, as him.

I wondered how Jasper was adjusting to his new position. I tried to picture it and failed. Jasper was charming, yes. Detail-oriented. But I'd never gotten the impression that he wanted to run the company. He may have butted heads with Graham on occasion in the past, but he'd always seemed content to play a supporting role.

Zara was quiet for a few moments, helping me fold. I hoped that was the end of it, but I sensed it wasn't.

"Well, you certainly have a type," she finally said.

I turned to her and frowned. "I do *not* have a type."

"Oh, come on," she said. "Wealthy. Charismatic. Emotionally unavailable."

That wasn't true. Was it?

Yes, Jasper was wealthy. Much, *much* wealthier than my ex. Charismatic. Yes. But emotionally unavailable?

If anyone was emotionally unavailable, it was me.

Jasper was the one who'd wanted to continue our relationship, and I was the one who'd pumped the brakes. Even though it had been a few years since my divorce, I wasn't ready to jump into another serious relationship. Let alone a long-distance one with potentially explosive consequences.

And I'd been right to put a stop to things before they

could get serious. We both knew what would happen—long-distance was meant to fail. And clearly, he wasn't willing to put in the effort. I might have ended things, but he'd let me go.

"So maybe the dating app is a good idea after all?" Zara nudged me. "You could do some research for me *and* find yourself someone nice and…uncomplicated."

"Uncomplicated." I laughed. "Right." That was putting it mildly. I'd slept with my boss's brother.

I told myself it was a lapse in judgment. I'd been going through a tough time. But who was I kidding? No amount of justification or mental gymnastics would change the fact that I'd fucked my boss's brother. And I'd fucked up.

But that was in the past. And it wasn't going to happen again.

It *couldn't* happen again.

"Just…" She lifted a shoulder. "Promise you'll keep an open mind. Everything's already set up. I even weeded out some of the guys."

I knew Zara meant well, but I didn't have the time or energy to date or hook up or whatever. I was moving to a new city, trying to build a new life, as I took on a new role at my company. I had enough *new*, enough changes going on right now, I didn't need to add to them.

"Zara," I chided. I mean, seriously? I knew she did this for her job, so it wasn't a big deal to her but… "You have to stop meddling."

Her gaze was piercing. "I'll stop meddling once you're happy."

"I *am* happy."

She gave me a look full of skepticism. I wanted to protest, but I wasn't sure I could honestly admit to being happy.

I was…content.

I had a well-paying job I enjoyed. I had a great relationship with my boss and felt like a valued part of a team. I had Zara and my parents. And Kai was the light of my life. I had the sweetest, cutest kid on the planet. Not that I was biased.

"And I don't need a man to be happy," I added. I had plenty of toys to keep me feeling good.

"You're right," she agreed. "You don't. And I know what you're going to say. That you're not ready to get back out there." I opened my mouth to protest, but she cut me off. "But clearly you are, considering—" she waggled her eyebrows "—what you did with Jasper."

"That was a mistake," I said, having to force out the word even though I knew it was true. "*Clearly*. And even if I were ready, I don't want to do anything that might cause even more disruption to Kai's life. I'm already moving him away from the only home he's ever known. Away from Craig."

I only hoped the move to LA would help with Kai's stomach issues. Over the past year or so, his pediatrician had shrugged off his frequent nausea and vomiting as a by-product of being a kid in day care. But I wasn't convinced, even if Craig thought I was overreacting.

Zara scoffed. "Not sure that will be much of a loss, considering the fact that you already do the lion's share of the parenting." She gave me a meaningful look.

She knew how aggravated I often got with my ex; hell, she was often just as frustrated on my behalf. Even before the divorce, Craig's attempts at co-parenting had often felt half-hearted. Sure, he gave Kai expensive gifts. But Craig wasn't there when it mattered. He never took care of Kai when he was sick, rarely attended his school events. And when Craig had, it often felt like an attempt to appease—or, worse still, manipulate—me.

I didn't want to discourage Kai's relationship with his dad, but I was sick of doing all the heavy lifting while Craig got to have all the fun. I was sick of rearranging my schedule last minute when Craig inevitably had something come up at work. I had a demanding, full-time job too. I hated having to comfort a disappointed Kai when his dad broke yet another promise.

Perhaps our new arrangement would be better than our current one. At least in the day-to-day aspects, not much would change. And maybe when Kai did visit his dad for two weeks over the summer and one week over the winter holidays, Craig would actually be more present. I only hoped that as Kai got older, Craig would make more of an effort. But that was likely wishful thinking.

"You're right," I said.

"I am?" Zara perked up.

"About Craig."

And if there was one thing I'd taken away from my marriage to Craig, it was that all the pretty words and expensive gifts would never make up for a partner who wasn't present. Or for a man who belittled me and my ideas, even if he'd done it so subtly that I'd questioned it and myself for years. No. I was better off on my own.

I grabbed a few more items from the closet, selecting a few dresses for the office. Some casual clothes for the weekends. Yoga pants. When I turned to drop them on the bed, Zara held out my phone.

"I never should've given you my passcode." I reached out to take the phone from her, but she tugged my hand, pulling me down onto the bed with her. "Hey!" I laughed from my position on my stomach.

"Look at these guys. Just look!" She held the screen in front of my face. "He's fit." She swiped. "And he's fit." She swiped again. "And he's fit as fuck. Mm."

"Yes, yes, I get it." I propped myself up on my elbow. "They're all hot. And half those pictures are probably fake. I mean, look at that one." I zoomed in on the photo. "That's totally AI."

"Fake or not, they're all interested in you."

I scoffed. "Um. Right."

"I'm serious, Halle. All three of them—and several others who don't count—messaged me. I mean, you. And they're interested in meeting up."

"Meeting up or hooking up?" I asked, still unconvinced.

"Does it matter?"

"I thought you wanted me to find happiness."

"Well, a few orgasms won't make you *un*happy." She shrugged.

I tossed a pillow at her, laughing the entire time. "You're terrible."

"Terribly awesome." She tossed it back at me.

"That too." I hugged the pillow to my chest.

"Is this because of Jasper?"

I handed her another dress and took a long sip of my rosé. "Jasper has probably moved on by now."

According to Sloan, Jasper had always been a bit of a player. But I didn't need my boss to tell me that. I'd seen the gossip blogs, the society papers. Jasper was almost always pictured with a different woman on his arm.

Zara arched her brow, probably trying to determine whether the idea of Jasper with someone else bothered me. It didn't. Or, at least, it *shouldn't*.

It doesn't, I told myself firmly, willing it to be true.

CHAPTER THREE

JASPER

I drummed my fingers on the conference room table, anxious energy coursing through me as I waited for everyone else to arrive for the board meeting. Today was Halle's first day in the LA office, and I was simultaneously eager to see her again and filled with dread.

"How's it going?" Nate asked, clapping a hand on my shoulder.

I jolted from the unexpected contact, my heart jump-starting once more. "Fine. You?"

"Good. You looked lost in thought."

I chuckled, returning my attention to my laptop. "Just thinking about Pops's favorite quote."

Nate started to recite it before I could. "True hospitality consists of giving the best of yourself to your guests."

He'd mimicked Pops's voice so well that if I'd closed my eyes, I could've imagined he was standing before me. It filled me with an ache so powerful, I almost couldn't breathe. Pops had repeated the line so often it had become ingrained in me.

"Eleanor Roosevelt."

Before I could dwell on my grief, Nate leaned into my

shoulder, keeping his voice low. "Remember that night we thought it would be a good idea to incorporate it into a drinking game?"

"How could I forget?" I chuckled.

Years ago, Nate and I had gotten wasted at the gala. Whenever Pops or Graham had repeated certain words or lines, we'd taken a drink. We'd ended up consuming a lot of alcohol.

Talking about that night was a good distraction, because every time someone new entered the conference room, I felt as if I might jump out of my skin.

He laughed. "Not sure we'll be trying that again soon."

Or ever. Especially not now that I was the CEO.

Several people filed into the room, including the board chair, Leith. I closed my laptop, spotting Knox at the back of the group. Knox and Nate had always been aware of what was going on with the company, but they'd made more of an effort to attend board meetings since Graham's departure. I knew they wanted to be there for me, to show a united front in the face of such a big change. I appreciated it more than they could know.

I often wondered how things would've turned out if Knox had been the one left in charge. When my grandparents named a successor, Knox hadn't been interested in taking over, and Nate's acting career had been taking off. At the time, Sloan had been too young, and I was too immature. Not that my grandparents had said that, but it was how I'd always felt.

Now, I was the CEO, and sometimes it felt like I'd gotten the position by default. I knew that wasn't entirely true, and those feelings of inadequacy were something I was working on with my life coach, Sumner. Still, the idea lingered.

I greeted the newcomers, standing when Knox joined us.

"Jasper." Knox gave me a hug. "You're coming to poker on Friday, right?"

"Wouldn't miss it," I said, taking my seat once more, now flanked by Nate and Knox.

"Good. Did you see Lily's new video?" Knox asked, resting his ankle on his knee.

I shook my head, wondering what shenanigans Lily had talked my brother into this time. Since Graham had stepped down as CEO, he'd moved to France to be with her. Together, they were developing a new line of historic properties for a new subsidiary of the Huxley brand, as well as restoring their personal French château.

Before they'd ever married, Lily had shared some of their adventures on her YouStream channel. I never would've imagined that Graham would've allowed her to post footage of him doing everything from walking out of the fog as it filtered through the trees to feeding a baby goat from a bottle while shirtless. My brooding older brother had officially become a thirst trap.

"Trust me," Nate said, his voice fading into the background as I caught sight of Halle through the large glass wall facing the hallway. "You don't want to miss it."

Sloan's head was bent in conversation with Halle as they approached. Everything in me focused on Halle. The sound of her voice. The click of her heels against the floor.

My heart thudded in my chest, feeling as if it might escape from the confines of my rib cage. I hadn't seen Halle since last summer. Now she was here. In my hometown. On my turf.

And damn did she look good.

Her red curls were swept back into a low bun. *Such a shame.* Her hair was one of my favorite things about her, though, in all fairness, almost everything about her was my favorite. And not just her physical appearance.

She was smart, and she saw things that other people didn't see. She was passionate about the company—our mission, our employees, our properties. A good friend to my sister. An amazing mom who adored her son.

I continued scanning Halle, drinking her in greedily. A few tendrils hung down over her cheeks, the color only high-lighting her freckles. And her lips... Those bee-stung lips were painted a warm orangey-red that matched the color of her blouse.

I moved to stand, my thigh banging into the table. *Ow. Shit.*

My eyes collided with Halle's, the effect of seeing her slamming into me. The table shook, the glasses on top rattling from the effect. Everyone's attention turned to me, and I realized I'd spoken the words aloud. *Jesus.*

My cheeks heated, but I tried not to let my embarrass-ment show. I was the fucking CEO, for crying out loud, not a boy who didn't even know how to talk to a girl he had a crush on.

But damn was Halle something. And she made me feel like a teenager again. Awkward. Tongue-tied. Desperate to make the pretty girl laugh.

Nate touched my arm, and I jerked my attention to him. One eyebrow was quirked as he assessed me. "You good?"

I nodded. "Yep. Yeah. All good."

"Everyone," Sloan said to the room, and I was grateful when they turned their attention to her. "I'd like to intro-duce Halle Lovejoy. Many of you have probably already interacted with her by email. But she's my chief of staff, and she just moved here from London, so please make her feel welcome."

Fuck. Halle was just as beautiful as I remembered, perhaps even more so. Dark, soulful eyes that saw right through me. Not that she was looking at me. If anything, she seemed to be doing her best to avoid looking directly at me. Or maybe I was imagining it.

That was fine—for now. It gave me an opportunity to observe Halle while Sloan introduced her to everyone. Halle smiled, but it seemed reserved. Almost cool.

Maybe she's nervous?

Halle's blouse nipped in at the waist, tucked into a camel-colored pencil skirt that flared over her luscious hips and ass. It ended just above the knee, and my eyes trailed down her bare legs—legs that had been wrapped around my head. My perusal finally ended at her shoes. And my mind immediately conjured a detailed image of her in nothing but those heels. My cock twitched in delight.

Fuuuuuck.

"Jasper," Sloan said, and her tone made it seem as if it wasn't the first time she'd said my name.

"Mm." I jerked my attention to her.

She inclined her head toward Halle. "Don't be shy."

I tried not to laugh. I was definitely not shy, especially not when it came to the woman standing before me. But I wasn't sure where Halle and I stood, and I was trying to be professional, when my thoughts were anything but.

"Yes. Of course." I stepped forward, smiling as I offered Halle my hand when all I really wanted to do was pull her in for a hug. *I am so fucked.* "Halle. It's good to see you." And I meant it.

She placed her hand in mine, a jolt of electricity shooting up my arm. I could smell her signature scent—roses and something warm and grounding, almost like sunshine. *Maybe ylang-ylang?* I wondered, thinking back to all the scent profiles I'd tested when trying to develop the Huxley Grand signature candle line. The tropical flower had always been one of my favorites.

What was probably only seconds felt like a lifetime, but I

relived so many memories in that moment. Emotions flitting through me like photos in an album. Happiness. Passion. Regret. Longing.

I'd missed her. God, how I'd missed her. Her smart mouth. The way she looked at me.

Well, not how she was looking at me now.

Right now, she was looking at me with something akin to disinterest bordering on disdain. I released her hand, remembering we weren't alone. Hoping I hadn't done anything to arouse suspicion. We'd kept our relationship a secret for this long, and I wasn't going to blow it now.

What would be the point anyway? I clenched my fists at my sides.

We were done. It was over.

She'd made that clear before, and she was making it abundantly clear now. And the fact that she could stand there and face me with no reaction whatsoever merely confirmed it. I inhaled slowly and tried to let it out calmly.

All these months of wondering if she ever thought of me. If she missed me. Still wanted me.

Ha! Clearly, I was the only one still hung up on her.

I turned and headed for my seat, suddenly desperate to be done with this meeting. I couldn't completely avoid Halle, but I could sure as shit use my own chief of staff to run interference so as to minimize our interactions.

I sighed, remembering that I had no chief of staff and my current assistant was a temp who wasn't particularly adept at her job. If only I'd been able to convince Darla to return.

Graham joined us via video, and the meeting began. I tried to pay attention. I did. But throughout the meeting, my eyes kept straying to Halle.

She was killing me. *It* was killing me—knowing that she was so close, and yet I'd never felt the distance between us so keenly.

Before our fling, we'd been friends or at least on friendly terms. And every year when I'd gone to London so Sloan could take her annual sailing trip, Halle and I had worked together without incident. But last summer, everything had changed.

Halle gripped my tie, wrapping it around her wrist and tugging me forward until my lips met hers. Her kiss was passionate and needy. And fuck...I was right there with her.

Right. Fucking. There.

She hastily unbuttoned my shirt, her lips swollen. Hair mussed. "Why do you have on so many clothes?"

"Why do you?" I smirked, tugging at the zipper on the back of her dress.

I stripped off my suit jacket and tie, desperate to give her exactly what she wanted. But I also wanted to take things slow. To savor her and what little time we had left together.

It wasn't enough. I wasn't sure it would ever be enough. I was in over my head.

She finished with the buttons on my shirt and shoved the material down over my shoulders. I yanked it off and tossed it aside, not caring where it landed. And then I helped her out of her dress.

Fuck me. She was gorgeous. Standing there waiting for me in that sheer bra, her nipples poking through the material. Matching black thong and sky-high black heels.

She moved to kick off her shoes, but I shook my head. "Leave them on."

NATE CLEARED HIS THROAT, AND I JERKED MY ATTENTION AWAY from Halle, feeling as if I'd been caught. Everyone was looking at me expectantly, including Leith.

Shit. Had he asked a question while I wasn't paying attention? And if so, what was it?

Nate leaned in and murmured, "Keyless entry."

Right. The new technology.

I was going to have to figure something out because this couldn't happen again. I couldn't allow myself to be so distracted by Halle that everything else became background noise.

I responded to Leith's question and didn't look at Halle again for the rest of the meeting unless she was speaking. Because when she did speak, it was impossible to look away. She was confident and persuasive, and the rest of the board seemed equally captivated.

When the meeting wrapped up, I closed my laptop and stood.

"Ready?" Nate asked, watching me in a way that was unnerving.

My siblings and I always tried to have lunch together after our board meetings. Since our schedules were so hectic, it was an easy time to schedule something. Out of the corner of my eye, I saw Halle typing on her laptop.

"Give me a sec to finish up a few things, and then I'll meet you there."

"Sounds good." Nate patted me on the back.

Everyone else filed out, leaving me alone with Halle. When she looked up from her laptop, I glanced away, trying to hide the fact that I'd been staring, studying her as I searched for a clue to her thoughts.

She tilted her head. Why did she have to be so goddamn beguiling? "Is this going to be a problem?"

"What?"

She gave me a meaningful look as if to say, "Oh, come on."

"Us working together?" I asked, wanting to make sure there was no miscommunication.

She nodded, her eyes tracking someone as they walked past the glass windows of the conference room. Everything about her was so buttoned-up; there was no way anyone watching would guess at the true topic of our conversation.

I supposed I should be thankful.

I wasn't.

I tucked my hands into my pockets, debating my response while telling my body to ignore its reaction to her. "Why? Is it a problem for you?"

I really hoped it wasn't, but I didn't know where we stood after all this time. Did she hate me for what we'd done? Regret it? Wish for a repeat like I did?

I doubted it.

It had been nearly eight months since our fling, and we hadn't spoken since. At least not about anything meaningful, not about anything other than work.

Before I'd left London, I'd tried to talk to her about our future, but she'd shut me down. I'd tried to tell myself it was because she wasn't interested in a long-distance relationship. But now, I wasn't sure if distance had been our biggest obstacle.

"I don't want it to be." Her words were heavy with meaning, her eyes practically begging me not to create an issue.

"Then it won't." I forced out the words. "We're both professionals, right?"

She closed her laptop and stood. "Right." I wasn't sure if the skepticism I heard in her voice was imagined or real.

"So we'll just…" I stepped closer, drawn to her as if tugged by some invisible force. "Keep it professional."

"Exactly," she said in a chipper voice. "Professional."

"But friendly," I added. After all, we'd been friends and colleagues before we'd become lovers.

"Professional," she said again, this time more firmly.

I held up my hands. "Of course. We'll be nothing but professional in all our interactions." *God. Stop saying professional!*

I'd known Halle for years, and it had never been so fucking awkward. I hated it.

While I didn't want to erase last summer together, I would if it meant that I could still have her in my life in a meaningful way.

She gathered up her things and tucked her laptop beneath her arm. "Great. I'm glad we got that cleared up." Her tone was dry and impersonal.

"Me too," I said, wondering if I sounded as miserable as I felt. "How's Kai?"

I'd never met her son, but I'd heard so many stories and seen so many pictures that I felt as if I knew him.

Halle smiled, her shoulders relaxing. She seemed lighter for the first time all afternoon. "Good."

"Jasper," Sloan called down the hall. "You coming?"

Shit. I turned to face her, feeling as if I'd been caught doing something I shouldn't.

You were just talking. You weren't doing anything wrong, I reminded myself. But if that was the case, then why did I feel so guilty?

"Right. Yes. Coming," I said to my sister before turning back to Halle. But she had already turned and was walking in the opposite direction.

With a heavy sigh, I strode down the hall toward Sloan,

clenching and unclenching my fists. It was almost as if Halle couldn't get away from me fast enough.

I jabbed the button for the elevator, feeling unhinged. "Is Jackson joining us?"

Sloan shook her head, her attention on her phone. "He has a meeting."

The elevator chimed, and I held the door open for her. Once we were inside, Sloan sagged against the wall, placing her hands on her stomach. It looked like she was carrying a basketball around in there.

"You okay?" I asked, trying not to let my panic show.

I'd read up on pregnancy so I could be a supportive brother, and it had been…enlightening. But I wasn't a doctor, and so much of what was happening with Sloan felt out of my control.

After her health scare in France, I felt as if I was always on high alert. I didn't know how Jackson did it. How he coped with the anxiety.

"Just tired. The third trimester of pregnancy is no joke."

I could only imagine. "Maybe you should get a prenatal massage from the spa," I suggested.

"Ooh. That sounds heavenly. Maybe I will." She leaned her head back against the wall with a heavy sigh. "I'm just so relieved that Halle agreed to relocate."

"I bet." I kept my eyes on the mirrored glass doors in front of me, trying to maintain a neutral expression.

I was still getting used to the fact that Sloan was here. Not for a visit or a longer stay, but permanently. We hadn't lived in the same city since before she'd gone off to college. Growing up, we'd always been close, and it was nice to have her home. Especially now that she was going to be having a baby.

"I couldn't do this without Halle. She's taken care of

everything," Sloan said. "She keeps my life running smoothly."

Sloan's comments were a reminder of why Halle and I needed to maintain a good working relationship—nothing more. My sister relied on her. Trusted her.

"Have you talked to her yet about the SVP role?"

Sloan had suggested that we temporarily promote Halle while she was out on maternity leave. I'd agreed because I knew it was the right thing for the company and for Halle, even if it would be torture for me. The board had already given its approval.

"Not yet, but soon. How's it going with your new assistant?" Sloan asked.

"Not great," I grumbled. "I'm finding it incredibly difficult to replace Darla."

"I can imagine. Halle's been with me for five years, and I rely on her so much. Darla was with the company for thirty."

And she'd been my chief of staff for the past decade. Not only was I trying to find my footing as the CEO, but I was trying to find my groove without a chief of staff.

"I'm surprised Halle decided to relocate," I said, attempting to keep my tone neutral.

"Me too. She might have loved London even more than I do, but I suppose this opportunity came at a good time."

"How so?" I hedged, hoping I didn't sound too eager.

"Between you and me, her dad was diagnosed with Alzheimer's last summer."

Last summer. Last. Summer. Before or after we'd had our fling? *Fuck.*

"I'm sorry to hear that," I said, hoping my tone didn't betray my anguish.

"We're lucky we never had to deal with that," Sloan said, and I nodded.

Our grandparents had still been very independent up

until their deaths. And it had all happened swiftly. That didn't necessarily make their loss easier, but in a way, knowing that they'd maintained their quality of life until the end was a blessing.

"It's been hard on her, as you can probably imagine," Sloan continued.

"She's an only child, and she's always been close to her dad," I mused, wondering how Halle was coping.

Sloan furrowed her brow. "Yeah." She paused. "How did you—"

"You mentioned it in the past," I added quickly, hoping my sister wouldn't dwell on it.

Sloan gave me a curious look, but I ignored it, grateful that the elevator doors had just opened. Sloan hadn't told me about Halle's relationship with her parents; Halle had.

Be professional, I reminded myself.

CHAPTER FOUR

HALLE

My phone chimed from my nightstand, and I fumbled around for it, eager to hit snooze. I squinted at the screen, the bright light harsh in the dark room. It was five in the morning. A text from Zara had awoken me, not my alarm.

I sighed and flopped back onto the bed, knowing I wouldn't be able to fall back asleep. Not when I had to be up in an hour anyway. I might as well take advantage of this window to chat with my best friend, even if I was still half asleep.

It was… I squeezed my eyes shut and calculated the time difference. It was one in the afternoon in London. I supposed I should be grateful she hadn't texted even earlier.

Zara: How was your first day?

I YAWNED AND TAPPED OUT A REPLY.

Me: Busy. Exhausting.

Zara: I'll bet.

Zara: How did it go with Jasper?

I HUFFED AND STARTED TYPING.

Jasper is even hotter than I remember.

Erased it.

Jasper... I blew a raspberry.

I don't trust myself to be alone with him.

Definitely not sending that one.

I deleted it as well, finally settling on something basic, even though I knew it would infuriate her. Maybe *because* I knew it would drive her crazy.

Meh. I considered it payback for creating a profile on a dating app without asking.

Me: Fine.

Zara: Oh, come on, Halle! You know how much I hate that word.

I SMIRKED AND ROLLED ONTO MY SIDE, TUCKING A PILLOW beneath me.

Me: It was…interesting.

Zara: God, I wish I could call right now. I'm really struggling to read your tone through the screen.

Me: Honestly, it was fine. We agreed to keep things professional.

Zara: And you honestly think you'll be able to do that?

Me: I don't have another choice.

Zara: Even so…

Me: Nope. That's the way it has to be.

Me: Today, Sloan and I are meeting with an art dealer to select some pieces for the newly renovated VIP suites.

Zara: Nice attempt to change the subject. I'll allow it for now, but we're not done talking about Jasper.

Zara: Also, that's amazing, Halle. I bet you're excited.

EXCITED WAS AN UNDERSTATEMENT. I WAS ECSTATIC.

I loved working at the Huxley Grand, but art was my passion. I had a degree in art and art history, and I'd curated for a gallery before having Kai.

Me: For sure. I have a huge budget, and Dimitri's collection is a dream come true.

Zara: Is he single?

I ROLLED MY EYES, THOUGH I WAS LAUGHING AS I DID.

Me: Why? Are you thinking of opening an LA office?

Zara: Sure. You can be my first client.

Me: Ha. Ha.

Zara: I've gotta get back to work. Chat later?

Me: Sounds good.

I PUSHED OUT OF BED AND STRETCHED BEFORE HOPPING IN THE shower. I spent longer than I should've in my closet, selecting what to wear. Finally, annoyed with myself and the mess I'd made, I tossed a hanger to the floor with a huff.

Professional. That was what I'd told Jasper, and that was exactly how I planned to keep things between us. So then, why was I agonizing over what to wear?

Enough. I yanked on the first thing I saw. It didn't matter what I wore; nothing would change the fact that he was completely off-limits.

Too bad he was just as handsome and charming as I remembered. It had been physically painful to sit across the table from him in yesterday's board meeting. To know what it felt like to be in his arms, to have his full attention focused on me.

And now…to know it could never happen again. To try to

smother the insane attraction I felt toward him and act like we were colleagues and nothing more.

We weren't more. We'd never been *more*. But for a brief time, I'd felt like the center of his universe.

I sighed and went to wake Kai. It was only my second day, and I was already running late.

I grabbed his favorite stuffed animal, an axolotl named Figgy.

"Morning, Kai!" I said in a high-pitched voice that Kai always found funny.

He grumbled and turned so he was facing away from me.

I had Figgy pounce up his arm to his shoulder, peeking over to look at Kai's face. "Time to get up. I'm ready to go to school. I like to axolotl questions."

He giggled, finally peeking his head out of the covers.

After that, we rushed through the morning routine, and I was grateful we didn't have a long commute. As part of my relocation package, the company had put us up in one of the Huxley Grand LA suites. It had a full kitchen, living room, and two bedrooms with their own bathrooms. It was nice, but it wasn't home. As I often reminded myself, it was temporary.

After I dropped Kai off at the on-site employee childcare center, I headed up to the office. I was grateful that Kai would be close, but also, that he'd be getting a good foundation for when he started kindergarten in the fall, thanks to the pre-K program here that was led by a retired kindergarten teacher.

I peeked down the hall at Jasper's office, relieved the door was closed. I'd survived one encounter with him; I wasn't sure I could handle another.

After I checked in with Sloan, I set to work. I was so immersed in my report that I didn't realize how late it had gotten until my laptop chimed with a calendar alert. I logged off my computer, my excitement growing. I'd pored over the art dealer's extensive catalogue, and I couldn't wait to see his collection in person.

Dimitri was known to be a shrewd businessman, but I wasn't easily intimidated. So I shoved my laptop into my tote bag and practically floated down the hall to Sloan's office. I rapped on the open door and peeked my head in, unable to hold back the smile from my face. I felt like a kid on Christmas morning. The art wasn't even for my home, and yet, it felt like I was receiving a gift.

I was honored that Sloan had entrusted me with such an important project. But when I caught sight of her, I frowned. "Hey." I stepped closer. "You okay? You look flushed."

"I'm—" She moved to stand but then promptly sank back down into the chair. She looked as if she might faint. "Yeah. I just need a minute, and then I'll be fine."

I wasn't so sure about that, but Sloan knew her body better than anyone else. So, I gave her a minute, trying not to stress about how late it was and how much time traffic would add to our commute. I didn't want to heap even more anxiety onto the situation. Nothing was as important as the health of Sloan and her unborn child.

"Do you want something to eat? To drink?"

"Maybe some water," she said, standing.

"Sit," I barked, the word coming out harsher than I'd intended.

I hadn't been with her when she'd had her health scare in France, but I knew it had been bad enough that she'd had to go to the hospital. The fact that Jackson had been scared was just as worrisome. After they'd returned, he'd asked me to keep a close eye on Sloan.

I'd already been monitoring the situation, but I tried to be even more proactive about Sloan's workload after France. She and I had discussed ways to manage her stress, but there was only so much that could be done, considering her role in the company. And once Graham had stepped down as CEO, she had even more on her plate.

I handed Sloan a glass of cold water, watching her. Waiting. For what, I didn't know, but I hoped it didn't get worse.

Sloan sipped the water slowly, closing her eyes briefly. "Thank you." Her shoulders relaxed. "I'll be ready in a minute."

I narrowed my eyes, watching her like a hawk. I got the feeling she was trying to downplay her symptoms. And after what had happened in France, I wasn't taking any chances.

"Maybe we should reschedule," I said, doing my best to make it sound like a suggestion. She was my boss after all, but she was also my friend.

She shook her head. "I don't want to reschedule. You know how difficult it was to get this appointment in the first place."

"We'll get another one," I said. "Your health comes first."

There was a knock at the door. "Hey, Sloan. You got a—"

I looked over my shoulder, and Jasper froze mid-step. I briefly registered his navy pinstripe suit. It was tailored to perfection, showcasing his trim but muscular form.

His hazel eyes bounced from me to Sloan, and then he sped toward her. "What's wrong? Blood sugar? Blood pressure?"

"Jasper," she sighed. "I'm fine."

"You don't look fine." He turned to me. "Does she look fine to you?"

He seemed...on edge, and his obvious concern wasn't going to help the situation. I placed my hand on his arm, and his muscle twitched. "Hey. Take a breath."

"I—" He locked his eyes on mine, and I nodded slowly, encouraging him. He inhaled deeply. Let it out slowly. "I. Yeah." His shoulders relaxed a fraction. "Thanks."

I nodded, retracting my hand. "Sloan, do you feel well enough to contact your doctor, or do you want me to do it?"

She groaned. "This seems like overkill. It's not like I'm going into labor. I'm just a little light-headed."

"Just to be on the safe side," I said.

"Fine." She sighed. "I'll call her."

"Great." I turned to Jasper, sensing that he needed something to do before he spiraled. "Can you give Jackson a heads-up?"

He nodded and started typing on his phone.

"What about the appointment with the art dealer?" Sloan asked. "You need someone at an SVP level or above to sign off on the financials."

Before I could tell her that I'd reschedule, Jasper blurted, "I'll go."

"Isn't your calendar packed this afternoon?" Sloan asked.

Jasper waved a hand through the air. "It's always packed. But it's fine. It'll be a good test for my new temp. We can see how well she does with rescheduling. I'm going to email her now."

Jackson rushed through the door, laser focused on his wife. He was a former Navy SEAL who was now the head of Huxley Grand security. For a man who was usually so calm and collected, he looked as if he might lose his shit.

"*Hayati?*" He rushed to her side. "Are you okay?"

"I'm fine," Sloan insisted. "I wish everyone would stop making such a big fuss. I got a little light-headed. I'm already feeling better."

"Here." Jackson pulled a protein bar out of his pocket. "Eat this."

"Come." I grabbed Jasper's arm, trusting that Jackson had the situation well in hand. "Let's give them some space."

"Are you sure we—" Jasper asked, seeming reluctant to leave.

"Come on." I tugged on his arm. "Sloan is going to talk to her doctor, right?" She nodded, chewing some of the protein bar. "And Jackson—" I met his gaze "—will let us know if they need anything."

Jackson nodded then returned his attention to Sloan.

Jasper hesitated a moment more then followed me into the hall. I shut the door to Sloan's office softly behind me.

"Is this normal?" he asked, and I could see the concern etched into his features. "It doesn't seem normal."

"It's not abnormal," I assured him. "When I was pregnant with Kai, I experienced light-headedness. Especially during the third trimester. She's going to be okay."

"You don't know that," he said. "You can't promise that."

"You're right. I can't." I placed my hand on his arm, wanting him to know that I was listening. I wasn't dismissing his concerns, but I also wanted to calm him. "But Sloan has a good medical team and a loving partner. All we can do is support her and hope for the best."

"I know." He blew out a breath, his shoulders relaxing. "I need a distraction. What's this meeting I promised to attend?"

"Sloan and I were supposed to meet with an art dealer to select some art for the newly refurbished presidential suite and the new Golden Key Penthouse."

He nodded. "Ah. Yes. Okay. Where do we need to be and when?"

I pulled up the Maps app on my phone and typed in the address. A quick peek at the estimated arrival time as well as the amount of red snaking over the traffic map, infecting it like a virus, had me squeezing my eyes shut.

"There's no way we're going to make it to the meeting in time." My shoulders slumped.

I'd told Sloan we could reschedule, but I'd only said it to

keep her calm. This art dealer was a stickler for punctuality, and if I was late, he wasn't going to see me.

"Show me," Jasper said.

I handed him my phone. He nodded, his entire demeanor focused. "Can you contact the art dealer and see if we can have permission to land a helicopter?"

"What?" I widened my eyes.

"You heard me." He handed the phone back to me, and I immediately texted the dealer.

When I looked up, Jasper was already halfway down the hall. "I… where?" I tracked his movements. "Where are you going?"

"Helipad. Come on."

Helipad? He couldn't be serious. Could he?

I practically had to run to catch up. He stopped in front of a private elevator I hadn't even noticed, it was so discreet. Jasper placed his palm on a scanner then punched a button marked "H." This was serious James-Bond-level shit. I glanced at Jasper askew. *The hell?*

The elevator climbed up and up, and when the doors opened, bright sunlight poured into the small vestibule. Jasper put on a pair of sunglasses, and I did the same. Through the glass doors, I spied a gorgeous navy helicopter, its gold accents glinting in the afternoon sun.

I scanned the roof, noticing that we were alone. "Where's the pilot?"

"You're looking at him." Jasper grinned from behind his aviators.

Jasper was a pilot? How did I not know this? I kept waiting for him to tell me he was joking.

"Come on." He grabbed my hand but quickly dropped it.

It didn't matter how brief the contact had been; my skin was branded by his touch. My breath hitched. "I—"

"Sor—" he started to say at the same time, and I waved it away.

"Are you sure you're in the right frame of mind to fly?" I asked, thinking of how worried he'd been for Sloan only minutes ago.

"If I weren't, I wouldn't fly. I don't fuck around with safety, especially not when it comes to you."

I—*what?*

I ignored the butterflies that fluttered in my stomach at his statement.

I wanted to argue that his love of sports cars contradicted that, but then I remembered how insistent he'd always been that I wear my seat belt. Or the way he'd gently guide me away from the street when we walked together.

In ways both big and small, Jasper had always looked out for me. Protected me. If he said he was focused, then I believed him.

"Let's go." I practically shouted, crossing the helipad as quickly as I could.

I was determined to get to that meeting, and my adrenaline was pumping. It wasn't until he'd opened the passenger door and I'd climbed in that I started to panic about the fact that we were going to be flying in a tiny aircraft with nothing more than a giant fan holding us aloft.

Jasper shut the door then rounded the aircraft, doing what I assumed was a preflight check. Finally, he climbed inside the cockpit, and suddenly, it felt a whole lot smaller. His cologne permeated the space, and I inhaled slowly, allowing a sense of calm to settle over me. Or at least, I tried to.

He checked the controllers and then told me to put on my headset. He placed his helmet with a built-in headset over his ears, but I was frozen. Maybe this was a bad idea. I mean…a helicopter?

"Are you sure this is safe?" I asked around a tight knot of fear.

"Halle," he said, waiting until I turned to look at him. "Do you trust me?"

I held his gaze, and then I nodded. I did trust Jasper. He'd always treated me with respect. He'd always been honest. And he'd always put my needs first.

That reminder had me clenching my thighs together. *Seriously, Halle? Now?*

I told myself the threat of dying was the only reason I was thinking about sex. I mean, wasn't that a thing?

"I promise to keep you safe," he said, and it felt like he was talking about more than the impending flight.

I swallowed past the lump in my throat and nodded. "Okay. Let's do this." I placed my matching helmet over my head, my gaze snagging on him.

He looked like danger and money and sex. And I shouldn't have been attracted to that, but something about the way he'd taken charge, coupled with the way he'd stopped to check in with me, had those butterflies swirling in my stomach.

My phone buzzed in my lap. "Sloan says thank you. She's going home to rest."

"Good," Jasper said through the headset. His voice was in my ear, and it was...unnerving. "Any update from the owner?"

I nodded, my attention on my phone. "He said there's a field behind the warehouse where you can land."

"Perfect."

"Right. But, um, don't you need a flight plan or something? I didn't think you could just take off in a helicopter like you can with a car."

The corner of his lips curled into a smile. "You don't need

a flight plan as long as you're using visual flight rules and flying below 18,000 feet."

I pressed my lips together and nodded.

Jasper flipped some switches, and the blades whirled to life. He rattled off some information into his microphone, alerting air traffic control that he was going to take off and requesting VFR, which I assumed stood for visual flight rules.

Oh my god. We're really doing this. He's going to fly this thing.

I braced myself as we lifted into the air, the ground disappearing far below. I'd never flown in a helicopter, but it was a lot smoother than I'd expected. Slowly, I released my grip on the leather seat, relaxing as I grew more accustomed to the sensation.

Once we seemed to have reached our flying altitude, I chanced a glance over at him…and immediately regretted it. The man was hot on a normal day. But Jasper sitting at the controls of a helicopter, radiating confidence and control from behind his aviator sunglasses, was devastating.

Hoooly shit. How did I not know this about him?

He met my eyes briefly. "You good?"

I nodded, unable to hold back a smile at the absurdity that was my life. I was flying over the Hollywood sign with my billionaire boss, who happened to be a badass helicopter pilot. And I got to go shopping for art—for my job. Talk about a dream come true.

"It's fun, right?" he asked, glancing over at me.

Now that I'd gotten over the initial shock of being in a helicopter, I could admit that it was pretty cool.

"Definitely." God, Kai would love this. I couldn't wait to tell him I'd gotten to fly in a helicopter. He was going to freak!

Jasper smiled a boyish smile, and his dimple popped.

"How long have you had your pilot's license?" I asked,

mostly out of curiosity, but also to distract myself from the sight of him.

"I've had a helicopter rating for the past ten years. And my private pilot license since I was eighteen."

My attention jerked to him. "I... I had no idea. Is that what you wanted to be—a pilot?"

He turned, smooth and arcing. "No." He laughed.

"Then why go through all that training?"

"Fear can be a powerful motivator," he said in a quiet voice.

"Fear?" I asked, frowning.

The sun glinted off the windscreen, Jasper's voice crackling through the headset. "After my parents' crash, I was terrified of flying. But I also loved to travel. And I knew that flying was an inescapable part of my life."

I placed my hand to my throat, my heart aching for him. For the family he'd lost and the fears he'd had to overcome.

"My gran suggested I learn more about airplanes to help with my fear. And that led to me wanting to get my pilot's license. I absolutely fell in love with it. I loved learning something new. I craved the sense of control."

"That's both understandable and admirable."

"I had no idea you were this easy to impress," he teased. "Maybe I should've taken you for a helicopter ride sooner."

I rolled my eyes, not that he could see them behind my sunglasses. "I'm not impressed." When he turned to me, eyebrow raised in challenge, I said, "Okay. Maybe a little impressed." I held up my thumb and forefinger. "You have to land us safely first."

"Then you'll be impressed." I wasn't sure if it was a question or a statement.

"We'll see," I said, trying not to laugh.

"I hadn't planned on getting my helicopter license, but I

was sick of LA traffic. And if I'm in the air, I want to be the one in control."

It wasn't the only place he liked being in control, but I didn't mention that. I didn't have to, judging by the heated way he was looking at me. I squirmed in my seat, feeling my skin heat.

"Eyes on the sky." I straightened in my seat, adopting a prim posture.

Sloan was relying on me, and I wanted to prove that Jasper and I could work well together. Or maybe I just needed the reassurance.

"What about the private jet?" I asked, trying to keep our conversation focused on work-appropriate topics. "You don't typically fly that, do you?"

"No, but I rigorously review the flight plan and the crew."

I knew the plane crash had affected Jasper and his siblings —how could it not? He'd lost his parents and his aunt and uncle in one cruel, tragic accident. But I hadn't realized how deeply scarred he was by it until now.

Something from his childhood, from decades past, had such a profound impact on him. Understandably so. And it made me wonder how Kai would feel about the divorce as he got older. Would it push him to avoid love or romantic relationships? Would he find it difficult to trust?

"There it is," Jasper said, breaking me out of my thoughts.

We gradually descended until we landed in a field next to the warehouse. As the blades slowed, their incessant buzz whirling to a stop, I removed my helmet.

"Are you okay?" Jasper asked, removing his helmet. "You got quiet on me there at the end."

I forced a smile, opening the door. "I'm great."

Even from behind his sunglasses, I could feel him studying me. Someone emerged from the warehouse to greet us, and I was grateful for the escape—from my thoughts, from the proximity to Jasper. Because his admissions had me making some of my own.

I wasn't comfortable with the way Craig had treated me, and I didn't want my son growing up thinking that was okay. I also didn't want Kai to be afraid of love and connection. To avoid it or become jaded because of how I'd responded in the wake of the divorce.

And if I didn't want Kai to follow in his parents' footsteps —at least how they'd been up to this point—then I had to show him another way. A different way.

CHAPTER FIVE

JASPER

"Mackenzie," Dimitri said with a glint in his eye, his heavy accent dancing with each syllable.

He was impressed by the helicopter, even if he wasn't willing to admit it. Money talked. And seeing him now, I was that much happier about our grand entrance.

He turned his gaze to Halle, and I didn't like the way he appraised her. Like a beautiful piece he wanted to add to his collection. She was breathtaking, but she wasn't a possession. And we were here on business.

"Dimitri," I said, my jaw clenched tight. I wished I'd realized he was the art dealer we were coming to meet.

"And you must be Halle." Dimitri shook her hand. "A pleasure to finally meet you." He brought her hand to his mouth for a kiss. Dimitri was smooth, I'd give him that.

Halle dipped her head. "I'm looking forward to seeing your collection."

"And I am looking forward to showing it to someone who will appreciate it as much as I do."

I rolled my eyes behind them. Was this how we were

going to spend our entire visit? Him fawning over her? And her… What? Enjoying it?

Fuck me.

We followed him into the climate-controlled warehouse that was more like an industrial art gallery. I'd never been inside, but I'd heard of it. On and on, Dimitri droned about different pieces and their merits, and Halle seemed completely enthralled.

"I have a few more pieces I think will be to your liking," Dimitri said, but I'd had enough. We'd been wandering around for over an hour, and if I had to listen to him much longer, I was going to punch him in the face. "They aren't here, but I'd be happy to give you a private tour this weekend."

His thinly veiled intent was clear, and I was fucking done. I must have let out a noise of annoyance, based on the way Halle's cheeks flushed with color. But she didn't otherwise acknowledge Dimitri's invitation.

While that was a relief, I still couldn't believe he was asking her out in front of me. Well, not *me*. In front of her boss. But it was the only choice left to him since I wouldn't leave her side.

"I think we've seen enough," I said in a curt tone, eager to put an end to this. We'd seen enough art to fill every suite in my hotel.

Halle's gaze snapped to mine, a warning in her eyes. I ignored it.

Dimitri was oblivious to Halle's ire. He was too busy smirking at me over his shoulder. The fucking nerve.

Halle glanced at her watch. "I was having so much fun, I didn't realize how late it had gotten. But we need to wrap this up so I can get back to pick up my son on time."

"No rush." Dimitri placed his hand on Halle's lower back,

and I fucking saw red. "I'm happy to resume our discussion at a later date."

Not if I have anything to say about it.

Dimitri's phone rang, and he glared at the screen, clearly annoyed by the interruption. "Excuse me."

Once he was out of earshot, Halle spun on me. "What is your problem?" she hissed. "Why are you being so rude?"

I pulled her aside so we were hidden from the view of Dimitri's office by a large sculpture.

"What's *my* problem?" Her back was to the sculpture, our mouths inches apart. "For someone who's so intent on being *professional*, you're awfully flirtatious with Dimitri."

She scoffed, turning her head to the side. "Jealous much?"

"Yes," I blurted.

Maybe she'd been teasing, but I was serious.

She turned back to me, wide brown eyes meeting mine as her lips parted in shock. "Oh."

Yeah. *Oh.*

I crossed my arms over my chest. "Maybe I should just handle the negotiations from here forward."

"Jasper." She glared at me, fire and anger blazing in her eyes. "Don't fuck this up. You have no idea how difficult it was to set up this meeting. I'm not going to blow all my hard work because you feel some ridiculous need to act like a caveman."

"I'm not—" I took a breath and smoothed down my tie. That wasn't what I was doing, was it?

Fuck.

She was right. I was being jealous and territorial, and I hated feeling so irrational.

"You're right. I'm sorry. You clearly put a lot of effort into this, and I would never want to undermine your hard work."

I could see how my jealousy had clouded my view of the situation. Dimitri's flirting was annoying but not completely inappropriate. But my behavior had been, and I couldn't believe how quickly the situation had spiraled out of control. I had no right to be jealous, no claim over her. And the fact that I'd acted like I somehow did was deeply problematic.

"Thank you," she said.

"Do you know which pieces you want?" I asked, eager to get this over with.

She'd done such a good job of fawning over everything we'd seen that I had no idea which ones she was truly interested in. Well, that wasn't entirely true. There'd been one item she'd definitely lingered on. It had been smaller, more of an artist's sketch than a finished piece. But something about it had spoken to Halle.

She took a breath and then held up her tablet. She indicated to the pieces in an online catalogue. I had no idea how much this was going to cost—the prices weren't listed. But I had a feeling it was going to be expensive.

It didn't matter. Halle had incredible taste, and I could already envision the pieces in both the presidential suite and the Golden Key Penthouse. Both suites were reserved for the most prestigious and wealthiest guests, and when it came to their experience, money was no object.

Fortunately, the next time we needed to trade the pieces out, we could move the art to another property or sell it. At this level, art was an investment. Not that I viewed it as such, at least not when it came to the pieces I personally owned. In my opinion, art was meant to be enjoyed, not traded like a commodity.

Halle and I had discussed the topic at length when I'd taken her to some of the museums in London. I loved seeing her gush over art, confidently sharing her knowledge of the pieces and artists on display.

"What about this one?" I asked, pointing to the one she'd lingered at on her phone.

She shook her head. "It's not right for either space."

"But you liked it."

"Yeah, but it doesn't complement the other works."

I furrowed my brow, prepared to press her on it, but then Dimitri called out.

Halle darted out from behind the sculpture, flashing him a megawatt smile. "We've made our decisions."

I joined them, my fists clenched, body wound tight. It didn't matter if she was interested in him; I was her boss. And I could act like the goddamn head of the company that I was. Even so, I figured it might be best if I just kept my mouth shut and let Halle do the talking. I didn't want her to think I was trying to sabotage the sale.

"Excellent." Dimitri rubbed his hands together, gleaming with smug pride at the date he anticipated with Halle while counting up the money he was about to make on this sale.

Bastard.

I ADJUSTED MY HEADSET. "HAVE YOU HEARD ANYTHING MORE from Sloan?"

Halle had been quiet on the flight back to the office, and I felt like the silence was slowly suffocating me. Typically, flying cleared my head, forcing me to focus solely on the task at hand. But after our meeting with Dimitri, I found myself more distracted than ever by the woman next to me.

If I hated the idea of another man asking Halle on a date, I could only imagine my reaction to her being in a relationship with someone else. The mere thought of it had me feeling as if I were suffocating. I loosened my tie, but it did nothing.

So far, keeping our relationship focused on business had been a lot more difficult than I'd anticipated. I figured it best to focus our conversation on appropriate topics.

"She's home resting. The doctor said everything looks good."

"That's a relief." I hesitated a moment then said, "You know my sister pretty well. Do you think she's okay?"

Halle wasn't a doctor, but she'd been pregnant. And she spent a lot of time with Sloan. If anyone knew what was really going on with my sister—besides Jackson—it might be Halle.

"I hope so. She's definitely been better about taking breaks since France."

"But…?" I prompted.

"Pregnancy is unpredictable, and everyone has a different experience."

"Did you have any of those symptoms when you were pregnant with Kai?"

"No, but I had my fair share of fun. Lightning crotch. Swollen ankles. It was super awesome."

I recoiled. "What the hell is lightning crotch?"

"A nerve pain that comes out of nowhere and shoots into your groin. It hurts, and it comes on with absolutely no warning. It was often so bad it would take my breath away."

Wow. Shit. "That sounds painful."

"It is. But it's still not as bad as being in labor."

Whatever expression I made must have shown my fear. "Maybe you should focus on flying," Halle said with a laugh.

The fact that Sloan might go into labor early had me on high alert. LA traffic was awful. And while I knew Jackson would do everything in his power to get her to the hospital safely, I reassured myself that if it came down to it, I could always fly her to the hospital in the helicopter.

Halle and I were quiet for a moment, enjoying the view of the city from high above. I'd taken a longer route than was necessary, just so I could spend more time alone with her. Maybe it was selfish, but after how things had gone down earlier, I wanted to smooth things over. Besides, she would still get back in time to pick up Kai.

"So…how do you like your new role?" she asked.

That was a loaded question. I wasn't even sure how I felt about it yet, so I settled for something diplomatic. "It's different, challenging at times."

"Oh, come on," Halle prodded. "I know you better than that. Tell me the truth. I promise not to tell anyone."

I sighed. "Today, getting out of the office, getting to focus on guest experience and design details, that's what I enjoy."

"And you don't get to do that as much now that you're CEO."

I shook my head.

I loved coming up with new, creative ways to elevate our guests' experiences, like pillow menus and custom scents. I always tried to celebrate our employees too. They were just as important as the amenities we provided. Our employees made the hotel feel like a retreat, a sanctuary, a home away from home.

We consistently had some of the highest employee satisfaction ratings in the industry. In *any* industry. And it wasn't solely because we paid a higher-than-average wage. We treated our employees like family because that's what they were. It was something I'd always overseen, and something I'd prided myself on. But now that I was running the company, I no longer had the luxury of focusing on the finer details.

"I'm not sure anyone's told you this," she said, "but being the CEO means *you're* the boss. You get to do what you want."

I chuckled, guiding us back down to the helipad on the roof of the Huxley Grand. Back to where we'd started. "So you'd think."

"You miss your old role," she said in a matter-of-fact tone. It was an observation, not a question.

I met her gaze as the propeller came to a halt. Our eyes locked and held. "There are a lot of things I miss."

Her eyes searched mine, different emotions flitting through. And then she bit her lip and looked away. I wanted to kiss her so damn bad.

I didn't know how Graham had done it all these years. Served as CEO. Put aside his wants and his needs to do what was best for the company.

It was fucking exhausting.

Staying away from Halle was fucking exhausting, and we weren't even a few days in. She'd wanted to keep things professional, and I agreed it was for the best. It was far from what I wanted, even if I knew it was necessary—for her, for me, for the company.

I shut off the aircraft and went around to open Halle's door for her, resigned.

"Will you take a picture for me?" she asked, surprising me. Then she tacked on, "For Kai."

"Of course."

I held up her phone, snapping a few shots before discreetly AirDropping my favorite one to myself. Halle looked so confident and carefree. She was on top of the world, and I hadn't seen her this happy, maybe ever. At least not since last summer.

I wanted to believe it had something to do with me, but I had a feeling it had more to do with the art. Halle had always been passionate about art.

As we rode down in the private elevator, I dreaded the end to what had been a fun afternoon—at least if I ignored the part with Dimitri. It was the most carefree I'd felt since taking over as CEO, and I knew most of that was thanks to Halle.

I was still trying to find my footing since Graham had stepped down from the position after fourteen years. I'd always lived in his shadow. And now that I'd been thrust into the spotlight, I was floundering. When I wasn't questioning my decisions, I was comparing myself to him.

How could I not? He'd expanded the company while increasing profits, all without sacrificing the luxury and sustainability our hotel brand was known for. And now... now, it was my responsibility.

If I fucked it all up, I'd only have myself to blame.

But right now, I was more focused on Halle. I wanted to see her smile like she had today. And I had an idea of a way to get more time with her without technically crossing any lines.

I cleared my throat. "I liked the pieces you selected for the VIP suites. You have exquisite taste."

"Thank you." Her attention was focused on the elevator doors, not me.

I shoved my hands into my pockets, struggling to formulate my request. Why was this so difficult? I usually had no problems talking to women, but then again, the stakes had never felt so high. I wasn't even asking her on a date, yet I dreaded the idea that she'd shut me down.

"I've been wanting to add some art to my personal collection, and I'd love your help."

She turned to me, lit up. "I'd have to see the space to get a sense of your style and the size requirements."

"What are you doing tonight?" I blurted.

"I, uh—" She stared at her feet as if her shoes were a novelty. Her earlier enthusiasm had been snuffed out. "I don't think that's a good idea. Besides, I have to pick Kai up from pre-K."

"Tomorrow, then?" I pressed. I was pushing my luck. But

after having to spend the afternoon watching her flirt with another man, I was at the end of my tether.

"I can't."

"Come on."

"You're forgetting that I have Kai, and I don't have anyone to watch him."

"Bring him with you."

She arched a brow. "Bring him with me? Jasper," she sighed. "He's a five-year-old boy with a lot of energy. I'm—" She shook her head. "I don't think that would go very well."

"Why not?"

What was she concerned about? Kai in my apartment, or introducing a man to her son? It wasn't like we were dating. This was a friendly visit.

"I just… I wouldn't want him to be in the way."

I leaned in. "He could never be in the way. Promise."

Her shoulders softened. "Maybe."

I wasn't above playing dirty. Which was how I found myself saying, "I'll give you an unlimited budget and carte blanche in selecting the pieces."

"Oh, that's dangerous." She grinned, and I could tell she was considering it.

My phone buzzed, an incoming slew of new messages. I barely held back a groan. "I have to take this, but I'll see you tomorrow?" I asked, hoping I didn't sound as desperate as I felt.

"Unlimited budget?" she asked.

"Unlimited," I said.

I didn't want to give Dimitri another cent. But I would give him my fortune if it meant I got to spend more time with Halle.

CHAPTER SIX

HALLE

"Wicked!" Kai ran to the floor-to-ceiling windows after I'd introduced him and Jasper.

We'd barely crossed over the threshold into Jasper's penthouse, and my child was acting as if he'd never been somewhere new. Granted, the view really was spectacular, especially with the sun low in the sky. But still…I'd hoped he'd be able to exercise some restraint.

"Kai," I chided. He lowered his hands, and I cringed at the smudge marks. His fingerprints were everywhere.

Before I could apologize to Jasper, Kai spied the oversized sofa and took a running jump and hurled himself onto it. I braced myself for Jasper's reaction, but he seemed completely unbothered, as if he had children running around his penthouse all the time. If it had been Craig, he would've been red-faced and yelling.

"I'm so…sorry," I said to Jasper through gritted teeth as I tugged on Kai's pants. Finally, I got my son's attention, and he knew he was in trouble.

"Hey." I crouched down to his level. "I know you're excited, but we need to be respectful of Jasper's home."

Kai dropped his chin, eyes on the floor. "Sorry, Mum."

"Thank you. But I think you owe someone else an apology. Hm?" I nudged him.

Kai turned to Jasper, twisting his hands in front of him. "Sorry, Mr. Jasper."

"Hey." Jasper crouched down, smiling a bright, wide smile. Big enough to show off his dimple. *Ugh. Why?* Was the man not hot enough, he just had to have a dimple too?

What was I thinking? Coming to his apartment when I'd admitted that I didn't trust myself to be alone with Jasper. I tried to tell myself this was a work obligation. I'd been to Sloan's house hundreds of times. And besides, I wasn't alone; Kai was here with me.

When Kai's attention remained on the floor, Jasper placed his hand on Kai's shoulder. "You're not in trouble. At least, not with me."

Finally, Kai lifted his head. He gnawed on his lip, evaluated Jasper, then nodded.

Jasper seemed completely unfazed by Kai's energy. If anything, Jasper seemed to welcome it.

Maybe he's just being polite?

But the easy smile on Jasper's face told me it wasn't an act. He was genuinely relaxed, and it all seemed so natural.

"Come on," Jasper said, steering Kai by the shoulder. "Let me give you a tour."

Jasper glanced at me over his shoulder, and I mouthed, "Thank you."

Jasper winked at me and then turned his attention back to my son. I tried not to read too much into that wink. Into the things he'd said yesterday. Instead, I turned my attention to my surroundings.

His home wasn't at all what I'd expected. It was a lot more…cozy.

The furniture looked expensive, but inviting. There was

even a slight indent in one of the couch cushions, like he actually used it. He had a few pieces of art, and they were colorful and quirky. The artists were unknown to me, something that would've immediately disqualified them from Craig's consideration.

It had been one of my ex's favorite party tricks—having me call out flaws or forgeries in the artwork on display. It didn't matter whether we were at a museum or a private home. He'd always put me on the spot, even though I'd told him many times that it made me uncomfortable.

Jasper continued the tour, and I wondered why he'd chosen those pieces. Maybe he'd purchased them as investments, like Craig and so many of his friends. Maybe an interior designer had made the selections. But if I knew Jasper like I thought I did, I seriously doubted that.

He was too detail-oriented. Too focused on guest experience to leave something as personal as his home up to someone else. And while it had an undercurrent of quiet elegance and luxury, the space felt both intentional and welcoming. It suited him.

"Here's my favorite room," Jasper said, interrupting my musings. "The game room."

"Oh sweet!" Kai's eyes pinged between the giant beanbags, the even bigger TV, and all the game consoles. "You like video games?"

"Love them." Jasper leaned in, getting more at Kai's level. "My brothers and I like to play together sometimes. What about you?"

"Oh yeah. But Mum won't let me play too much."

"That's because your mom's a smart woman. But if she's okay with it, maybe the next time the two of you come over, we can play."

Kai turned to me, a hopeful expression on his face. When

I looked at Jasper, he was wearing a similar one. *Oh lord. These two.*

They'd just met, and they were already conspiring against me.

I wasn't sure what I'd expected, but Jasper had quickly hit it off with Kai. Jasper and I were no longer together, but it made me wonder if… No. I shook my head to clear it. It didn't matter. I should just be grateful things were going so well and not read anything into it.

"Mum?" Kai tugged on my wrist.

Oh right. He'd asked me a question about video games.

"Maybe."

It was a completely noncommittal response, and yet they both hissed out a "Yes," complete with matching fist pump. It was both unnerving and adorable.

I wasn't sure how I felt about my son playing video games with my ex-lover slash boss. I should be putting distance between Jasper and me, not entangling our lives even more.

Then why are you here?

"Come on," Jasper said. "We have more to see."

Throughout the tour, Jasper indicated some of the spaces where he wanted to add art. He showed us his outdoor terrace with a gorgeous pool, before finally leading us through a set of large glass doors to his bedroom. The room was dominated by a huge bed that screamed debauchery even though it was perfectly made. I wondered how early his housekeeper must have arrived to make sure everything was just so.

Black-and-white pictures lined one wall, images of Jasper and his family at various ages. While Jasper was busy showing Kai all the settings on his adjustable bed, I stepped closer to admire the photographs. A group of kids piled on top of each other. I could easily pick out Sloan—the only girl. Graham was tall and brooding, with dark, curly hair. And Jasper lay on the top of the pile, mischief in his eyes. I shook my head and laughed to myself before moving on to the next one.

Jasper and Sloan dancing at her wedding. They looked so happy and carefree. Another of Jasper and his grandmother. I recognized her from the company website and pictures I'd seen around Sloan's flat.

Kai let out a giggle, and I turned to find him pressing the buttons on Jasper's bed remote, his legs and head going up and down. I rolled my eyes with a smile. "He's going to break your bed."

Jasper merely shrugged.

"You're such a pushover."

He chuckled. "Actually, it was my idea. Why do you think I'm the favorite uncle?"

"Because you're a big kid."

"Only one of those things is true." He kept his eyes on Kai as he said it, but the corner of his mouth lifted into this delectable little smirk. *What a tease.*

And now I was thinking about Jasper breaking *me* with just how *big* he was. My core quivered with longing, and I tried to ignore it. I wasn't supposed to be thinking about that at all, let alone in Jasper's bedroom.

"So this is your place," I said, trying to return us to safer territory.

"This is my place." He rocked on his heels.

"Don't you ever want more separation between home and work?"

"Sometimes, yeah. And I've considered getting a place out near Knox and Nate. But the idea of having that much space all to myself seems somehow lonely."

"Maybe you need a pet," Kai offered. His little ears were always listening, even when you didn't think he was paying attention.

"Maybe," Jasper said. "I've actually been thinking about getting a dog."

"Yes!" Kai shouted, popping up to his knees on the bed. "You should definitely get a dog."

Jasper laughed. "Yeah? Why don't you tell me what kind of dog I should get while your mom decides how much of my money to spend?"

Kai scrunched up his face. "Why is she spending your money?"

Jasper leaned in as if he was imparting some big secret. "Because she's got a good eye for art, and I want her to buy me some."

"I'll give you some of mine," Kai said. "It won't even cost you anything."

I stifled a laugh. "You're good if I go measure?"

He nodded then turned his attention back to my son. "Come on," Jasper said to Kai. "Let's fix the bed, and then you can tell me."

Surprisingly, Kai popped off the bed and handed Jasper the remote without argument or complaint. I stood there, shocked. Seriously? Kai was rarely ever that compliant with me. He was a good kid, but he was five. He had his own, often strong, opinions on things.

But for Jasper, Kai had done exactly as asked. The first time. First. Time.

It had to be a fluke. Beginner's luck on Jasper's part. Kai was trying to impress him; that much was sure. It wouldn't last. At least, that's what I was telling myself.

"Okay, so I'm going to show you a magic trick," Jasper said.

"Ooh, really?" Kai leaned in as if Jasper were imparting some great secret.

"Yes, but only if you'll be my assistant."

I was definitely intrigued, even if I was trying not to show it. It made me wonder why Jasper had never had children. He was clearly good with them. Enjoyed spending time with them.

"Yes. Yes!" Kai bounced on his toes.

"Okay. So, you stand over there at that corner." Kai darted over to where Jasper had indicated. "And I'll stand here. And once I say the magic words, you'll pull it snug. Ready?"

Kai gripped the edge of the comforter, and I bit back a laugh. He was so enthralled, he didn't even realize he was doing chores. *Clever, Jasper. Very clever.*

"With a tug and a pull." He and Kai tugged the comforter, smoothing out some of the wrinkles. "And a little hocus-pocus too." Jasper hovered his hands over the mattress as if he were casting a spell. "We'll make this bed good as new."

And with a final flourish, they stepped back.

"That was fun!" Kai said. "Can we do it again?" I watched the two of them, marveling at Jasper's sense of play and order, Kai's eagerness to assist.

"Sure!" Jasper grinned.

"I won't be long," I said, schooling my face into a more neutral expression. Kai had no concept of time, and Jasper was a busy man. I didn't want to encroach on his space—or his schedule—any more than we already had.

And honestly, I needed to get out of his apartment. It felt too personal, too intimate, being in his space. I was about to exit the bedroom when I heard Kai shout, "Sick! That bathtub is as big as a swimming pool!" Unable to resist looking, I cringed as Kai hopped into the tub. "You could have a party in here!"

"You could," Jasper answered Kai, but he was looking at me. His eyes were hooded, and I knew he was imagining the last time we'd taken a bath together.

Great. And now, so was I.

My cheeks heated, and I spun away. I'd said we needed to

keep things professional, and yet here I was. A few days in and more than a few lines crossed.

"Thanks again for coming to help me," Jasper said to my back. "I know you have a lot on your plate, and this is outside the normal scope of your duties. I'll make sure you're compensated for your time."

"That's not necessary." When he opened his mouth as if to protest, I said, "I'm serious. I don't want or expect anything in return."

"Maybe that's the problem." He held my gaze, and I sensed there was so much more loaded into those four words than what he was saying.

Slowly, I opened my eyes, feeling as if it was…late. I sensed it was still the weekend, but I was adjusting to a new time zone, and the first week of work at the LA office had been intense. Plus, I'd stayed up way too late last night, scrolling through Dimitri's art catalogue as I put together a plan for Jasper's home. I couldn't remember the last time I'd felt so invigorated.

Now, I just felt tired. But something about the way the light filtered through the curtains of my bedroom made me wonder just how late it was.

I blinked my eyes open, and Kai was standing beside me, peering down at me. *Blink. Blink.*

"Jesus." I startled, placing a hand to my chest. "What are you doing, Kai? You scared me."

I was definitely awake now. My heart was racing. So much for a relaxing Sunday morning.

"I'm hungry."

"Okay." I stretched, trying to calm myself. "Give me just a

minute, and then I'll come make breakfast. Do you want to cuddle first?"

He shook his head. "I'm sooo hungry."

I yawned and rolled to my side, clutching my pillow to my chest, still not eager to get out of bed. "How long have you been up?"

"I think the clock said six-one-two. I was working on my new Hulkbuster. Come see!" He bounced on his toes, full of energy.

6:12? Jeez. He was going to be a mess later.

"What time is it now?" I massaged my temples.

He picked up my phone, and I squinted against the bright screen. I held up my hand to shield my eyes, and he said, "Seven three nine. Oh look! There's a new message from Dad."

"Seven thirty-nine," I said, taking the phone from him.

Kai was learning how to read, and I didn't want him to see what Craig had sent. Not until I'd screened the contents of the message first.

Kai pouted, and I knew he missed his dad. "But I wanted to read his message."

I opened Craig's message. It was too damn early for this. But Craig was Kai's dad, and I was glad to see him making the effort. Hell, if our roles were reversed, I'd be trying to call Kai every day. Probably multiple times a day.

> Craig: Is now a good time to video chat
> with Kai?

I wasn't sure there'd be a better time. We needed to run some errands. Get some things ready for the week ahead.

And hopefully do something fun together. I didn't want all of Kai's memories with me to be of me working or us doing chores.

Me: Yes. Call anytime.

Almost immediately, the phone started buzzing in my hand. *Jeez. That was fast.*

I handed it to Kai; he could answer it. His dad was calling to speak to him, not me. And I needed some coffee before I dealt with anything, let alone my ex.

"Hi, Dad!" Kai waved at the screen, a big smile on his face.

"Mate. How are you? Have you been working on the Hulkbuster I sent you?" Craig asked. Because, to him, being a good parent meant spoiling your son. Though, at least he'd asked to chat with Kai without any prompting on my part. That was something.

"Yeah." Kai hopped up. "Want to see?"

"Of course," Craig said, and I let out a breath of relief when Kai took my phone—and Craig—down the hall to see it.

I pushed out of bed with a groan. I gathered my hair and twisted it up in a clip before padding out to the living room. Kai was sitting on the floor, with the pieces laid out on the coffee table before him. My phone rested against the box so he and Craig could talk while he assembled it.

I couldn't believe he'd spent almost an hour on it. I supposed I should be grateful to Craig for the extra sleep. As if he'd really had anything to do with it.

I went to the kitchen and started gathering the supplies for chocolate chip pancakes, keeping one ear on the conversation between Kai and Craig. Craig was asking him about LA and the things he'd done. The kids he'd met. Kai gushed about Jasper, and then Kai gave him a tour of our accommodations.

When Kai made it to the kitchen, he held up the camera so I filled the screen. "Say hi, Mum!"

I waved, forcing a tight smile. All the while, I tried not to let my annoyance show. It wasn't Kai's fault that he was excited to show off our current living space. I just didn't know why I needed to be part of the tour.

"Hi, Hal. Nice place," Craig said, the nickname grating on me. "Think there's room for me?"

Kai was so excited he nearly dropped the phone. "Are you coming to visit?"

I narrowed my eyes at Craig. What was he up to? "Can I please have the phone?" I said to my son, taking it before either of them could discuss it further. Kai pouted, but I ignored it. "I'll be right back," I said to Kai. "See how much you can get done on the Hulkbuster while I'm gone, 'kay?"

"Okay." Kai slunk back to his seat on the floor.

I went into my bedroom and closed the door. "What was that about?" I hissed, hoping Kai wouldn't overhear.

"What?" Craig lifted his shoulder. He was dressed in a button-down shirt, as polished as ever, while I was fresh out of bed with messy hair. Since I was still in my pajamas sans bra, I kept the camera angled so that he could only see from my neck up. "I have some business in LA in a few weeks, and I thought Kai and I could celebrate his birthday early. Even if not, I want to see Kai. See both of you."

I frowned. "I really wish you hadn't said anything to him without talking to me first. What if something comes up or your plans change?" It wouldn't be the first time it had happened.

"My flight is booked. I'm coming. And I was hoping I could stay with you for a few days while I'm there."

He...what?

The fact that Craig planned to come to LA had my heart pounding. But asking to stay here… What the hell was he thinking?

"I don't think that's a good idea," I said. *For my own personal sanity.* "I wouldn't want to give Kai the wrong impression."

"I only asked so I could have more time with him."

"I understand that," I said, though I was doubtful. "But I think you'd be more comfortable in one of the other rooms at the Huxley Grand. And you'd still get to spend plenty of time with him. You could even have him stay with you in your room for a few nights if you'd like."

For a minute, I didn't think Craig was going to let it go without more of a fight. But then he said, "Fine."

I made a note to myself to book him a room, just in case he "forgot." It wouldn't be the first time Craig had pulled something like that—completely ignoring my wishes in favor of his own. All while playing it off as an "accident."

I was done letting Craig—or any man—dictate my life. And how it had taken me so long to see what he was doing and to put an end to it was beyond me. I might not be ready to look for love, but I could certainly show my son what it meant to love and respect yourself.

CHAPTER SEVEN

JASPER

We'd just finished our weekly poker game with the guys when I pulled Pierce aside. "I need to ask your advice on something."

Pierce wasn't just Graham's best friend; he was part of the family. He was also our family lawyer, the "fixer." He often devised elegant solutions to various PR issues.

"Sure. What's up?"

"It's—" I did a quick check to see if anyone was nearby. Jackson had already headed out, home to Sloan. Knox and Nate and Jude were talking in the kitchen. "Private."

Pierce led me down the hall to Knox's office, shutting the door behind us. "What's up?"

"Hypothetically speaking… Say I wanted to date someone who works for the Huxley Grand."

His entire demeanor shifted, and I tried not to be intimidated by the fact that he'd gone into lawyer mode. It was why I'd come to him for advice after all. Because I knew he'd be honest about the risks.

"Hypothetically speaking…" he repeated. "Has anything happened between the two of you?"

I debated how to phrase my answer, finally settling on, "In this example, yes. But it happened in the past."

"Before she was an employee?"

I shook my head, wishing that were the case. I knew it could potentially make things easier. Though nothing about this was simple.

"Jesus, Jasper." He pinched the bridge of his nose. I shoved my hands into my pockets, sensing that it was best to keep my mouth shut. "Consensual?"

I glared at him. "Of course."

Definitely consensual.

"Jasper," Halle whimpered as I trailed my fingers over her collarbone. "I need you."

We'd been touring one of the newly renovated hotel rooms at the Huxley's main London location. She'd stayed behind after all the other staff had left, helping me make any notes on details that were missing. Brainstorming ideas for ways to enhance the guest experience.

Being alone with Halle was a bad idea. Especially after all the tension that had been building between us since my arrival a few weeks ago. Spending time with only Halle in a luxury hotel room was fucking insanity.

And yet here we were, her ass on the desk. My cock straining against the zipper of my trousers. Her legs spread, skirt rucked up. Lips swollen from my kisses.

God. She was something.

Pale thighs sprinkled with freckles. Her shirt rumpled, the top few buttons undone to reveal the flush of her chest. But it was those eyes—deep, soulful, rich chocolate eyes—that got me every time.

"This is a bad idea," I rasped, as if that would stop me. We'd been dancing around this for weeks.

Sloan would kill me.

Halle was my sister's chief of staff. My employee.

Halle grabbed my tie and wrapped it around her fist, pulling me close. Reeling me in. And god, I was such a sucker for her.

I'd been trying to avoid her—this. Not because I didn't want her, but because I wanted her too much. I couldn't do it anymore. I just... I dropped my head to my chest. I couldn't.

She pulled me even closer, the scent of sunshine and roses floating from her. When I met her gaze, the way she was looking up at me was the perfect mix of demure and sexy, and I nearly came in my pants.

I had a firm rule against sleeping with anyone who worked for the Huxley brand. It was something Pops had drilled into me—into all of us, really. The need to make sure our actions were always above-board. To treat employees with respect.
And here I was, about to break it.

Fuck.

Looking at her, I knew I was fooling myself to think I could resist.

"You're sure?" I asked, even though I already knew the answer. She might regret this later, but she definitely wanted it now.

"Positive," she said, looking me dead in the eye.

"Any doubts?" Pierce asked, snapping me out of the memory.

I shook my head. "None. I would never be with someone without their enthusiastic consent."

His shoulders relaxed a hair. "That's good because I sure as shit don't want to be dealing with a sexual harassment lawsuit on top of everything else we've had to weather the past few years."

Everything else, meaning lapses in security, especially for high-profile guests. Then there were the anonymous threats Sloan had received, the escort scandal, an attempted hostile takeover, Graham's sudden marriage and the board shake-up, and my taking over as CEO. It was a lot.

The last thing I wanted was to add to the scandal that had swirled around the brand for the past few years. But I also knew that my feelings for Halle weren't going away, and it was getting harder to ignore them. And so, I'd sought Pierce's advice. If anyone could help me navigate this situation, it was him.

"And in this scenario, you're not together now, correct?"

"Correct," I said. "We were together briefly. In the past."

"Did things end on good terms?"

I nodded.

"You want my advice? Let it go. Let *her* go. Move on and consider yourself lucky that things ended amicably and discreetly. The board likes you right now," Pierce said. "Don't fuck that up."

"I know," I said. "Trust me. I saw what Graham went through with them."

"Your family may have secured a majority, but you still

need the board's support. The board is always on high alert for anything that could pose a risk to the company's reputation or finances. And the CEO having an affair with an employee definitely falls into that category."

"Knox slept with an employee who was also his son's ex."

"Yes, but as the sole owner of the Leatherbacks, he doesn't have to report to a board or shareholders." Right. Because he owned the damn team.

"What about Nate?" I asked, trying to plead my case. If my siblings could find happiness with someone who was considered "inappropriate" or "forbidden," why couldn't I? "He slept with his daughter's nanny."

"I hate to say this, but he's a movie star, and it's sort of expected. And again, no board runs his production company."

Fuck. I rubbed the back of my neck. This conversation wasn't going at all how I'd hoped. Instead of helping me find solutions, Pierce was pointing out all the reasons why I shouldn't go for it.

"Sloan?" I asked. Her situation was probably the most similar to mine, though there were differences.

"First of all, Jackson was her bodyguard. And he was hired through Hudson Security—an independent contractor. Jackson wasn't an employee of the Huxley brand."

"True, but it was still against Hudson's rules."

"Yes, and Jackson had to resign because of it. Do I need to go on? You want to talk about Graham? Your brother, who decided to step down as CEO because of his relationship with Lily."

"Yeah, but that was different, and you know it."

"I do," Pierce said, and I sensed there was something he wasn't telling me.

I'd always suspected there was more to Graham and Lily's marriage, but if my brother was happy and the board had forked over the shares, I wasn't going to pry. What was done was done, and sometimes it was better not to know.

"She was his former assistant."

"Exactly," Pierce said. "Former. As in she didn't work for him anymore. Because he always put this company first."

Well, shit. If Pierce was trying to make me feel guilty, it was working. My brother, Graham, had asked me to be his successor. He'd trusted me to lead the family business and protect the family legacy, and here I was threatening to undermine all of that. And for what? A woman I wasn't even sure wanted a relationship with me.

"You're right," I said, feeling defeated. "It's a bad idea."

"The worst," Pierce said in a stern tone. "You asked for my advice, and I'm telling you flat out. Don't do it."

"I know. I know." I dragged a hand through my hair. "I get it. Okay."

"Do you?" He leaned forward, gaze homed in on mine.

I nodded.

"Good," he said, and I knew it was meant as a threat. Stay in line or else this ends badly for all of us.

THE SUN GLINTED OFF THE WATER AS WE CRUISED AWAY FROM the shore. My family and I, along with a few guests, were spending the afternoon on Knox's yacht, enjoying some time together.

I was half paying attention to the conversation because I was too distracted—yet again—by Halle, who was sitting on the other side of the deck. At least, I was, until Kendall's question caught me off guard.

"A bachelor auction?" I practically choked on my beer. I was careful to keep my voice low so Halle wouldn't overhear. "You want me to participate in a bachelor auction?"

"Bachelorx," my sister-in-law Kendall corrected, adjusting her son, Leo, on her hip. "The steering committee wants it to be an inclusive event."

"So does that mean there will be both men and women on the auction block?" Astrid asked, joining us, wiggling her fingers at Leo, and he gave her a big, toothy smile.

Astrid was family by extension. Her twin, Emerson, was married to Nate. And while my family had not-so-gently hinted that Astrid and I should date, I wasn't interested. I wasn't interested in anyone who wasn't Halle.

"Yes," Kendall said. "But they also want it to be welcoming to all, including gender nonconforming, queer, or nonbinary people."

"It's going to be amazing." Emerson gave Kendall a squeeze. "I know it."

"I hope so. This is my first year serving on the board of the Huxley Family Foundation." Kendall smiled as Knox took Leo from her, but her attention remained on me. "And I really want it to be a success."

She twisted her hands together, and I got the feeling she was anxious. I softened, empathizing with her now more than ever. I understood what that was like—taking on a new role and needing to be successful.

"I appreciate your dedication, *mi cielo*," Knox said, wrapping his free arm around Kendall and pressing a kiss to her temple. "We all do. But it's not all on you." He might be talking to her, but he was looking at me when he spoke those words.

"He's right," Nate said. "This is the family charity, and we all need to do our part." He gave me a meaningful look.

Well, shit. Talk about peer pressure. This was beginning to feel like an ambush. I needed to shut down this conversation before it went any further.

I peered over my shoulder. Currently, Halle was occupied

with Kai. They were playing a game with my niece, Brooklyn, as well as my nephew, Jude, his wife, and their son Ezra.

Halle looked so open and carefree. And yet with me, she'd put up a wall, and I had no idea how to break it down or if I even could. But every time she ruffled Kai's hair or smiled, I wanted to try.

I wanted to be the person Halle came to with her problems. The person she trusted to let herself fall apart. To come undone.

She'd let me be that for her once—briefly. And it was something I'd never taken for granted. Something I would've given anything to have again.

There has to be a way.

She met my gaze, held it briefly, then glanced away all too soon. I watched her out of the corner of my eye, gratified by the way her porcelain skin bloomed with color. My head instantly went to the last time I'd made her blush like that.

Before I could let my mind travel too far down that path, Pierce's voice popped into my head. His words from our conversation the other day, rebuking me. *Don't do it.*

"You hate the idea," Kendall said, looking downcast. It snapped me back to the present, making me realize that I hadn't spoken and they were all staring at me.

I didn't hate the bachelorx auction—in theory. But I also wasn't interested in participating.

That said, I could tell that Kendall had put a lot of effort into the event, so I tried to choose my words carefully, settling on the most diplomatic response. I found myself doing that a lot lately—tempering my statement, concealing my true thoughts. It was fucking exhausting.

"This is a bit out of the norm for the Huxley Family Foundation," I said, wondering if Sloan knew about this.

I would've asked her, but she was resting in one of the cabins. Her doctor had threatened to put her on bed rest, but

Sloan had promised to take even better care of herself. And being on the water had always put her at ease.

"Which is why it's so great," Nate said. "We've been doing the same thing for years. It's time to shake things up."

A bachelorx auction would certainly do that. I wondered who had approved the idea in the first place. In the past, I'd served as the family's liaison to the steering committee responsible for the annual event. Right now, it felt as if they were driving the foundation into a ditch.

"I appreciate ingenuity, but it feels..." I didn't know how to say it without just coming out and telling Kendall that a bachelorx auction, despite trying to be more inclusive, would always feel outdated and cheap.

I closed my mouth before I could voice that thought. In the past, I wouldn't have held back. But now...*now*, I was the CEO. I was the public face of our brand, and I had to be diplomatic and brand-focused at all times.

Like how you slept with your sister's chief of staff?

I resisted the urge to cover my face with my hands and groan.

I couldn't stop thinking about her. I *had* to stop thinking about her. I knew that. Halle was forbidden. Off-limits.

And you just love to push the limits, don't you? Gran's voice rang through my head.

Her voice was loving, almost teasing in tone. Because even when Gran had been exasperated with me—and rightly so—she'd always loved and embraced me just as I was. Where many had seen an unruly kid and a troublemaker, Gran had helped me find outlets for my energy, anger, and grief. I missed her. Her and Pops.

I rubbed the back of my neck, knowing this had to stop. *I* had to stop.

Pierce had told me it was a bad idea. I knew it was a bad idea.

Nate clapped a hand on my shoulder, startling me from my thoughts. "I thought you'd jump at the chance to participate," he said. "All those eligible women—"

"And men," Knox piped in.

"People," Astrid corrected.

I glared at them. All of them.

"Practically begging for you to sleep with them," Nate finished.

Too bad there was only one woman I wanted, and she was unavailable.

Last summer with Halle had been a one-off. And yet, it had felt like the beginning of something. At least to me.

"Oh no, no, no," Kendall rushed to respond. "That's not what this is. There's no—" Her cheeks pinkened. "We make it very clear that it's a date only. No…"

"Sexual favors involved," Emerson added, laughing.

I would've been amused by Kendall's obvious discomfort, but I was too busy trying to finagle my way out of the event.

"You've been so uptight lately," Nate said, ribbing me.

Of course I'm uptight, I wanted to bite out. I was still adjusting to my new role as CEO. The pressure. The expectations. I was barely sleeping, just trying to stay on top of it all. I had so much to learn. So much to oversee.

And then there was the situation with Halle. I was trying to maintain my distance, but she was fucking everywhere. At the office. In the helicopter. On Knox's yacht.

Then why'd you ask her to come to your penthouse to help with art?

"Are *you* participating?" I asked Nate in an attempt to stall. Though I suspected I already knew the answer.

Nate draped his arm around his wife, looking inordinately pleased with himself as his wedding band glinted in the sunlight. "I'm not a bachelor."

I wanted to punch the smug grin off his face. *God, I'm tired.*

It was probably a good thing Nate wasn't participating. Because if he had been on the auction block, I could only imagine how high the bidding would've gone. But he was married now and, therefore, exempt from this ridiculous fundraiser. *Lucky bastard.*

He pressed a kiss to Emerson's temple, and she smiled up at him in response. They were so sickeningly in love. I was happy for them, truly. But it felt as if everyone was moving on with their lives. Getting married. Having children. While I was the odd man out, pining after a woman I could never have.

"Holden Hansley is participating." Kendall beamed, and Astrid started coughing.

"You okay?" Emerson asked her.

"Yeah!" Astrid chirped. "Yep!" Astrid held up a hand, and her face was beet red. "Sorry. Went down the wrong pipe."

"Dad recruited a few of the players from the Hawks," Emerson explained, as if I didn't know who Holden Hansley was.

Everyone knew who Holden Hansley was. He'd recently been traded to the Hollywood Hawks, and he was a fucking legend on the ice. I couldn't wait to see him lead our team to a long-overdue Stanley Cup win.

"And several of the Leatherbacks volunteered," Knox said, referring to players from the pro soccer team he owned.

"Or got voluntold." I coughed the words into my hand, letting out an "oomph" when Knox elbowed me.

I wanted to help the family foundation, of course I did. I was passionate about its mission to provide low-cost or free temporary housing to those in need. Donating money was great, and I could admit that a bachelorx auction would likely generate a shit-ton of money. But did I really need to participate?

I didn't mind being in the public eye. But no fucking way did I want to stand on a stage and have someone value my worth. Or worse still…find me lacking.

I examined my family. For years, they'd given me shit for my playboy reputation, and now they were asking me to what? Lean into it?

"Graham would never agree to something like this," I said to no one in particular. And not only because it would sully the Huxley brand. My older brother was too serious and brooding. He absolutely detested small talk. Just thinking of him squirming onstage and during the auction and then suffering through the date had me smiling.

But Graham wasn't here. I was still trying to wrap my head around that fact. Not just that he was married, but that he'd left. The country. His position at the company. *Me.*

I kept waiting for him to change his mind. But the longer he was gone, the more my new reality sank in. He wasn't coming back.

"Maybe not," Knox said, his warm gaze meeting my own. "But you're not Graham."

"No, but I am the CEO, and I have to be more careful about how I'm perceived."

And even if I wasn't my brother, I was still trying to fill his shoes. An impossible task.

I missed my brother more than I ever dared to admit. Now that I'd taken over his role, I held an even greater appreciation for him and all that he'd done for the company.

It wasn't that I didn't want to be CEO. I just had never envisioned myself in this role. And the suddenness with which it had all happened was still a lot to wrap my head around.

"Pierce?"

"Sounds like an excellent idea if you ask me." He gave me a knowing look. Another warning from our conversation the other day. His message was clear: forget about the employee and go out with someone else.

Conversation turned to other matters, and I drifted over to the railing. I stared out at the water, enjoying the feel of fresh air on my skin. Kendall joined me, placing her hand on my arm. Her diamond ring sparkled in the fading sunlight, and I glanced up to find her wearing a sheepish expression.

"I'm sorry if it felt like I put you on the spot by mentioning the auction in front of everyone."

"It's fine." I twisted my hands on the railing, appreciating her concern.

I didn't want to make her feel bad. Especially not when she was putting in so much work to make the event a success.

"I honestly thought you'd be happy to do it." She removed her hand, resting her elbows on the railing.

I sighed. "I'm probably overthinking it, ever mindful of my new role and the responsibility that comes with representing the family brand."

She nodded, her expression thoughtful. "I'm sure it's been a lot to take on. How are you doing?"

I'm an anxious, exhausted ball of stress. But yeah, I'm just peachy.

"I'm—" I was tempted to tell her the truth. To blurt it all out. But I knew that wasn't what she wanted. That wasn't what anyone wanted. So, I smiled my charming smile and said, "I'm great."

Kendall evaluated me, and for a minute, I thought she'd push the matter, but she dropped it. "We'd love to have you participate, but only if it's something you're comfortable with. Just…think about it."

I didn't need to think about it. Kendall was family, and

this was for a good cause. Everyone else thought it was a great idea. I was the only one who had a problem with it.

Because of Halle.

Which was ridiculous, really. Halle might have moved to LA, but she'd made it clear that nothing would happen between us. Pierce had reaffirmed how foolish such a decision would be. And with my only recently taking over as CEO and Sloan going on maternity leave in the next few months, I would need Halle's help.

Auctioning myself off to the highest bidder might force me to go on a date, spend time with a woman who wasn't *her*. Because now, more than ever, I needed to maintain my distance from Halle.

So, despite my reservations, I said, "Thanks for asking me to participate. Of course I'll help."

Kendall tilted her head. "Only if you're sure."

"I'm sure," I said, trying to project a certainty I didn't feel. Lately, I wasn't sure of anything.

CHAPTER EIGHT

HALLE

"Thanks for coming to lunch with me," Sloan said from across the table.

I glanced up from my menu. The food looked delicious, and I was hungrier than I'd realized.

"It's always nice to get away from the office for a little bit. How are you feeling?"

"Good." She smiled, placing her hand on her stomach. "Honestly, I'm just ready for the baby to be here. I'm sick of everyone acting like I need to be swaddled in bubble wrap. And my belly is getting so heavy."

I laughed. "Not much longer now. And then everyone's focus will shift to your little one."

"Thank god." She laughed. We both did. "But if it's a girl, she's going to be screwed."

I shook my head. "All those overprotective uncles. Not to mention her dad."

Sloan's smile turned wistful. "She will have Jackson wrapped around her little finger."

"Can you even imagine?"

If it was a girl, Jackson was going to lose his shit. I couldn't wait to see him absolutely melt for their daughter.

"Honestly, I'm just really excited to meet this little one."

"We all are," I said, beyond thrilled for my friend. She was going to be a great mom. "Are you looking forward to the baby shower?"

"Yes, but I'm completely overwhelmed by the registry. Who knew something so tiny needed so much stuff?" Her eyes bugged out.

I laughed. "Yeah. I remember feeling the same way. Do you want some help?"

"That would be great. My best friend Greer offered. But so much has changed, even since she had her kids."

"It's been a while for me too, but we can go through it together."

After we ordered, I held out my hand. "Show me what you've got so far."

She handed me her phone. I scrolled through the registry website. "Okay, so this—" I pointed to the screen where an item was displayed "—total gimmick."

"Really?" Sloan scrunched up her nose.

"Definitely. A waste of money."

"It's gone. Delete it. Next."

I deleted it and offered a few more suggestions.

"I feel silly even having a registry," she admitted after a while. "I don't want to ask people to buy things for us when we can more than afford to get them ourselves. But Greer insisted on it, and she's throwing the shower with Kendall and Emerson."

"Let them have their fun. People love buying stuff for babies."

Sloan laughed. "That's what Jackson's mom said too. I just want to have a party to celebrate, but everyone keeps insisting on gifts."

"At least you know your baby is very loved."

She smiled, her features softening. "Yes. They are. And the baby loved being on the water this past weekend. What about Kai? I hope he had fun on Knox's yacht."

"A blast," I said. "And your family was so wonderful to make him feel welcome and let him explore."

Everyone had gone out of their way to include my son. I knew I wasn't part of their family, but they'd certainly welcomed me into their fold. Kendall and Emerson had invited me to join them for yoga. And Jasper had continually surprised me—holding Ezra, his great nephew, and making him laugh. Watching out for Kai and keeping him entertained. Answering every one of my son's endless questions about his helicopter or the yacht or whatever else popped into his head.

"We loved having him there," Sloan said.

"Thanks. He thought it was beyond cool, but he's obsessed with Lego and transportation. I showed him a picture of me with Jasper's helicopter, and now he won't stop asking to fly in it."

"Jasper took you in the helicopter?" she asked, surprise lighting her tone. "When?"

"Oh, um—" I smoothed my napkin over my lap. "The day we went art shopping. Traffic was awful, so Jasper suggested it."

"Having a brother who's a helicopter pilot definitely comes in handy sometimes."

I nodded. "We would never have made it on time otherwise."

"I can't wait to see the new pieces once they arrive."

I was so excited, I felt as if I might burst. I only hoped Sloan and everyone else would like them as much as I did. "They're supposed to deliver them later this week."

"Excellent. And thank you again for handling everything."

"Absolutely."

Her expression turned more contemplative. "Can I ask you something?"

"Of course."

"You worked with Jasper in the past when he was still an SVP. How do you think he's handling his new role?"

I, uh…I hadn't expected that question. It felt as if it had come out of left field.

"Why do you ask?" Maybe I was stalling, but I was also curious.

"He hasn't been acting like himself lately."

"Hasn't been acting like himself…how?" I asked, hoping I didn't sound overly curious. I was merely a concerned friend and employee inquiring after the welfare of her brother.

"He seems more reserved or withdrawn or something. It's weird. Honestly, I don't like it."

"He's had a lot of big life changes recently," I said, understanding her concern but feeling defensive on Jasper's behalf. "He's taken on a huge new role, somewhat unex-pectedly. Graham's suddenly out of the picture. You're about to have a baby. Any one of those things would be a lot. But all three at once…" I let my statement hang in the air.

Not to mention the fact that with Graham focused on a new subsidiary of the brand, Jasper and Sloan had had to redistribute the workload as well as look for a new SVP to help share that burden.

"Yeah. I guess when you put it that way," she sighed. Sloan skimmed something on her phone then smiled. "Sorry."

She typed a response to someone; I assumed it was Jack-son. Then she slid her phone back into her purse and returned her attention to me. "Where were we? Oh right… Jasper." She rolled her eyes, but her smile was warm. "I'm just worried about him, that's all."

"He seems to be adjusting well. At least from what I can tell."

Was he stressed? Sure. Who wouldn't be in his position? And while I didn't want to betray Jasper's confidence, I couldn't help but wonder… What if I could help?

"You know how you're sick of everyone treating you like you're fragile because you're pregnant?"

She nodded. "Yeah."

"And there are probably other things you miss about not being pregnant. Like wine."

"God, I miss wine," she groaned.

We both laughed.

"I think…well, I can imagine, that Jasper has certain things he misses about his life before he was CEO."

"Huh." She sank back against her chair. "I guess I never thought about it that way. And what about you? Are there things you miss about London?"

"Of course," I said. "But I'm excited about this new chapter in LA."

"How are you settling in?"

I straightened my silverware. I couldn't believe we'd already been living in LA for almost two weeks. But after spending the past decade living in London, I found LA a bit of a culture shock. There was so much sun, especially moving here in the midst of winter. It was so warm, it didn't even feel like winter. At least, not the dark, blustery winters I'd come to know in London.

And everyone was so…shiny. That was a bad description, but everyone here was so beautiful. I was living in a sea of actors and wannabe actors. Models. Everyone seemed to have perfected that no-makeup look that actually took two hours to achieve. I couldn't imagine how exhausting it was to maintain that façade.

"I'm sure I'll feel more settled once we have a more permanent home."

"I'm sure you're right," she said. "And Kai? How is he doing with the move?"

"Good." He'd adapted more quickly than I had. But he was a kid. They were resilient. "His birthday is coming up, and I'm hoping he'll make a few friends at pre-K that he'll want to invite to celebrate. And I need to find us a house before the school year starts."

I wanted to be settled before Kai started kindergarten in the fall. I wanted a space that was ours. A home we could invite friends over to visit that wasn't attached to my office, even if it was convenient. Maybe a little too convenient, considering the proximity to Jasper's penthouse.

A few steps. A short elevator ride. And we were at his place.

Finding a home for Kai was something that had been weighing on me, but I wasn't even sure where to start. I had a generous relocation package, but LA real estate was expensive. Renting seemed like my only option for now, especially considering the uncertainty surrounding my parents' situation.

I still hadn't convinced my mom that moving my dad to a facility was a necessity, despite offering to pay for it. She knew the circumstances better than I did, so maybe I was overreacting. But I knew the day would come—probably sooner than later—when we'd have to move him to assisted living. I didn't know how I was going to afford that plus a place for Kai and me, but I was determined to figure it out. I had to.

"I can't help with the friends, but as for the house, have you talked to Alexis?"

Alexis Black. Black Realty. Nate's friend and owner of one of the top residential real estate brokerages in LA.

I nodded. "I have. I really like her."

"I had a feeling the two of you would hit it off. You have a lot in common."

I took that as a compliment. Because Alexis was a badass. Strong, independent, a successful businesswoman.

"She found Jackson and me an amazing home on fairly short notice. I'm sure she'll help you find what you're looking for too."

What if I wasn't sure what I was looking for? Or what if I found it, but it came at too high a price?

Like Jasper?

I shook my head, wondering where that had come from. Though, honestly, could I really say I was all that surprised? Lately, he was unavoidable.

I shut down that line of thought and tried to focus on the conversation at hand. "I'll touch base with her. Thanks."

"It's strange to be back in this city after such a long time away," Sloan said. "Visiting LA isn't the same as living here. It's definitely an adjustment."

"I'm sure it'll get easier," I said, wondering when I'd start to believe it.

Our meals arrived. I hadn't realized how hungry I was until the plate was before me. It had been a busy morning packed with meetings and obligations, and I'd barely stopped to breathe.

After I'd inhaled a good portion of my meal, I glanced up to find Sloan watching me curiously.

"Sorry." I used my napkin to wipe my mouth. "I guess I was hungry." I laughed.

"It's okay, but we're not in any rush. I know we work in a fast-paced environment, but we all need to slow down some-times." When I gave her a pointed look, she added, "I know. I know. I need to be better about taking my own advice."

I knew she was right, but I also knew—like Sloan—that it

was easier said than done. I was a single mom. It was all on me. I often ate my food on the run, and I couldn't remember the last time I'd actually sat down for a meal at a nice restaurant with only adults for company for something that wasn't related to work.

"Actually, that's a big reason why I asked you to join me for lunch today. I know I've been putting off making decisions about my maternity leave, but I think I've been in denial."

I could understand that. I'd had similar feelings after my dad's diagnosis. Denial. Anger. Disbelief. Heartbreak. I was still grappling with it.

"With my due date approaching, we need to put some things in place," she said.

Finally.

I let out a small exhale of relief. Living in limbo while waiting for Sloan to tell me how she wanted to handle her maternity leave had been weighing on me. At least now, hopefully, we'd be able to make a plan and move forward for the four months that she'd be gone.

I folded my napkin in my lap. I'd anticipated this, and I'd wondered how she'd want to approach it. "Let me know how I can help."

"Thank you. I appreciate you more than you know."

I tucked my hair behind my ear, wishing the curls would stay put. "I know you do." But it was always nice to hear it.

"I know you just moved here and you have a lot on your plate, but the annual Huxley Family Foundation gala is coming up. Since I'm not allowed to travel, I was hoping you'd go in my place. You'd travel on the private jet with my family, and you'd get a clothing allowance."

"How long would I be gone?" I asked, thinking about Kai and how he often struggled when I traveled for work.

Fortunately, it wasn't often that I had to go on overnight

trips. But to say the last one hadn't gone well would be an understatement.

"Leave Friday. Back Sunday."

Two nights. Okay.

A quick review of my calendar confirmed that Craig was supposed to visit around that time. Maybe he could stay with Kai while I went to New York. If not, well, I'd cross that bridge when I got there.

"That shouldn't be an issue," I said, trying to infuse my voice with a confidence I didn't feel.

"Great." Sloan flashed me a relieved smile. "Thank you so much, Halle. It really puts my mind at ease, knowing you'll be there."

"Of course," I said, grateful I could help. "Apart from serving as your representative, is there anything else I can do?"

"The foundation is doing this whole bachelorx auction. So maybe check in with Kendall to see if she needs anything."

I arched my brow. "Bachelorx auction?"

She laughed. "They wanted to try something new. Jasper's participating."

Of course he is.

I shouldn't have been surprised, and yet her words felt like a punch to the gut. I had no right to feel jealous. No claim over Jasper, and yet… I felt like a fool.

I'd lost count of the times he'd looked at me, flirted with me, over the past two weeks. And the entire time, he'd been planning to auction himself off to other women. It was yet one more reminder of why I needed to maintain my distance.

"Good. That's one thing taken care of." Somehow, though, she didn't look all that relieved. "And now for an even bigger ask."

I was used to juggling a lot, and she was my friend. She'd

given me an opportunity when most people had slammed the door in my face. Lack of relevant experience. Too big a gap in my résumé. "Tell me what you need while you're out, and I'll handle everything."

"I know you will." She rolled her lips between her teeth in a rare moment of hesitation. "Which is why I want to name you as acting SVP in my absence."

"You…" I blinked a few times. "What?"

"While I'm out, I want to put you in charge," Sloan said.

"Me?" I swallowed hard. She was putting *me* in charge? "But I'm not…"

She shook her head. "Don't say you're not qualified. You are more than qualified. I know it's a lot to ask, but I trust you to do what's best for the company. And the board is in agreement."

"Wow." I blinked a few times, stunned. "I don't know what to say."

Yes, it would be more responsibility, but it was also an amazing opportunity. When I'd taken a break to stay at home with Kai, I could've never dreamed I'd be given a chance like this.

"Say yes." She grinned. "You'll get a temporary pay increase as well."

"That's very generous." I was already thinking of what I could do with the extra money. I could put some of it away in savings. I could hire in-home help for my dad. I could…

She leaned forward—well, as much as she could with her stomach in the way. "It's what you deserve. And between us, it would be a huge relief to know that you'd be there to keep an eye on Jasper."

I paused with my fork midway to my mouth. *Jasper.*

Hearing his name was like being doused with a bucket of ice water. Because this opportunity would require me to work even more closely with him. If I were the SVP—even temporarily—spending time with him would be unavoidable. It would be a *requirement* of my job.

Fuck!

Perhaps sensing my hesitation, Sloan said, "No. No. No. Not—" She held up a hand. "I didn't mean to make it sound like he needed a babysitter. I just know that he likes and respects you, and I worry he doesn't have the support he needs, especially with Graham in France and me out on maternity leave."

I tilted my head back in understanding, because what could I say?

I couldn't say no. Sloan needed me. But I wasn't sure—in good conscience—that I could say yes either.

"You've been there for me, and I can only hope that you'll be a friend to him too," she added.

I didn't know if I could commit to being Jasper's friend. Not after...well, not after everything we'd shared. I'd put space between us for a reason, and now Sloan was asking me to close that gap.

If she only knew...

"Would it require much travel?" I asked, thinking of Kai. He was still adjusting to living in a new city. I couldn't leave him in the care of a stranger, no matter what their qualifications were as a nanny.

I didn't want to mention that to Sloan, especially since I'd just agreed to go to New York for a weekend. I'd never want her to question my commitment to the job or my ability to perform my responsibilities. Being away from Kai wasn't ideal, but he was a little older now. And besides, Craig would be there with him.

I really hoped I wasn't putting too much faith in my ex. History told me that I couldn't count on him, but he'd been different since the move. More involved. More proactive, even if it was from afar.

"It shouldn't," Sloan said. "Jasper has a few trips planned since we knew I'd be unavailable. And if something else comes up, we can always see if Graham could handle it."

"Who would do my job?" I asked, my wheels spinning.

"We could temporarily promote someone from within the company, or we could hire a temp."

I scrunched up my face. "I'm not sure I'd want a temp, based on Jasper's experience."

She laughed. "Oh, please. Jasper selects them based on attractiveness not competence."

It was an offhand comment, and she probably meant it in jest. But my stomach churned, my lunch threatening to reemerge. That wasn't really true, was it?

Based on the fact that he wanted to rehire Darla, I had my doubts. She might be an attractive woman in her sixties, but I knew Jasper had no romantic interest in her. Maybe I was just believing what I wanted to believe. Or maybe Jasper's family didn't know him as well as they thought they did.

"We will find someone." Sloan patted my hand, perhaps misinterpreting my horrified expression. "I don't expect you to manage your job plus mine all on your own. That wouldn't be good for you or the company."

Or Kai.

That said, I wasn't really in a position to turn it down. The extra income could help offset the cost of my dad's care but also give me more wiggle room with our finances. More options when it came to buying a home.

I nodded. "I appreciate your faith in me, but I also have to consider what's best for Kai."

I wanted to give her offer careful consideration. I wanted to make sure it was something I could actually commit to. Something I could manage to the level of excellence Sloan expected. The level I expected of myself.

"Of course." Sloan placed a hand over her stomach. "I get

that. Think it over. We still have a little time before my maternity leave."

"Thank you," I said, though I didn't want to leave her hanging.

If I wasn't going to take the role, she'd need to find someone else—and fast. But I knew Sloan, and she wouldn't have offered it to me unless she thought I could handle it.

Could I handle it?

I had reservations. Not just about the responsibility but about what it would mean for Kai and me. My life was already hectic. I worried that accepting the position would mean time with my son would be even more limited.

Perhaps most concerning of all, though, was the fact that the role would require me to work even more closely with Jasper. I was already struggling to keep our relationship professional, and the last thing I wanted was to spend more time with him.

Liar.

Okay. Rephrase that. The last thing I *should* be doing was spending more time with Jasper.

CHAPTER NINE

HALLE

"You ready, Kai?" I called out as I finished cleaning up the dishes.

"Ready for what?" he asked.

"To go to Jasper's."

"Really?" he practically squealed down the hall from his bedroom. "We get to see Jasper? Are we going to play video games? Will we get to swim in his pool or ride in his helicopter?"

"He has some artwork arriving, and I need to be there to help the delivery team install it."

"Can Jasper and I go for a ride in his helicopter while you do that?"

I tried not to laugh. "Probably not. But maybe he'll let you play video games."

"Okay."

"Is your bed made?" I asked. "We need to finish bedtime chores before we go to Jasper's since I'm not sure how late it will be when we get back."

"Does that mean I get to stay up past my bedtime? Can I stay up until midnight?" He was practically buzzing.

"I don't know. And no." I laughed. "Is your bed made?" I asked again.

Since we were working on establishing routines, we had a rule that it had to be made before bedtime. I didn't care if he made it in the morning before pre-K or as part of his evening chores. I just wanted him to practice making his bed every day. Eventually, I'd work on making it a morning chore. But for now, I was happy if it was done.

"No," he said, followed by giggles. "Will you come help me?"

"Kai, bud, we talked about this. In the evening, you're responsible for your bed, putting away your clean laundry, and one 'notice and do.'"

"I know. I just…" Was he grunting? "Can you come here for a sec?"

"Sure." I set down my purse and headed back down the hall to his room. "What's up?"

He stood in front of his bed, beaming. The quilt was pulled up, the pillows were fluffed and in the right places. And he looked so cute and proud.

"Tricked you!" He grinned.

"You sure did." I smiled and ruffled his copper curls, so like my own, completely okay with this turn of events. "Good job."

"Thanks, Mummy. I used Jasper's tricks."

I wondered what else I could get Jasper to "trick" Kai into doing. Eating more vegetables? Brushing his teeth for the whole two minutes without being asked?

"Ready?" Kai asked, placing his hand in mine.

"Yep," I exhaled.

I couldn't wait to see the new art in Jasper's penthouse. I was both anxious and excited for him to see my selections. I'd put a lot of effort into choosing art that spoke to me for him, and I hoped he'd love them.

We rode the private elevator up to Jasper's floor. I stared at my reflection in the mirrored doors. I'd changed out of my work clothes and into a pair of linen shorts, a matching tank with a square neckline, and slide-on sandals. Nothing too fancy. I didn't want to look like I was trying too hard.

Right. So that's why you refreshed your hair and makeup?

I rolled my eyes at myself in the mirror. My makeup was minimal, but that wasn't the point. The point was that I'd gone to any additional effort with my appearance because I knew I'd be spending time with Jasper.

It annoyed me that I didn't just say yes to going out with Dimitri when he'd asked. It annoyed me that I couldn't look at another man without comparing him to Jasper. It annoyed me that…

The elevator chimed, and the doors slid open. I took a deep, steadying breath. *Get it together.*

I was tired, that was all. It had been a busy week, and I'd spent more nights than I cared to admit thinking about Jasper and whether I should accept the temporary promotion.

I'd be crazy not to; Zara had said as much. And I'd told myself that I'd never let a man dictate my choices, but Jasper was definitely a big factor in my decision. There was a difference between working in the same office as him and working *closely* with him.

We'd gotten along fine when we'd gone art shopping, which was reassuring. Well, at least when he hadn't been openly hostile toward Dimitri. When Jasper hadn't cornered me and admitted he was jealous.

Apart from that, it had gone well. When Jasper and I were alone, things had been cordial, friendly even. But that was one interaction on one day. Not months of conversations and decisions and…

My phone buzzed; I had a new text message from Alexis.

She'd been sending me questions about houses, but we'd also talked about her favorite places around LA and the challenges of being a working mom. It was nice, and it felt like I'd made my first new friend in LA.

Kai skipped down the hall to Jasper's door.

"Kai," I whispered.

"Hm?" he asked, turning back.

"What kind of behavior are you going to be on today at Jasper's?"

He straightened. "Best behavior."

"That's right," I said. "So that means no hands on the windows. No jumping on the couch. Got it?"

"Got it." He gave me two thumbs up and the biggest smile. But then he winced, his hands flying to his stomach as he curved inward on himself.

"What's wrong, baby?" I crouched to his level.

"My tummy hurts." He groaned, clutching at his abdomen.

His stomach did look bloated, but I couldn't understand why. We'd eaten the same thing we'd had a million times. And he had no reason—at least none that I could tell—to be anxious.

"Do you want to go back home?" I didn't want Kai to be uncomfortable. And while I was excited about the art, we could always reschedule.

Kai shook his head, fervent in his refusal. "No. Please. I want to see Jasper."

I wondered how much of Kai's enthusiasm for spending time with Jasper had to do with missing his dad. Or if he really liked Jasper that much. They'd definitely connected, even in the short time we'd been in LA.

"You're sure?"

He nodded. "Please, Mum."

I straightened. "Okay." After a moment's hesitation, I rang Jasper's doorbell.

It didn't take long for him to answer. He swung open the door. "Welcome! Welcome. Come on in."

He looked casual and effortless in a pair of white chino shorts and a short-sleeved Henley in this sumptuous oatmeal color. The material clung to his chest, beckoning me to touch him.

He was hot in a suit, but this look might be my favorite. Casual. At ease. Feet bare and posture relaxed.

"Hi." His eyes finally met mine after a leisurely perusal that heated my skin. "Can I get you anything to drink? Water? Wine?"

Wine sounded good, even if I knew it was a bad idea.

"I'm good. Thanks."

"What about you, Kai?" Jasper gave him a high five. "Want anything to drink or eat?"

"No thanks. Can we do those magic tricks now?" Kai practically bounced on his toes.

I studied him, searching for any signs of stomach troubles. Did he already feel that much better, or had he forgotten? It was a relief that it wasn't bothering him—regardless of the reason. But he complained about his stomach often enough that I was worried, even if no one else took my concerns seriously.

Jasper chuckled. "In a little bit. I actually need your help with something while we wait for my new art to arrive." Jasper placed his hand on Kai's shoulder. He was so warm and affectionate, so unlike Craig.

God. Stop comparing them.

"What is it?" Kai asked.

"Actually, there's someone I want you to meet." Jasper turned to me, and I wondered what he was up to. "She's through here."

She? Why did the idea of another woman in Jasper's home irk me so much?

Sloan hadn't mentioned that her brother was dating anyone. But that didn't mean Jasper wasn't involved with someone. Last summer, we'd snuck around for weeks without anyone knowing. Was he doing that now but with someone else?

My stomach clenched—both at the idea that he was seeing someone else and the thought that maybe what we'd had wasn't that special to him.

It was supposed to be a fling. Casual. Carefree. Easy.

The opposite of my current feelings. This was why it had been a mistake to get involved with anyone, let alone…him.

But he made it difficult to resist. Jasper was charismatic, detail-oriented, and fun. God, I'd had so much fun with him. Last summer, our fling, was the first time in years I'd felt like myself. I'd felt as if I could breathe again.

He'd made me laugh. He made everything feel so…easy. When I'd been drowning, he felt like a lifeline.

As Kai and I followed Jasper into his bathroom, the sound of sniffing and panting threw me. And then I spied a little gated area with towels on the floor. A cute little dog jumped up and barked, and Kai froze.

"Oh. My. Gosh," he whispered. "Oh. My…" He turned to me, his eyes bulging. *"Mum!"*

"I know." I laughed, that bubble of anxiety that had been building inside me popping.

"How cute are you?" Kai squealed.

And she was adorable. A small wire-haired Dachshund with a brown-and-black coat. Her ears had curly fur, and she was so expressive.

"Is she yours?" Kai asked Jasper.

"Yep." Jasper beamed. "A rescue pup."

I narrowed my eyes at Jasper. What was he playing at?

But Jasper's attention was on Kai, a warm smile on his face. "Here," he said, stepping forward. "Let me open the gate, and you can play with her."

"Really?" Kai looked between us as if he couldn't quite believe his luck. "Can I, Mum?"

"If it's okay with Jasper, sure."

"You'd be doing me a big favor," Jasper said. "She's been whining all night because she's lonely, and I wouldn't let her sleep on the bed. I'm fu—" He stopped himself. "I'm exhausted."

I patted Jasper on the shoulder. "Welcome to parenthood."

His expression changed, and the shift was so subtle I would've missed it if I hadn't been watching him so closely.

"Ack!" Kai shouted. "She slobbered on my face. Yuck!"

"Where are your washcloths?" I asked, opening a few drawers. Razor blades neatly in a row. Bars of soap with the Huxley Grand logo. And...oop! Condoms. I slammed the drawer shut. Damn. That was a lot of condoms. All labeled with the Huxley Grand logo.

"Here you go." Jasper handed me a washcloth, and I prayed that he hadn't seen me open that drawer.

I held the washcloth under the sink and then wrung it out before handing it to Kai. "Here you go."

Kai was in heaven. And the dog seemed pretty happy too, clambering over his lap, playing tug-of-war with the edge of a towel.

"Mum, look!" Kai giggled as the pup licked him. "I think she likes me."

I laughed. "Yeah. I think she does too." I turned to Jasper. "Does she have a name?"

"Not yet." He leaned his hip against the bathroom counter, looking sexier than any man had any right to. "Any ideas?"

Why did he have to be so handsome? A strong jawline,

high cheekbones, full lips. A wayward curl that often fell over his face.

Professional. Just be...professional.

To distract myself, I leaned over the fence and smoothed my hand down the puppy's fur. Though she kept trying to nip or lick me. "Fiddlesticks."

"Fiddlesticks?" Jasper asked.

I peered at him over my shoulder, only to find him staring at my ass. I quirked an eyebrow, and his eyes met mine. He didn't even try to hide the fact that he'd been checking me out.

Oh, this is bad.

"Fiddlesticks," Jasper said again.

"Yeah. Why not?"

"Seems like a mouthful when I need to call her." He shifted, ever-so-subtly adjusting himself. Had that... Had *I* made him hard?

"Did you have any names you were considering?" I asked, still pondering that as I loved on this sweet little dog. She was too cute for words. And keeping my attention on her was safer than watching her owner.

"How about Pom-Pom?" Kai said.

"That has potential," Jasper said, while I went over to the sink to wash my hands.

I shot him a look as if to say, "Really?"

"Why not?" he asked.

I lifted a shoulder, marveling at the way we could have an entire conversation with only a handful of words. Craig and I had never been that in sync, even after all the years we'd been a couple. In fact, it seemed like the longer we'd been together, the more disconnected we'd become.

While Kai played happily with Jasper's new pet and suggested names for the puppy like Rosemary and Tuxedo, Jasper stood with his back against the counter, arms and legs crossed before him. He looked so relaxed, and part of me was tempted to muss his hair. Make him look as out of sorts as I felt every time I was in his presence. Every time I had to pretend I felt nothing for him.

Jasper glanced at his phone then said, "Dimitri's team is on their way up."

His words snapped me out of my daze. "Kai. Are you good here while I help Jasper?"

"I'm great!" he practically squealed.

I laughed. "Okay. Come get us if you need us."

As Jasper and I headed for the front door, he said, "Thanks again for doing this."

"Are you kidding? It was a dream come true. Getting to shop for art with an unlimited budget," I sighed.

But it was more than that. It was the fact that Jasper had given me free rein. He hadn't micromanaged or second-guessed me. He'd trusted me.

Though, now that the delivery crew was actually here, carrying the wrapped pieces to their designated homes, my nerves were bubbling up. What if Jasper hated them? I rolled my lips between my teeth, directing the crew where each piece was supposed to go.

As each one was unveiled, I watched Jasper's reaction closely. When he saw the first piece, his eyes widened, and he leaned forward. He said nothing, following me to the next piece and the next. There were five pieces in total, and by the time he'd seen four of them, sweat was dripping down my back. I had no idea what he was thinking. Did he love them? Hate them?

He was so detail-oriented, and he put so much care into everything he did, that part of me was still surprised he'd wanted my help.

The last piece was one of my favorites. I held my breath, anxiously awaiting his reaction.

"Is that…" He stepped back and rubbed a hand over his mouth. "A dragonfly wing?"

I nodded. "Isn't it beautiful? So delicate and sculptural. I can't believe the level of detail the artist captured."

He smiled. "My gran used to wear the most beautiful dragonfly brooch."

I watched him. "I know. It was in the image of her on the website. And her portrait in the lobby."

"I—" He turned to me. "Yeah." He rubbed the back of his neck. "That's right. She always told me that dragonflies symbolized transformation and new beginnings. But now it feels like…" He sniffed. "Like she's saying hello."

I smiled. "That's lovely."

"These are incredible. Thank you." His expression was full of such intensity that it nearly stole my breath.

My body lit up at his praise, and the effect could've powered the entire building. "I'm glad you like them."

"I love them." But when he said the words, he was looking at me. It felt as if he was saying the words about me.

I dipped my head, unable to meet Jasper's eyes. The moment felt both too intense and too delicate. As if one wrong word would ruin everything and send our fragile relationship over the edge.

Did I want to fall over that edge?

Sometimes.

Sometimes I didn't want to restrain myself. Sometimes I wanted to give in. To let go.

Sometimes I wanted to go back to how we were last summer. Easy and carefree and fun.

It was tempting. *He* was tempting.

There was a long, silent pause, and then my phone started vibrating in my back pocket. I startled then peeked at the screen. It was my mom, so I figured I'd call her back later.

I pocketed my phone, but as soon as it had stopped buzzing, it started again. Mom, again.

"Everything okay?" Jasper asked.

"I just—" I hooked my thumb over my shoulder. "I should take this call."

"Sure." He furrowed his brow, scanning my face for clues. "You can use my office. I'll keep an eye on Kai."

"Thanks." I pressed the button to connect the call and dashed down the hall to his office, closing the door softly behind me. "Hi, Mom. Is—"

I barely got the words out before my mom cut in. "I can't find your dad." She sounded frantic, and my pulse instantly shot up.

"What do you mean, can't find him?"

"I-I don't know. I went to shower, and when I came out, he was gone. I'm sorry to bother you with this, but I'm just so worried. He usually comes back by now."

"Usually?" My pitch rose. "How many times has this happened? How long has he been gone?"

I was practically shouting at this point. I couldn't believe she'd kept this from me, and I was upset that it was happening, period.

"Oh. He just went to see Ms. Foster last time. It was no big deal."

"No big deal?" I scoffed. "Mom, he has a progressive disease that affects his brain. He could've been hurt or…" I swallowed hard, not willing to go there. Right now, the only thing that mattered was finding my dad. We'd deal with next steps once he was safe. "Look. Let's focus on finding Dad. Did you call his phone?"

"It keeps going straight to voice mail."

"I thought you installed the app to track his phone."

"I did, but that only works if he has the phone on him and the battery is charged. Last time, we got lucky."

I wasn't even going to touch that statement. Not yet. "Neighbors?"

"I texted them, and they're keeping an eye out for him. I drove the main road several times but didn't see him."

"Do you think he's in the woods?"

She started crying when I mentioned that possibility.

That was it. I'd had enough. He was missing. He could be confused or hurt. "We need to call the police and have them issue a Silver Alert."

"He'll come back." She sniffled. "He always comes back."

If I'd been in denial, it was nothing compared to my mom. And I worried that there was even more that she hadn't been telling me about my dad's condition. About the true state of things.

"I'm going to call the police, and then I'll call you right back."

"No. Wait."

Why was she fighting me on this? "Mom, it's getting dark. The longer we wait, the greater risk of harm. Once I alert the police, I can try to book a plane ticket to come help."

"No. It's Dad. He's…he's here. He's in the backyard."

It was too much to process too quickly. Relief. Concern. Despair. My hands were shaking so badly, I almost dropped the phone.

"Is he okay?" I asked, trying to focus on what mattered. He was home.

I could hear the hinges of the back door as it creaked open. "Oh, thank god, Daniel," Mom said to him in a rush of relief.

"Minnie?" Dad asked. Concern mingled with confusion in his tone, and it was heartbreaking.

"Why don't you sit down at the table, sweetheart, and I'll get you some water?" I could hear my mom bustling around the kitchen, could picture it in my mind.

"Mom?" I called, then louder still, "Mom!"

"Yes. Sorry. He's back." She exhaled, keeping her voice low. "Just a small cut on his hand, but he's okay. Thank god."

"Go take care of Dad, but I want you to call me later."

I held it together long enough to tell my parents I loved them and end the call. And then I covered my face with my hands, my heart fracturing into a million pieces.

"Halle?" Jasper called through the door.

"Yeah? Yep."

I sniffled and straightened, frantically wiping away my tears. *Get it together.*

"The delivery team is gone, and Kai fell asleep."

Oh my god. I'd been so immersed in my call that I'd neglected to help Jasper with the delivery. With my own son. I didn't know if that meant I was negligent or just that I trusted Jasper. When I thought about it, I was surprised to realize the latter was true.

"Okay." My voice warbled, and I clapped a hand over my mouth.

Jasper opened the office door before I could add that I'd be right out. He took one look at me and frowned. And then, without another word, he crossed the room and pulled me into his arms.

I considered backing away, but I was too weak to protest. Especially not when Jasper was offering me comfort that felt like home.

CHAPTER TEN

JASPER

"I'm so sorry." Halle backed away from me but kept her hands on my chest. "This is so…" She shook her head. "And…" She sniffled, and I hated seeing her so upset. "I probably ruined your shirt."

I couldn't stop touching her. I kept my hands on her shoulders, needing that connection. "The shirt doesn't matter."

"I, um—" She spun away from me, grabbing her purse. "I need to get Kai. We have to get going." Her movements were frantic, and I itched to fix whatever was bothering her. To beg her to open up to me. Trust me.

Before her phone call, it had felt as if we were on the precipice of something. But whatever she'd intended to say was now lost. And it didn't matter. What mattered was that Halle was upset.

"Halle." It was a plea. "Halle," I said again, more of a command. "Stop."

"I-I—"

What the hell had happened on her phone call? Who or

what had made her cry? My mind raced with possibilities, none of them good.

"Stop." I guided her over to the sofa, taking a seat next to her. I placed my hand on her thigh, desperate to ground her. "Take a breath." I waited until she did so. Until she'd taken a few slow, deep breaths.

"There," I said. "That's better."

She nodded. "Yeah." Her shoulders relaxed by a hair. "Thanks."

"What happened?"

She focused on the skyline, and I could see her reflection mirrored back at me in the large single-pane windows. "It's getting late."

"And you're upset." I tried to keep my tone gentle, open. "Talk to me. Please."

Her shoulders relaxed, but she still wouldn't look at me. "Do you think I should take the temporary promotion?"

Whatever I'd been expecting her to say, it hadn't been that. I didn't want to sway her, and I was surprised she'd asked for my opinion. Halle always seemed so confident when it came to her career. And that confidence put others at ease. Whether Halle realized it or not, she was already a leader. People within the company looked to her for answers and reassurance.

"Do you want to take it?" I asked.

"Jasper," she huffed, turning to face me. "You can't answer a question with a question."

"I believe I just did," I quipped. She gave me a flat look. "I wouldn't have voted in favor if I didn't think you'd do a good job."

She seemed to brighten at that. Was she surprised I'd been in favor of the promotion? Surely she knew she had my vote of confidence.

"Thank you. I appreciate that. But that's not what I asked. Why are you dancing around my question?"

"Because I'm trying to understand why you're asking for my opinion in the first place. You earned the promotion. If you want the job, it's yours." To me, it was as simple as that. Halle would do a good job, and I knew I could count on her.

When she didn't offer up any more information, I finally asked, "Halle, what's this really about?"

"I *need* this job. But I also need to know that we can work together."

"We've done a good job lately, haven't we?"

She scoffed. "You're kidding, right?"

"What?" I asked, genuinely mystified. Okay, so maybe I'd flirted a little. Pushed the boundaries. But there'd been no touching. No kissing. We were friendly; that was all.

She shook her head and glanced away once more. "Nothing. It doesn't matter."

"It does matter." It mattered to me.

"I'm scared," she whispered, a tear streaking down her cheek.

I wanted to wipe it away, but I had a feeling that would only make her clam up. Pull away. Withdraw. It would undo all the progress I'd so painstakingly made the past few weeks. Especially when she was finally letting me in.

"What are you scared of?" I asked in a gentle tone.

"I'm scared I'm going to screw it up. I'm scared we won't be able to work together. I'm scared because my family needs me. Kai needs me. And I know this position will require even more of me than my current role."

It was as if she was mirroring my emotions from the past few months back at me. "You don't think I feel those same things?"

"I—" She opened her mouth and gaped at me. "You do?"

"Yes." God, it felt good to admit that. "Every fucking day. The pressure. The fear. I'm drowning in it."

Ever since I'd taken over for Graham, I felt as if I were going through the motions. I attended meetings, I made all these decisions, but I kept waiting for someone to expose me as a fraud. To tell everyone I had no fucking clue what I was doing.

I didn't want to make this conversation about me, but I wanted Halle to understand. I wanted her to know that she wasn't alone. And now that I'd confessed my struggles, I found myself wanting to tell her more.

"I never expected to be in this role. And to take over after someone like Graham?" I shook my head. "Someone who's perfect."

"First of all," Halle said, giving me a dubious look. "No one's perfect. Not even," she added when I opened my mouth to protest, "Graham. Have you talked to him about this? Asked him how he handled the pressure? The expectations?"

"He entrusted the company to me." Because there was no one else. "This is my responsibility. And besides, he deserves a break."

"You should talk to him," she said. "I bet he experienced similar feelings when he took over as CEO."

I seriously doubted that. Graham had prepared to take over as CEO his entire life. "When he was CEO, he didn't ask for help."

"And that was a problem. You even mentioned in the past that it was an issue."

Damn. She had me there.

"You have to stop comparing yourself to your brother," Halle said. "You also have to remember that the version of Graham you're comparing yourself to had been in this role for fourteen years! You've been doing it less than four months."

What Halle said made sense, but still... This was Graham we were talking about. But this wasn't about my brother. I wanted to know why Halle was so upset.

First, though, I wanted to reassure her. "I'm not trying to persuade you, but I know you'd be an amazing SVP. And even though we have—" I cleared my throat, hating the words I knew needed to be said. "Despite our history, we can make this work. We have to. Because Sloan needs you, and so do I."

Halle was quiet a moment, considering. "I need this to work too. My dad..." She rolled her lips between her teeth. "Last summer, he was diagnosed with Alzheimer's."

"I'm sorry." I didn't want to let on that I already knew. Halle was opening up to me, trusting me. And I didn't take that lightly. "I know you're close."

She nodded, tugging at the corner of her eye. "I've been trying to convince my mom to move him into an assisted living facility, but she keeps dragging her feet. After tonight —" She stared at the ceiling, looking as if she was trying not to cry again. "Well, I'm hoping she'll realize it's time."

"What happened tonight?"

She dragged a hand through her hair. "Dad went missing. Thankfully, he found his way back home, but apparently, it wasn't the first time he'd done this."

I cringed, imagining someone with memory issues just... wandering off. "That sounds terrifying."

"It was." She gnashed her teeth. "I can't believe my mom kept this from me."

"Why do you think she's hesitant to move him?" I asked.

"A lot of reasons. Some of it emotional. Some financial."

I nodded. "Ah. I see."

"The pay increase from the temporary promotion means that maybe I'll finally be able to convince my mom to move forward with getting the care my dad needs."

As in…she was going to help bear the financial burden. I rubbed a hand over my mouth. *Damn.*

I was tempted to offer Halle the money she needed outright, but I knew she'd never take it. In fact, the mere offer would probably piss her off.

My hopes for a future with Halle were sinking with every passing moment as the reality of the situation dawned on me. We both needed her position as SVP to work out, and the stakes were even higher than I'd realized.

"I didn't want to tell you all of this—"

I placed my hand over hers, stopping her. "I'm glad you did."

She studied the place where our hands were connected then met my gaze. "Thank you. I just, I guess I wanted you to understand why I need this to work. I want to do this for myself and for Sloan and the company. But I *need* to do this for so many other reasons."

I remembered everything she'd said about needing this job. Needing us to maintain our distance. So even though I didn't want to stop touching her, I removed my hand from hers.

"If you want the job, you should take it. You've earned it."

She folded her hands in her lap. "And you really think we can do this?" she asked, clearly still skeptical.

I rested my arm on the back of the sofa, needing to infuse some levity into our conversation. "Afraid you can't resist me?"

She narrowed her eyes at me. "As far as I'm concerned…" She hesitated for a beat. It wasn't long, but it was enough for me to doubt her commitment. "We're done."

I stilled, remembering us saying those two words under completely different circumstances. And somehow, despite her bravado, I wasn't buying it. She didn't mean it now, just like she hadn't meant it then.

. . .

We stood just outside the door to my hotel room. Well, my second hotel room. The one I'd reserved at a competitor's hotel so Halle and I could be together without the risk of being seen by any of the Huxley Grand London employees.

"We're done," she said. And yet, she was still standing there. Watching me with heat in her eyes.

I wanted to ask, "Then why are you here?" But I didn't. If she wanted to pretend this was over, fine. I would play her game. I leaned in, swiping the keycard in front of the lock, my words a whisper along her ear. "So done."

She shivered and turned to look at me, and I saw my own longing reflected back at me. I slanted my mouth over hers as I opened the door, knowing that we weren't done. Not yet. Maybe not ever.

She grabbed my lapels and tugged me inside with her. "I mean it, Jasper," she panted, breathless from our kisses.
The door shut behind us, and I guided her farther into the room, shedding clothes as we went.

"Mm." I kissed my way down her neck. "So do I."

I MET HER GAZE, AND I KNEW SHE WAS REMEMBERING THAT moment too. And the look in her eyes told me far more than the words she'd spoken. We weren't done. Far from it.

∽

THREE WEEKS PASSED. THREE LONG WEEKS IN WHICH HALLE and I stuck to our agreement to "be professional." Neither of us mentioned that night in my penthouse or our past. I knew she was under a lot of pressure at home and at work, and I didn't want to add to it.

I might want more, but a relationship with her was impractical for so many reasons. So, I'd tried to keep my distance.

It was fine. I was fine.

I wasn't fine.

I was on edge. I'd seen her on and off—passing her in the halls, smiling between meetings. But every time our eyes locked, that knot of ache in my chest both intensified and loosened. It was pathetic.

I could barely look at Halle without thinking of what could've been. So I'd avoided her, mostly. I knew that wasn't a winning strategy, nor would it be workable when Sloan went on maternity leave. But I didn't have much of a choice. I was now the CEO, and Halle had agreed to be the acting SVP in Sloan's absence. We were both committed to our jobs and the success of the company.

Halle deserved to be the SVP, even if it was temporary. But if anyone found out about our relationship, even if it was all in the past, people might question the true reason for her temporary promotion. They might doubt her abilities.

And then there was the matter of my position as CEO and the impact that my relationship with an employee could have on the company. This wasn't just about me and my feelings for Halle; it was about all one hundred and seventy-five thousand employees who were employed by the Huxley Grand, not to mention the communities that relied on the tourists our hotels attracted to the area. Even more than that, it was about my family. Our legacy.

I'd never fully understood Graham's obsession with

legacy until now. And if he'd had any idea what was going on, he'd kill me.

"You seem distracted today," Sumner said, dragging me away from my thoughts.

Distracted? I wanted to bark out a laugh.

Unfortunately, it wasn't just today. It was every fucking day since Halle had moved to LA. Before that, even, but it was worse the closer our proximity.

"Want to talk about it?" Sometimes it felt more like Sumner was my therapist than my life coach. I'd tried talking to therapists in the past but with mixed success. None of them got me, but Sumner did. Halle did.

I sighed. What was there to say?

"Do you ever find it difficult to remain committed to your goals?" I asked, opting to keep it vague.

"Who doesn't?"

"Emerson," I muttered.

Sumner laughed. "This again? Yes, your sister-in-law is an Olympic gold medalist, but she's not a machine. I bet if you asked her, she'd admit to struggling with her goals."

"But she didn't give up."

"Doesn't mean she didn't feel like it." Sumner shot me a look. "Are you finding it difficult to remain committed to your goals?"

Don't talk about Halle. Don't...

"I, uh—" I tugged on my collar.

Sumner arched one eyebrow. "Jasper?"

"Last summer, I was seeing someone. And she recently came back into my life."

Sumner smiled. "Ah. I see. Is it serious?"

I lifted a shoulder. "She's not interested in anything serious."

Sumner lifted her chin in understanding. "But you are."

I toyed with one of my cuff links, a gift from Nate for my

birthday last year. "I want to be, but there are a lot of obstacles standing in the way. And I'm afraid she doesn't completely trust me or my intentions."

"So, prove her wrong. And be the man you want to be—for yourself but also for her."

If only it were that simple. If only Halle weren't my employee. But would I honestly stand a chance, even if she didn't work for me?

"You don't seem convinced," Sumner said, observant as ever.

I barked out a laugh, dragging a hand down my face. "I can't even get my shit together at work. If my work life is a mess, how can I have any hope of getting my personal life in order?"

"Start with what you can control. If you want everyone to see you as the boss, you have to take charge. Stop looking over your shoulder for your brother. Stop second-guessing yourself. You're the CEO." She held my gaze. "You're in charge."

I nodded, letting myself believe her words. "I'm in charge."

Sumner passed me a business card. "It's time to get serious about finding Darla's replacement."

I hung my head. I knew Darla wasn't coming back. I'd known that for a while now. But I'd finally admitted it to myself.

"Call the Hartwell Agency. They'll be able to help."

The Hartwell Agency was a reputable staffing agency known for their service and discretion. Knox used them to staff his yacht. We used their services to staff the family jet. My family had hired a number of outstanding employees through them, including Kendall and Emerson.

"Is there a reason why you're hesitating?" Sumner asked.

"Besides the fact that you've been dragging your heels about hiring a new chief of staff."

"Just want to make sure they can help me find the right type of person. Because hiring some young, attractive assistant is *not* going to help me convince everyone that I've changed."

Sumner rolled her eyes. "Yes, a lot of their staff is attractive. But you can request certain things in your intake form. Ask for someone with twenty-plus years of experience. Hell, ask for a man if you want, if you're worried about the perception of having a woman working for you."

I set the card on my desk. I knew I was being unreasonable. The Hartwell Agency had an excellent reputation. I needed to stop making excuses.

"Okay. I'll reach out to them."

"Good." Sumner brightened. "I think once you have a new chief of staff, a lot of things will fall into place. And before you know it, you'll be well on your way to accomplishing your goals."

"I want to believe that," I said. "But to be honest, dating this woman is one of the biggest things that could derail everything." And I did mean *everything*.

I considered leaving it at that, but I knew if I didn't talk about this, the situation would continue to fester. If I couldn't talk to Sumner about it, who could I talk to? Not Graham—he'd blow a gasket and regret leaving me in charge. Not Sloan. It would unnecessarily stress her out when she was supposed to be limiting her anxiety. Not to mention create friction with Halle. And Pierce... Well, he might actually kill me.

So I finally said, "The woman in question is important to the company and my sister."

"Ah. Now I understand."

"I didn't mean for this to happen." I crossed and

uncrossed my legs at the ankle, trying to dispel some of my restless energy. "Yes, I knew the risks when we were together last summer. But at the time, I was an SVP with no thought of taking over as CEO. And we both agreed it was just for the summer."

"I've been there."

"Really?" I asked, leaning forward and resting my forearms on my thighs. Now I was intrigued. Maybe Sumner would have a solution for my predicament.

"I suppose I can tell you. Fair warning, it doesn't paint me in the most professional light, but it's also not something I'm ashamed of."

"Okay," I said, hoping that I sounded nonjudgmental. Accepting. Sumner had repeatedly shown me empathy, and I wanted to give her the same in return.

"When I was younger, I slept with my boss at the time." She bit her lip, and I wondered how things had turned out for them. Then she added, "Who also happened to be my dad's best friend."

I tried to mask my reaction. "What happened?"

She laughed. "I married him."

"Wait." Record scratch. I held up my hand. "Jonathan, as in your husband? Your husband used to be your boss and your dad's best friend?"

"Fortunately, he's still my dad's best friend."

"Damn." I shook my head.

Maybe there was hope for Halle and me after all. Sumner's dad had gotten past her relationship with his best friend. Hell, even Sloan was married to her best friend's brother. Of all people, Sloan would understand, right?

Maybe.

Maybe if they were just friends and didn't work together, my sister wouldn't have an issue with it. But it wasn't quite so simple.

"Feel any better about your situation?" Sumner teased.

I laughed. *If only.*

"The trouble is, we're going to be working closely together once my sister goes on maternity leave."

"Do you think you can do that—successfully work together?"

I thought back on the past few weeks. Seeing Halle at the office. Shopping for art together. Spending time with her and Kai. It was both wonderful and excruciating.

"Spending time with her is…difficult. The more time I spend with her, the harder I fall." And avoiding her was no better. Either way, I couldn't win.

Sumner let out a low whistle. "Look, I know I said you should prove her wrong. And I would never want to discourage you—or anyone—from following their heart."

"But…" I prompted, knowing there was definitely more to that statement.

"But that was before I fully understood the situation. And now that I do, I would caution you to remember your big-picture goals. You've told me time and again that you want people, your family especially, to see that you've changed. You want to prove that you're capable of running the company. Based on what you've told me, I don't think it's the right time to pursue a relationship with her."

What Sumner said made sense, even if I didn't like it.

"You're right." I blew out breath, disappointment coursing through me. "I know you're right. I just… I guess I needed to talk to someone about it." And realize how crazy the idea of pursuing a relationship with Halle truly was once I spoke the words aloud.

"Well—" Sumner placed her hand on my shoulder "—I'm glad you confided in me. And I'm not saying you should never pursue her. I just think you and your family and your company are already going through a lot. Starting a new relationship—and one that's sure to make waves—would be better left until things are more…settled."

I considered Sumner's words. Considered what Halle had told me about her wishes to keep things professional. Remembered how I'd consistently pushed those boundaries —by asking for her help with art. By ingratiating myself with Kai. By inviting them to my home.

"Thank you," I said. "I appreciate your honesty."

Sumner nodded. "Always. And look, I, of all people, know that sometimes the heart wants what it wants and it will not be dissuaded. But I think you should give it some time. Trite as this is going to sound, if it's meant to be, it will be."

I laughed. "Trite as fuck." But she joined me.

Time. Give it time.

I didn't want to be just friends with Halle, but if it was in the best interest of Halle, my sister, and the company, then I could be patient. If I had to wait a little longer, then I would.

CHAPTER ELEVEN

HALLE

"So—" Kendall leaned in, keeping her voice low so the other guests wouldn't overhear. "I'm not sure how you'll feel about this, but one of the team doctors for the Leatherbacks is single. And I really think you'd hit it off."

Oh god. I sincerely hoped I'd held back my groan.

Why was everyone so intent on fixing me up? First Zara and now Kendall? We were at her house for Sloan's baby shower, for crying out loud.

I tucked a curl behind my ear. How the hell was I supposed to respond? Kendall and Emerson had been kind enough to invite me to their weekly yoga sessions, and I'd enjoyed getting to know them. But part of me always felt different from them. Separate.

Not because of anything they'd done. In fact, they were both so warm and welcoming. It was more the fact that I was almost a decade older. I was at a different point in my life. They'd been best friends long before they'd married brothers. And I was an employee of their family.

Perhaps taking my silence as an indication of my interest, Kendall tapped on her phone then showed me the screen.

"Isn't he handsome? He's also the sweetest guy and helps coach a kids' soccer team."

He was cute. And he sounded really nice. But I just… couldn't.

I could try to blame it on my new job, my busy life, the situation with my parents—though, thankfully Mom had agreed to move Dad to Green Acres. I'd done all the research, and she finally felt comfortable with the decision. Maybe not at peace per se. But at least she'd relented.

And while those were all completely valid reasons for not wanting to date, I was trying to put myself first. I was trying to show my son what it meant to love yourself. And right now, putting myself first meant focusing on myself and my family, on my career, not starting a new relationship.

No matter how difficult it might be to resist Jasper.

"Thanks for thinking of me, but I'm not looking to date right now." I didn't want to lead Kendall's friend on, but I also couldn't share that I was hung up on her brother-in-law. "I don't even know where I'd find the time, let alone someone to watch my son."

Emerson turned to me with a brilliant smile. "You know if you ever need someone to watch Kai, he's always welcome to come hang at our house. He was so sweet with Ezra."

"And Leo," Kendall said.

"Or our place," Alexis said. "The girls had so much fun with him the other weekend."

"Thanks. That's so nice of you," I said, trying to backpedal. "Both of you. But I couldn't possibly—"

Alexis smiled. "The offer stands." And then she walked off to say hi to someone else.

Emerson placed her hand on my arm. "I wouldn't have offered if I didn't want to."

"She used to be a nanny," Kendall said. "Nate's nanny, in fact."

Emerson rolled her eyes. "I wasn't *Nate's* nanny. I was Brooklyn's nanny."

"Semantics." Astrid popped a carrot slice into her mouth, crunching on it loudly. Even though they were twins, they had very distinct personalities. "Brooklyn's his daughter. Therefore, you were Nate's nanny."

"My point is," Kendall said, giving them both a look, "she's trained in CPR and first aid, and kids love her."

"Thank you." Emerson blew her a kiss. "And Brooklyn would love to hang out with Kai."

"I—" I didn't know what to say. "That's really kind of you to offer. Thank you."

"I've never been a single parent, but I can imagine it's tough, based on what Nate's told me. Take support when you can. It's freely offered," Emerson said.

I nodded. These women were so authentic and down-to-earth. I found myself wanting to confide in them. "It is tough. Sometimes, I honestly don't know whether to be upset or grateful that my ex isn't more involved."

Though Craig had certainly been making more of an effort lately. He'd called every Saturday morning since we'd moved to LA. And as far as I could tell, he was still planning to come visit later this week. I sure hoped so because I was relying on him to watch Kai while I went to New York for the charity auction.

"Nate's ex is a piece of work," Emerson said. "Thankfully, she signed away her parental rights."

"I can't even imagine…" That made me sad for Brooklyn, even though I knew she was so loved by Nate and Emerson and all of their family.

"Unfathomable," Kendall said, probably thinking of her own son.

"In this case, it was definitely for the best," Emerson said.

"One hundred percent," Sloan agreed then turned to me.

"And you'll know when you're ready to put yourself out there. For now, just enjoy being single."

I said nothing, instead sipping my drink. Was I enjoying being single? I mean…now that I thought about it, I hadn't really dated that much. Jasper was the only man I'd been with since Craig.

"Enjoy being single?" Astrid laughed. "The dating world is terrifying. You must have forgotten now that you're blissfully married to Jackson."

Sloan laughed. "Oh. I haven't forgotten. I think I'm scarred for life by the thumb-sucker."

"Oh god." I shuddered.

"Wait." Emerson placed her hand on Sloan's arm. "What do you mean, thumb-sucker?"

Sloan and I looked at each other and tried not to laugh. Finally, she said, "So I'd gone on a few dates with this guy, and I was going to spend the night at his place. When we went to go to sleep, well…" Her cheeks pinkened. "He rolled up in the fetal position and put his thumb in his mouth."

"Oh my god," Astrid said at the same time Emerson exclaimed, "He did not!"

"Oh, he definitely did," Sloan said.

"What did you do?" Kendall asked, looking as if she was struggling to contain her laughter. Or maybe her horror.

"I said that I'd forgotten I had an early meeting, and I got out of there as fast as I could."

We all started laughing. When Sloan's laughter cut off, her face suddenly serious, I frowned. She stood, and everyone fell silent.

Oh shit.

Everyone seemed to realize at the same time that her water had broken. And then all hell broke loose.

~

Zara's eyes were wide as I recounted the story of Sloan going into labor. "I can't believe Sloan's water broke at her own baby shower."

I adjusted my robe, tightening the belt on it. "I know. It was crazy, but everyone sprang into action. And luckily, her family got to meet the baby before we left for New York."

"Boy or girl?" Zara asked.

We'd spoken briefly a few times over the past month, but this was the first time we'd gotten to video chat for an extended time in a while. I was in my room at the Huxley Grand New York getting ready for the Huxley Family Foundation gala, and she was relaxing on her couch. I'd missed hanging out with her.

"Girl. Evie. Evelyn was Sloan's mother's middle name." I'd gone to visit them the day after Evie was born, and she was darling. Mom and baby had been doing well, and Jackson looked absolutely besotted.

"Oh, I know that look." Zara pointed at my face on the screen. "Does someone have baby fever?"

"What?" I pulled a face. "No."

"You sure about that?"

"I can admire a cute baby without wanting another one of my own."

"If you say so." She didn't sound convinced.

I laughed at the absurdity of it. "As if I don't already have enough on my plate."

"True," she said. "How's your dad settling into his new place?"

"It sounds like it's going well." I'd spoken with the staff at Green Acres several times. "I think my mom is the one who's struggling the most with the transition." I grabbed my makeup palette and started applying my eye shadow.

"That's understandable. How's Kai? What's he up to this weekend?"

"He and Craig are dog-sitting for Jasper."

Her eyes widened, and she sat up. "Um. Excuse me. What?"

"Jasper adopted a puppy a while back, and Kai is obsessed with her."

Zara stared at me, mouth agog. "I don't know what's more surprising. The fact that Craig actually followed through on his visit. Or the idea that your ex-husband is dog-sitting for your boss slash ex-lover." She leaned forward. "He *is* still your ex-lover, right?"

"Craig?" I laughed, intentionally misinterpreting her question. "Of course."

She narrowed her eyes at me. "Jasper. I thought you were trying to avoid him. How the hell did you end up dog-sitting for him?"

"I'm not. Kai is." I bit back a grin.

And I couldn't be more grateful to Jasper for suggesting it. Kai often got anxious when I traveled, and I knew Jasper's dog, Rosie, would be both a good companion and a good distraction.

"And Craig was okay with that? And Jasper and Kai..." She furrowed her brow. "...have spent time together?"

"Craig only knows that Jasper is my boss. They've never met. And Kai hung out with Jasper after he asked me to select some artwork for his penthouse. I guess I forgot to tell you that."

"Forgot?" she scoffed. "Um, yeah, you definitely *neglected* to mention that. How did that come about?"

I gave her a condensed version of the story. By the end, she was grinning. "Ooh, babes. An unlimited art budget and the freedom to choose whatever you wanted?"

I laughed. "It was amazing."

"It or *him*?" she asked.

"It," I said in a firm tone. "As in the art shopping. That's all."

"Mm-hmm." I sensed that she was holding back a laugh. I pretended to be too busy applying makeup to notice.

"We agreed to focus on work," I said, hating how defensive I sounded. "And we've both adhered to that."

"Mm." She didn't sound convinced. She leaned forward, squinting at the screen. "Is that your dress?"

I gestured over my shoulder to where the gown was hanging. "Yeah. I have to get going soon, but do you want to see it on?"

"Um, yes. Is that even a question?"

"Be right back."

I grabbed the dress and stepped out of the frame, donning it before staring at myself in the mirror. I wasn't even sure I recognized myself.

This dress was an architectural wonder. I'd never worn something so exquisite, not even on my wedding day. The emerald silk fabric hugged me in all the right places, emphasizing my best attributes. As if that weren't enough, it was actually fairly comfortable. And, best of all, it had pockets.

I could've kissed Sloan's stylist, Jay Crowe, for selecting this for me. He'd nailed it. I'd never felt more beautiful or powerful.

I'd gotten a blowout earlier in the day at the hotel salon, and my hair cascaded down my back in loose waves. And while I'd tried to tell myself I was merely following Jay's styling suggestion, I knew how much Jasper loved it when I wore my hair down.

I stepped into my heels and smiled, surprising myself. Then, shoulders back, head held high, I sauntered toward my phone to let Zara see the full effect.

"Holy shit." Zara gaped at me. "Turn." I did so, letting her see the dress from all angles. "Babes, you look hot."

"Isn't this dress amazing?" I asked, showing off the pockets.

"It is, but I love your confidence even more." She smiled. "Jasper won't know what hit him." When I glared at her, she quickly added, "Not that you're trying to impress him or anything."

"I'm not," I said, though even I could admit that was a lie.

Jasper had been nothing but professional lately. Yes, he'd asked Kai if he wanted to dog-sit. But I'd definitely seen less of him the past few weeks. It almost felt as if he'd been avoiding me.

We'd both been busy, and he didn't owe me anything. But it felt as if he'd put up a wall between us, firmly delineating our positions as employer and employee. This was what I'd asked for after all—professionalism. I should've been happy or, at the very least, relieved. And yet, it felt so hollow.

"Besides," I added. "I'm representing my boss."

"You can represent your boss while ogling her brother."

I rolled my eyes, remembering the purpose of the evening. "Jasper's going to have more than enough people ogling him. Did I tell you it's a bachelorx auction?"

"What?" Her eyes widened. "No. If you had, I would *so* be there right now."

I laughed. "I've been a little busy. Must have slipped my mind."

Okay. A lot busy.

Evie had been born several weeks early, but fortunately, she hadn't ended up in the NICU. Even so, her unexpected arrival meant that Sloan's maternity leave had come sooner than expected. I'd thought I'd have more time to prepare myself for being an SVP, but I'd thrown myself into the role.

In addition to juggling all that, I was helping my parents from afar, managing the move for my dad and the endless associated paperwork. Trying to house hunt, though that had definitely been put on the back burner lately. Even so, I'd texted regularly with Alexis, and she'd invited me out with some of her girlfriends. I also needed to find a new pediatrician for Kai, though I hadn't had much time or success so far. I needed to ask Alexis and Emerson who they took their kids to.

"Mm-hmm. Sure. So…" Zara leaned in. "Who else is on the auction block?"

I listed off a few names, her eyes growing wider with every celebrity or pro athlete I mentioned. Finally, I asked, "Wanna trade places?"

I might love this dress and the way I felt in it, but I would definitely consider trading places. It was my first major event as the temporary SVP, and most of the board members would be in attendance. But that wasn't even why I was dreading the evening ahead. I was going to have to stand in the audience and watch while gorgeous, wealthy women bid on Jasper.

But at least I would look fabulous while doing it, thanks to Jay.

"Yes! But also—" She narrowed her eyes at me. "No! Halle, you have worked your butt off for this promotion. You deserve it. And you look fucking amazing."

Before I could respond, Sloan's name popped up on my screen.

"Shit. I have to go. Sloan's calling."

"Go. *Go!* And have fun tonight. Find a hottie to let loose with. Preferably one who's not your boss or anyone related to your job."

I laughed, though there was a bitter edge to it. Zara was right. I needed to stop being so hung up on Jasper. But how could I not be when he made me feel seen and safe and…

"I'm serious, Halle," Zara said.

"Yeah. Yeah. Talk soon." I ended the call before answering Sloan's. "Hey, Sloan."

"Hey! I just wanted to thank you again for attending the gala for me."

"Of course. Is everything okay?" I was surprised she'd called. I knew she trusted me to handle it, and I figured she'd be busy with Evie.

She looked tired, defeated. Her shoulders rounded. "Yeah. I'm just… I've never missed one of the Huxley Family Foundation events."

"You have a good reason for not attending," I said. "You just had a baby. I know everyone will miss you, but they will understand."

"It's not everyone else I'm worried about." She frowned. "So much for the Three Musketeers," she said more softly.

"The Three Musketeers?" I asked.

"That's what we used to call ourselves—Jasper, Graham, and me. We're close with Knox and Nate, of course. But the three of us were a unit. Especially after our grandparents died and we took over running the company."

I couldn't imagine what they'd gone through. First, losing their parents at such a young age. And then—many years later—losing both of their beloved grandparents in quick succession. I was still trying to cope with the fact that my dad had Alzheimer's.

I was grieving the man I knew and the memories we'd shared. Memories that he no longer retained—at least, not reliably. Sometimes when we'd video chat, he seemed to be able to recall so much, and yet others…nothing at all. It was a painful experience to know that he was there—at least in body. But there were many times that he didn't feel like "my dad."

I was so much older than Jasper and Sloan and the rest of their family had been when they'd had their lives completely upended by loss, and yet, it was still heartbreaking. I still felt woefully unprepared to cope with it. I couldn't even imagine trying to do so as a child.

"I just hate to think that Jasper would feel like he's all alone." She sniffled, and I was surprised by how emotional she was. It was out of character, but I chalked it up to postpartum hormones and lack of sleep. "He's always been there for me. And he's taken on a lot these past few months. I just want him to know that I'm there for him too. But it's kind of hard to show him that when I'm not physically there, you know?"

"I do. But Knox and Kendall will be here. Nate and his family. Jude and Chrissy." Since it was a quick trip, Knox and Jude had left Leo and Ezra with Kendall's mom and her husband back in LA.

Graham had skipped the event, claiming he had too much to do at the château. I didn't doubt it, but Sloan was convinced his absence had more to do with not wanting to take the spotlight off Jasper. I had a feeling she was right.

"And you."

My heart stalled out. "What about me?" I hoped the words didn't sound as forced as they felt.

Did Sloan suspect something? *Know* something?

"You're going to be by his side tonight. And on that note…" Her breath gusted out of her. "I'm probably keeping you from getting ready."

"I still have a few minutes before I need to go. What's really bothering you?"

"I'm worried about Jasper," Sloan admitted. "Taking over as CEO has definitely been a big adjustment—for all of us. And he's doing a great job." I only wished Jasper could've heard her say that.

I sensed Sloan had more to say, so I remained quiet, giving her space to process her feelings.

"I guess I just don't want anyone to look at my absence from this event and question my support for Jasper as the new CEO." Then in a quieter voice, she added, "I don't want Jasper to question my support."

"I'm sure he doesn't," I said. "But if you're that concerned, maybe send him an encouraging text."

"That's a great idea. I'll do that. Thanks, Halle."

"Anytime." There was a knock at my door, and it set my heart racing. "I have to go. Give Evie a kiss for me and try to get some rest."

"Have fun tonight."

We ended the call, and then I checked myself over one more time in the mirror. I peered through the peephole, using the opportunity to take Jasper in, even if it was through a fish-eye lens. He peered back at me, almost as if he could sense me standing there.

He was downright devastating in his tux, and I knew he'd be popular tonight. Even if he weren't a billionaire, the man was damn attractive. Charming. Kind.

Okay. I straightened. *Enough gawking.* I'd met my quota for the evening. I was done. So, I took a deep breath and opened the door.

He stood in the hallway, hands in his pockets, eyes on the floor. Slowly, he lifted his head, his eyes skimming me from the tips of my toes to the top of my head. I felt it as if it were a caress, and it left goose bumps skittering over my skin.

"Damn. You look…" He fell silent, as if searching for the right words. He was so rarely at a loss for words that I found it amusing and immensely gratifying. "You look phenomenal."

"Thank you," I said, feeling self-conscious about my dress. I was showing more skin than I typically did, especially for a work event, but I felt sexy and confident. "So do you. You just have something—" I stepped closer, reaching up to push his hair into place. "There."

He grabbed my wrist before I could lower my hand, clasping it gently. "Halle." It was a prayer. A plea.

This was already hard enough—having to spend an evening with him when he looked like…well, this. He was so handsome it hurt to look at him.

Jasper had this quality about him. He was charismatic, yes. But when he entered a room, he didn't just step into it; he commanded it.

And he was about to have all eyes on him as the CEO of the company. I needed to distance myself at the event before someone caught me looking at him. I didn't trust myself to be near him without signaling my inappropriate thoughts.

I closed my eyes, allowing myself a moment to revel in his touch. One moment. That was all. I could smell his cologne—rich, smooth, warm.

For a minute, I got caught up in the fantasy of it all. And then I remembered why we were here—the family foundation gala and the bachelorx auction. My stomach soured because I knew I wouldn't be the only one unable to keep my eyes off him.

I shook my head, silently begging him to let it go. To let me go.

Jasper wasn't mine, and he never could be.

CHAPTER TWELVE

JASPER

I couldn't fucking take it anymore.

All evening, I'd had to watch Halle smile and flirt with other men, and I was at my limit. I wasn't thinking rationally. I was only thinking of getting to her.

My smile was tight as I crossed the room, my fists clenched. I tried to bypass the crowd, annoyed every time someone stopped me to wish me congratulations. I wasn't sure what they were congratulating me on—becoming CEO or the fact that I'd stood up onstage like a piece of meat and someone had purchased an evening with me.

I just needed to…

Someone blocked my path, and I was two seconds away from losing my shit. The auction was taking an intermission, and if Wyatt Anderson didn't get his hands off Halle, I was going to explode.

I didn't care that he was the owner of the Hollywood Hawks, LA's NHL team. Nor did I care that the Huxley Grand was the official hotel for the team. I saw red, and the word "mine" went screaming through my head.

Finally, I made it over to her, barely acknowledging Wyatt before saying, "Excuse us. Urgent matter."

I hooked my arm through Halle's, ushering her through the crowd. There were people everywhere. On the balcony. In the hallway. *Fuck!*

"Jasper," Halle hissed. "What on—"

I searched for an escape. *There.* Down the hall was a stairwell. I pushed open the door, the music and laughter echoing into the concrete chamber. I gestured for Halle to go ahead, the door shutting behind us.

"What is going on?" Halle asked as soon as we were alone. "What's wrong?"

"I—" Oh shit. I really hadn't thought this through. I started pacing. All I'd wanted was to get Halle away from Wyatt Anderson and every other man in the room who'd dared to lay eyes on her tonight. I should've been more prepared. I should've—

"Jasper?" She gripped my arm to pause my movements. "Is it Sloan? The baby? Is everything okay?"

Now I really felt awful. I hadn't meant to worry Halle. I just… I shook my head, my thoughts a jumbled mess.

"You lost," I blurted the first thing that came to mind. "You weren't supposed to lose."

Her lips were in a flat line. She was unamused, and now that I realized just how close we were, her perfume was fucking distracting. Part of it was the fact that she smelled delicious. The other part was my aggravation that I still couldn't put my finger on the scent profile.

Roses. Vetivier? Or maybe ylang-ylang. And something else.

I couldn't focus. This was a problem.

Whatever her scent was, it was intoxicating. I wanted to kiss that spot behind her ear where the scent was strongest. I wanted to draw it in deep and hold it in my lungs to sustain me.

No. No. I smoothed a hand down my shirt, trying to get my head on straight.

I was focused on my goals. I was focused on… *Fuck me, she was gorgeous.* Like a movie siren from the golden age of Hollywood. Her hair. Her gown. It was maddening.

But even more than all that, it was the way she carried herself. She was a fucking queen, and everyone had been captivated by her tonight. All the while, I'd had to stand across the room and pretend to give a fuck about anything as I watched other men hit on her.

"You dragged me in here, interrupting my conversation— so you could berate me for losing?" She scoffed.

Well, when she put it that way, it did sound pretty ridiculous. But apparently, she wasn't done.

She planted her hands on her hips. "You asked me to find a way to bid on you. You never said you wanted me to win."

I groaned, dragging a hand down my face. "Of course I wanted you to win." Even if she'd been using someone else as her proxy.

Halle crossed her arms over her chest and leaned against the wall. "Then you should've said so."

The music thumped through the door, only slightly muted by the thick concrete walls of the stairwell. I'd avoided her for weeks, but I was at my breaking point. And tonight had finally pushed me over the edge.

I threw my hands in the air. "Why else would I have asked you to bid on me?"

"I don't know. I figured you wanted to make things interesting and start a bidding war. It'd be good for the charity and your vanity, right?"

I pressed the heels of my hands into my eyes. Was that

truly what she thought? That I was so self-absorbed that I cared how high the bidding went for an evening with me? *Jesus.*

Apparently, I had some work to do when it came to my image with Halle. Yes, I'd played to the crowd when I'd been onstage. But fuck me, did she really believe that was who I was? It stung…to think she didn't know me as well as I thought she did.

And then it dawned on me. Her irritation. Her…digs.

I pushed, grinning as I took a step forward. "You're jealous."

"Jealous?" she scoffed. "No." But her chest flushed with color, and victory thrummed through my veins. *She was, wasn't she?*

I found myself wanting to push her. Break her. Until she spilled open and admitted the truth—she wanted me. Just like I wanted her.

"You were jealous," I pushed.

Her cheeks pinkened—anger or desire, I couldn't be quite sure. Her chest was heaving, her tits nearly spilling over the top of her gown. *Jesus.* I knew I shouldn't look, but I also couldn't look away.

"Enough." She briefly dropped her head to her chest. "Enough. I can't keep doing this with you. First Dimitri and now Wyatt? You have to stop, Jasper. *Please.*"

Her voice cracked on the last word, and it was the "please" that nearly broke me.

She was right. God, she was right.

I was doing the exact opposite of what I'd promised—to myself, to Halle. And I'd been trying, damn it. For weeks now, I'd been doing my best to treat her just like I would any other employee.

"I'm sorry." I ran a hand over my head as I took a step back. "You're right." I wasn't being fair. I wasn't respecting her boundaries. But it was damn near impossible when I knew we belonged together. I just needed her to see that too.

"I should go." She hesitated a moment then sighed, her shoulders dropping as some of the fight went out of her.

She turned and reached for the door handle. But when she pushed down on it, nothing happened. She cursed under her breath then tried again, jerking on the handle a few times.

"Need some help?" I offered, only slightly amused by her predicament. The other part was hurt that she couldn't seem to get away from me fast enough yet again.

She tried one more time before stepping aside with a heavy sigh. I pushed on the handle, only to discover it was locked. I tried a second time, thinking it must be some mistake. But it wasn't. And the handle didn't budge.

I held up my phone to the security panel, hoping my room key would unlock it. Nothing happened. The sensor stayed red. The lock remained engaged.

I squeezed my eyes shut briefly. "The door's locked."

She stepped forward, nudging me aside. "It can't be." She jiggled the handle, but nothing happened. She kept trying anyway, as if by sheer force of will, she would be able to free us.

I checked my phone. No service. *Shit.*

"Fine," she huffed, blowing some of her hair out of her face. "We'll just…"

"Call someone?" I held up my phone and shook my head. "I don't have any reception. The walls must be too thick."

She removed her phone from a pocket hidden in the folds of her dress, her movements frantic. She peered down at her screen and cringed. "Okay, so, we'll just bang on the door until someone hears us."

I leaned back against the concrete wall and crossed my arms over my chest. "Good luck with that."

"You're not even going to try? We can't just…sit here and do nothing."

"The music's too loud for anyone to hear us. All it will do is wear us out." I surveyed up and down the stairwell. "I'll try the other doors." There had to be ten floors. *Fuck me.*

"Okay," Halle said. "I'll stay here and see if I can do anything about the lock."

I removed my jacket and draped it over the railing. And then I started my descent. I tried the first door with no success; I had a feeling they'd all be locked.

"Any luck?" Halle called down to me, her voice echoing off the concrete.

I leaned over the railing. "Not yet."

"Keep trying," she gritted out.

I went to another level and another. When I finally reached the ground floor, I pushed on the crash bar, expecting it to open. It gave a little squeak of protest, but it barely budged. The door remained firmly shut.

"The fuck." I pushed at it again, ultimately deciding to kick it.

"Jasper?" Halle called down. "Are you okay?"

I moved so that I could peer up at her. She seemed so far away. "I'm fine. Just trying to kick the door open."

"Be careful," she said.

I attempted a few more times, finally admitting defeat and sinking down on the step. *Fuck.*

I was ten flights down and still no closer to getting us out of this mess. By this point, I'd shed my bow tie, loosened the top buttons of my shirt, and rolled up my sleeves. I took a deep breath and stood. I climbed the stairs until I was sweating, only to end up back where I'd started.

Halle was sitting on the steps, her shoes on the floor beside her. She perked up when she saw me. "Any luck?"

I shook my head. "The ground floor should be unlocked.

This is a fire escape, and it should allow us to exit to the outside."

She grimaced. "It should be, but it isn't?"

I nodded. "I'll definitely be demanding answers as soon as we get out of here. And I'm going to have Jackson ask the security team to run checks at all our other locations. This can't happen again."

"I bet Jackson would know how to get out of here." She glared at the door as if her gaze alone would burn a hole through it and allow us to escape. "Apparently it's more difficult to pick a lock than TV shows and movies would have you believe."

I laughed despite the absurdity of the situation, or perhaps because of it. "Yeah. I'm surprised the old credit card trick didn't work," I joked.

I didn't mention that Jackson would probably shoot the lock with his gun.

"Right?" She laughed. "Shocking. I also tried a bobby pin. Nothing happened. Well, I suppose I broke the bobby pin."

I went over to the door, evaluating the handle. The lock. The Huxley Grand New York was housed in a historically listed building. The structure had been built in the late 1800s and had been operating as a hotel almost continuously since its opening. The interior had been restored, but many original details remained.

While the fire doors weren't quite as old as the hotel, they'd only been fitted with electronic security keypads in the past decade or so. Which was why Halle had probably hoped to be able to pick the lock.

I tried to rack my brain for a solution. A way out. Before I could brainstorm any more great ideas, Halle said, "Face it. We're stuck."

I sank down beside her, needing a moment to regroup. I didn't want to admit defeat.

She groaned, bracing her head on her hands. "I have to get out of here. Kai will worry if he doesn't hear from me. I promised I'd call."

"I'm sorry," I said, feeling even worse about dragging her in here. "This is all my fault."

"You couldn't have known we'd get locked in."

I appreciated her saying that, but it didn't change the fact that we were stuck. And we would've never been in the stairwell had it not been for me.

I didn't know how to fix this. Not just our current predicament, but all of it. I was going to be working closely with Halle for the next few months, and I couldn't keep living like this.

Avoiding her didn't work. Being friends with her was painful when I wanted so much more. And waiting, hoping, for a future together while fighting my attraction was proving to be a losing battle. But what choice did I have?

"Hey." Halle perked up. "Do you think someone would realize you're gone and come looking for you?"

"Maybe," I said, not wanting to burst her bubble. "But I doubt it."

This was one of the few times I wished I'd listened to Jackson when he'd suggested I hire personal security. I had a residential security team for my penthouse, but I preferred not to be followed around by a bodyguard at all times.

"But you're the CEO," Halle said.

"I know, but it's not like someone is monitoring my every move." At least, I hoped they weren't. That would be creepy.

"But what if…" She stood and started pacing. "What if someone happened to see us go off together? What if they think…" She spun on me. "What if they think we're sleeping together?"

"I doubt anyone saw us," I said, hoping to allay her fears as well as my own. "If they had, they would've heard us banging on the door."

"Yeah. And assumed that we were *banging*." Her tone was rife with innuendo and concern.

I sighed. I was fucking it all up. Yet here we were—thanks to my actions—trapped in a stairwell together, and I was compromising Halle's reputation and integrity. Not to mention my own.

Even though we weren't sleeping together—now—I still wished we were. I wished for so much more than that where Halle was concerned. But this definitely wasn't the way to go about it.

I pressed my hands to my thighs and stood. "They aren't going to assume that."

"They're certainly going to assume *something* happened. It's the logical conclusion given…well…" She gestured to me.

Right. Given the fact that she, and everyone else, thought I was a player.

"Given what?" There was an edge to my voice.

I understood that we were judged by our past actions, but we should also have space for transformation. I'd changed—I was still changing and evolving—but no one seemed to want to give me credit for it. Hell, the board—not my siblings, but the other members—seemed to want to lean into my billionaire playboy image. They liked that I was, well, liked.

Sometimes it pissed me off. Not only because I wanted to be valued for my contributions, but because it felt as if they were undermining Graham's as well. His past few years as CEO had been contentious with the board. They'd been so focused on his reputation as a cold, heartless billionaire that they'd often ignored all the amazing things he'd done for the company, especially at the end.

Graham wasn't cold or heartless, but I could understand why people had that perception of him. And now that I'd stepped into his role, I was beginning to see just how difficult it could be to change people's opinion of you. Especially people who had known you a certain way for a long time, like my family. Or even Halle.

It was disheartening, but I liked a challenge. And I wouldn't easily be deterred.

She gestured to me. "I mean, look at you."

"What about me?" I asked, unwilling to let it go.

She stepped closer, and I could feel the air thickening with the unspoken tension. If we weren't careful, we'd suffocate in the stairwell.

"Your skin is flushed." She lifted her hand as if to touch my face then dropped it. "Your hair is mussed. And your clothes are rumpled."

I looked down at myself. Oh. *Oh.*

Maybe that's what she'd meant by people assuming we'd slept together. Not because of my playboy reputation but because of my current state.

Maybe I was the one jumping to conclusions, not Halle. Maybe she hadn't meant anything by her comment. She'd literally been making an observation, but I'd taken it as an insult.

"Well, I did climb down ten flights of stairs then back up."

"Thank you for doing that, by the way."

"I wish one of the doors had been unlocked." I sighed. "We'll just have to wait until the music dies down and start banging on the door."

Was I happy we were stuck? No. But I'd accepted the fact that there wasn't much to be done about it. At least for now. Maybe later, after the party had wound down, we'd be able to get someone's attention, assuming the cleaning staff would be within hearing range of the stairwell.

She shivered, wrapping her arms around herself. I lifted my jacket from the railing and placed it over her shoulders.

"Thanks." She shoved her hands in her pockets. Then she paused, frowned, and removed something from one of them. "Do you often carry around protein bars?"

"These events can be hectic. Now that I'm the CEO, I find even more people making demands on my time. So I try to be prepared in case my meal is interrupted, as it so often is."

"I can understand that," she said, handing over the bar. Sometimes I didn't know how she did it. If I was struggling to find time to eat because of my position in the company, Halle had it even worse. She was a single mom on top of a busy executive.

I shook my head, refusing to take it. "I'm fine. You should eat it."

"I'm not hungry."

"You sure about that? You picked at your meal."

"Have to be able to fit into the dress." She gestured to herself, and I couldn't not look.

"That dress looks like it was made for you," I said with all sincerity. "But I'd be happy to help you remove it if that would make you more comfortable."

"Jasper," she chided, but she was fighting a smile. Maybe I shouldn't have said it, but at least it had lightened the mood. And I was grateful to be on more familiar footing. We'd been tiptoeing around each other lately, and I missed her sharp tongue and her quick wit.

I held up the protein bar. "Want to split it?"

"Maybe we should save it. Who knows how long we'll be stuck here."

Instead of making a promise I wasn't sure I could keep, I opened the bar and handed half of it to her, determined to show her that I was confident we would get out. Surely someone would come.

She hesitated a moment then took it. "Thank you." After she finished it, she dusted off her hands. "I'm sorry for snapping at you. I promised Kai I'd call, and I'm worried what will happen if I don't."

I couldn't change our situation, but I could focus on the things I could control, just like Sumner and I had talked about. I hated that Halle was worried. I hated that I'd put her in this position. So I did the only thing I could—I tried to reassure her.

"Kai is going to be okay. His dad is with him. And Rosie."

"True." Halle smiled, perhaps thinking about how excited both Rosie and Kai had been when I'd dropped her off for their weekend together. "But…Kai relies on me."

"Of course he does. You're his mom."

"No." She shook her head. "You don't understand. Kai loves his dad, but he's not used to my being away. Plus, he's still adjusting to living in a new city. He's always been attached to me, but after the divorce, well…" She blew out a breath. "Let's just say that he will freak out if he doesn't hear from me."

"Freak out how?" I asked.

She nibbled on her nail. I took her hand in mine, desperate to comfort her.

"The last time I had to travel with Sloan on business, Kai lost four pounds. He was sick to his stomach for days because he was stressed by my absence."

I frowned, not liking the sound of that. "I'm sorry it's been so difficult on him. On both of you." I was tempted to drape my arm around her and hold her, to try to comfort her, but then I thought better of it. It was enough that we were holding hands.

"Thanks." She dropped her head to her chest. "He's always had stomach issues, but the doctors have yet to find a cause, apart from anxiety."

She sounded so…defeated. I hated it—for her, for Kai. I

hated that he was suffering. He'd never even let on. He always seemed like such a happy, carefree kid.

"Does being away from Craig trigger that reaction?" I asked, her ex's name bitter on my tongue. Maybe it was because he was in her suite that I suddenly felt so threatened.

I still couldn't believe he was even in LA. After everything Halle had told me of her ex, I would've never expected him to fly across the world and spend the weekend with his son. I was happy for Kai, truly. But I was also mistrustful. Cautious on Kai and Halle's behalf.

"Just me."

"But you're not convinced his stomach troubles are all down to anxiety," I said.

She shook her head. "No, but everyone else—the doctors, Craig—thinks I'm being ridiculous."

I gnashed my teeth, hating everyone who had ever made her doubt herself. "You're Kai's mom. You know him better than anyone. And if your gut tells you it's something else, then trust it."

When she met my gaze, she looked so…fragile. "You mean that?"

"Yes." I gave her hand a squeeze before releasing her. "One hundred percent."

"Thanks."

I wanted to ask more questions. I wanted to find a solution. But I sensed that wasn't what Halle needed. She had enough people who made her question herself. So I kept my mouth shut, giving her space. Trying to be there for her in the best way I could—for now.

There was no way Sloan knew about this, or she would've found a way around having Halle travel. But now that Halle was going to be acting SVP, at least temporarily, we'd have to come up with a solution for any trips that arose. In the meantime, I wanted to reassure her and keep her calm.

"When I was a kid, I developed a lot of anxiety after my parents died," I said, wanting Halle to know that she wasn't alone, and neither was Kai.

She turned to me, her expression one of sadness but also understanding. It made me feel safe to continue, and I found myself sharing things with her that I'd never shared with anyone outside of my family. And even then, not all of my siblings knew or understood the extent of what I'd gone through. They'd been dealing with enough of their own challenges. Their own grief.

"Anytime my grandparents left, even just for an evening, I panicked. I couldn't fall asleep until they returned. And the entire time they were gone, I was afraid they would never come home."

I could remember the absolute terror I felt anytime they left, even if it had been scheduled and discussed ahead of time.

"I'm sorry, Jasper." Halle placed her hand on mine. "You were so young to have your parents ripped away from you. And so suddenly."

I nodded. "It was hard on all of us. Sometimes I don't know how my grandparents did it." I blew out a breath. "They lost both their children and their spouses, all at once. They became the guardians of their five orphaned grandchildren."

It had been a shock, and it had sent ripples through my family, affecting all of us in different ways.

"I'm sure you and your siblings are what kept them going."

I chuckled. "We didn't always make it easy on them."

As the eldest, Knox had taken on the role of peacemaker. Caretaker. He always took care of us, watched out for us. Nate was just as protective in his own way.

Graham had always been brooding and serious, but he

had turned inward even more so. Sloan had been so young… she'd barely gotten to know our parents. And that was its own kind of loss. The grief of lost memories and stolen moments.

And I was the jokester, determined to make everyone laugh when all they wanted to do was cry. I was so sick of seeing them be sad. Not that I hadn't been devastated myself —I was. But I'd made it my goal to keep my family entertained, even at my own expense.

"You miss them," Halle said.

I nodded. "I was really close to them, especially my gran. Even before my parents' crash, she was the one person who always seemed to get me. I took her death really hard."

When I was in my twenties, coping with the death of my grandparents, humor had no longer been enough. When Pops and Gran had died, one right after the other, the pain and grief had been all-consuming. So, too, had the fear.

It was then I'd realized that there was nothing I could do, nothing I could learn, to prevent the death of someone I loved.

I felt as if I'd been kidding myself all along, foolishly believing that knowing how to fly an airplane would protect me. Or thinking that learning CPR would save the life of someone I loved. My grandparents' deaths couldn't be prevented. No one's could.

Halle gave my hand a squeeze. Before she could pull away, I flipped my hand so it was holding hers. "I made some really stupid decisions. Ones I'm not proud of."

I remembered how it had become easier to numb the pain. With fast cars, alcohol, late nights, and other questionable escapades. While my siblings were lauded for their achievements, I'd become known as the playboy billionaire brother.

Sometimes it grated on me—that everyone had such low

expectations of me. But there had been a string of years when I hadn't given anyone a reason to believe I was capable of anything else. Over time, the playboy lifestyle had certainly lost its shine, and I'd finally had to admit to myself that I wanted more out of life.

I was scared shitless of the idea of losing someone I loved, but I also didn't want to miss out on life because I was afraid. It wasn't until Halle that I'd felt brave enough to try.

CHAPTER THIRTEEN

HALLE

I shifted on the step, the cold concrete hard and unrelenting. "I think anyone who's experienced devastating news or loss knows that grief can make you do things you might not ordinarily." I kept my eyes on the floor. "I know that was certainly the case for me last summer."

I was thrown back to a memory from my summer with Jasper. One of the bright spots in an otherwise dark time.

"Stay the night." Jasper dotted kisses up my spine.

We'd spent the day in bed, kissing, laughing, exploring each other's bodies. It had been glorious, but he was going home to LA tomorrow. And I was going back to reality.

Back to the office, where my boss, his sister, was in charge. Back to the real world, where I didn't have flings with billionaire hotel moguls who also happened to be my boss's brother. I was responsible and professional, and I didn't make reckless decisions that could ruin everything.

I sighed. "I can't. You know I can't."

Even if I wanted to. God, how I wanted to stay. To avoid reality for a little longer.

My dad had been recently diagnosed with Alzheimer's, and these past few weeks with Jasper had been the only thing keeping me sane. Jasper had been my escape. My salvation.
"Because of Kai."

And my dad, I thought. But I didn't want to think about that. Not now. Not when Jasper's hands were still caressing my skin. Not when our naked bodies were intertwined.

I nodded. It was true—I needed to get home to Kai. But it wasn't the full truth.

There was no way Jasper and I could be together in the real world. And spending the night with him was merely prolonging the inevitable.

"I just..." He sighed, his fingers tracing mine. "I don't want this to end. Not when it feels like the start of something..."

I kissed him. I would always wonder what he'd wanted to say, but I couldn't bear to hear it. So I'd kissed him.

Passionately. Deeply. Pouring everything I felt into that kiss.
Devastating. *The man was absolutely devastating.*

What had started out as a way to escape reality, to numb the pain, had turned into something else entirely.

When I pulled back, Jasper opened his mouth to speak. I cupped his cheek and shook my head, hoping he'd understand.

This had already gone on long enough. It had to end.

"Last summer?" Jasper's question was an echo, and I could see a million questions swimming in his bottomless eyes.

"Last summer, after my dad was diagnosed with Alzheimer's, I wasn't in the best place mentally. Honestly, there are still many days that I struggle."

He swallowed hard. "I'm sorry. The grief will always be there, but with time, it will get easier."

He gave my hand a squeeze before releasing me. I felt the loss of his touch, his warmth. He leaned back to rest his elbows on the step behind him.

I clutched his jacket to me, its scent familiar and calming. I'd forgotten what it was like to be enveloped by him, and I ached to hold him after his earlier confession. I ached to be held by him, to feel that comfort and warmth and protection that he so willingly gave.

"And your fears? How did you get past them?" I asked. "Or did you?"

"There are times it still affects me. Not to the extent it once did. But grounding myself in the present always helps. It reminds me that I can't control life, but I can appreciate the time I have with loved ones. Focusing on sensory details or doing mindfulness exercises helps."

"I can see that. You're always so aware of your environment and putting people at ease."

He smiled at that, and my heart lifted a little. He'd been through so much; all of them had. But it also made me admire him even more. He was strong and resilient, but he wasn't afraid to be vulnerable.

"Connection also helps center me, touch. Adopting Rosie has been a game changer. I used to spend a lot of time with Graham's Irish wolfhounds, and I didn't realize how much I'd missed having a companion to come home to."

"And Graham?"

He kicked at a piece of lint on the stairs. "Yeah. I miss him too."

It was the first time he'd admitted as much, but I wasn't surprised. Jasper and Graham might be as different as night and day, but they had an unshakable bond.

"I'm sure he misses you as well."

Jasper's expression turned more serious. "Not likely. He's so busy with Lily and the château and the new Fleur-de-lis line of properties."

"You're busy too," I said. "And yet you still miss him."

Jasper tilted his head, seeming to consider my words. "True."

"And I know Sloan hates that she couldn't be here tonight," I said, seeing an opening to remind Jasper that his family loved him. Supported him.

"I know." He sighed, rubbing a hand over the back of his neck. "She texted me earlier, wishing me luck tonight."

"Oh. That reminds me." I pulled out my phone. *Still no service.* "Kai asked me to show you this."

I pulled up the photo Kai had texted me, grinning at the sight of my son. He was holding Rosie, and he was laughing as she licked his face.

"Adorable." Jasper smiled down at the photo, his expression full of fondness. "He's a good kid. You're doing a great job."

"Thank you," I said, touched by his compliment. "Though I might have to hit you up for some tricks. You got him to make his bed without me asking. And now, he's taking on the responsibility of watching Rosie."

"It's all him," Jasper said.

"The only downside is that he's always wanted a dog. And now he's going to be begging me for one."

"Well, he now has hands-on experience with caring for a pet."

I glared at him. "Hey! Whose side are you on?" I teased.

"What?" He shrugged. "Rosie loves Kai."

"Yeah, but—" I tucked my phone back in my pocket "—what happens when we move out?"

"Did you find somewhere?"

I shook my head. "I've been too busy to even look." Alexis had sent me several listings and offered to set up some showings, but I hadn't had time.

"Well, until then, he's welcome to hang out with Rosie as much as he wants. And even after. He can always hang out with Rosie."

"Thank you. She's been a ray of sunshine for both of us, especially with everything that's been going on with my dad."

"I'm glad," Jasper said. "I've been meaning to ask how your dad has been, but I didn't want to overstep."

I smiled sadly. "My mom finally agreed to move him to a facility, which is good."

Fortunately, the increased pay from my temporary promotion would help alleviate some of the stress, but it still wouldn't be enough to relieve the constant pressure I felt in my chest. Though most of that was due more to my dad's situation, rather than the financial aspects. It wouldn't matter if I had as much money as Jasper—nothing would reverse time and the effects of Dad's disease.

"But honestly, it's been hard. Every time we talk, I never know how much he's going to remember. I moved to LA so I could be closer to help and to let Kai spend time with his grandparents while he can. We visited over Christmas, but it feels like so much has already changed since then. And I don't want to wait much longer to visit again."

I straightened, trying not to get choked up at the thought that the day might come when my dad might not even remember his grandson.

"What does Kai say about all of it?"

I lifted a shoulder. "I've tried to shield him from it as much as possible, but I can't completely hide my dad's confusion."

Jasper nodded, and I realized I didn't want to talk about this anymore. It was too depressing.

"You mentioned mindfulness exercises earlier," I said, eager to change topics. "Can you give me some basic examples? Ones that might work for a five-year-old."

"Mindfulness is all about grounding yourself in the present. You could try finger breathing."

"What's finger breathing?" I asked.

"I'll show you." He held out his hand.

I hesitated a moment. He smirked. I cocked my head. It was almost as if we were playing a game of chicken, and I couldn't help but bite back a smile.

Finally relenting, I placed my hand in his. He slid his hand down to my wrist, and I tried to fight the response his touch had provoked. Heat. A shiver of desire. Something settling deeper within my core.

With his fingers around my wrist, he positioned me so my fingers pointed toward the ceiling. He used the index finger of his other hand to trace up the outside of my thumb, eliciting another shiver.

"Each time my finger traces up your finger, breathe in," he said, pausing at the tip of my thumb, waiting for me to do so.

I inhaled a shaky breath, every single cell—no, every single atom—focused on the point of connection.

"Now, exhale," he said, followed by another shaky breath out from me as he traced down the opposite side of my finger.

"Good," he coaxed, his voice liquid honey. "And breathe in."

Up my index finger he went, and when he paused at the tip of my finger, I finally lifted my gaze to his. I licked my lips, and his eyes tracked the movement. His nostrils flared, and when his eyes met mine again, they were hooded.

"Breathe out," he rasped, sliding his finger down the other side of mine. "Focus on your breath." He ascended my middle finger. Another breath. Another pause. My heart felt as if it might beat out of my chest. Another descent.

As he traced up my ring finger, he said, "Focus on the feel of my finger tracing yours."

I had no problem focusing on the feel of his skin on mine. I was, however, struggling to remember why this was a bad idea.

Finally, he finished with my pinkie finger, slowly releasing my hand. "Feel calmer?"

I certainly felt…something. And while I wouldn't say I felt calmer, I definitely felt a lot more present. It was as if we had zeroed in on this moment, and I was fully in it.

But since I wasn't willing to admit all that, I merely nodded. The exercise had had its desired effect. Well…at least partially.

"Think Kai could manage that?"

Right. Kai. Jasper had been demonstrating the five-finger breathing for Kai.

I was flirting with danger. And Jasper's question was a powerful reminder of everything that was at stake. Kai. My family. Jasper's family. At the end of the day, I could want Jasper, but I couldn't have him. Not in any meaningful way.

I cleared my throat. "Definitely. I like how simple it is. He could do it anywhere, at any time."

"Precisely."

Do you have any others?" I asked, needing to distract myself while keeping the focus firmly on my son.

Kai was a huge reason why I needed to maintain my distance from Jasper. Even if everything in me wanted to beg for more.

"You can do the 5-4-3-2-1 method." Which Jasper explained as a grounding exercise using the five senses. "But here's a condensed version. What's one thing you smell?"

I closed my eyes and inhaled deeply. "I smell...cookies." I furrowed my brow. "No, almond extract. That's what it smells like. Like the cookies my mom makes every Christmas." *Like home.*

Jasper's dark chuckle threaded through me, lighting me up, not allowing me to dwell on thoughts of my parents or how different Christmas might be this year.

"That's my soap."

My eyes popped open. "You—" I cleared my throat, quickly trying to backtrack and cover my misstep. "I mean, *it* smells good."

The corner of his mouth twitched. "What's one thing you feel?"

I was tempted to mention the soothing warmth and weight of his jacket wrapped around me, but I was determined to get back on track. So instead, I said, "The cold, hard concrete beneath my ass."

"Agreed. These stairs were not designed for comfort."

"Definitely not." I wiggled a little, trying to get comfortable. My body was sore from sitting so long on the chilly surface. "God." I groaned. "I hope we aren't stuck in here all night."

"What's one thing you taste?" Jasper asked, perhaps in a bid to distract me.

I tried to concentrate on the exercise. There was nothing I could do about our predicament, and stressing about it wasn't going to help. "The lingering sweetness of the chocolate from your protein bar."

"What's one thing you see?" Jasper asked.

I took a moment to scan my surroundings. Gray walls. Gray floor. Black railing. I turned my attention to Jasper, allowing myself a moment to look at him. *Really* look at him.

I'd been so intent to avoid gawking at him all night that it was nice to finally take him in. His top button was undone, his bow tie loose around his neck. His black pants had a nice sheen to them, and I followed the line of his legs until I reached his ankles. I smiled at the sight of his socks, which were peeking out from beneath the hem.

"Dragonflies," I said, barely realizing I'd spoken the word aloud. "In honor of your gran?"

He nodded, and I fell a little harder. The man had selected his socks because of his grandmother. And then he leaned in so that his arm brushed against mine, his breath caressing my ear when he whispered, "What's one thing you hear?"

My heartbeat. It was pumping so hard, I was surprised he couldn't hear it too.

I turned my head to face him, which had the effect of putting our lips mere inches apart. I wanted to kiss him. He cupped my cheek, and I closed my eyes, reveling in his touch.

And then the music from the party shifted, swelling as the crowd let out a loud cheer.

I opened my eyes and leaned away, reality encroaching on the moment. "I hear—" I laughed, though nothing about this situation was funny. I was stuck in the stairwell with the man I was trying to avoid being alone with. If that wasn't a metaphor for my life lately, I didn't know what was. "The music from the party."

I held his gaze, and then I took a breath and forced myself to stand. To put some much-needed space between us.

But I wobbled, only then realizing that my leg had fallen asleep. Before I could grab the railing, Jasper was there, supporting me.

"You okay?" he asked.

I glanced up at him, and my breath caught.

Jasper was hot, yes. But he had this way of looking at you, of seeing you. And when he gave someone his full attention, well… My heart fluttered just thinking about it. I'd never felt as beautiful or as smart or as incredible as I did when I was with Jasper.

"Yeah. I'm good." I pressed myself into the corner, letting the concrete hold me up. "Thanks. I wonder who's on the auction block now."

"Fortunately, not me," he groused.

"Why agree to participate if you didn't want to?"

He frowned. "Because it was Kendall's first year on the steering committee, and I wanted to show my support."

"That's really nice of you," I said. "And I wouldn't stress too much about it. Your assistant can arrange everything, and besides, everyone knows it's not a real date. It's a chance to spend the evening with a celebrity or a billionaire. To show off."

"You think the woman who purchased me doesn't expect to be debauched in addition to being wined and dined?" He sounded bitter.

My eyes widened. "Does she?"

He stood, dragging a hand through his hair. "I wouldn't be surprised if she suggested something to that effect, if she tried something."

I knew Jasper probably had gorgeous women throwing themselves at him all the time, but I felt as if I might be sick. But then I remembered all the times Sloan had mentioned Jasper's latest flavor of the moment, and the idea of him spending the evening with another woman made me irrationally angry.

"You are LA's billionaire bachelor," I teased, though it wasn't funny. At least, not to me.

"First of all, my reputation was exaggerated," he said in a bored tone, though I sensed that my accusations had needled him. "But even if it weren't, that's not who I am. Not anymore. I haven't been with anyone since last summer."

Was he saying what I thought he was? And why did I care so much? It wasn't like it changed anything.

And yet, I still found myself seeking confirmation. "No one?"

He shook his head, his eyes locked on mine as he inched closer. "No one."

"Why?" I leaned toward him, my body drawn to him like a magnet.

But also, why was I torturing myself? This couldn't lead anywhere, but something about being trapped in this stairwell made it easier to ignore that. It had me forgetting about my job, the company, everyone who was relying on me. It was just Jasper and me.

He gave me a look. "You know why."

"I want to hear you say it." My voice was breathy, my heart fluttering madly.

He arched an eyebrow, challenging me. "You sure about that?"

Yes. No. Ugh. I'd never been so torn between doing what I wanted and what was right.

Nothing felt "right" anymore. Trying to be professional

with Jasper felt stiff and unnatural. Keeping him at arm's length was even worse. Wanting him was the only thing that made sense, and yet...it was the one thing that wasn't an option.

"Halle?" he asked, closing the remaining distance between us until I was backed into a corner—both literally and figuratively.

I was so tired. Tired of shouldering all the responsibility. Tired of doing the right thing. Tired of denying myself the one person who could give me comfort.

Getting trapped with Jasper in the stairwell had reminded me of how happy I'd been. How supported I'd felt. It might have been a fling, and yet I'd never had a partner who had made me feel more seen—in or out of the bedroom.

Last summer when he'd been in London, he'd always make sure to have a coffee waiting for me at the office. He'd not only listened to my opinion but sought it out on matters that affected the company. And he'd worshipped my body, always putting my wants and needs before his own.

My body said to go for it. My heart said to be careful. Since moving to LA, I'd been listening to my brain, but maybe it was time to start trusting my gut like Jasper had suggested.

So instead of fighting it like I usually would, I said, "Yes." The word was a wisp of air, a promise, a plea.

He smelled so good. Like almond extract and vanilla and...bourbon. It was somehow both light and masculine. And it reminded me of all the times in the past I'd been in his arms, in his bed.

"What happened to being professional?" he asked.

I'd been fooling myself all along.

I sighed. "I'm not sure I know how to do that with you. Not anymore anyway."

"Meaning?" His voice was gravelly, and I could feel the heat radiating off his body.

I was so tired of being professional. Of pretending I felt nothing for him when he made me feel *everything.*

He was going to make me say it, wasn't he?

"I'm so tired of fighting this." I dropped my head to my chest, feeling defeated.

He shuffled even closer, his shoes coming into view. "And I don't want what we had last summer."

My heart went into a free fall, my stomach swooping. How had I so misread the situation?

But then his hand was beneath my chin, lifting. "You said you weren't in the best place mentally. I don't want to be an escape or a regret."

"What?" I gasped. "No. I could never regret our time together. Is that what you think?"

He studied me intently, his eyes searching mine, as if seeking the truth. I hated that I'd ever made him question how I felt about him.

"Jasper." I placed my hands on his cheeks, desperate to reassure him. Even if this didn't go any further, I needed him to know. "You were the one thing that kept me going. The one thing that got me through."

How could I regret the only thing that had kept me sane when my world had been spinning apart?

"What do you want from me, Halle?" I could hear the anguish in his voice, and it gutted me. Because I felt it too. I felt torn between doing what was best for everyone else and what was right for me. "Because I've been here, waiting for you."

The bridge of my nose stung, and I hadn't realized how badly I'd been holding on to hope. I'd told myself time and again that we were over. Done. But after all this time apart, his words were a balm to my soul.

"And I will keep waiting for you if that's what you need." He rested his forehead against mine, one hand curling around the curve of my waist. "But I don't want what we had before. I want to know that you're all in."

CHAPTER FOURTEEN

JASPER

alle peered up at me, and I was dying to know what she was thinking. I was dying to touch her. Kiss her. But that was nothing new. It was pretty much my default setting.

"Jasper," she whispered, and I nearly groaned at the sound of my name on her lips. Followed by my second favorite word, "*Please.*"

She was beautiful. A fucking smokeshow in her emerald-green silk dress that flowed over her curves in the most tantalizing way. The color contrasted perfectly with her creamy skin and red hair.

Every cell in my body was attuned to her. My hand rested on her hip, and her palm was pressed to my chest. If I moved an inch, we'd be kissing.

I hadn't felt this alive in months. I couldn't let her slip through my fingers, not again.

I smoothed my hand over her hip until it was resting on her lower back. "Please, what?"

She clutched my shirt, gathering the fabric as if to hold on to her control. I wanted her to give it up, to give it all to me.

Please. Please. I was all but holding my breath. *Give in to this. In to me. Us.*

She was so damn close. I could sense it, and I wanted it.

Fuck my goals. Fuck the company. None of it mattered—not without her.

It all felt so hollow. Empty.

And I was so damn tired. Of tempering my thoughts. Of being diplomatic. But all that seemed easy in comparison to pretending I felt nothing for Halle.

But I also knew I couldn't just turn my back on the Huxley Grand. I couldn't—and wouldn't—ignore the welfare of our employees, the future of the brand, my family's legacy, Sloan. I was unwilling to give up one for the other. I was determined to find a way to have both.

I was determined to find a way to run the family business with Halle at my side—not just in the office, but in my life in every way that mattered. Because I couldn't do this without her, and I didn't want to.

She drifted closer, so close that our lips were practically touching. It was agony. It was ecstasy. She was a rose garden in bloom—lovely and full of promise, her scent luring me in like a bee to nectar.

It was almost impossible to ignore her pull, but she had to take that next step. I needed to know that she wanted this.

"I want you," she whispered, and my heart stuttered at those words, "to kiss me."

I'd waited so long for this that I wanted to take my time. Savor it.

I cupped her cheeks, marveling at the constellation of freckles scattered over the bridge of her nose. She tilted her head, leaning into my touch. And I reveled in it. In the fact that she trusted me. Wanted me.

I stroked her jawline, scarcely holding back. I was so tempted to seize her mouth like a man desperate for oxygen.

I wanted to press my lips to hers, pry her mouth open with my tongue and taste it for myself. I knew what it would taste like—decadent, rich, and sinful. Because that's what it felt like when I kissed Halle.

But then I realized she still hadn't answered my question. At least, not with the sort of clarity I needed. There could be no room for misinterpretation.

It was great that she wanted me to kiss her. And I was relieved she'd finally admitted it, but I didn't want just sex with Halle—though the sex was amazing. I wanted it all. I wanted lazy Sunday mornings in bed. I wanted time with her and Kai. I wanted to know her innermost thoughts and her deepest desires. And I wanted to be the one to give her everything.

Her eyes fluttered closed, lashes fanning out, dark and inky. I moved in, desperate to claim her mouth.

"Answer me, Halle," I rasped, mere centimeters from her lips. "Tell me that you're all in." It was a plea, a wish. And only she had the power to grant it.

I was weak for this woman, but I vowed to stand firm. I'd meant what I'd said—I would wait for her. So until she confirmed that was what she wanted, I wasn't willing to kiss her. It might kill me, but the idea of not having all of her, of her leaving again, was even more painful.

She parted her lips as if to say something. But before she could, the door to the stairwell swung open.

I froze, and so did Halle. We stared at each other, suspended momentarily. And then I dropped my hand, and she backed away. *Fuck!*

A waiter stood in the doorway. "Sorry," he said, eyes ping-ponging between us. Relief and regret mingled within me. "I didn't realize—" He backed away as if to close the door behind him.

I lunged for the exit, sobering. I didn't want to leave, not with everything so unsettled, but I also didn't want to be stuck anymore. But seriously? Why now?

"No. Wait." I grabbed the edge of the door, not willing to let it close again.

Halle needed to get back to her room so she could call her son. Whatever we needed to discuss could wait until later. For now, it was enough that we'd started the conversation. She knew what I wanted, and I'd promised to be patient if that was what she needed.

The waiter paused, holding the door open for us while we gathered our things. Halle slipped on her shoes and gripped the trash from the protein bar in her hand. I waited for her to go through the door before following.

"Thank you," I said to the waiter. "We really appreciate you rescuing us."

"Yes. Thank you," Halle said, her cheeks flushed with color. She turned to me. "I have to go call Kai."

"Yes. Go. Go." We could talk more later, if that's what she wanted.

She held my gaze a moment, and I wondered if I imagined the look of regret in her eyes.

Halle excused herself, her phone already held to her ear. As she rushed down the hall toward the elevator bank, I hoped Kai was okay.

I removed several bills from my wallet and handed them to the waiter. "Sincerely, thank you."

He laughed, staring down at the cash in shock. "All I did was open the door. But hey, you're welcome."

"Take it," I said, pushing it toward him. He hesitated for another moment before finally accepting the money with a quiet thanks. "Tell me something. Is the door at the bottom always locked?"

The waiter furrowed his brow. "I don't usually go to that

level, but it should be unlocked. It wasn't?" I shook my head. "I'll have the maintenance staff check into it."

"So will I," I said. "It's a safety hazard."

The waiter returned to his duties. The party was still going strong, but I was in no mood to socialize. There was only one person I wanted to see, and she'd already left. As much as I wanted to see Halle again, to know what she was thinking, I didn't want to push too hard. If experience was any indication, that would only make her run away.

Instead, I forced myself to focus on my responsibilities. If I was serious about balancing my relationship with my new role in the company, I needed to find out why that crash bar at the bottom of the stairwell was locked and get it rectified immediately. It was a safety hazard and a fire code violation.

I glanced at my phone, my eyes bulging at all the messages I'd missed. I skimmed them while waiting for the elevator. My new assistant, Charlie, had sent me a few updates. The family text thread was going wild with auction updates from Knox and Nate to Graham and Sloan.

I opened a text message to Graham. It was nearly three in the morning in France, but I knew he'd probably silenced his notifications. Now that he was no longer CEO, he had the luxury of unplugging. And somehow, knowing that he might not be up to respond made it easier to send my text.

Me: We missed you tonight.

THERE. IT WAS A START.

I went to the hotel control center and spoke with security, management, and operations. A group of us went down to ground level and discovered that the door had been blocked from the other side. A pile of things had been stacked in front of it, essentially using the area as a storage space.

"This is unacceptable," I seethed, enraged. To think that people could have been trapped in the stairwell in the event of a fire made me sick. "I want this cleared immediately. And I want all the other stairwells checked."

"Yes, sir," the manager rushed to respond.

"I also expect a report by Monday, explaining how this happened and how it will be prevented in the future."

"Absolutely."

He was lucky I wasn't going to fire him—for now. But I would certainly be keeping a closer eye on things at this location—and every location. Right now, my priority was making sure he understood how serious this was. I was satisfied that he seemed just as appalled as I was by the situation.

With that done, I headed back to the elevators. I needed to update Halle and Mike, who was standing in for Jackson as chief of security during Jackson's paternity leave. I opened my email on my phone and sent them both a message about the stairwell situation, asking Mike to look into it at every location.

Then, I navigated to my text messages, tapping on Halle's name. I didn't like to leave things unfinished, especially not with her. I was so tempted to rush up to her room, to demand she tell me what she'd planned to say before the waiter interrupted us in the stairwell. But I knew she had responsibilities of her own, and I'd never encroach on her time with her son.

Even so, I wanted her to know that I'd meant what I'd said—I was here for her. Her and Kai. I was worried about him after everything she'd told me. I could only imagine how she felt as his mom. When I got back to my room, I texted her.

> Me: I hope you got to talk to Kai and that he
> was well.

I KNEW I'D DRIVE MYSELF CRAZY IF I SAT BY THE PHONE waiting for her to respond. So I tossed my phone aside and headed for the shower. As soon as I was out, I heard my phone buzz.

> Halle: Thanks. He was actually asleep. Craig
> sent me this picture.

A SENSE OF RELIEF WASHED OVER ME. KAI WAS FINE. ROSIE WAS good. And Halle wasn't avoiding me.

An image appeared on my screen of Kai and Rosie. They were curled up in bed together, his arm around her little body, holding her close. It made me smile.

> Me: So much for the no-sleeping-on-the-bed
> rule. 😜

> Halle: Don't even try to pretend that you
> don't let her sleep on the bed with you.

A LAUGH BURST OUT OF ME. HALLE WAS RIGHT. I WAS TOTALLY a sucker when it came to Rosie. She was just too cute.

And something in my chest eased at the fact that Halle was teasing me. I was hanging on to her words like a lifeline.

Fuck me, I was so desperate for this woman I'd take any morsel she'd give, no matter how small.

Me: Looks like I have some serious competition for Rosie's affection.

Halle: I love how you're worried about that. Because here I am thinking I'm going to have to get him a dog if it helps him relax like that. Thanks. A. Lot.

I KNEW SHE WAS TEASING. BUT I WAS GLAD THAT ROSIE HAD helped Kai. I sank down on the edge of the mattress, still staring at the screen.

Me: Like I said, he can hang with Rosie whenever he wants.

THREE DOTS APPEARED ON THE SCREEN, DANCING BEFORE disappearing. Then danced again. I wondered what she was thinking. About the almost-kiss. About what I'd said. Did she want to give us a chance? Was she even considering it?

When her message finally came through, I damn near dropped my phone.

Halle: Thanks, Jasper.

I STARTED TYPING OUT A NEW MESSAGE. DELETED IT. TRIED again. Cleared it again.

Instead of asking her what I really wanted to, I ultimately resorted to talking about work. I updated her on what I'd discovered about the stairs. I figured if she'd checked her emails, she would've already said something about it by now.

> Halle: Unbelievable.

> Halle: I guess it makes me feel better and worse that the door wouldn't open.

> Me: Same.

I WAS TEMPTED TO APOLOGIZE AGAIN FOR GETTING US STUCK, but in the end, I realized I wasn't sorry. I regretted the fact that she'd worried about Kai. But I would never take back the time we'd spent together or the things I'd said.

With my fingers poised over the keyboard, I wondered if I should mention it or leave it be? If we'd just had a minute more… I sighed. Maybe I would've known what she was going to say. Maybe…

Another message came through, and my hope inflated like a fucking balloon. And then it deflated just as quickly when I read it.

> Halle: It's getting late, and we have an early flight tomorrow. I'm going to head to bed.

Fuck.

What did that mean?

Maybe it just means that she's tired. Maybe it means that she needs more time. Either way, I knew now wasn't the time to push.

AFTER A FEW MINUTES, WHEN NO NEW MESSAGE CAME, I flopped back on the bed with a groan. *God, I'm pathetic.*

THE NEXT MORNING, I CLIMBED THE STAIRS OF THE JET, feeling tired and stiff and cranky. I'd barely slept, and my body was sore from sitting on the concrete for all that time. I'd gone for a run and done a brief yoga and stretching video in my room, thanks to our company-wide in-house workout library. But I could definitely use a sauna and a massage and a good night's sleep.

I'd jacked off in the shower this morning, but it hadn't done much. The kind of release I craved was something only Halle could give me. I sighed, still not sure where we stood after last night.

I tucked my bag into one of the overhead compartments and greeted the pilot before Tabitha emerged from the galley, smiling. She was our family's preferred flight attendant, and we asked the Hartwell Agency to staff her almost exclusively.

"Morning, Jasper. Can I get you anything? A drink or some breakfast?"

"Morning." I studied her. Something about her always seemed so...familiar. Though I didn't know why, and I couldn't put my finger on the reason. Whatever it was, it put me at ease. "Maybe some coffee after we take off."

"Of course. Latte with oat milk, right?"

"Exactly. Thanks."

Kendall was next to board the plane, talking to someone behind her before Halle appeared. She turned to face me, and when she lifted her head, I was hit with such a pang of longing that it felt as if my heart had stopped. Halted and then restarted at double speed.

Fuck. I clutched my chest. *Fuck me.*

"You okay?" Knox asked.

I'd been so distracted, I hadn't even noticed he'd boarded the plane. "Yeah. I'm good. You?"

"Glad to be going home." He gave me a hug just as Nate and Emerson boarded.

Emerson joined Halle and Kendall. I took a seat while the crew finished their preparations for takeoff. Restless energy thrummed through me, and I tried to study Halle without attracting notice.

"Where did you disappear to last night?" Knox asked, taking a seat across from me.

Nate gave me a knowing look. "Did you find someone to keep you company? Give the winning bidder a preview of the bachelorx date?"

"I—" *Shit.*

I could feel Halle's gaze boring into the side of my head. Halle and I hadn't discussed how to handle this because we hadn't expected anyone to even notice we'd gone missing. So instead of telling them that I'd found myself locked in a stairwell, which would've inevitably led to more questions, I decided to keep it vague.

"Something like that." The words felt wrong the moment I said them aloud.

But what else was I supposed to say?

I felt as if I'd surpassed everyone else's ideas on who I was and what I was capable of. It felt like…like how it felt to outgrow your clothes. They were tight and uncomfortable and no longer reflected your style.

But for now, these were the clothes I had to continue to wear. If it meant protecting Halle. Even if lying to my family meant gaining Halle's trust, then I would do whatever it took.

"How was the rest of the evening? Any surprises?" I asked, eager to refocus the conversation away from me.

Knox chuckled. "Apparently one of the rookies from the Hawks had been running a social media campaign to hype up interest. He went for almost as much as Holden Hansley."

I chuckled. "Which rookie?"

"Kovi." And then he added, "Carson Kovalsky."

The pilot announced that it was time for takeoff, and the plane turned, likely angling toward the runway. I tapped on my phone, navigating to Carson's social media. The guy was photogenic; I'd give him that. And he knew how to use social media to his advantage. He had a mix of videos and stills, and he was shirtless or holding a hockey stick in most of them.

"How much?" I asked once we were in the air. Halle and I had been locked in the stairwell long before any of the players from the Hawks had taken the stage.

"Twenty-three thousand."

"Damn." I whistled low. "Good for him."

"The audience was rabid when he went onstage," Nate said as the plane leveled out.

The captain announced that we were free to move about the cabin. Tabitha delivered my latte, and I thanked her. Then she circulated the cabin, taking drink orders.

I inhaled slowly, taking a sip as a memory from last night floated through my mind. Me tracing Halle's fingers as I explained the mindfulness exercise. Each inhale had been shaky. Each exhale just as much so. I'd done the exercise countless times, but it had never felt so…erotic.

"Were you talking about Carson?" Kendall asked. When Knox nodded, she added, "Because he's definitely getting invited back next year." She then turned to Halle to resume their conversation.

Emerson unbuckled and moved over to take the seat next to Nate. He draped his arm over her shoulder, and I'd never felt more jealous than in that moment. I was happy for Nate, truly. But I wanted what he and Emerson had. I wanted to be able to show Halle affection in front of my family. Fuck. Even just not having to pretend I felt nothing for her when she was in the room would be a welcome change.

"I was thinking we should try to get Carson to do some classes for the Huxley Grand's in-house exercise program," Emerson said.

"Yes." I pointed at her, loving that idea. "Yes. Do that."

Since marrying Nate, Emerson had taken an active role in the wellness component of the brand. She had so many great ideas and contacts in the industry, and I was always impressed with the experiences she developed. She and Lily were also working on some wellness retreats for the Fleur-de-lis line that were brilliant.

"Awesome. I'll reach out to him," Emerson said, making a note in her phone.

"Great. Thanks." I set my coffee mug on the side table, and Tabitha quickly whisked it away before asking if I'd like anything else.

I had to hand it to Kendall; the auction had been a huge success. It had not only raised a ton of money but garnered a lot of positive attention for the foundation and its mission. I still wasn't looking forward to my charity date, but I hoped it would be a fun, easy afternoon. Maybe a helicopter ride, lunch on the terrace at the hotel.

Even so, I resented the idea of giving up some of my limited free time to a stranger. No matter how much she'd donated.

Maybe next year I will no longer be a bachelor.

The thought came to me unbidden, and I couldn't help but hope that it might be true. That Halle and I would find a way to be together, because I was done with being apart. And I was going to do everything in my power to show her that she could trust me. To remind her how great we were together.

CHAPTER FIFTEEN

HALLE

"$40,000. That's forty thousand. Can I get fifty?" The auctioneer scanned the room, all eyes on the stage.

When I looked up, I realized that the spotlight was directed at me. I was the one onstage. I was the one people were bidding on. My skin felt tight.

From the back of the room, someone said, "Stop."

The crowd gasped, and the auctioneer seemed irritated. But then the spotlight focused on him. On Jasper. "She's mine."

Jasper's eyes were on me when he said those words, and I felt his voice reverberate through me like a tuning fork. His declaration sang through my blood with the very truth of his words. Of all the people in the room, he was the only one who saw me. Truly saw me.

His eyes never left mine, and I knew he was checking in with me. Trying to make sure I was okay. I was far from okay, but having him here with me made everything seem better.

"You have to win her first," the auctioneer stated.

"I will," Jasper said, and there was no doubt in my mind that he would. My nipples pebbled at the command in his tone.

The setting changed, shifted. The next thing I knew, Jasper and I were in his office, and he was staring down at me. I wanted him so much I felt as if I were going to burn from the inside out with longing.

"Beautiful." He knelt between my legs, kissing his way up my calves, my thighs. His touch was reverential. Every stroke of his hands was done in a way to comfort me. Please me. "Absolutely beautiful."

I shivered from his touch and the intensity of his expression. He was so...resolute. So focused on doing everything he could to bring me pleasure.

With his hands midway up my thighs, Jasper peered up at me, seeking permission. Confirmation. He might be the one in control, but he was making it very clear that I held all the power. I watched his hazel eyes swirl with desire. And when I inclined my head in assent, something in him seemed to both relax and coil tighter still.

He kept his eyes locked on mine as he glided his hands the rest of the way up my thighs. His palms were smooth, strength radiating through his hands on my skin. My breath gusted out of me the closer he got to my center. And when he used his fingers to spread my folds, inspecting me, I let out shaky, "Fuck," finding it increasingly difficult to remember words. What they meant. Anything.

Jasper continued teasing me, circling my clit. He alternated his pressure, his tempo, until it felt as if my heartbeat were centered between my thighs. When I gasped, he latched on to my reaction, holding that tempo. Slowly, ever so slowly, increasing his speed.

"That's it," he coaxed. "I want you to scream my name as you come on my fingers."

I held his gaze as long as I could, my body unraveling. I held his gaze until my legs were shaking and everything in me was clenched tight. It was such a strange sensation—this feeling of tension and release.

"I'm so close." My head fell back against the chair on a moan. "Take your time," Jasper said, leaning forward to tease my nipples with his mouth as he inserted one finger into me. "Take all the time you need."

My skin flushed with heat, my pleasure rising with every stroke of his finger. He added another, using his thumb to circle my clit at the same time. Oh god. I'm going to come. I need to come.

I groaned, rocking my hips, seeking more friction. More...something. "Please," I whined.

"Please, what?" he asked, a smirk playing at the corner of his lips. When I said nothing more, he added, "Don't be shy, love."

My head dropped, and I jolted awake with a start. *What the...*

I blinked a few times, trying to reorient myself. I was on the private jet with Knox, Kendall, Nate, Emerson, and Jasper. I blinked a few more times and tried to slowly, discreetly, slide to a more upright position.

Because...*fuck.*

I'd just had a sex dream about my boss. In front of him and his family. In front. Of him. *And* his. Family.

Oh god. I felt as if I might throw up.

The dream… It had felt…so real. I'd woken with a start, horny and confused.

What if they'd noticed me sleeping? What if I'd moaned in my sleep? Or said something embarrassing? Oh god. What if I'd said something incriminating?

My cheeks heated, and I wanted to hurl myself out the nearest emergency exit, parachute be damned.

I knew what Zara would say. She'd tell me it was my subconscious trying to force me to see the truth of the situation. She'd claim that my mind was telling me what my body —and my heart—already knew.

And I'd tell her it was a dream. Nothing more.

But in my gut, I'd know she was right.

Right. Okay. Just…stay calm. No reason to freak out.

Or at least, I didn't want anyone else to realize I was freaking out. About the dream. About what it meant. About my feelings for Jasper.

I tried to settle myself, using the condensed version of his five-finger exercise. I peered out the window. I concentrated on the fluffy shape of the clouds dotting the blue sky. *Feel.* I could feel the smoothness of the leather seat beneath me.

I inhaled slowly. I could smell…coffee? Not the usual cheap airline coffee, not for this billionaire family. It smelled like something out of a fancy Italian coffee shop. Rich and creamy. It made me long to visit the Huxley Grand in Bergamo again, walking down the cobblestone streets as the church bells rang.

And taste. I could taste my minty toothpaste. I let out a slow, measured breath and turned to my fifth sense. I could hear the hum of the private jet.

Feeling a little calmer, though still a bit off-kilter, I blinked a few more times as if to clear my vision, hoping no one had noticed. Knox and Kendall were so lost in each other, they were oblivious to anything else going on. Emerson was working on her computer while Nate read what I assumed was a printout of a script. Jasper, however, was staring right at me.

When I met his gaze, he arched his brow as if to ask, "Everything okay?"

"Yeah. Yep." I turned away. My cheeks were so hot I thought they might burst into flames at any moment.

How he could look so put together was beyond me. I was a wreck and not just because of that dream. I'd barely slept last night, my mind spinning with fantasies about what might have happened had the waiter not interrupted us.

I'd tossed and turned, twisting the sheets around me while I'd replayed our conversation in the stairwell over and over. Jasper's voice, raspy and full of anguish as he said the words that had left me stunned.

"I've been here, waiting for you."

"I want to know that you're all in."

All in. Those two words had circled my mind like a record on repeat. *All in. All in. All in.*

What did that even mean?

Part of me was disappointed he hadn't come to my room last night. The other part was relieved because I still didn't have an answer for him.

I'd tried to picture it. Us—together. I was thrown back to a memory from last summer, from the last time he'd tried to suggest *more*.

I appreciated that he'd offered, but it didn't change anything. My life, my friends, my job, were in London. I couldn't abandon Sloan, and my ex would never agree to let me move so far away with our son.

"My life is here," I said, misery marking my tone.

I didn't want it to end either, but we had to be realistic. And a long-distance relationship was not realistic. Not with the demands of our work schedules or my home life. And not when I needed this job, now more than ever.

If having an affair with my boss's brother was reckless, wanting a relationship with him was even more so. If anyone found out... I didn't want to think of the consequences for either of us.

Which was why I had to end this. I couldn't let Jasper believe we had a chance. I couldn't let him hope for anything more than this moment.

He dropped his forehead to mine, a somber expression on his face. I hadn't expected to see him again before he'd left, but he'd surprised me by coming to the office before his flight.

"You know where I am if you change your mind."

And you know where I am, *I thought. He didn't mind if I was inconvenienced, but he wasn't willing to make the sacrifice to be with me? It was just like something my ex would do.*

And in that moment, I realized that I was falling into my same old patterns. And I refused to do that. I didn't want to be in another "relationship" where I was putting in all the work. I didn't want to let myself fall for another man who would never be the partner I deserved.

These past few weeks, they weren't reality. And leading Jasper on—giving him false hope—wouldn't be good for either of us. So I forced myself to say the words, "I won't."

"WOULD YOU LIKE ANYTHING TO DRINK?" TABITHA ASKED, snapping me out of the memory.

"I'm okay for now." I smiled. "Thank you."

I stood and headed for the bathroom, stumbling in my eager attempt to escape. She tried to help me, and I declined the assistance, embarrassed. I darted inside and quickly locked the door, hating how frazzled and out of control I felt. I prided myself on having my shit together. And right now, I was a hot mess.

I braced myself on the edge of the sink and stared at my reflection in the mirror.

Why? Why did it have to be him?

Why did our chemistry have to be so strong?

Was it, as I'd often wondered since our fling, the forbidden element that made everything that much hotter with Jasper? Or was it just...him?

I had a feeling I knew the answer, but I hadn't been willing to admit it to myself. It seemed like there were a lot of things I hadn't been willing to admit to myself, including how much I liked Jasper and not just because the sex was amazing. Which it was.

Finally, accepting that I couldn't stay in here forever, I washed my hands and dried them before exiting the bathroom.

Jasper was waiting just outside. He reached out as if to touch me, before retracting his hand. We were out of the line of sight of his family, but it was a small plane, and it would soon become obvious that we were both missing. He scrutinized me, and I wanted to squirm beneath the intensity of his stare.

He opened his mouth as if to say something, but then the plane hit a spot of unexpected turbulence, and I lost my balance. I stumbled forward, straight into Jasper. And he remained there, strong, unshakable, his touch gentle yet firm as he steadied me. I sucked in a sharp breath at the unexpected contact.

He looked hungry. Desperate, despite his buttoned-up appearance.

Images of my dream flashed through my mind in lurid detail. His hands on my skin. His mouth on my…

My knees wobbled, threatening to give out. And he kept holding me. And I didn't want him to stop.

There was a chime on the overhead speaker, and I jolted. *What am I doing? What are* we *doing?*

"Well, folks," the captain said, while Jasper watched me with concern, "we've hit a pocket of unexpected turbulence. Please take a seat and buckle up. We'll try to navigate us to smoother airspace."

"Here," Jasper said, ushering me toward the private office and lounge. His hand was on the small of my back, and it sent a bolt of lightning down my spine.

"Shouldn't we—" I paused, giving the main cabin where the rest of his family was seated a pointed look.

"This is closer. And besides, you heard the captain." Jasper smirked, clearly pleased by this turn of events. "We're supposed to take a seat."

When the plane hit another bump, I ducked into the lounge without further comment. I took a seat in one of the leather seats and buckled in. Jasper closed the door then buckled in next to me.

"Are you okay?" he asked.

"I'm—" I wasn't sure what I was. "Tired. I didn't sleep well," I admitted, surprising myself.

"Neither did I." He scrubbed a hand over his face, his fatigue showing for the first time. It made me realize how often he donned a mask, even with his family.

He always seemed so blasé about everything, but I knew it was an act. And I felt privileged that he didn't feel the need to be anything but himself with me. Just as I'd never felt the need to be anything but myself with him.

It was a big reason why I'd almost agreed to his terms last night. No. Not terms. His demand. Because when I was with Jasper, he made me believe that anything was possible.

It was part of the reason he'd been so good at his job when he was an SVP. He was so creative and passionate about the guest experience, and he came up with unique and creative ideas. And the guests delighted in them.

I stared at the door, my mind on work. On his family just down the hall.

Almost as if sensing my thoughts, Jasper said, "I locked it, and this room is soundproof."

My shoulders relaxed. "Can I ask you something?" When he nodded, I asked, "Did you mean what you said?"

Gold swirled with hazel, desire, and promise. "Every. Fucking. Word."

His words sent a thrill through me that I tried to ignore. I'd tried to tell myself that it was because I hadn't slept with anyone in the past eight months, but I knew it was the fact that it was Jasper. And he wanted more than just sex with me. It was both exhilarating and terrifying.

I swallowed, feeling completely unprepared for this conversation. "Last night caught me off guard."

"Before I left London last summer, I told you I wanted more. I thought I'd made that clear."

"Yeah, but…" That had been months ago. "I figured you'd moved on by now."

He took my hand in his. "At first, I'd hoped you'd change your mind. Eventually, I tried to move on. I did. But it only made me realize that I didn't want to move on even if I could. Because there's no one else for me but you."

My heart soared at his words, even as my mind tried to shoot it down. I was surprised. Flattered. Confused.

"But why wait for me?" It was something I was still trying to wrap my head around. Not only the fact that he'd waited, but the idea that he'd been holding out hope for us all this time. "You couldn't have known that Graham would step down and that Sloan and I would relocate to LA."

He rubbed his thumb over the back of my hand. "No, but I kept hoping something would change so we could be together."

That seemed like a pretty huge leap of faith.

"And now that you're here," Jasper continued, "I don't want to let you go. Not again."

For a moment, I let his words wash over me. Letting myself revel in them. In the idea of being with him. When I'd ended things before, it was because we'd been living in a fantasy.

The distance might no longer be an issue, but there were still so many additional obstacles standing in our path.

Jasper was still my boss's brother. Last summer, he'd been an SVP. Which, admittedly, wasn't great. But now, he was the CEO of the company, which made our situation even worse than before. He had a lot of attention focused on him and his actions.

Attention that I didn't want or need, especially since I wanted to keep my job. I *needed* to keep my job. Not only did I love working with Sloan, but not many companies offered such generous health insurance, benefits, and paid time off.

"I—" I didn't know what to say to that. I was still trying to process everything. "I can appreciate where you're coming from, but I also can't just jump to being 'all in.' What does that even mean? How would that even work?"

It was something that had been plaguing me since last night. What Jasper expected. What he really wanted. And how he thought that might actually be possible.

I'd come too far since my divorce to risk my career, my future—and my son's—for a man. In the past, I'd given up my wants and my dreams for Craig. And while Jasper wasn't my ex, I refused to compromise my reputation, my hard work, my career for anyone, let alone a man. There was too much at stake. I couldn't afford mistakes, especially not with Kai and my parents relying on me.

"We can go at whatever speed you need." Jasper threaded his hand through my hair, and I relaxed into the contact. "But it means no more running away."

Was that what he thought I was doing? Was that what I had been doing?

"Just give me a chance," he continued, his gaze so open, imploring. "Give *us* a chance. I'm not saying we need to announce to the world that we're together—yet. Because I do want us to tell our families at some point." He cupped the back of my neck, his eyes searching mine. I held still, unable to speak because his words filled me with such joy and hope. "I just need to know that you're in this. With me." He tilted his forehead to mine, and I closed my eyes briefly. I just wanted to be here, with him. "That when you get scared, you come to me. That when problems arise—which they inevitably will—we'll figure them out—together. Do you think you can do that?"

Did I think I could do that?

"Because I want you, Halle." His voice nearly shook from the conviction in his tone, and I felt it from the top of my head to the tips of my toes. "I want to be a part of your life and Kai's life. I want it all."

"I…" My throat clogged with emotion. I wanted to, but I was scared. Scared to hope. Scared to believe it could be possible. But despite my fear, I found myself wanting to say yes.

CHAPTER SIXTEEN

JASPER

Halle was on the edge, and my heart was in her hands. My breathing was shallow, and I was trying not to push her any more than I already had. But I was done holding back. This was my chance, and I was putting it all on the line in the hopes that she'd agree.

All in.

Come on. Say yes, I pleaded. Hoped. Prayed. I wasn't sure I'd ever wished more for anything in my life.

"Jasper," she sighed, and my heart sank. I'd been so hopeful, and now I was mentally preparing myself for rejection. She took her hand and placed it over my heart. Something about her action soothed me, even as I braced for impact.

"I'm… I want to be with you. *Truly.*" She met my eyes. "But I don't understand why this has to be all or nothing. Why can't we just let things evolve naturally?"

I placed my hand over hers, relieved, grateful, but also… concerned. "Maybe we could if we were a normal couple. Do you have reservations about me? About us?"

"No." She shook her head. "This has nothing to do with you—and everything to do with our jobs."

That was a relief. Sort of.

She gnawed on her bottom lip. "I know you want to tell our family and friends, but I'm not ready for that. And even if I were, we need to tread very carefully. This is a delicate situation."

I wanted her to know that I took her concerns seriously. She was a single mom, supporting herself and her son. I had nothing but admiration for how hard she worked to provide for them. Let alone everything she was doing to help her parents. And I respected her dedication to my family's company.

"I looked at your employment contract, and it guarantees you cannot be fired at will. Technically, Sloan is your supervisor, not me. While I can suggest things regarding your employment, she will always have the final say. Though obviously, the board weighs in since you're now considered an executive."

Halle's shoulders seemed to relax slightly at that. "That's good. I feel better about the fact that I don't report directly to you."

"So do I. I don't like the idea of there ever being a power imbalance between us—at work or at home. I want us to be partners. Equals. And I want you to feel secure in your job, because you are important to this company." *And to me.*

"Thank you." She dipped her head. "It's nice to work for a company that values me. And I appreciate your looking at that. My job—our roles at the company—is one of my biggest hesitations."

"I understand that," I said. Because truly, I did. Our relationship could be explosive—for her, for me, for the company. It wasn't something I took lightly. "I do. And I'm not pushing for us to do a hard launch here, but I need to know that telling them is our end goal." Because she was the end goal for me.

She peered up at me from beneath her lashes. "But we could be discreet for now, right?"

"For now," I said, wanting to emphasize that point, even though I thought it might be best just to get our relationship out there. Part of it was impatience, but a bigger part of it was concern.

Last summer, we'd been having fun. There'd been no need to tell my family or the board because it wasn't going to amount to anything serious. Things had changed for me during our time together, and I'd realized I wanted serious. But Halle hadn't. Her life had been in London, and mine was in LA. She hadn't wanted a long-distance relationship.

Now… Well, I was going into this with an entirely different mind-set. Distance was no longer an obstacle, and I didn't want to let anything else stand in our way. I was thinking of the future—my future with Halle, with Kai. I wanted to do everything in my power to protect them. And that meant I had to think ahead when it came to our roles in the company, to Halle's career, to how we were going to handle this with Sloan and my family, as well as Pierce and the board of directors.

"What else?" I asked, wanting to assuage Halle's fears and reassure her. "What other concerns do you have?"

"Just—" She blew out a breath. "So many. What if things don't work out? What then?" I could see the fear in her eyes. "What about my job? What about Kai?"

"What about him?"

"I haven't dated anyone since the divorce. And this is all new territory for me. I don't want to confuse him or have him get attached to you, only for things to end."

I could understand that, even if I didn't like how much emphasis Halle was putting on things ending. I didn't even want to contemplate it, let alone discuss it. But I had to remember that she was divorced, and her reticence was understandable.

"Would you be okay with just being my friend or colleague for now?" she asked.

I tucked her hair behind her ear, wanting her to know that I understood her concerns regarding Kai. "He's your son, and you know what's best for him."

She smiled at that. "Thank you."

"Of course. You're a good mom, Halle. You probably don't hear that enough, but you are."

She leaned forward and pressed her lips to my temple. "You're a good man, Jasper Mackenzie. You probably don't hear that enough, but you are."

Something in me warmed at her compliment. Released. Eased.

Halle saw me, not only as the man I was but as the man I wanted to be. It was nice to have someone believe in me. Appreciate me just as I was.

"I'm scared too," I admitted. "I've never really done this with anyone. Never found anyone who made me want to try. Until you."

She smiled then, and I couldn't help it. I found myself saying, "I want to kiss you." It felt as if the words had been ripped from my chest. From my very soul. "So damn bad."

"Then kiss me," she said, as if it were that simple.

I'd wanted to kiss her since the moment she'd walked into the conference room all those weeks ago. I'd thought about little else since. Just one taste. One kiss.

I shook my head, releasing her hand so I could drag mine through my hair. "I can't…" I swallowed, trying to compose myself. "I want you. I want this. But I can't. Not unless you're sure." Because losing her had hurt too much.

She stared at me, unblinking. Stunned.

Hell, I was still a little surprised myself. But I knew what I wanted, and I refused to compromise. If I couldn't have all of her, then I wouldn't have any of her.

Yes, she'd said that she wanted to be with me. But I knew she still had reservations. It was understandable, and I was trying to show her that I wanted more than a physical relationship with her. And I was proving it to her in the only way I knew how.

She searched my eyes as if seeking the truth. And then she said, "You're serious."

I nodded. "I am. Because the way I feel about you isn't going away. I don't want it to go away. Tell me you feel it too."

Her eyes fluttered closed, and she looked almost pained when she admitted, "I feel it too."

I felt as if my heart was in free fall.

"I'm scared," she whispered.

"I know," I said. "But if you ignore everything else and focus on us, on me, it feels right."

She nodded. "It does."

She was so close to giving in. To saying yes.

"So let's just focus on us—for now. And forget everything else." Baby steps.

She nodded again, and something in my chest eased. "Just… I know I'm asking for discretion, but I won't share you," she said, and I couldn't hold back my smile. "I couldn't handle seeing you at an event with another woman."

"You'd never have to. I'm yours."

Her shoulders seemed to relax, some decision crystallizing. "Okay."

"Okay, what?"

A smile formed on her lips. "Okay." Her eyes met mine, pure and sincere and good as she finally, *finally*, uttered the words I'd been longing to hear. "I'm yours."

"Fuck yes, you are." I'd known that all along, but it was a relief to have her admit it too.

I unbuckled her seat belt and pulled her into my lap. I needed to touch her. Halle let out a yelp of surprise, and I chuckled, feeling lighter than I had in months. I kissed beside her eye. Her cheek. The edge of her mouth. Everywhere that wasn't her lips.

My cock was already hard and pushing against my zipper, but I took a deep, steadying breath and tried to think of something other than the feel of her on my lap. In my arms. Because nothing had ever felt more right.

As desperate as I was to kiss her, I hadn't waited this long to rush it. I was going to savor every fucking second.

I searched her gaze, drinking her in. The way she looked at me. The feel of her in my arms. She brushed my hair away from my face, and I closed my eyes, overcome.

"What is it?" she asked, tracing the lines of my face with her fingertip.

I let out a shaky exhale. I couldn't tell her the truth—not yet. But I could tell her part of it. "I've never wanted anything more than I want you."

She tilted her head, her expression softening. "I want you too, Jasper." She wrapped her arms around my neck. "I don't think I ever stopped wanting you."

With one hand on her back, I used the other to cup the back of her neck, guiding her mouth to mine. When her lips grazed mine, my entire body felt as if it had been jolted back to life. And as we danced and devoured and claimed each other, I knew that it had all been worth the wait for this moment.

Months of pent-up longing poured out of me. I wanted her. I'd never stopped wanting her. And I had a feeling that would always be the case. I would never get my fill.

We couldn't seem to make up our minds. One second, we

were gentle. The next, our kiss turned feral. Greedy alternating with playful and tender.

My hands were in her hair, on her ass. Everywhere I could reach. I'd never been more grateful for the soundproof walls and locked door.

She rocked against me, and I gritted my teeth. My cock was already aching to be inside her, but I was determined to stay focused. Meanwhile, she seemed just as determined to get me to lose control.

I cupped the back of her neck. "Say it again, Halle. Tell me you're mine." Because fuck…my restraint was so close to snapping.

"I'm," she gasped, gliding over me with just the right amount of friction, "yours." She gasped again when I pinched her nipple, and I let out a satisfied sound. "But should we really be doing this here? Now?"

I followed the direction of her gaze. To the door and my family beyond. I kissed her again. I didn't fucking care.

"We're playing with fire," she said.

"And you fucking love it." I unzipped her dress, pushing it aside to reveal her to me. "Tell me you don't. Tell me you want me to stop."

She shook her head. "Don't you dare stop, Jasper."

I stood, carrying her over to the couch, and she squealed. I chuckled and lowered her to the sofa, bracing myself over her. The turbulence had long since passed, but there was no way we were leaving this room. Not until the wheels were back on the ground. Halle was mine, and I was going to take advantage of every moment we had together.

She wrapped her arms around my neck, and I couldn't help but watch her. Revel in her. "Fuck, Halle."

"Yes," she whispered. "*Yes.*" Her smile was dazed, her cheeks flushed with color, eyes wild. "We should do that." *Fuck.*

"I, I—" I lost the ability to communicate. Words. What were words? What need was there for language when she made me feel like this?

"Fucking stunning," I said, taking her in.

She wrapped her legs around my waist, pulling me down to her so her breasts brushed against my chest. My cock was hard and aching, and I needed to be inside her. But that would have to wait—for now. I wanted all my attention to be on Halle—her desires, her needs, her everything.

"Oh god." She moaned. "This is even better than my dream."

"Dream?"

Was that what this was? A dream? Because after all this time apart, I couldn't believe she was in my arms once again.

Her cheeks turned an even deeper shade of pink. She sucked in a jagged breath, though I wasn't sure if it was from my words or our position.

I ran my nose along the shell of her ear, dipping my finger into her bra. "What happened in this dream of yours, love?"

She turned away as if trying to hide from me. From the truth. I wasn't sure.

"Halle?"

"I dreamed that I was on the auction block last night. And you…"

I arched my brow, intrigued. This I had to hear. "And I…?"

She shivered. "You claimed me in front of everyone."

"Claimed you how?" I asked, my voice dropping an octave. I had a sudden image of rutting into her like an animal. That was how she made me feel—savage and primal.

"You…" She gasped when I shifted, rubbing her pussy against my cock at a new angle. Harder.

I definitely wanted to hear more about this dream, but fuck me. Fuck, that felt good.

I rolled my hips, unable to stop myself. My body was acting on autopilot, and it had taken over the controls.

She reached for me, palming me. I placed my hand over hers then gently removed it. I shook my head. Though it wouldn't take me long to get off, I wanted this to be about her. Falling into bed wasn't the way to prove myself to Halle. This was about her and putting her needs first—not just in the bedroom, but everywhere. And I would show her that.

"You said I claimed you. Claimed you how?" I traced a circle around her nipple, and I hoped she didn't realize I was shaking. I was so excited and nervous that my hands had a tremor. I focused on the way her nipple puckered in response to my ministrations. "Tell me, or I won't let you come."

She narrowed her eyes at me. "You wouldn't."

"Don't try me, Halle," I warned. "You've made me wait a long time."

I peered down at her, my body on fire for this woman. I pressed down on my cock, drinking in the sight of her. Skirt rucked up on her thighs. Breasts exposed. Hair a wild flame.

"Y-You climbed onto the stage."

"And…" I prompted.

She swallowed. "You told everyone I was yours."

I moved so I was kneeling between her legs. *Damn right.* "Because you are."

She smiled, her cheeks flaming with color, and she gave a short, quick nod.

"Then what?" I asked.

She shook her head, her eyes skimming down my chest. "We were in your office. You were dressed about like you are right now."

"That's it," I purred in her ear before kissing my way down her chest. She thrust her breasts forward, and I eagerly peeled her bra aside so I could suck one nipple into my mouth, then the other. "I love hearing about your fantasies. Tell me more."

"You…" She panted, body thrashing. "You made me come."

"How?" I asked, mapping her body with my hands, recommitting every freckle, every birthmark, to memory.

"With your fingers."

I coasted my hand up her thigh until I reached her underwear. I dragged a finger over her slit. She'd soaked through the material. "God. You are so fucking wet."

She shuddered, closing her eyes as I peeled her underwear aside to play with her clit. "Yes. Yes." She let out a shaky breath. "Right there. Just like that."

I loved that she was telling me exactly what she wanted. I loved that she'd been dreaming of me. I loved sharing in her fantasy and helping act it out. Watching her like this was hot, especially when she arched her back, clenching her fists.

She was so damn close. She just needed something to push her over the edge. Before I could say anything, the captain came over the intercom system, startling us.

Halle's eyes went wide, but I didn't stop. I couldn't. If anything, it only made me more determined to make her come.

"Ladies and gentlemen," he said. "This is your captain speaking. Flight attendants, please prepare for landing."

"Come on, Halle," I taunted, taking the captain's announcement for the challenge it was. "Think I can get you off before we land?"

"You. Better," she gritted out.

I chuckled, taking in the state of her. She wasn't worried about my family, our jobs, or the future; she was firmly rooted in the present. And I fully intended to reward her for it.

"Don't worry." I brushed my lips over her nipple, gratified by her reaction. "I will."

I sped up my tempo, increasing the pressure of my thumb on her clit as I inserted another finger. We were running out of time. We needed to get cleaned up before we landed. But first, I needed to make her come.

I watched Halle's body for cues, picking up the pace and seeing how she responded. She was so tight. So wet. And I knew she was close.

"Oh my god. Oh my god," she chanted, hair splayed over the arm of the couch, legs parted.

"That's it, Halle." God, I was so hard. I felt as if I might explode from touching her alone. "Come for me, love."

And then she was clenching around me, panting as her release crashed over her. I pressed my mouth to hers, swallowing her pleasure. So beautiful.

The buzzer rang, indicating that someone was at the door, and Halle's eyes popped open. I reached over her and pressed the button on the intercom. "Yes?"

"Mr. Mackenzie," Tabitha said, but my attention was on Halle. She was a fucking sight to behold. Happy. Sated. *Mine.*

"We'll be landing soon," Tabitha continued as I pressed a chaste kiss to Halle's forehead. "Please ensure that you and any other passengers in your cabin are buckled in and your personal items are secured."

"Will do," I said, releasing the button to talk. As soon as I had, Halle and I looked at each other and burst out laughing.

I was relieved. Giddy. Ecstatic. We were really going to do this.

"I should get cleaned up." She smoothed my hair away from my face before kissing me. "Thank you."

"My pleasure," I said, giving her another quick peck before standing so that she could do the same.

I smoothed down my tie, righting my shirt, while she

adjusted her dress. When she turned to head for the attached bathroom, I gave her ass a playful smack. She glanced at me over her shoulder, biting back a smile. We might be coming back down to earth, but now that Halle had agreed to give our relationship a shot, I had a feeling I'd be floating in the clouds for a long time.

CHAPTER SEVENTEEN

HALLE

"Mummy!" Kai ran down the hall and threw himself into my arms. Rosie wasn't far behind. Her little nails clicked against the floor, and I couldn't help but smile at the sight of the two of them coming to greet me. "You're home."

I held him close, using my hand to measure where the top of his head came to on my body. It felt as if he'd gotten taller in just the few days I'd been gone.

My trip to New York had been quick, but so much had happened in such a short time. The stairwell incident. The… My cheeks heated as I thought about what Jasper and I had done on the jet. With his family not far away. Yes, it had been a soundproof room with a locked door, but it was reckless.

And yet, I couldn't quite find it in me to care. Maybe it was the oxytocin, the dopamine, or the endorphins. Hell, maybe it was the adrenaline from having sex on the jet. And while I wanted to blame it all on the orgasms, I knew that wasn't it. At least, not entirely.

I was happy.

Jasper wanted us to be together, and I wanted that too.

More than I'd wanted anything in a long time. I had to believe we'd find a way to make it work.

"Halle, hey," Craig said, rubbing the back of his neck. He seemed more relaxed, and it wasn't just the casual clothes he wore.

"Hey." Rosie was jumping at my ankles, so I picked her up and gave her a cuddle. "Hey, Rosie girl." She licked my hand, and I laughed.

"Wait till I show you the new trick I taught her!" Kai said.

Rosie squirmed to get free, so I set her down on the floor. "I can't wait."

Kai ran off with Rosie, leaving me alone with Craig. "I'm glad the timing worked out for you to stay with Kai while I was out of town. Seems like he had fun."

"He did. We both did." Craig leaned forward, pressing a kiss to my cheek. I stood there, frozen in shock. "Did you have a good trip?"

"I—" I swallowed hard, taking a small step back. "Yeah. Yep."

Act normal, Halle. Jesus.

I grabbed the handle of my suitcase, eager to escape to my room. I probably still smelled like Jasper. Like sex. And my ex was kissing my cheek, acting like this doting partner.

"I should get unpacked." I took a few steps, but then there was a knock at the door. "Did you order room service?"

"Oh, right." Craig bypassed me to answer it. "Kai was getting hungry, and you know I can't cook."

I laughed. No joke about that. But it was nice to see him admitting he wasn't perfect for once. Nice, but also…strange.

"Plus," Craig continued. "I figured you might be hungry when you got in, so Kai helped me pick something you might like. We added it to the order in case you wanted it."

"Oh. Um. Thank you." Who the hell was this considerate man, and what had he done with my ex?

"Let me just get changed, and then I'll come eat with you and Kai," I said, rolling my suitcase behind me.

Craig swung open the door, and I nearly tripped when I heard Jasper's voice coming down the hall. I dropped my suitcase and spun back toward the door, trying not to panic.

Be calm. Act normal. Be...

"Who are—"

"Jasper, hey." I forced myself to smile, wishing I could've avoided this confrontation even as I inserted myself into their conversation. "Is everything okay?"

Did my voice sound weird? High-pitched and breathy?

Be calm. Act normal.

"I came to get Rosie." Jasper smiled, charming as ever. Though his eyes kept darting between Craig and me.

"*You're* Jasper?" Craig asked.

Oh right. They'd never met because Craig had never attended work functions with me, even when we were still married. Despite expecting me to accompany him to his.

"Yes." Jasper held out his hand. "And you must be Kai's dad."

I laughed nervously as they shook hands, sizing each other up. "That's right. Okay. Great." I turned back toward the living space, eager to put an end to this awkward situation. "Kai," I called. "Jasper's here to pick up Rosie."

"Jasper's here?" Kai called before bounding in, Rosie at his heels.

Jasper smiled, and this time, it was a genuine smile. "Hey, kiddo."

Kai threw his arms around Jasper, and I could practically feel Craig's eyebrows rise as they lifted to the ceiling. I shifted from one foot to the other, trying not to freak out. Trying not to do anything that might spark unwanted questions.

But it felt as if it didn't matter what I did. Craig was certainly taking it all in. Jasper. Me. Kai. Rosie. *Crap!*

Jasper picked up Rosie and gave her a cuddle. "Thanks for taking such good care of Rosie." Jasper opened his wallet and held out some cash to Kai.

Kai's eyes went wide. "Whoa!"

I frowned at Jasper. "What are you doing?"

"Paying him for dog-sitting."

"You don't have to pay him anything. It's a win-win situation. He got to hang out with Rosie, and you had someone to take care of her while you were gone."

"Exactly," Jasper said. "If Kai hadn't volunteered to watch Rosie, I would've had to pay someone. He earned this money."

This wasn't a conversation we should be having in front of Kai, let alone my ex. But before I could say anything, room service arrived. The guy did a double take when he saw Jasper standing at my door. "Mr. Mackenzie."

"Ethan, hi." Jasper smiled, stepping aside so Ethan could roll the room service cart through. I'd always been impressed by Jasper's memory for names and faces. It was part of what made him such a great leader. He made everyone feel important.

"Let's go eat, Kai," Craig said, turning our son toward the kitchen. Then to me, he said, "Join us when you're ready, Hal."

Kai's shoulders slumped. "But what about my money?"

"Come on, mate." Craig clamped his hands on Kai's shoulders and steered him away. "Lunchtime. Your mom will sort it out."

"Hal?" Jasper mouthed.

I shook my head. *Not now.*

I stepped into the hall, letting the door close behind me. I pinched the bridge of my nose, a headache forming.

"I'm sorry," Jasper said. "I didn't realize paying Kai would cause an issue. I should've talked to you about it first."

"I get why you wanted to offer it to him, but I don't want your relationship with Kai to be based on a foundation of money or expensive gifts." *Like Craig.* "Besides, are you going to pay him every time he dog-sits?"

"I should," Jasper said. "Don't you think it's important for him to value his time? To be compensated for providing a useful service?"

What Jasper said made sense, but still…

The door to my suite opened, and Ethan stepped out. I smiled politely and thanked him before he rolled his cart down the hall toward the service elevators.

"We really shouldn't—" I said at the same time Jasper said, "This isn't the place—"

We laughed.

He made sure the coast was clear then leaned in, careful to keep his voice low. "Can I see you later?"

"I wish, but…" I frowned, thinking of all the things I needed to do to get ready for the week ahead. Let alone the fact that, "I need to spend some time with Kai."

"I understand," Jasper said. "I'd never want to encroach on your time with Kai. Maybe after he goes to bed?"

I laughed, wanting so badly to touch him. "Craig's staying with us, and—"

Jasper jerked his head back. "Your ex is staying at your place?"

"Just for a few nights. I booked him a room here, but we thought it was more important for Kai to be comfortable while I was out of town."

"But you're back now," Jasper said.

"And Craig's only here for one more night. He's staying on the extra bed in Kai's room."

Jasper shook his head, his displeasure clear. I understood

where he was coming from. I wouldn't be pleased about the situation if our roles were reversed.

"I'm not happy about it either," I said. "But I want what's best for Kai. I moved him away from his dad, and Craig made the effort to be here. I want to give them time together."

Jasper frowned, and Rosie wiggled in his arms, letting out a yip.

"I should get going," I said. "Before someone…"

"Right." Jasper straightened as if suddenly remembering where we were. "I'll see you tomorrow."

I nodded, feeling there was so much left unsaid. "See you…tomorrow."

I hated that we had to stand here and pretend we were nothing more than colleagues. I hated that I couldn't invite him into my apartment and ask him to join Kai and me for lunch. At the very least, I wanted to hug him, kiss him good-bye. And I couldn't do any of that.

It hadn't hit me until that moment how much I wanted to have that with Jasper. Sure, sometimes it was fun to sneak around. But there were situations—like now—when I just wanted to spend time with him. And I didn't want to have to come up with a cover story. But I also wasn't ready to blow up my entire world and everything I'd worked so hard to achieve.

I sighed, shoulders curving inward. "This sucks."

He glanced around then linked his pinkie finger with mine. It was so subtle no one would've noticed, and yet that simple touch lit me up inside. Gave me hope.

"We'll figure it out. Okay?"

I hesitated a moment, then nodded. I trusted Jasper, and I wanted to have faith in us and our future. I might not see how it would all work out, but that didn't mean it wouldn't.

It was a big part of the reason why I'd ultimately agreed to this. Because Jasper made me believe that it could. Because

I wanted to find a way to be with him. He made everything better, brighter.

"Okay."

His shoulders relaxed. "Also, I know you don't want me to give the money to Kai, but he earned it. So what if we gave him a small amount each time and put the rest into a bank account for him?"

I considered it a moment. Jasper was right—Kai had earned that money. And giving him some now while putting the bulk aside would teach Kai about delayed gratification and saving. It was an elegant solution.

"Okay." I nodded. "Thank you. That seems like a good compromise."

"I'll see you tomorrow," he said, lingering.

"Tomorrow," I echoed, thinking it sounded so far away.

"You have to go inside," he whispered. "Or I'll never be able to leave."

I laughed, loving that he felt the same struggle to say goodbye as I did. I'd just spent the flight home with him, and I would see him at the office tomorrow, but it wasn't enough. And it wasn't the same as spending time alone together outside of work.

"See you," I whispered.

I opened the door, and when I checked over my shoulder, Jasper was still standing there. Rosie was in his arms, her ears drooping. They both looked sad to say goodbye. It took everything in me to make myself go inside.

I closed the door softly behind me, pressing my back to it with a sigh. This wasn't like before. This was…so much more. I took a minute to compose myself then headed to the kitchen.

"Come sit by me, Mum! I saved you a seat." Kai smiled, bouncing in his chair.

"I would love to. Let me just wash my hands first." I went

to the sink and washed and dried my hands before joining Kai and Craig at the table.

When Kai asked me about the money, I explained the bank account solution. He seemed disappointed at first, but then Craig pointed out how it would allow Kai to save up for a bigger Lego kit he'd been wanting or, even better, a trip to Legoland. That seemed a bit ambitious, but I was more surprised by the fact that Craig had backed me up. In the past, he would've offered to buy Kai a Lego kit to get him to calm down.

Conversation moved on to what they'd done while I was gone. And when Kai finished, he popped up and went to his room to grab something, leaving Craig and me alone.

"Mum," Kai called from down the hall. "Granny's calling on my tablet. Can I talk to her?"

"Sure," I called out.

Craig leaned forward, resting his elbows on the table. "How's your dad?"

"Hanging in there," I said, not wanting to get into it. It was nice that Craig had asked, but I didn't have the desire or the emotional energy to go into detail.

He nodded, seeming to contemplate something. And then he asked, "Does your boss often visit you at home? He and Kai seemed awfully...familiar."

"Jasper's not my boss. Sloan is," I said, feeling that the distinction was more important now than ever.

"Hal," he scoffed, "Jasper's the CEO. He's everyone's boss."

I shoved a bite of salad into my mouth to avoid responding. This reminded me of my conversation with Jasper on the jet. The mental gymnastics made my head ache. He wasn't my boss, but he was the CEO. The only consolation was that I reported to Sloan, though she was out of the office for the foreseeable future.

"Doesn't it bother you that Jasper can just drop by your

suite at any time? It seems like he's encroaching on your personal time."

"We're friends," I said. "Just like I'm friends with his sister, Sloan. They're a family company, and they like to treat their employees like family."

"Mm." He leaned back in his chair, crossing his arms over his chest.

I stood, done with this conversation. Craig had no right to butt into my life. He was here to spend time with Kai; he wasn't allowed to judge me or my decisions.

I returned my plate to the room service tray and navigated to the Huxley Grand app on my phone. I went to the room service menu and selected the button for "finished with meal."

"This is temporary. I'm working on finding a place for Kai and me to live. I just haven't had much time."

"I know, and I understand that. I just…think it will be good for you both to have some space from your work."

"My work—or Jasper?" I asked.

"Jesus, Halle." He stood, his chair scraping against the floor. "I'm just trying to find out more about the people my son's spending time with. If roles were reversed, you'd be doing the same."

That was fair. But I worried about what Craig was hinting at. And I worried if he suspected something between Jasper and me, others might too. I needed to shut down anything that might suggest an improper relationship, at least until Jasper and I figured out what we wanted for the future. And only then, how we wanted to handle it.

Jasper's words floated to me once more. *We'll figure it out.*

I tried to be a little less defensive, but that was difficult when it came to Craig. I'd spent years retreating into myself or feeling the need to defend myself. I might not care what he thought anymore, but it was a difficult habit to break.

"Jasper has several nieces and nephews who adore him. Kai adores him. Him and Rosie."

"And what about you?"

"What about me?" I asked, sweat dripping down my back. Was he insinuating that something was going on between Jasper and me?

"I don't know. You seem…different, happier, lately. And I guess I just wondered if you're seeing anyone."

I jerked my head back. And here I'd been worried that he suspected something between Jasper and me. But holy shit. Was Craig…?

He held up his hands. "Not because…" He shook his head. "Not because *I*…" He dropped his hands. "This is coming out all wrong."

He cleared his throat, and I wondered what the hell was going on. "I, um—" He tugged on his collar. "This isn't easy for me, but I'm working on it. A few months ago, I started going to therapy."

I couldn't have been more shocked if he'd told me he'd taken a trip to Mars. "That's, uh, that's great, Craig."

I wondered what had finally prompted him to go to therapy. I'd asked him to go with me or on his own many times, and he'd always been completely opposed.

"Therapy, Kai moving away, it's made me realize how much I've missed with him. Not just lately, but for the past five years. And with his birthday coming up, well—" He sighed. "He's growing up so fast."

I leaned my hip against the counter, using it to prop myself up. Craig had never said anything like this. And while pretty words were empty without action, this was definitely a step in the right direction. This was everything I could've wanted for Kai. For my son—and his relationship with his father.

I only hoped Craig would follow through this time.

Because he'd disappointed Kai in the past, broken promises, and Kai had been heartbroken.

Craig stepped closer, attention darting down the hall toward Kai's bedroom. I could hear Kai giggling at something my mom had said, but I appreciated Craig's effort to be discreet. "Ever since you and Kai moved to LA, I feel so far away from him."

"I can imagine," I said. "And I think it's great that you've been trying to call him more regularly. That you came to visit. It seems like you spent some quality time together this weekend."

"We did." He smiled. "It was really nice. But I don't want to watch him grow up through a screen. And two weeks in the summer and then a week over Christmas isn't enough."

A pit formed in my stomach. I was going to be sick. Craig was going to try to take Kai from me. It wouldn't be the first time, but I'd fought like hell, and I would do so again.

I tried to remain unruffled. I needed to appear calm, cool, and in control.

"Which is why—" Craig spread his arms wide, his smile almost hesitant "—I'm moving to California."

"Wait. What?" Surely I'd misheard him. Surely I was imagining things. Because there was no way that Craig was moving here.

"I'm moving to LA. I want to be closer to Kai. I want to have the chance to get to know my son. That's why I was here, to meet with some of the company execs about transferring."

I was hit by a chill that went deep to my core. "I'm stunned. I had no idea you even felt this way."

"I know, and it's something I'm working on. Feeling my emotions. Expressing them."

"But…" I tried to figure out how to best word my response. "I'm glad, really." For him, for Kai. Hell, even for me since I'd continue to interact with Craig until Kai was an adult. And this was certainly a much nicer version of my ex. "But what's brought this on?"

Was he sick? Or dying? I didn't want to jump to the worst-case scenario, but I honestly couldn't imagine something short of life-altering to spur Craig to such drastic action. He'd always been a bit self-centered.

"Let me start by saying that I'm okay, but I had a health scare earlier this year." He focused on the table, and I sank back down into my chair. Despite everything that had happened between us, I still cared about him. As a person. As the father of my child. "It really put a lot of things into perspective."

"I can imagine," I said, thinking of my dad's diagnosis and how much it had thrown me for a loop. I didn't know what had happened to Craig, and I didn't need to know the specifics. "I'm sorry you had to deal with that."

"Thank you. I realized that I didn't want to be the kind of father my dad is. I realized that I had a lot of regrets." He gave me a meaningful look.

"I'm glad you're okay. And I'm glad that you want to be more present for Kai. That's all I've ever wanted."

"Thank you." Something in him seemed to ease. "I know Kai needs stability, and you do a great job of providing that for him," Craig continued, and I appreciated his saying that. "But I'd also love to spend more time with him."

"I'm not opposed to the idea," I hedged. Because I wasn't. I just knew better than to take Craig at his word. He had a habit of saying one thing and doing another.

He nodded, and he actually looked…nervous? "I know what the custody agreement states, and I also know that you don't owe me anything. But I was hoping we could come to an agreement between us, no lawyers. A weekend or two a month would be great. Or if you were going to be traveling for work, maybe I could stay with Kai. Or even if you just want a break, I could spend time with him instead of a babysitter."

"I…" I was still completely stunned by this entire conversation. "I think we'd have to try it out first. I want Kai to have more time with you, but I need to know that you're going to show up and follow through." I wasn't trying to be mean; I was trying to protect my son.

Craig considered it a moment. "That's understandable. I know I haven't always done the best job of that in the past. But I promise, things are going to be different this time."

"I hope so," I said, and I meant it.

He placed his hand over mine. "Thank you, Hal."

"Have you told Kai yet?" I asked.

He shook his head. "I wanted to talk to you first. And I figured we should wait to tell him until it's finalized. He's had enough changes lately."

I blinked a few times, seriously wondering if I'd tripped into an alternate universe. But then I spied my suitcase that needed to be unpacked and thought about all the things I needed to prep for the week, and I knew it was real. Even so, things were looking up for the first time in a long time.

Kai had spent a nice weekend with his dad, and Craig seemed to be serious about stepping up for our son. Jasper and I were going to give our relationship a chance. I'd gotten a fantastic promotion, and I loved my job. Dad was at his new facility and seemed to be settling in. So instead of dwelling on what might happen in the future, I decided to try Jasper's advice of focusing on the present. I was going to live in the moment.

CHAPTER EIGHTEEN

HALLE

I kept stealing glances at Jasper throughout the meeting. I'd tried to keep my attention on the head of hospitality, but I was finding it incredibly difficult to focus on anything but Jasper. We'd texted some last night before I'd gone to bed, and I couldn't wait to be alone with him again. Not that I was sure when that would be. We both had busy schedules, and my weekends were my time with Kai.

Jasper adjusted his tie, and I wondered if he was struggling as much as I was. When he met my gaze across the table, his eyes darkened. I shifted in my seat, seeking relief from this ever-present ache. His attention darted to my legs, and he smirked.

Was I being reckless? Most definitely.

But that was the thing about living in the present. It was freeing in a way. Consequences seemed like a problem for future me.

"Unless there are any other questions," said the head of hospitality, "I think that about covers it."

"No questions," Jasper said. "At least not from me. Halle?"

I shook my head, wishing I'd paid more attention there at the end. "I'm good. Thank you."

Jasper stood, signaling an end to the meeting. "Halle, can I see you in my office after this? I want to review those numbers."

"Of course," I said, hoping it was a pretext to spend some alone time together.

I grabbed my things and followed him down the hall to his office, greeting everyone we passed. As soon as we were inside, and the door was shut, he pushed me up against it. I reached for him at the same time he grabbed for me, and our lips collided.

It was electric, and I felt as if I couldn't touch enough of him fast enough. As if I'd been deprived of oxygen until now. Until him.

I reached behind me and pressed the button to lock the door. I didn't know how long we had, but I did not want any interruptions.

"That meeting was torture," Jasper rasped.

"All morning has been torture." I let my head fall back against the door as he kissed my neck, my collarbone, squeezing my breasts through my dress. I groaned my appreciation as my nipples hardened, brushing against the lace cups of my bra.

"Did you wear this dress to taunt me?" he asked, skimming his hand down my hips, over my ass.

"Maybe." I bit back a grin, and he squeezed my ass, his hard-on digging into me. We groaned in unison.

"And these shoes?" He lifted my leg, and my phone fell out of my pocket, landing faceup on the floor. It didn't matter. Nothing mattered in this moment but Jasper.

I wrapped my leg around his waist, rocking against him. Seeking more friction as our kiss became heated. Desire unspooling deep within me.

This. This was what I'd needed. Jasper.

When my phone rang, I was tempted to ignore it. But then I saw Sloan's name on the screen.

"Shit." I unhooked myself from Jasper and bent down to pick it up. "She's probably calling for our weekly check-in."

"Answer it if you need to," he said.

Even though Sloan wouldn't be able to see me, I smoothed back my hair, trying to regain my sense of composure. I hit the button to connect the call, turning so Jasper was behind me. Maybe I'd be able to concentrate if he was out of sight.

Doubtful.

But then Jasper smoothed his hands over my stomach, pulling me flush to him. Letting me feel the effect I had on him. Concentration shot.

"Sloan, hey," I chirped.

He gathered my skirt, lifting the material until it was bunched above my waist. I glanced at him over my shoulder, my eyes wide. "What are you doing?" I mouthed.

Jasper leaned in so his breath tickled my skin. He grazed the shell of my ear with his mouth. "Relax," he whispered.

I glared at him. How could he expect me to relax at a time like this? I was on the phone with my boss—his sister. And he was touching me. At work.

"I, um—" I swallowed hard when he slid his hand up my thigh toward my center. "I was just finishing up a meeting with Jasper. If you give me a minute, I'll be back in my office."

"Actually, that's perfect," she said. "I had a few things I wanted to loop him in on. Can you put me on speaker?"

"Give me just a second." I put the phone on mute and then said to Jasper, "She wants to talk to both of us."

"Good." He kissed my shoulder, sliding his hand beneath

my underwear. "That gives us an excuse to spend more time together."

"Jasper. You have…" I gasped when he circled my clit, my head falling back against his chest. "You have to stop."

I didn't want him to stop. Not when it felt like this. But Sloan…

He used the other hand to grab my breast, pinching my nipple. Arresting my attention. He always seemed to know exactly what I needed to get off.

"I'll stop when you come."

"I can't…" I squeezed my eyes shut, nearly overcome with pleasure. "This is so," I panted, "unprofessional."

"What's unprofessional…" His voice was low in my ear, dark, dangerous, and seductive. "…is keeping your boss waiting. Now hit the mute button again so she doesn't wonder what's up."

Crap! I'd almost completely forgotten about Sloan. I grabbed his wrist, but instead of trying to remove his hand as I'd intended, I found myself using it to hold on. Gripping his wrist as he plucked at my sensitive nerve endings. Was I asking him to stop? Keep going? I wasn't even sure.

"Halle," he chided, stilling his hand. A warning. "Unmute the phone."

My legs were shaking, but I tapped the mute button again so she could hear us.

"Halle?" Sloan asked.

"Sorry about that," I said, hoping the delay hadn't been too suspicious. "You're on speaker with Jasper and me."

There was a pause, and I briefly wondered if she'd heard something she shouldn't. The rustle of our clothes. The sound of him thrusting his finger into my body. The moans I was biting back.

"Are you okay?" Sloan asked. "You sound different."

"I'm—" My words were cut off when Jasper inserted

another finger, and I tried not to gasp. "I'm great. Yeah. Just busy. You know how it is, running between meetings."

"Of course. This won't take long."

No, it wouldn't. Not with the way Jasper was touching me.

"How was the gala?" Sloan asked. "I saw some of the pictures online."

I widened my eyes at Jasper, pleading with him to answer. We'd missed most of the gala because we'd been stuck in the stairwell.

"Successful," Jasper said, though his eyes were still on me. Was he thinking about the stairwell? Or our conversation on the plane? Or what had happened after? Maybe all of it.

"Good. We should do something nice for Kendall to thank her."

"Absolutely," Jasper said.

"Are you looking forward to your date?" Sloan teased.

"Mm," Jasper hummed, leaning in to nuzzle my neck.

Sloan continued talking, and I tried to stay focused on what she was saying. But all I could concentrate on was the feeling of Jasper's hands on me. The way he made me feel both weightless and secure.

Every so often, Jasper responded, his voice rumbling through his body and into mine. My eyes closed of their own accord as he continued coaxing my pleasure from me. What we were doing was reckless, but somehow the danger of getting caught only added to the thrill.

My release blazed through me, and I shattered, right there in Jasper's arms. In his office. Jasper clamped his hand over my mouth, silencing me as he continued to work my body until I sagged against him.

"Okay. Well, I think that's it for now," Sloan said. *Thank god.* "Any questions?"

The only thing holding me up right now was Jasper. My limbs felt heavy. My body buzzing with pleasure.

"Answer the question, Halle," he whispered, nipping my shoulder.

I jolted. "No. No questions."

"Great. I'll let you get back to it, then."

"Okay. Thanks." I'd never hit the end button on a call so fast. I lowered my dress and whirled to face Jasper. "What the hell was that?"

He smirked. "I told you. I was helping you relax."

I smoothed my hair and crossed my arms over my chest. "I thought we agreed that we wouldn't let our personal relationship compromise our professionalism."

"This wouldn't have happened if I'd gotten to see you last night." He was taunting me.

"Oh, so now you're going to blame this on me?" I teased.

"Pretty sure this—" he gestured to his erection that was tenting his pants "—is all your fault."

"Poor baby." I pouted, closing the distance between us. "Do you need some help with that?" I palmed him through his pants.

He groaned, dragging his thumb down my lip. "Yes. Always."

"Does that feel good?" I asked, continuing to touch him. Tease him.

"You know it does," he ground out.

My phone chimed, and I brushed my lips against his. I retreated to the desk, grabbing my phone before sliding it into my pocket. "Sorry. I have to go. I have a meeting in five."

"Seriously?" he asked.

I nodded, trying not to laugh at his stricken expression. "Afraid so." I grabbed my things and headed for the door.

He grasped my wrist. "When can I see you again? Outside of work," he added. "Do you have plans this weekend?"

"Not yet, but I have Kai."

"I know." He pulled me to him, gripping my hips. "I was

hoping we could do something together—the three of us. Well, and maybe Rosie too."

"Yeah?" I tilted my head, surprised by his eagerness to include my son. I placed my hand on his cheek. "I'd like that, and I know Kai would too."

"Great. Bring your swimsuits, and we can hang out by my pool. Unless…"

"Unless what?"

"Kai has been begging me to take him for a flight on my helicopter. I know his birthday's coming up. We could go to San Diego. Spend the day at Legoland."

"He would absolutely love that," I said, knowing how excited Kai would be about either one of those things. I could only imagine how he'd react about both. Still…what kind of message would it send?

"But…?" Jasper said, perhaps sensing my hesitation.

"But it seems…extravagant. Plus, aren't you worried about being seen together in public?"

"In San Diego?" He chuckled. "No. I'm not a celebrity like Nate or Emerson. And I don't think anyone would expect to see me at Legoland."

Could we really do this? Could we go out and spend the day together like a real couple? When we'd been in London last summer, Jasper had found ways for us to be together. The picnic at St Dunstan in the East came to mind, as did a weekend spent on a canal boat when Kai had been with Craig.

But those hadn't involved Kai. And I had no idea how we'd explain Jasper's presence. I wanted to say yes, but I needed to think through all the implications.

"Can I think about it?" I asked.

"Absolutely. And if you decide it's too much, we can do something more low-key. I just want to spend time with both of you."

I pressed up on my toes, giving him a quick peck. "I want that too."

~

IN THE END, I AGREED TO JASPER'S PLAN FOR KAI. IT SOUNDED like fun, and I knew Kai would love it. Besides, he hadn't made many friends yet, and I wanted him to feel special on his birthday. As long as Jasper and I acted like friends for the day, it would be fine. Wouldn't it?

I worried about Kai telling Craig, but not enough to stop us from going. If Kai mentioned it to his dad, I'd figure out how to handle it. Today was about Kai—not Craig, not anyone else.

The moment the elevator doors to the helipad opened, Kai's eyes widened. He turned to me. "Are we…"

"Flying in the helicopter?" Jasper clapped a hand on Kai's shoulder. "You bet!"

"Really?" Kai looked from one of us to the other.

I nodded, and he threw himself into my arms. Then he leaped into Jasper's arms. "Thank you!"

Was this excessive? Absolutely. But unlike with Craig in the past, I knew Jasper wasn't trying to win Kai over with expensive gifts or outrageous experiences. Jasper wanted to share something he loved with my son.

Jasper took him around the outside of the aircraft, telling him about the parts of the helicopter and asking Kai to help him perform his safety inspection. I knew Jasper had already come up here earlier to inspect the helicopter and perform his preflight checks, but he was so sweet to make Kai feel important and special.

I smiled, taking a few pictures as I watched the two of them together, Kai asking questions, and Jasper patiently answering each and every one. Jasper seemed to delight in my son, and Kai's confidence grew with every interaction.

"Come on, Mum!" Kai called. I joined them, setting down my backpack and climbing into the helicopter after Kai.

"Whoa. Cool." Kai scanned all the controls.

"I've got a special spot just for you." Jasper pointed to the back seat. It was then I noticed the child-sized restraint. Jasper had to have bought it just for Kai because I didn't remember seeing it the last time I'd flown with him. My heart melted. "And I've got some ear protection for you because it's going to be pretty loud once I fire up the engine. Okay?"

Kai nodded, and then Jasper buckled Kai in and double-checked that everything was secure. Jasper slid the ear protectors over Kai's head. Jasper flashed him a thumbs-up, and Kai smiled a toothy grin and gave him two thumbs up in return.

"One more thing." Jasper pulled out a stuffed dog from a backpack and handed it to Kai. It looked just like Rosie. "Will you hold on to her for me?" Kai nodded, clutching the stuffed animal to his chest.

I turned to look out the window, trying to hide my reaction to Jasper's thoughtfulness. I didn't know why, but it still surprised me. How much he cared—for a kid who wasn't even his own.

"You good?" Jasper asked, joining me in the front. He had on a pair of light tan shorts and a short-sleeve chambray button-down shirt. He looked ready for vacation.

I nodded, buckling myself in before slipping the headset over my ears. "I'm great. Thank you again for doing this."

"Of course." He lowered his aviator sunglasses then spoke to air traffic control through the headset.

When he fired up the engine, I scanned Kai, checking in.

His feet were swinging, and he clutched the stuffed dog to his chest. He was in heaven. I snapped a few more pictures.

The flight was smooth, and Jasper was a great tour guide, pointing out interesting landmarks during the hour trip down to San Diego. When we landed, Kai was talking nonstop. About the flight. About riding in a helicopter. About how cool it was that Jasper was a pilot.

"You ready for the next surprise?" Jasper asked as a luxury SUV pulled up to the helipad. He had a backpack slung over his shoulder, and he made it all look so effortless.

All I knew was that we were going to Legoland; he hadn't told me anything else. Jasper had planned the entire day for us, and it was so nice to let someone else handle the details for once.

The driver parked and opened the door to the back seat, where a booster seat was already installed in the third row and waiting for Kai. Jasper had done this, all of it. He'd not only planned the day for us, he'd put everything in place to make sure it would be safe and enjoyable for my son and me.

I could never imagine Craig doing something like that. I was so used to handling everything, even before my divorce, that I was touched. And if I hadn't been convinced before that Jasper was the right man for me, I definitely was now. When he'd said he was all in, he'd meant it. Not just with me, but with my son.

CHAPTER NINETEEN

JASPER

"Where are we going?" Kai asked from the third row of the SUV.

"We'll be there soon." I glanced over at Halle. I wasn't sure I'd ever seen her look more relaxed or at ease.

She was wearing these tantalizing denim shorts, and I itched to place my hand on her thigh. I was excited about spending the day with her and Kai, even if it meant I couldn't touch her. At least, that's what I kept telling myself.

The reality was that if I didn't touch Halle soon, I really might explode.

Those damn denim shorts were like waving a red flag in front of a bull.

Long bare legs.

Smooth skin.

It was torture.

But it was all worth it to see her smile. To hear Kai's delighted squeals as the helicopter took off. She rested her hand on the seat between us, and I placed my hand beside hers. Tension filled the air, but I waited for her to make the next move. For now, it was enough that we were together.

I turned my attention to the passing scenery. I was so keyed up that when she linked her pinkie finger with mine, it sent a bolt of lightning straight down my spine.

If such a simple touch could set me off, I was scared to think what having her touch other parts of me would do. I'd gotten a preview of it, the other day in my office. But we'd been short on time, and it had ended all too quickly.

I wanted to have sex with her. God, did I. But I also wanted our first time together, now that this was more than just a fling, to be special. I wanted Halle to know that our relationship was about so much more than the physical aspects. I wanted to prove to her that I was in this for the right reasons.

When the driver pulled up to the entrance to Legoland, Kai freaked out. "Are we—" He was kicking his feet. "We're going to Legoland?"

"We are." I grinned, delighting in his reactions. He was so much fun. "Happy birthday, kiddo."

Halle unlinked our fingers, sliding her hand back into her lap. As soon as the car had stopped, Kai unbuckled his seat belt. "This is amazing. Thank you!" He threw his arms around my shoulders. "Thank you."

"Your mom and I wanted to do something special to celebrate you," I said, and Halle's watery smile made me even more excited for everything I had planned. This was just the beginning.

When we stepped out of the car, a Legoland employee, Kayla, was waiting for us. "Welcome to Legoland. I'll be your tour guide for the day."

Halle peered at me over the top of her sunglasses. Okay, so maybe I'd gone a little too far. But I'd wanted to spoil them. So I'd reached out to the park and paid a generous fee to get the VIP treatment. No waiting in lines. We could ride as many times as we wanted. We had free run of the park and a personal tour guide.

"You ready?" I asked, tightening the strap of my backpack.

"Yeah!" Kai fist-pumped the air.

As Kayla ushered us into the park, Kai slid his hand into mine. My heart warmed at the contact and the fact that he'd initiated it. I smiled at Halle over his head.

When we bypassed the ticket booth, Halle leaned in and said, "I was planning to pay for the tickets."

"Thank you, but it's already taken care of."

"Mm. I'm going to owe you a big thank-you for this."

I placed my hand on her lower back. "While I'm not opposed to what I think you're suggesting, you don't owe me anything."

She grinned. "We'll see."

The rest of the day was spent going from one attraction to another. Kai loved the rides, and I loved seeing Halle let go. I couldn't remember the last time I'd had so much fun.

Every time Kai experienced something new—a ride or a show—he was full of delight. He was so animated, so funny. I'd always liked kids, and Kai was no exception.

"What a fun day," Halle said as we exited the theater. I placed my hand on her lower back, using every excuse to touch her. The park was closing soon, and we still had an hour flight back to LA. "Thank you."

I smiled, thinking back on how nice the day had been. Relaxing, easy, joyful. It had been everything I could've hoped for. We might have had this adventure to celebrate Kai's birthday, but today had felt like a gift to me. To get to spend time with the two of them. To get to spoil them. Well, it made me happy.

"It was fun."

Kai slumped forward, dragging his feet as we headed to where the SUV would pick us up. Kai's energy had started to wane after dinner, but he was trying to act like it wasn't. It was honestly pretty amusing to watch. That said, I had a feeling he was going to crash. It had been a jam-packed day of rides, shows, and so much more.

"I don't want to go." Kai pouted.

"The park is closing," Halle said. "We have to go. But didn't we have a nice day?"

He nodded, his lower lip still sticking out. So adorable. If it were up to me, I'd pay the park to stay open late just for us. But I knew Halle would kill me if I did something like that. And I also knew that Kai needed his sleep.

I'd considered asking Halle if she wanted to make it an overnight trip, but I figured that might be a bit much for our first outing as the three of us.

"I can't walk anymore," Kai whined.

"How about a piggyback ride?" I asked.

He perked up a little at that. "Really?"

"You don't have to do that, Jasper," Halle said.

"I want to." I moved my backpack to my chest then crouched down beside a nearby bench. "Come on, Kai. Hop on."

He stood on the bench then launched himself at me. Luckily, I'd been paying attention, so I caught him. I took off, and he cheered. "Woo-hoo! Look at me, Mum."

"I see you." Halle's smile was warm, relaxed.

As we rode back to the heliport in the SUV, Kai said, "I hope Daddy can come with us next time, now that he's moving here."

Craig? Moving here?

Halle's guilty expression all but confirmed it. *The fuck?*

"I'm sure Dad would love to come with you sometime."

Kai made it through takeoff, but he fell asleep soon after. I kept thinking about what Kai had said about Craig moving to LA, but it didn't feel like the right time to bring it up.

Besides, I wasn't going to let Halle's ex ruin what had been an otherwise perfect day.

"Thank you for today," Halle said as the LA skyline came into view. "Truly."

"My pleasure," I said, and I meant it.

We chatted about the day, and I tried to forget about Kai's bombshell. Craig didn't matter. Halle was with me, even if no one knew about our relationship.

Once we landed, I glanced back at Kai, who was somehow still asleep. I was surprised he hadn't woken up when the helicopter had switched off.

"He had a great time today. We both did," Halle said, giving my hand a squeeze. "Thank you."

"Thank you. For letting me spend the day with both of you. I had fun." I smiled. "Let me perform my postflight safety check, and then I'll carry him down to bed."

I rounded the outside of the aircraft, checking everything over before grabbing my backpack. I tossed it over my shoulder then went to the back door and opened it before carefully removing Kai's ear protection and gently unlatching his seat belt. He roused briefly.

"Shh," I whispered, picking him up. "I've got you."

Halle grabbed her bag, and we headed for the elevator. We were quiet on the trip back to her suite, mindful not to wake Kai. After she'd removed Kai's shoes and tucked him into bed, we returned to the living room.

Halle stood in front of the windows, her attention on the skyline. I went over to her, pressing a kiss to her shoulder. "You okay?"

"Yeah. Just thinking about how nice today was."

"It was," I said, though she seemed sad somehow too. I pushed away my questions about Craig and his move. Today, tonight, was about us. No one else.

"I wish every day could be like this," she sighed, leaning back into me.

"You want me to propose that we move our board meetings to Legoland?" I teased, though I knew that wasn't what she meant.

"No." She laughed, and I wrapped my arms around her. "Though, can you imagine Leith's face if you tried?"

I chuckled, enjoying the feel of her in my arms. I wasn't ready to say good night yet, even though I knew it was inevitable.

"Today was such a gift. Not because of the helicopter flight or the trip to Legoland, as fun as those were." She turned so she was facing me, looping her arms around my neck. "It was a gift to spend time with you and Kai. It was a gift that he felt good all day. That we got to just be together and have fun."

"One day," I said, cupping her cheek, "every day will be like today."

She held my gaze briefly before looking away. She still didn't believe it, but I believed enough for both of us. So I kissed her, trying to infuse my kiss with all the love and hope I felt.

"I have something for you." I'd been waiting all day for the right moment to give this to her. I removed a small velvet box from my pocket. "I know it's Kai's birthday, but you deserve to be celebrated too."

"Jasper." She tilted her head. "You didn't have to get me anything. You've already done enough. More than enough."

"You're always taking care of everyone else. I wanted to do something special for you."

She opened her mouth to protest, but this wasn't up for debate. "Open the damn box, Halle."

She took it from me with a huff, but I could tell she was curious. When she pried open the lid, she gasped.

"I had it specially made for you." I watched her reaction for clues. I had no idea what she was thinking.

"It's stunning," she said, running her fingers along the edge of the box. Nestled on the velvet was a delicate gold necklace with a dragonfly pendant dotted with natural purple diamonds. "It reminds me of your grandmother's brooch."

"Exactly," I said. I'd considered having the brooch made into a pendant, but it was too big. Besides, it would've been obvious who had given it to Halle. And I was trying to respect her wishes to be discreet. "I had this made with the stones from one of her necklaces."

"Jasper," she gasped. "You…what?"

"I know my gran would've loved you and Kai. She's the one who always told me that beautiful things are meant to be enjoyed. Wear your favorite outfit. Use your fine china. Life is too short not to."

"Still…" Halle peered up at me. "These stones have to have great sentimental value."

They did. All of Gran's jewelry did, and she'd left the most important pieces to me. Her dragonfly brooch. The purple diamond necklace. Her engagement ring.

"That's why I selected them. That, and I know how much you love the color purple. The stones are natural purple diamonds."

She ran her finger over the pendant, her expression full of awe. "I didn't even know purple diamonds existed."

"They're very rare," I said. "Like the color used to be in art."

She smiled. "You remembered."

"Of course I did," I said. Every conversation, every smile, every look from her was emblazoned on my heart. Including a conversation we'd had last summer about her love for the color purple and its use throughout art in history. And all the reasons it was rare. I'd found it fascinating. But that was probably because she completely lit up when she was talking about it.

"They're beautiful."

"You're beautiful." I brushed a curl behind her ear. *I love you.*

I knew it was too soon to tell her. I didn't want to scare her off, but I couldn't help it. I loved her.

"Do you want to try it on?" I asked instead.

She rolled her bottom lip between her teeth then nodded. I twirled my finger in the air, and she spun so she was facing the windows once more.

I removed the necklace from the box, then waited for her to pull her ponytail aside. I draped the necklace over her collarbone, feeling like a man starved. I'd been dying to touch her all day, and the occasional graze or linked fingers hadn't been enough. Far from it.

As I worked the clasp, I watched her reflection in the windows. "Many people believe that if you're lucky enough to have a dragonfly land on you, the universe is sending good fortune your way. But if that's the case, then I suppose I should be the one wearing the dragonfly, because I feel nothing but good fortune when I'm with you."

Her hand fluttered over the necklace, and when she turned to face me, I admired how the pendant looked against her skin. Like it was made for her.

"Even when we aren't together," I continued, "I want you to know that I'm thinking about you. Always."

"Jasper. I—" She inhaled slowly, and I swiped away a tear before it could make its way down her cheek. "I love it. Thank you."

I smiled, brushing my lips against hers. "I'm glad." *Because I love you.*

She linked our fingers, tugging me along with her toward

her bedroom. I followed behind, double-checking that Kai's door was closed, the hint of his night-light shining beneath.

When we got to her room, she closed the door and locked it. I arched one eyebrow, intrigued. Turned on.

"I'm not sure I've ever seen Kai as happy as he was today," she said, closing the distance between us, sliding her hands over my chest. "Thank you for making his birthday feel special."

"Thank you for letting me be a part of it." I kept my hands fisted at my sides.

Between the locked door and the way Halle was looking at me, I was pretty sure I knew where this was going, but I didn't want her to take that next step until she was ready. I never wanted Halle to feel like she owed me something or that our relationship was somehow transactional.

She frowned down at my hands. "What's wrong?"

"I don't want you to think that I arranged today or gave you the necklace because I expect something in return."

She laughed. "Thanks for clarifying, but I know that's not why you did it. And, just so we're clear, that's not why I want to have sex with you."

She slid her hands beneath the hem of my shirt, and I melted from the contact.

"I just…" God, she was making it impossible to concentrate. Especially when she stepped back and pulled her shirt over her head before tossing it aside. "This is about more than sex."

"I know." Her smile was so fucking coy. Somehow sweet but sultry. Fuck. She was hot.

Now she was in her denim shorts and a lacy purple bra, the dragonfly on her chest sparkling when it caught the light. *Mine.*

I was so distracted that when Halle gently shoved me toward the bed, I found myself falling onto the mattress. I watched her with rapt attention as she started unbuttoning those fucking shorts. I loved her confidence. Loved the way she looked. The way she moved.

She'd been confident last summer, but she was even more so now. She looked damn good, and she knew it. And I loved to see it.

I ran a hand over my face. How was this real? How was she even real?

"You're gorgeous, love," I rasped, already so close to losing it. My cock was hard, and I had a feeling if I pulled it out, precome would be dripping from the tip.

She smiled and slid her shorts over her hips. I loved that she was taking control. That she felt safe with me, trusted me, to let me in.

I let out a long, low "Fuuuuck," as I took in her matching bra and underwear. Fuck me, she was hot.

"Jasper?" she asked, and my eyes flicked to hers. "Clothes off."

I swallowed. Hard. "I don't think that's a good idea."

She stepped closer, her scent filling the air around me. Making it impossible to think. Especially when she looked like that, her breasts full and nearly spilling out of the cups of her bra, her curves on display, begging me to touch her.

She crawled onto the bed, over me. "What happened to being all in?"

"I, um—" I let out a shaky exhale. "I'm trying to move at your pace." *I was, but she was making it incredibly difficult.* Plus, I didn't want us to get so distracted by the physical aspects that we neglected the rest of our relationship.

She leaned down so her breasts brushed against my chest, her lips grazing along my jawline. I fisted the sheets in my hands, aching to touch her.

"Jasper."

"Mm-hmm?" I asked, squeezing my eyes shut, overwhelmed by the sensations, the emotions.

She placed a hand to my cheek. "Look at me. Please." I opened my eyes, peering up into hers. "Why are you holding back?"

"Because… I want our first time together to be special." My cock was so hard, it was a wonder I could even speak.

"First time?" She laughed. "I think we're well past that."

I grazed my hand along her hip, resisting the urge to bring her even closer still. "I meant our first time as a couple."

"This is special," she said. "At least, it is to me. It's special because we're together. But if you're not ready… If you don't want to have that kind of intimacy yet—"

I rolled us so I was on top, hating that she even had to question where I stood. "I want to be as close to you as possible." I ground against her, letting her feel my arousal. "I want to be buried so deep inside you that I can no longer tell where I end and you begin."

She arched up against me, and I thought I might explode. "Then what are you waiting for?"

I'd waited so long for this—for her. And for a while, I'd feared it would never happen.

Unable to resist any longer, I crushed my mouth to hers. We raced to undress the other. My shorts and shirt were gone, followed by my boxers. Her bra and underwear were tossed aside until she was naked except for her dragonfly pendant.

Seeing her in nothing but the necklace I'd given her was one of the hottest things I'd ever witnessed. I was so keyed up, I felt as if I might come on the spot.

Shit. I squeezed my eyes shut.

She paused. "What's wrong?"

"I don't have a condom."

"Seriously?" She scoffed. "You have a drawer full of them in your penthouse."

I'd suspected she'd seen them, but I hadn't gotten the chance to explain. Not while Kai was there. "They were a promotional thing. A new brand we were trying out for the intimacy kits."

"'Trying out'?" She gave me a meaningful look.

I shook my head. "I wasn't testing them personally. The only reason I have so many is because the company sent all the executives a thank-you box, and I didn't know what else to do with them since they already had our logo on them. It's not like I was going to use them, but I also didn't want them just floating around."

"Mm-hmm." Her tone conveyed skepticism, but her mouth twitched with a smile.

I took a breath, wanting her to know how important this conversation—and she—was to me. "As I said before, I haven't been with anyone but you since last summer." *And you're it for me.*

"Same." She placed her hands on my chest, and something in me settled at her confession. How could one simple word convey so much? "I have an IUD, and the test results at my annual physical this January came back negative."

"As did mine." I took her hand and brought her palm to my lips, pressing a kiss there. "But I don't want you to feel pressured to do anything you're not ready for."

We'd always used a condom in the past, and this wasn't a decision I took lightly.

"Jasper." Halle pressed her lips to my jawline, wrapping her legs around my waist. She pulled me down to her. "I meant what I said. I'm all in. I trust you, and I don't want to use condoms. Unless you do."

Something eased in my chest at her words, at the look in her eyes. She trusted me. I leaned forward, brushing my mouth against hers, wanting to commit this moment to memory. To remember exactly how she looked—so full of love and trust.

She opened herself to me, and I slid into her, slid home, feeling whole in a way I hadn't for the past eight months. And the fact that Halle trusted me with her body made me believe that maybe—with time—she'd trust me with her heart as well.

CHAPTER TWENTY

JASPER

"Jasper," Halle chided. "Focus." But she was smiling as she said it.

I met her gaze from across my desk, knowing mine was full of hunger. "I am focused." *On you.*

She rolled her eyes. "Focus on the report." She jabbed the paper with her pointer finger. "We're supposed to be reviewing this together."

How was I supposed to focus on a report when I'd been half hard the entire morning? How was I supposed to focus on anything when I hadn't been alone with her in days?

After our weekend together celebrating Kai's birthday, I'd been desperate to see her again. But we'd both been so busy that our stolen moments alone together had been few and far between.

I supposed that was the reason why she'd insisted on sitting on the opposite side of my desk. But every time I looked at her, my focus was shot. Even when I wasn't looking at her, just having her in my office, alone, was tempting enough. Her scent. Her presence. Everything else faded into the background.

"There are many other things I'd rather be doing *together*," I muttered, my attention on said report. We were supposed to be reviewing some documents, but all I could think about was her.

Halle sighed and came to stand before me. Her back was bracketed by a wall of windows, the sun making her hair look like a halo of burnished copper. I had a sudden urge to strip her naked and take her against the glass. The windows were covered in tinted film that was reflective, but I knew she'd still enjoy it. So would I.

I was about to stand and suggest doing just that. But then she knelt to the floor, spreading my thighs apart as she did so. That got my attention. If my cock hadn't been hard before, it definitely was now.

"Maybe we can do both." She looked so sexy there, on her knees, ready to do my bidding. Eager to please me.

"Mm." This was more like it. "What did you have in mind?"

"You tell me about the report." She unbuckled my belt, and my breath quickened. "And I'll…listen."

She peered up at me, her brown eyes beguiling as she sought my permission. I couldn't have looked away if I'd tried. And I didn't want to.

I groaned, dragging my thumb down her bottom lip. *Fuck. How did I get so lucky?*

Were we really doing this?

Technically, I had blocked off some time for lunch. I was supposed to go to Sloan's to hang out with my sister and my new niece. And while I hated ditching Sloan, I knew she'd understand if I had to cancel last minute. I just wasn't going to tell her what exactly had come up.

"Lock the door." I almost didn't recognize my own voice. It was deeper than usual, commanding.

We might be taking a lot of risks, but I would always do

everything in my power to protect Halle. Besides, I sure as hell wasn't going to get caught with my pants down like my brother. I'd once walked in on Graham fucking Lily on his desk. And even though she'd no longer been his assistant—she'd been his wife—there was no way I was going to let anyone else see Halle like this.

I shuddered at the memory. It had been shocking enough to walk in on them. But to think that Graham—my uptight, brooding, older brother—had been so impulsive. Well, it gave me a whole new respect for him. Even if I wished I could erase the whole incident from my mind.

While Halle locked the door, I grabbed my phone to text my assistant that I did not want to be disturbed. Then I texted Sloan that I wouldn't make it for lunch after all. I would've suggested that Halle and I go to her suite or my penthouse, but I didn't think I could make it that far. My cock was already aching to be inside Halle, and if we left my office, I had no idea how to hide my hard-on. I also wouldn't be able to guarantee that someone wouldn't interrupt us on the way, asking for my attention to something.

No. This would have to do for now.

This past weekend had been slow and sensual, full of passion and love. I vowed that, soon, I would have her in my bed. I would take my time with her. I would worship her body fully and in the way she deserved. But this was not that moment.

And I knew that while she enjoyed sweet and sensual, Halle also craved reckless and passionate. So did I. That was part of what made us such a great match. She didn't try to suppress my wilder instincts; she encouraged them.

I stood and loosened my tie while I drank in the sight of Halle as she walked toward me. She was fucking stunning.

A lavender silk button-down blouse draped over her breasts, tantalizing me with the promise of what lay beneath the smooth material. A black pencil skirt clung to her hips. And those legs. Fuck me. Those legs.

But it was the dragonfly necklace that made me the happiest. She was mine. And even if no one else knew it, she was wearing my necklace.

"Shirt off. Now." I wanted her naked, but that would have to be enough for now. Anything more was too risky.

Oh, who the hell was I kidding? I was about to have sex with an employee. In my office.

But all thoughts of risk and consequences fled my mind the moment Halle started unbuttoning her shirt. Slowly. Deliberately. Teasing me with every button loosened from its slot.

I crooked my finger, enjoying the way she watched me with a heated expression. "Come here."

She came to stand before me but then shoved me gently in the direction of my chair. "Sit."

I readily complied, sinking into my chair, more than willing to do her bidding.

"I thought I was going to be the one doing the talking," I teased as she slid to her knees before me. Though the only thing I wanted to use my mouth for was kissing her.

"What are you waiting for?" She started unbuttoning my pants.

What was the question again?

She laughed, and I realized I'd said that aloud. I loved the sound of her laughter, light and effervescent. Even when it was at my expense. I'd make a fool of myself for this woman, all to hear her laugh.

I eased up so she could work my slacks and boxers over my hips, my cock springing free. She grinned, her lips curving into the most delicious smile. She was a sight to behold. Confident. Taking exactly what she wanted. I loved to see it. I loved her.

"Halle, love," I rasped, threading my fingers through her hair.

She leaned into my touch, and I loved that we had these tender moments mixed in with the passionate ones. "Jasper."

She took me in her hand, a smile playing at her lips. "So… are you going to talk?"

She licked me from root to tip, teasing, sampling, taunting. I gripped the armrests. *Fuck me.*

"I'm a little…" I hissed, "distracted at the moment."

She peered up at me, lapping at the tip of my cock. "Should I stop?"

"Fuck no." I slid my hand to the back of her neck, cupping her there. Pleasure infused my blood, making me feel light-headed. My hold on her was the only thing keeping me grounded in reality.

She tapped her index finger on my thigh—not too hard, but hard enough to get my attention. "Then I suggest you find a way to multitask."

"You are so fucking beautiful," I choked out the words, even though I knew that wasn't what she meant. I didn't fucking care. "On your knees for me, sucking my cock like you were made to do it."

She moaned around me, and I felt it to the center of my very being. She squirmed a little, and I could tell she was seeking friction.

"You like that, don't you?" I gave the back of her neck a quick squeeze, and she leaned forward, letting me guide her. "My praise."

She nodded, head bobbing around me. Her mouth felt fucking amazing. So warm and wet and hot. I continued using my hand to guide her as she cupped my balls, sending a shiver down my spine.

I was… My muscles tightened. Fuck, that felt good. Too good. If she didn't stop, I was going to come.

I signaled to Halle that I wanted her to stop. Well, I didn't *want* her to stop, but I also didn't want to come in her mouth. Not this time anyway.

She released me with a pop, sinking back on her knees. She held her chin high, letting me—inviting me—to look my fill. "You make me feel…powerful."

"You *are* powerful," I said, wanting her to see herself like I did. As a fucking goddess—eyes bright, cheeks pink.

But it wasn't just about her looks or the effect she had on me. Halle was a force to be reckoned with at the office—confident, intelligent, and passionate. She was an amazing mom to Kai. But even if she weren't any of that, if she were just *Halle*, she was incredible.

She gave my cock a few lazy pumps. "As much as I love your praise, that's not exactly the type of talking I had in mind. If you don't want to tell me about the report, then at least tell me what's bothering you."

Bothering me?

At the moment, absolutely nothing was bothering me except for the fact that I wasn't inside her.

I rubbed my thumb across her bottom lip before pressing it inside. She sucked it briefly before giving it a playful bite, and my cock twitched in delight.

"Halle," I commanded, low and deep. *Enough teasing.*

She sucked the tip of my cock into her mouth, and I let out a sound that was unintelligible. She smirked. "My mouth may be occupied, but yours is not."

She swirled her tongue around me, lapping up precome. I cupped the back of her neck again, gentle but commanding. Her eyes met mine, encouraging me. I used my hands to guide her.

Yes. There.

My eyes rolled into the back of my head at what she was

doing. I let my head fall against the chair, reveling in this stolen moment alone with her.

"Is this about Craig moving here?" she asked.

I practically growled at the mention of her ex. "I don't ever want to hear another man's name when you're touching me." *Me. No one else.*

And I sure as shit didn't want to think about him moving here. Or the fact that Kai—not Halle—had been the one to tell me. And judging from Halle's guilty expression at the time, it seemed like she'd known for a while.

I growled. *Enough about Craig.*

There would be time for questions later. Right now, my focus was on Halle.

I grabbed her beneath her arms and hauled her to her feet. She let out a little squeak as I turned her to face the desk. My movements were rough—angry, even—as I pulled up her skirt so it bunched around her waist.

Halle glanced back at me over her shoulder, her eyes wild with excitement and desire. "Wh-what are you doing?"

I didn't answer. Instead, I yanked down her underwear, keeping it around her knees, holding her in place. She let out a shaky exhale, and I grinned. I finally had her right where I wanted her.

I pried her ass cheeks apart, her body slick with desire. "Who does this pussy belong to?" I asked, blowing cool air.

She shivered. "You."

"Damn right, it does." Hearing her say those words unleashed something inside me. Something raw and animalistic. This urge to claim her as mine. Because that's what she was. *Mine.*

Halle belonged with me. Just as I belonged with her. And I hated the fact that we were keeping this a secret. I understood it, of course. But I still didn't like it.

So instead of focusing on the things I couldn't control, I

decided to ground myself in the present. In this gorgeous woman who had offered herself to me. Who trusted me.

I had to have faith that, with time, the rest would sort itself out.

I would find a way to make it. Because I'd spent months without her, and I wasn't going back to that. We were together, and I would move heaven and earth if that's what it took for us to stay together. To truly *be* together. Not just in secret, but as a couple. As a family, with Kai.

I pressed my mouth to her, licking and sucking until her legs were shaking. She braced her arms on the desk, resting her cheek on the surface.

"*This* is mine," I said, easily sliding two fingers into her. "This gorgeous body—" I pumped my fingers inside her, listening to her whimpers, feeling the way she clenched me tight "—is mine." I lined my cock up with her entrance. "*You are mine.*"

"Yes, Jasper. Yes. *Please.*"

I ran my hand down her spine, wishing we were naked. Longing for a lazy day in bed together. Just us. Unrushed. Uninterrupted.

"Hurry," she whispered, desperate.

I didn't know whether it was her eagerness for me to be inside her or her desire to finish before anyone suspected something. Either way, I needed to get moving. I'd already let this go on longer than I'd intended, but when I was with Halle, time ceased to have meaning.

She braced herself against the edge of the desk as I slid home. "Fuck. Do you feel that? Feel your pussy gripping my cock?"

"Yes." She arched her back, hands pressed to the surface of the desk. "Yes. Right there."

This position was hot, but I liked it even more when I could see her face. I pulled out, ignoring her cries of protest as I spun her to face me. With her back to the desk, I placed a hand to her cheek, guiding her focus to me.

"Look at me, Halle. When I'm inside you, I want your eyes on me."

"Mm. Somebody's awfully possessive today." She grinned as I slid home once more.

I brushed my lips against hers. "You like it."

"I hate to admit it, but I like seeing you a little unhinged."

I could understand the feeling because I certainly enjoyed seeing Halle come undone. So I pressed my fingers to her clit, rubbing circles as I pumped into her from behind.

"Yes. Yes. Yes," she chanted, and I gave her a bruising kiss to silence her.

Pleasure blazed through me, and I was so damn close to coming. But I wanted to wait for her. I wanted her to go first.

"I'm going to—" I started to say, feeling control slipping away from me, my pleasure spiraling, swelling until it was this storm I could no longer tame. "Tell me you're close."

"Yes," she whispered, our kisses desperate, almost frantic. "Yes."

She was so beautiful when she let go. Back arching. Creamy skin flushed with color.

And then I hurtled over the edge, following her into oblivion. My body convulsed as she clenched around me, my cock pulsating as waves of my pleasure filled her.

With our bodies still joined, I captured her lips, needing that connection. That…grounding.

And god, when I pulled out of her and saw her pussy dripping with my seed, I groaned. "Fuck me. That's hot."

I swiped my fingers through her slit, pushing it back inside her. She moaned her appreciation, falling back on the desk. I lingered for a second more, taking in the scene. Halle, splayed out on my desk, sated and flushed. She was something.

I pressed a kiss to her thigh then tucked myself back into my pants, giving her a moment to collect herself. Maybe a moment to collect myself too. She pushed herself off the desk, putting herself back to rights.

She buttoned up her shirt. "Feel better?"

"Much." I grinned, giving her a quick peck. "Time with you always makes me feel better."

"Time. Right. So the sex had nothing to do with it."

"It might have helped a little," I teased, holding up my thumb and forefinger.

She smirked, taking my tie in hand. I peered down at her, watching as she retied it.

"Why didn't you tell me about Craig?" I asked, finally circling back to that, even though I didn't want to. But I needed to know.

Halle sighed, her attention focused on my tie. "Because I didn't think he was going to actually follow through on it. It wouldn't be the first time Craig said he was doing something and then his plans changed."

I gnashed my teeth, my emotions shifting with this new revelation. I hated that Kai or Halle had ever been disappointed by a man who was supposed to protect them, love them. Not hurt them. I vowed that I would never give them cause to feel as if I'd let them down. And what Halle needed from me wasn't judgment or accusations but support.

"How do you feel about it?" I asked, placing my hand on her hip.

Her shoulders relaxed. "Surprised. Maybe a little disbelief. I still won't believe it till I see it."

"Do you think he's trying to win you back?"

She barked out a laugh. "He already tried once and failed." I wasn't sure if that made me feel better or worse. Maybe a little of both. Perhaps sensing my mood, she placed her hand over mine. "There's nothing between Craig and me. Not anymore. There hasn't been for a long time. But Craig is Kai's dad. He's going to continue to be a part of my life."

"I get that," I said. "And I respect it. Kai deserves all the love in the world."

"Thank you," Halle said. "I don't expect you to be friends with Craig, but it would be nice if we could all get along."

Everything would be fine as long as Craig didn't act like a dick.

"Does that mean you're going to tell him about us?" I asked, trying not to sound too hopeful.

"When the time's right."

I wanted to ask if she had any ideas on when that might be, but I didn't. Instead, I pulled her in for a hug, holding her close. I knew we needed to return to our workday, but I wasn't quite ready to let her go. And if I had my way, I'd never would.

CHAPTER TWENTY-ONE

HALLE

Weeks had passed in the blink of an eye. I was settling into my new life in LA. I'd gone to lunch with Alexis and her friends a few times, and I loved getting to know her better, as well as Juliana and Lauren. I had yet to meet Harper, but that was only because she lived in a small town up north with her son and husband, a retired pro soccer player.

I was also busy. I was juggling calls with my parents and the nursing staff at my dad's facility, taking care of Kai, serving as the temporary SVP. And then there was my secret relationship with Jasper. But I seemed to thrive in the chaos, even if I often felt I was on the verge of losing control.

And as much as I wanted to believe I had it together, the fact that I hadn't talked to Zara, apart from texts here and there, was like a check engine light. Reminding me to nourish my own needs. We texted almost daily, but it wasn't the same as a phone conversation.

"Hey," I said, accepting Zara's request to video chat.

It was early, and I was sitting at the counter drinking

coffee while reading through some emails. Kai was still asleep, and I was about to get ready for the day.

"Oh my god. Halle." Zara leaned in, squinting at the screen. "Is it really you?"

"Ha-ha." I rolled my eyes, but I was smiling. "Yes, it's me."

"I was beginning to think I'd have to fly to LA if I ever wanted to talk to you again."

"I mean…you're more than welcome to visit anytime. I think you'd love it here. And I know you'd hit it off with Alexis, Lauren, and Juliana."

"I'm glad you've made some friends there. And thanks, babes. Be careful, I might take you up on that offer."

"I'd love that. Kai would too." Zara was like a sister to me and an aunt to Kai. It felt strange to be so far away from her.

"I miss my sweet boy. How is he? How's everything going?"

"Good," I said. "Craig is still planning to move to LA."

"Think he will actually follow through?"

"I think so." Sometimes I still couldn't believe it myself, but he really seemed to have turned over a new leaf this time. "Ever since his visit, he's been consistent in his efforts to connect with Kai. They'll build the same Lego kit together over video chats. Sometimes they play video games together." It was nice to see Craig making more of an effort. And Kai definitely seemed happier from his dad's attention.

"How do you feel about it?" she asked.

"Assuming it happens, conflicted. I'll be happy for Kai, of course. I want Kai to have a good relationship with his dad. But I'm worried about how much time Craig might expect to spend with him."

"That's understandable. Craig's lucky you're as nice as you are."

I barked out a laugh. "This isn't about what I want. It's about what's best for Kai."

"I know. I just hope he remembers that."

I nodded then asked her about work and some of our friends. We chatted for a while before she said, "And your parents?"

I toyed with my necklace, sliding the dragonfly charm along the chain. "My dad is holding steady. Mom seems to be finding her new rhythm now that she no longer has to worry so much about Dad."

Then, I listened as she told me about a client's wedding she'd recently attended. It sounded amazing and over the top, and it reminded me of one of the stories Juliana had told us recently about a wedding her firm was planning for a client.

I peered up from the phone, momentarily distracted by the sight of Rosie padding toward me. She drank some water from her bowl then came to my side and whined up at me.

"Is that..." Zara furrowed her brow. "Your stomach?"

"No." I laughed, bending over to grab Rosie from the floor. "It's Rosie." I set her on my lap, cuddling her.

"Interesting." Zara watched me. "What's Jasper's dog doing at your place?"

"Jasper asked Kai to dog-sit for him while he's in Colorado touring the newly renovated Huxley Grand at Beaver Creek."

"Mm." She gave me a pointed look. "What's going on there?"

"Potential expansion of the ski amenities," I said, intentionally misinterpreting her question. "It would be a huge project."

"You're sleeping with him, aren't you?"

"Actually..." I rolled my lips between my teeth. "It's a bit more than that."

She blinked a few times. "You're in a relationship with him?"

"I am." I smiled. And it felt so good to finally admit it to someone. "But it's still new. And we're being discreet."

"How long has this been going on?" she asked.

"About a month. I'm sorry I didn't tell you sooner. We've both just been so busy, and it didn't really feel like the kind of news you drop over text."

"You don't have to apologize. I'm happy for you." She smiled. "So I take it Sloan doesn't know?"

I shook my head, smoothing my hand over Rosie's fur. "You're actually the only person who knows."

"But you're going to tell people eventually, aren't you?" She sounded cautiously hopeful.

"That's the goal," I said, though the idea made me feel sick to my stomach.

"How do you think Sloan will take it?" Zara asked.

"Honestly," I sighed, "I'm not sure. I want to think she'll be supportive, especially based on her own relationship history."

"She married her best friend's brother, right?"

"Yeah. But I don't know how she'll feel about me dating her brother. Especially since we all work together."

She winced. "Oof. That's dicey. I mean…you love that company. And it surprises me that you'd do anything that could jeopardize your position with Huxley. But also your friendship with Sloan."

"I know. And I know it seems crazy and reckless and whatever, but…" I shrugged. I didn't even know what to say.

"Wow." She watched me, cautious. Assessing. "I knew you liked him, but I didn't realize you wanted anything serious."

"I didn't realize I did either." Or maybe I just hadn't ever thought it would actually be a possibility. "But here we are." Even so, I couldn't help but smile. "I just…" I sighed. "I've never felt like this. I didn't know it could be like this. He's amazing with Kai, an incredible partner. And when I'm with

Jasper, he makes me feel like I could do anything. Be anything."

She smiled.

"What?" I asked.

"I'm glad you found someone who knows your worth. You deserve to find happiness and love."

"Thank you," I said, warmth filling me as I patted Rosie. "I know it's complicated, but I'm trying to live in the moment."

After my conversation with Zara, the rest of the day passed by in a blur of meetings and emails and so many other things. Despite how busy I was, I kept watching the clock, waiting until Kai was in bed so I could finally talk to Jasper. We'd texted throughout the day, and I knew he had a dinner meeting, so I'd stayed up to work on some reports.

When my phone finally rang, I leaped to answer it when I saw it was Jasper calling. I hit the button to connect the video call, drinking in the sight of Jasper's face. He looked tired but happy, handsome as ever in his suit with the tie undone. I'd missed him. We all had. Me, Rosie, and Kai.

"Hi, love." His voice was deep and rich.

The sound of the word "love" on his lips sent a thrill through me, even though he'd called me that almost from the beginning. But lately, it felt as if it had taken on a different meaning. It wasn't some offhanded pet name common in London. It felt like he meant it.

"Hey." I cleared my throat, trying to dislodge the emotion suddenly stuck there.

Life just wasn't the same without Jasper. He'd been away for the past week, and I was ready for him to come home. Especially with the way he was looking at me now.

His smile was warm, his eyes softening at the sight of me. And then his gaze dropped to my chest, where my navy silk nightgown dipped low. My nipples pebbled in response to his attention.

"How was dinner? Did you just get back?" I asked. It was an hour later in Colorado.

"Yes." He swiped a hand down his face. "It went well, but it dragged on." He sighed, and I could tell he didn't want to talk about work. Neither did I.

I wanted to crawl into bed with him, nestle in his arms, and fall asleep talking about our day. More and more, I craved those simple moments. But then I'd remember everything that was at stake, and I'd send him home before morning. Before Kai would wake. Before someone could find out about us. But I didn't want to think about that—not right now.

"I miss you," I admitted, trying to ground myself in the present. I could neither predict nor control the future. But I could enjoy this moment.

Jasper's eyes crinkled at the corners. "I miss you too. I wish I were there with you."

"Oh yeah?" I shifted, and my nightgown slipped even lower. God, he looked hot. "And what would we be doing if you were here?"

"Mm." He was sitting against the headboard, and he tucked his arm behind him. Relaxed. Confident. Sexy. "What would you want me to do?

"Everything," I breathed. My eyes darted to my bedroom door, and I was grateful I'd locked it earlier.

"I'd start by kissing you. I've missed that mouth of yours." He grinned. "And then I'd kiss my way down your neck, inhaling your perfume."

I trailed my fingers down the same path, aching for his touch. His kisses. Just...*him.*

"I'd pull your nipple into my mouth, sucking through the silk." My nipples hardened at his words, at the intense way he was looking at me. "And then I'd pull it aside and swirl my tongue around you until you were panting."

"Yes." I squirmed in the sheets. I rubbed my thighs together, but it did nothing to ease the ache. Nothing would except the man staring back at me on the screen.

"Show me," Jasper said.

I didn't even have to ask what he wanted; I knew exactly what he meant. But as eager as I was to come, I wanted to draw this out—for both of us. So I set my phone against a pillow, making sure I remained in the frame.

I took my time, dragging one of my straps down my shoulder, tantalizing him with glimpses of my skin until I had removed the second strap. And then I let go, allowing the silk to slide over my skin until my breasts were revealed.

"Fuck, Halle." He was practically salivating, and I was just as needy, filled with a yearning so strong it nearly overpowered me. "You're so gorgeous."

I preened at his words. "Your turn." I gestured toward him.

He adjusted his phone then undid the top few buttons of his shirt. I watched as he stripped out of it before reaching behind his neck and tugging his undershirt over his head. He was bare-chested, his skin tanned and toned with a light dusting of hair. He was perfect.

"I want to see you. All of you." He gave me a meaningful look.

"Same," I said, waiting until he agreed.

He started unbuttoning his pants, quickly shucking them aside. He returned to his position at the headboard, cock in hand. Hard and waiting.

I laughed, loving his enthusiasm. And then I slid out of my nightgown before removing my underwear.

"That's better," he sighed, drinking me in. "Now show me how wet you are for me."

I nearly whimpered at his demand. Something about his

commanding voice and the idea of being on camera—on display—for Jasper, made desire rush to my core. If I hadn't already been soaked, I definitely would be now.

I swiped a finger through my folds then held it up to the camera. It glistened with my desire, and Jasper watched me through hooded eyes.

"Taste yourself," he demanded.

I slid my fingers into my mouth, imagining his cock instead. I moaned.

"Delicious, right?" he asked. "Like heaven." I nodded. "You're so good, Halle. Following my instructions."

My breath hitched, and I waited for his next command. Jasper gave his cock a few lazy pumps, and my eyes pinged from his lips to his chest to his hands and back to his face. I found him smirking, sexy and devious and so hot I thought I might combust.

"Spread those legs, love. Show me what I'm missing."

I did as he asked, using my fingers to trace circles on my clit. I shuddered at the sensation, the way he was looking at me. As if I was his everything.

"That's it, love." He gnawed on his bottom lip, stomach muscles clenching as he watched me. I liked watching him, and I liked him watching me.

"If I were there, my mouth would be on that pretty pussy. My tongue flicking your clit." Shadows played on his face, making his jawline seem even sharper.

I shuddered, my pulse quickening. I could picture it exactly, just as he'd described. "Yes. I want that too."

"Show me how much you want me," he demanded, his voice gruff. "Make yourself come."

I continued touching myself, my pleasure rising. I wanted him. Not just on the screen but here with me. "Only if we can do it together," I said, my skin growing slick with sweat.

"Yes. God, yes," he panted, his strokes coming faster now, his movements less controlled.

Jasper coaxed me to my climax, taunting me with promises of all the things he intended to do to me when he got home. I couldn't wait. I couldn't…

"Tell me you're close," he said.

"I'm…" I trailed off, overcome. "Yes," I hissed.

My toes curled into the sheets, a wave of pleasure cresting over me. When I opened my eyes, Jasper was watching me, his hand moving faster than ever as he grunted out a stream of curses along with his release. The veins of his forearm flexed, and I couldn't believe he was mine.

"Don't stop." His voice was gravelly. "Not until you come again."

"I ca—"

"Halle—" He cut me off, and I knew he wasn't going to relent. When I placed my hand to my clit, it was already so sensitive that a whisper of touch was almost enough to set me off again. I whimpered.

"That's it, love," Jasper said. "That's it."

And the next time I came, it was with him.

He relaxed against the headboard with a sated smile. I melted into my mattress. At least I did until my door handle rattled.

"Oh shit," I whispered. "I think Kai's trying to come into my room." I scrambled to grab my nightgown.

"Mum," Kai groaned, rattling the door. Thank goodness I'd locked the door earlier. I just hoped he didn't ask me about it.

"Give me just a sec," I said, quickly righting my night-gown and hoping I didn't look too flustered. "Hey," I said to Jasper. "I can call you back or…"

"It's fine. I'll wait. I should get cleaned up anyway."

"Sorry." I mouthed to Jasper.

He chuckled, and I left my phone on the bed while I went to open the door. I took one look at Kai and frowned. "What's wrong?"

"I don't feel good." He flopped on the bed, and Rosie trotted in a moment later. He picked her up, and they cuddled on the bed together.

I brushed Kai's hair away from his face. "What's bothering you?"

"My stomach." He curled up into a ball, his little face racked with pain. I hated seeing him go through this time and again with no way to help him.

I had a feeling this wasn't going to be a quick thing, and I didn't want to keep Jasper waiting. It was even later there, and I knew he had a lot of meetings in the next few days before he came home.

I picked up my phone, my heart still pounding. "Hey. Sorry. I'm going to have to go."

"Who are you talking to?" Kai asked then leaned over to see my screen. Fortunately, everything below Jasper's waist was covered up. "Oh. Hi, Jasper."

Rosie also decided to jump into the frame, and I laughed. This call wasn't going at all to plan. My kid and Jasper's dog were hijacking the conversation.

"Hey, kiddo." Jasper's hair was mussed, and he was shirtless. He looked relaxed. A little smug. And deeply satisfied. "How are you?"

"Not so good." Kai hugged a pillow to his chest.

"I'm sorry to hear that, bud." Jasper frowned. "I hope you feel better."

"When are you coming home?"

"Two more days," Jasper said. "And it can't come soon enough."

I nodded my agreement and mouthed "Miss you," while Kai's attention was focused on Rosie. He mouthed it back.

"Mummy." Kai groaned again, clutching his stomach. "I really don't feel good."

Jasper's eyes darted between the two of us as he tried to assess the situation. I could tell that he didn't want to hang up, but he was also trying to respect my wishes about keeping our relationship a secret from Kai.

We spent time together as the three of us—well, four with Rosie. But we didn't want to confuse Kai or risk spilling the secret until we were ready.

Finally, Jasper said, "I should let you get some rest."

Before I could hang up, Kai said, "Mum. I think I'm going to—" And then he threw up all over my bed.

"You hungry?" I asked Kai.

"Not really," he said from the couch where he was watching a show with Rosie.

I decided to order some food anyway, hoping it would entice him to eat. When the on-site doctor had visited earlier, he'd suggested a mild diet, hydration, and then referred us to a pediatric gastroenterologist. I wasn't sure whether to be relieved or concerned that he wanted me to get Kai into the gastro right away, but it was nice to have my concerns taken seriously.

My stomach growled, and I realized I also hadn't eaten all day. I'd been up most of the night taking care of Kai, worried about him and trying to figure out how to juggle everything. Because with Jasper in Colorado and Sloan still out on maternity leave, my calendar was jam-packed.

I'd had my assistant cancel all my meetings, but I couldn't

completely shut off work. And I also couldn't devote myself fully to it. Not with a sick kiddo.

Pre-K was out. Even if Kai hadn't had a fever, he'd been throwing up. And I also wasn't going to leave him in the care of a nanny I'd never met before, even if I could call the Hartwell Agency and secure someone at the last minute.

But between taking care of Kai and trying to squeeze in work where I could, I'd barely had time to breathe, let alone eat or get dressed. I paused in front of the mirror, evaluating my messy topknot and oversized cardigan. I was still wearing my silk nightgown from the night before. And my call with Jasper seemed like a lifetime ago.

I sighed and placed the order for room service. Some oatmeal for Kai and a sandwich for me.

Kai was watching TV when there was a knock at the door. I went to answer it, grabbing some ones for a tip from my wallet as I opened the door.

I blinked a few times, stunned. Surely I was seeing things. Because there was no way Jasper was standing at the threshold to my suite. He was supposed to be in Colorado. For two more days.

I didn't even question it. I walked toward Jasper's outstretched arms, closing my eyes as he held me. And as we stood there, embracing, I realized just how much I'd come to rely on him. And while the idea of relying on anyone, especially a man, terrified me, another part of me felt so…at ease. Because it was him. Because he was a supportive partner.

This is what love is.

The thought gave me pause. But the more I thought about it, the less surprised I was. The more it all made sense.

I loved him. I loved Jasper, and even though he may not have said the words aloud, there was no doubt in my mind that he loved me. The fact that he'd dropped everything to fly home to be with Kai and me was further proof of it.

Jasper had chosen to miss a major, important meeting to be with Kai and me. He'd chosen us over his job. He'd put my son above everything else.

But when the elevator chimed, I remembered that we were standing in the hallway where anyone could see us. As much as I wanted to revel in Jasper's presence, I knew we needed to continue being discreet for now. So I grabbed his arm and pulled him inside with me, closing the door behind me.

Kai peered over the back of the sofa, and Rosie came running to greet Jasper, her little collar jingling from the movement.

"Hey, kiddo," Jasper greeted Kai while picking up Rosie.

"I thought you were out of town," Kai said, his voice lacking its usual enthusiasm.

"My trip ended early. Is it okay if I hang out with you?"

"Really?" Kai asked.

"If it's okay with your mom." Jasper turned to me for confirmation.

"Of course," I said, still shocked that he was here. "He shouldn't be contagious."

He waved away my comment, as if to say, like I'd let anything come between spending time with Kai.

As I watched Jasper with Kai, my heart melted a little more. At the way Jasper treated my son. At the care and attention and patience Jasper showed Kai. He listened as Kai told him about Lego Star Wars. And he subtly encouraged Kai to drink. Jasper was a good caregiver. Nurturing.

When room service arrived, I pushed off from the barstool. I collected our order at the door and thanked Ethan before returning inside. I didn't want to risk anyone seeing Jasper here, not when he was supposed to be in Colorado. I wondered what he'd told everyone, how he'd explained his abrupt departure. But I supposed that was one of the perks of being the CEO—he could do whatever he wanted. He didn't have to justify his decisions to anyone except maybe the board. But they weren't going to weigh in on something like this.

"Here you go." I handed Kai his oatmeal before turning to Jasper. "Do you want me to order something for you?"

"I'm fine. I had lunch on the flight. Besides, you don't need to be worrying about me. I'm here to help you."

Since Kai was preoccupied with his show and oatmeal, Jasper came to join me in the kitchen. Kai's back was to us, and he was so invested in the characters, he wasn't paying attention to anything else. The TV provided enough background noise that I wasn't overly concerned about him overhearing our conversation.

I updated Jasper on what the doctor had said, ultimately referring us to a pediatric GI. I'd made an appointment, but the earliest I could get in was in six weeks. It seemed so far away, too far away, but they'd promised to call if something opened up sooner.

Jasper slid his arms around my waist, resting his chin on my shoulder. "I missed you." He pressed a kiss to my neck.

"I missed you too," I said, placing my hands over his. "I'm glad you're here, but how did you explain your sudden need to leave?" I asked as the TV droned on in the background.

"I said I had a family emergency."

"Yeah, but…"

"Halle." He pulled me into him. "When are you going to realize that you're my family? I love you and Kai, and I would do anything for the two of you."

I turned to face Jasper, my heart in my throat. I tilted my head back to look at him, to really see him. This wonderful, caring, loving man who adored my son and me. Who would do anything for us.

"I love you too."

He smiled and cupped my cheek, glancing over at the couch before pressing his lips to mine. The kiss was sweet and chaste, but I could feel his love all the same.

I turned so we were both facing the couch, sliding my arm around his waist. He draped his arm over my shoulder. He was so solid and reassuring. I knew I could do this on my own, but it was nice that I no longer had to.

CHAPTER TWENTY-TWO

JASPER

I drummed my fingers against my desk, impatiently waiting for an update from Halle. My assistant and I had just finished going through my calendar, and she was getting closer to confirming a date with the woman who'd won me in the bachelorx auction. To say I wasn't looking forward to spending an evening with another woman was an understatement.

The only woman I wanted to spend time with was Halle. I might be at the office, but my mind was on her and Kai. I could only imagine how she felt after dealing with this for as long as she had. For having doctors, her ex, doubt her instincts.

And poor Kai. If last night was any indication, he'd been through a lot. I'd spent the night at their place, though I'd slept on the couch. Kai had thrown up a few more times, but we'd kept him comfortable and hydrated. I could see the exhaustion in Halle's eyes, and I felt it too. The worry. The love.

Kai couldn't keep living like this. Halle either. I didn't want her to have to continue to wait for answers. Nor for

Kai to have to continue to wait for relief. So, I'd pulled some strings and gotten a next-day appointment for Kai with one of the best pediatric GIs in the city. She was usually booked solid, but her office had been able to work them in this morning.

Halle: I like the GI a lot. She's ordering some blood tests and wants Kai to have an endoscopy.

AN ENDOSCOPY? SHIT. THAT SEEMED LIKE A BIG DEAL, BUT I didn't want to alarm Halle.

Me: How do you feel about that?

Halle: I'm glad my concerns are finally being taken seriously.

SO WAS I. I COULDN'T BELIEVE CRAIG HAD DISMISSED HER fears. There was no way the symptoms Kai was experiencing were normal or acceptable. And the idea that Kai's father—the man who was supposed to be looking out for him, protecting him—had ignored or downplayed what his son was going through made me irrationally angry.

Me: Me too. Let me know if I can do anything to help.

Halle: Thanks. I'll tell you the rest of what she
said later. Sorry I had to miss the meeting
today.

I DIDN'T GIVE A SHIT ABOUT THE MEETING, AND I DIDN'T WANT
Halle to worry about it either. Kai absolutely came first.

Me: Focus on Kai. Work will be here when
you get back.

Halle: Thanks.

Me: Rosie and I would love to see you and
Kai tonight.

WHO WAS I KIDDING? ROSIE PRACTICALLY LIVED WITH HALLE
and Kai. There were many times, especially lately, that I
found myself jealous—of a dog.

Halle: We'd love that.

I SMILED, BUT BEFORE I COULD RESPOND, THERE WAS A KNOCK
at my office door. I was surprised to find Pierce standing at
the threshold.

"Pierce, hey." I stood, rounding the desk to greet him with
a handshake and a hug. "How are you?"

"Good. And you?"

"I'm good." Better than good. I was still worried about Kai, but I knew he was in good hands.

"And your family?" Pierce asked, though I wasn't sure why. He was practically family himself. He could've called up any one of my siblings and asked how they were. Hell, sometimes I wondered why he wasn't part of the family group chat.

"They're good."

"You sure?" he asked.

I eyed him. What was his deal? "Yeah. I'm sure."

"I'm glad to hear it, though I was surprised to learn that you came back from Colorado several days early for a family emergency." *Ah. That.* I tried not to react as he continued speaking. "As far as I can tell, Sloan and Jackson and Evie are good. Graham and Lily are fine. Knox and Nate. So you can understand my confusion, as well as that of some of the board members who passed along their concern."

"Please feel free to reassure any interested board members that all is well."

"Mm." He crossed his arms over his chest. "Is it?"

"Yes," I said, trying not to let my exasperation show.

"Does this 'family emergency,'" he said, using air quotes, "have anything to do with that situation we discussed previously?" He gave me a meaningful look.

I knew he was referring to Halle even if he hadn't mentioned her specifically. I couldn't help but smile at the thought of her, though I knew that was the exact opposite of what I should've done.

"Oh, fuck me." He dragged a hand down his face. "It does. Doesn't it?"

When I didn't deny it, he closed the door to my office. I settled in behind my desk, trying to appear calm when I was anything but. It felt as if reality was pushing in on the bubble Halle and I had been living in, trying to burst it.

"I thought I told you to drop it," Pierce said.

"I tried. I really did. But…" I lifted a shoulder. What else was there to say? I was in love with Halle.

"I need details," Pierce said, taking the seat across from me. "Who is she? What's her position in the company? How serious is it?"

I shook my head, unwilling to answer his questions. I couldn't do that. I'd promised Halle. I wouldn't make decisions that could impact her career without talking to her first.

"I can't betray her confidence."

"Jasper." Pierce pinched the bridge of his nose. "I can't help you if you don't talk to me. And when—not if—this blows up, you're going to want my help."

I dragged a hand through my hair, knowing he was right. Halle might not be ready to tell anyone about us, but Pierce might be the one person who could help us navigate this situation. I understood her reservations, and I hoped that by talking to Pierce, we'd be able to devise solutions to overcome them.

"This stays between us?" I asked, needing confirmation. I would never intentionally do anything to put Halle or her job at risk. But it was my hope that this would help her. Help us.

"Of course. Though, I have to remind you that I'm your family's attorney, not just yours. So if your relationship creates a conflict of interest, and it's more than minor, I might be required to disclose it to the others. Especially if it could harm their interests in the company. But, of course, I'd give you the opportunity to disclose it first," he said.

"I understand." And I respected him for stating his boundaries.

"Who is she?"

"A higher-level employee."

He groaned. "It's Halle, isn't it?"

I supposed there was no use trying to lie to him, not when he'd already guessed. But still, I was protective of her. "And if it is?"

"Is it serious?"

I knew Halle loved me. And while she seemed to know that we'd need to tell my family about us at some point, she was always evasive when I brought it up. Not that I'd broached the subject in a while. We'd been busy with Kai's birthday, my travel, and now navigating Kai's health issues.

"Yes, but she's concerned about the impact to our jobs and the company."

"Rightly so," he said, and the pit in my gut widened. "After our last conversation, I reviewed the bylaws and employee policies. There is no policy outright prohibiting a relationship between the executive and a subordinate—"

"That's good," I said, relief settling over me.

"You would think so, but it's still a potential conflict of interest. And it's subject to review by the board."

I scrunched up my face, seriously disliking that idea. Halle would hate it.

"Look. I get it," Pierce said. "But if you want to keep seeing each other, you're going to have to bring it to the board. You'd have to recuse yourself from voting, which means that your family would lose their majority. But at least you'd still have a huge advantage."

"Realistically, what kind of action could the board take?"

"They could put you under review. Ask for your resignation. With regards to Halle, they could demote her, put her on leave without pay, demand her resignation."

I gulped, the consequences suddenly feeling that much more real. "Do you think they'd do that? Halle's good at her job."

"You know how these things go. It's all about politics and

perception. Which is why you need your family on your side more than ever."

I winced, and Pierce massaged his temples. "I take it you haven't told any of them?"

I shook my head. "Not yet."

"What are you waiting for?" he pushed.

"I would, but she's opposed."

"I don't know about you, but that feels like a red flag to me."

Red flag. The fuck?

I tried not to overreact, but Jesus.

"I understand her reasons," I gritted out. Even if I didn't like them.

"Right. But surely you can see how that makes you more vulnerable, legally speaking. Because if you go to the board, that puts her on record for saying the relationship is consensual. And if that's the case, it can undercut any potential claims to the contrary that might later…arise."

"Pierce," I warned.

I understood it was his job to protect me and my family, which included the company by extension, but I didn't appreciate the way he was talking about Halle. Questioning her motives. Doubting our future together.

He lifted his hands as if in surrender. "Look, I know that no one wants to think about a relationship ending while they're in the throes of it. But you have to."

He might be right, but I didn't like it. I didn't want to think about things ending with Halle. The idea of not having her—or Kai—in my life was too painful.

"You saw the fallout from Nate's divorce. It was bad enough that Trinity was his wife. Can you imagine how much worse it would've been if she'd also been his employee?"

I shuddered. Trinity was a manipulative, toxic woman

who only cared about herself. I hated what she'd done to Nate. To Brooklyn. And I was glad Trinity was no longer able to poison their lives with her bullshit.

"First of all, H—" I swallowed, smoothing down my tie. I was still unwilling to admit that it was Halle. "She is nothing like Trinity. And I'm not a celebrity like Nate." I hadn't won Sexiest Man Alive or a Golden Globe. "The paparazzi don't hound my every move."

"No, but you are worth billions."

"She's not—"

He held up a hand. "When Trinity and Nate fell in love, do you think he would've ever believed the level of destruction she was capable of?"

Point taken.

"And you're not a celebrity, no. But your family has notoriety, and you've had a lot of press since taking over as CEO. Even if you hadn't, don't you think a story like this—CEO and his employee—would garner some attention?" He arched a brow as if in challenge.

"I should've talked to Knox," I muttered. At least Knox tempered his advice with compassion. With Pierce, the hits just kept coming.

"You asked my advice, and I'm giving it. You need to find a way to assure the board that it's not a conflict of interest. And they're going to care more about how it reflects upon the company—to employees, the industry, and our guests."

Right. So, no big deal, then.

"Let me ask you something," Pierce said. "Take away the fact that you're the CEO and she's your employee. If you were just a regular couple in love, do you think she'd still insist on keeping your relationship secret?"

She wouldn't. Would she?

She and Sloan were close. Keeping this from my sister felt like a betrayal, and we were both afraid how it might affect our working and personal relationships with her. "She knows that telling my family is ultimately the goal."

"Has she said that?"

I considered it a moment, then I said, "She agreed to it when we first started dating, but I promised to go at whatever pace she needed."

"Mm. And have you tried broaching the subject since?"

"Yes, but—"

"Let me guess. She always has some excuse?"

"I—" I opened then closed my mouth. Yes. He was right, but also…he didn't fully understand the circumstances. And he was approaching this from the standpoint of what was best for me, for the company. Not what Halle wanted or needed.

"Are you listening to yourself? It's like you're doing my job for me. Red flag after red flag." He pretended to throw flags in the air like a referee at one of the Leatherbacks' soccer matches.

I wanted to protest and tell Pierce that none of this would be an issue but for our positions. But the fact that I had to question it gave me pause.

Was she questioning our future? Me?

No. I shook my head. She loved me. We loved each other.

And yet, she kept finding reasons to keep our relationship a secret. From Kai, from her family. From the people who mattered most to us.

"And that, my friend—" Pierce pointed at my face "—is further proof of why you need to protect yourself."

I groaned. I didn't want to believe there was any truth to his claims. I wanted to love Halle wholeheartedly without any obstacles standing in our path. But I was coming to realize that maybe Halle's mind-set was the biggest roadblock to our future.

I didn't know what more I could do to convince her that I

would do everything in my power to protect her. To make her see that we could find a way to be together *and* keep our jobs. Maybe I was being naïve, but Halle offered so much to the Huxley brand. I wanted to believe that our relationship wouldn't undermine all her hard work. But Pierce's warnings about potential outcomes had certainly put me on edge.

"I hope she's worth it," Pierce said. I knew he wasn't trying to sound callous or mean. It was his job to consider what was best for me. Best for my family and our company. And the idea of my dating an employee was definitely a huge risk.

And yet, I was determined to have faith in us. Because nothing mattered without her. "She is."

Pierce seemed to consider it a moment. "If you won't protect yourself, protect the brand."

I sighed, knowing I owed it to my family. To the company and all our employees. "What do you suggest?"

"The company can't handle another CEO change in such quick succession."

"Nor do I have any intention of stepping down," I said firmly. He needed to remove that idea from his mind.

"You need to be ready for a fight. Start by getting your siblings on your side before you approach the rest of the members. It would be best not to catch your family off guard."

"Oh, you mean how Graham stunned everyone by announcing that he was *married* to Lily?"

Pierce covered a laugh with a cough. "Yeah. Something like that."

"Did you know they were dating?" I asked. Of all people, Pierce would've known. He was Graham's best friend.

It was something I'd wondered for a while—how much Graham had told Pierce about his relationship with Lily. Because the rest of us had been shocked to discover that

Graham was not only in a relationship but married. It seemed as if it had all happened so suddenly, but I was happy for Graham.

For the first time in as long as I could remember, my brother seemed…content. Settled. Grounded.

Pierce tapped the side of his nose. "Attorney-client privilege."

I rolled my eyes. "How convenient."

"Mm." He tugged on his tie. "You'll be grateful when I give the same answer to anyone who asks about your relationship with Halle."

"I never said it was her."

He chuckled, though he didn't seem amused. "You didn't have to."

"Your comment suggests that Graham's relationship with Lily wasn't all that it seemed." I studied Pierce, but he didn't so much as twitch.

This was why I hated playing poker with Pierce. He kept his cards close to his chest, and he was damn near impossible to read. At least with Graham, I knew his tells. But even after years of playing with Pierce, I was still no closer to discovering his.

Pierce's phone rang. "Speak of the devil." He flashed me his phone, where Graham's name was displayed. "I need to take this. And you need to talk to Halle and your family before you tell the board. *Soon.* Got it?"

I gave him a thumbs-up, my voice dripping with artificial excitement. "Got it."

He exited my office, closing the door behind him. I slumped in my chair. Ending things with Halle wasn't an option. Which meant…I needed to find a way to convince her to go public with our relationship. I only hoped I could get her to agree before it was too late.

CHAPTER TWENTY-THREE

HALLE

"What's an andopoppy again?" Kai asked while we were getting ready for bed the night before his procedure.

I tried not to laugh at his pronunciation, though this was no laughing matter. When we'd met with the doctor previously, she'd suggested a battery of tests to try to determine the cause of Kai's tummy trouble. Blood tests, an upper GI endoscopy, and a biopsy.

She'd mentioned the possibility of Kai having celiac disease and had recommended having Kai go gluten-free as a precaution. It had been a lot to take in. But for the first time, it was nice to have a clear path forward. And the new diet did seem to be helping.

"It's an endoscopy," I said, smoothing his hair away from his face. Rosie grunted in her sleep from the foot of the bed. "And it's a special test. It will help the doctors figure out what's going on, so you can get to feeling better."

I didn't want to go into too much detail. I didn't want to freak Kai out about the idea that they'd sedate him and then feed a camera down his throat. *I* was trying not to freak out about it. About what it might mean—the results, the prognosis. I had to be strong and calm for him.

"But they have to put me to sleep?" Kai asked.

"They do," I said. "And then you'll wake up, and they'll be able to tell us what they discovered."

His face crumpled, and he looked as if he were going to start crying. "Mummy," he whispered. "I'm scared."

"I know, baby." I pulled him in close, kissing the top of his head. I wished I could take away his pain, his worries. "But I'll be there with you every step of the way. I promise. And Daddy is thinking about you."

We'd talked to Craig earlier in the day, and I could see the concern in his eyes. He'd even offered to fly to LA to be with us, but I'd told him it wasn't necessary. Though I'd promised to send frequent updates.

"And Jasper too?" Kai asked.

I followed Kai's gaze to the doorway, where Jasper was leaning against the doorframe. Jasper often came over for dinner and stayed until bedtime. After Kai was asleep, Jasper and I would catch up on the day, cuddle, make love. It all felt so normal, so domestic. Apart from the fact that Jasper would sneak out late at night or early in the morning before Kai woke.

That was the only part that sucked, and I was over it. I could tell Jasper was too, even if he didn't say it. It made me love him all the more—for his patience, for his willingness to go at my pace.

"And me too," Jasper said, stepping into the room. "If…" He paused, glancing at me. "That's okay with your mom."

"I—" I wasn't even sure what to say. I still wasn't used to having support, especially not when it came to Kai's health. For all these years, even before the divorce, I'd been on my own in that department. But now, Jasper was here, and he'd consistently shown up for my son.

He'd researched gluten-free foods and cooked some recipes with Kai that Alexis had sent me. Her eldest daughter, Sophia, had a gluten allergy, though she didn't have celiac disease. But they'd been navigating a gluten-free diet for years and were full of great tips.

I so appreciated their support. And I was grateful that Jasper had taken my concerns about Kai's health seriously, even going so far as to make the appointment with one of the best doctors in the area. Jasper had advocated for Kai. A child who wasn't his son, wasn't even related to him.

He loved Kai. Kai adored Jasper. And that terrified me.

I should've been happy about it, and I was. But I was also scared at how attached Kai had become to Jasper in such a short time. And Rosie.

But I also knew that I had to be brave—for my son. For the future of this relationship. I had to trust Jasper, and he'd given me every reason to believe he'd be there for us.

"And Jasper," I finally said, adding, "when he can."

Jasper frowned, and I was hit with a pang of guilt. I didn't want Jasper to think I doubted him or how much he cared for my son. I just… I worried about the future. About how devastated Kai would be if things didn't work out. And while I hoped that wouldn't be the case, I often questioned how our relationship would be possible, considering our jobs.

"It's late. Why don't you try to get some sleep?" I said to Kai.

"Can Jasper stay and keep telling me his story?" Kai asked, peering up at me. "Please, Mum?"

Jasper said nothing. Instead, he inclined his head, deferring to me.

"Okay," I said, giving Kai one last cuddle. I stood and tucked him in. "Ten minutes," I said to Jasper on my way out. "That's it."

He mock-saluted me. "Got it."

I tried not to roll my eyes, even as I bit back a smile.

I padded out to the living room and grabbed my phone from the counter. I had a few new messages.

Alexis: Sending all the positive vibes for Kai's endoscopy.

Zara: Call me anytime, babes. Sending you and Kai all my love. Xx

Mom: I love you, Halle. You and Kai. I'm here for you.

Sloan: I hope Kai's procedure goes well tomorrow. I'll be thinking about him.

I'D DEBATED TELLING SLOAN ABOUT THE ENDOSCOPY, BUT SHE was my friend, and I knew she'd want to know. That said, I didn't want her to worry about it affecting my work, even if my focus was shot.

I tidied up the living room, trying to keep myself distracted. Because if I thought too hard about tomorrow, I'd never get any sleep.

Jasper finally joined me, closing the door to Kai's room softly. "He was tired." Jasper came over to me, wrapping his arms around me. "You okay?"

I shook my head, at a loss for words. But he didn't push; he simply continued to hold me.

"I think I should go with you tomorrow," he said.

"I wish you could," I said, pulling back. "But we both know you can't."

"Sure I can," he said, leading me over to the couch. "I'm the boss, right?" he joked, parroting back my own words.

I sank down next to him, still holding his hand. "I appreciate your offering—more than you could know. But I don't think it's a good idea."

"Because you don't want me there?"

"Of course I want you there." I placed my hand over his. It scared me how much I wanted him there—at my side, lending his support. "But the company needs you. Sloan's out on maternity leave. I'm going to be off for Kai's procedure. Someone has to stay to hold down the fort."

"It's one day," he said. "I don't think everything will fall apart without us. At least, it shouldn't. If that's the case, then the company has even bigger problems."

"It's more than that, and you know it." It was our secret relationship. It was the perception. It was everything.

He sighed, dragging a hand through his hair. "If our relationship weren't a secret, this wouldn't even be up for debate."

"You don't know that. I mean, look at Sloan and Jackson and what they had to do to take leave for the new baby. Yes, they're executives, which gives them more power. But it's also more limiting in some ways because so few other people in the company are at that level."

"I should be able to take off one day."

"I'm not saying you shouldn't or can't. I'm just saying... not for this. I'll be okay."

"Maybe I won't." He jabbed his chest with his thumb. "Maybe I offered because *I* need to be there. For you and Kai. But also, for me."

Oh. I should've considered how he might be feeling about this. I'd been so wrapped up in my own thoughts and concerns that I hadn't realized how this might be impacting Jasper as well.

"Jasper." I cupped his cheek, in awe of this tenderhearted man. Jasper had confided in me about his anxiety in the past, and I could only imagine how much he was struggling with this. I kicked myself for not realizing it sooner.

Somehow, everyone had it wrong about Jasper. And I was grateful that he'd let me see the real him. A man who was gentle and passionate and nurturing. A man who stood by me in life's difficult moments and loved me through them.

If there was one thing Jasper had taught me, it was to ground myself in the present. And I knew that mindfulness and physical touch helped him when he was feeling anxious.

I stood, tugging on his hand. "Come on."

"Where are we going?" he asked, standing.

"To bed." I pulled him toward my room. "Stay with me tonight. I don't want to be alone tonight, and I don't think you do either."

He followed me to my room, and we undressed each other slowly, taking our time. There was nothing rushed or hurried about our movements as we explored each other, acting as if it were the first time. In some ways, it felt like a revelation. A new discovery. Because the more time I spent with Jasper, the harder I fell.

"ALL RIGHT, MOM," THE HOSPITAL ADMIN SAID, "WE HAVE SOME paperwork for you."

"Sure," I said. "Whatever you need."

Kai was sitting on the hospital bed watching TV while I spoke with the nurses and staff. We reviewed his health history and my insurance info, along with all the other basic stuff like the risks and outcomes. It was daunting, but I was trying to remain positive and calm for Kai.

"Just sign here," she said, and I did. "And then your estimated co-pay is $250. Of course, the doctors and anesthesiologists might bill your insurance separately, and then you'll have to pay that as well."

"Right," I said, handing her my credit card. "Thanks."

I was grateful my portion was only $250. If I hadn't had such good health insurance, I'd be paying a heck of a lot more. It wasn't something I took for granted.

She handed my card back to me. "One of the nurses will be in soon to place his IV. Until then, hit the call button if you need anything."

I thanked her then joined Kai on the bed, holding him close. He cuddled the stuffed dog Jasper had given him during his birthday weekend, and we waited. Jasper texted every so often to check in, and he and Kai sent funny memes back and forth. Jasper might not be here, but his presence and love were very much felt by Kai and me.

After the nurses came, things started to move quickly. Before I knew it, Kai was being rolled back to the operating room, and I was a nervous wreck.

I breathed in deeply. *I am strong.* I exhaled slowly. *It will be okay.* Then I repeated it again.

"Okay, sweetie." I kissed Kai's cheek, trying to remain upbeat even as the bridge of my nose stung. "I'll see you soon."

"Okay, Mum." He was already half asleep as the nurse assured me they'd take good care of him.

I returned to his room, swiping away a tear. Before I could even send a quick update to Craig and Zara, I saw a message from Alexis.

> Alexis: I'm showing some houses near the
> hospital. Let me know if you want company.

ANOTHER TEAR SLID DOWN MY CHEEK. ALEXIS AND I HADN'T known each other long, but she'd become a good friend in a short amount of time.

Me: Thanks. You're the best.

I SENT AN UPDATE TO CRAIG AND ZARA BEFORE OPENING MY messages with Jasper.

Me: They just took Kai back to the OR.

Jasper: I'm thinking about him. Call me if you need to talk. I love you.

Me: Thanks. I love you too.

I OPENED MY LAPTOP AND LOGGED ON, BUT THEN I JUST stared at the screen. As much as I wanted answers, I was scared of what the doctors would find. And I hoped that Kai would do well with the anesthesia.

My phone buzzed. *Mom.* She was asking to video chat.

"Hey, Mom," I said, answering the call. "They took Kai back a little while ago. How are you?"

"Dad and I just wanted to call and let you know that we're thinking about you. Both of you."

She panned the camera so Dad came into view. I smiled, but his brows furrowed in confusion.

"Hi, Dad." I forced myself to continue smiling even as he maintained his bewildered stare.

Dad turned to Mom. "Who is that?"

My heart fractured into a million tiny pieces, and self-ishly, I wished I hadn't answered the phone. I was already feeling emotional, thanks to Kai's procedure, and the fact that my dad didn't recognize me was absolutely heart-breaking.

When Mom tried to explain who I was, Dad started to get agitated. To the point that she had to call one of the nurses. I watched all of it with increasing horror—for him, for them, at the reality of the situation. I hadn't realized how much his disease had progressed. Or maybe I'd just been in denial. Ultimately, Mom left the room and went out to the hallway while the staff tried to help Dad calm down.

"Sorry." Mom frowned, glancing over her shoulder. "I thought it was a good day."

I was scared to ask, but I needed to know. "Has this been happening more lately?"

"We can talk about it later." She smiled brightly, and I knew she—like me—was trying to hold it together. "Right now, your focus needs to be on Kai."

"Mom. Tell me, please." If she didn't, my mind would keep spinning out with countless terrible scenarios.

She sighed. "The facility wants to bump Dad up to the next level of care."

Jesus. The next level? We'd visited my parents when we'd first moved to the States, and I was concerned by how quickly Dad's disease seemed to be progressing.

"What do you think?" I asked Mom. "Does he need it? Is he getting worse?"

"Honestly?" she sighed. "Yes. I just wish it weren't so expensive."

"Don't worry about the money," I said, unwilling to contemplate the cost. "I'll take care of it."

"Honey, I can't ask you to do that." Her eyes met mine, full of gratitude and sadness and love. "Especially not when you're already doing so much. Your father and I would never—"

"I wouldn't offer if I couldn't do it. 'Kay?"

"Okay. It's just…" She twisted her wedding ring on her finger. "There are options. We could move him somewhere else. Somewhere less expensive."

I'd researched other places online before we'd decided to move him into his current facility. The reviews on some of the others were terrifying, especially considering my dad's potential inability to advocate for himself. I didn't want to worry her, not when she was already dealing with so much. Plus, we both knew that another move in such a short amount of time would only add to my dad's confusion and agitation. My dad's care, and my mom's and my peace of mind, was worth more than anything.

I would figure out how to pay for it even after my temporary promotion ended. Maybe I'd rent an apartment instead of buying a house or not put as much into my 401(k). The point was, I would figure it out.

"I want the best care for Dad," I said. "And Green Acres is the best fit." The doctor entered Kai's hospital room. "Mom. I gotta go."

"Okay. Of course. Let me know what the doctor says. And I'll see you in a few weeks."

I nodded. "Looking forward to it. Love you."

"Love you too, honey."

I ended the call and stood, smoothing my hands down my thighs.

"Kai is in recovery now. He's doing great. We're going to let him wake up some more, and then we'll bring him back here."

"Thank you," I said, relief coursing through me. That had been the longest twenty minutes of my life. But Kai was a champ. He'd made it through the procedure. And I could only hope the test would help.

"We won't have the results of the biopsy for a few days," the doctor continued. "So I'll call when I have a more definitive answer. For now, Kai needs rest. And continue to avoid gluten as a precaution."

"Will do," I said.

She gave me some more information on his care at home following the procedure. It was a lot to take in. As soon as the doctor left, I dropped into a nearby chair. I was emotionally wrung out from the events of the morning. Worrying about Kai. The call with my parents. Trying to figure out how I was going to pay for my dad's care as it continued to get even more expensive.

I sagged, covering my face with my hands. *I wish Jasper were here.*

Before I could talk myself out of it, I picked up the phone and hit the button to connect the call to him. I knew he'd be waiting for an update, and I needed to hear his voice.

"Just a sec," he said, answering the call after the second ring. I could imagine him excusing himself from his current meeting, holding the phone to his ear as he went somewhere more private. "Okay."

All the emotions of the morning poured out of me, and I started crying.

"Halle?" he asked. "What's wrong? Is it Kai? Is he okay?"

"He's—" I sniffled. "I'm sorry. Yeah. He's in recovery. They said it went well, and we should have the results in a few days."

"Oh good. That's good." Relief threaded through his words. "What about you? Are you okay?"

"I—" I hiccupped around a sob. "I wish you were here."

Jasper had insisted on hiring a driver to transport us to and from the hospital. I hadn't even fought him on it. I'd appreciated the help, and I knew he needed to do it for himself.

"I can be there in thirty minutes," Jasper said. "Ten, if I can get the hospital to clear me to land on the helipad."

I laughed at the idea, but I knew he'd do it. Even if he had to donate enough to fund a new wing of the hospital, Jasper would gladly do it to be here for Kai, for me.

"I'm serious, Halle."

"I know," I said, feeling lighter from his support. "Will you come over when we get home?"

"Of course," he said. "And you're right. It's probably best if I stay here. Pierce was already pissed about my leaving Colorado early for a family emergency."

I frowned. When it came to Jasper and his family, Pierce was always very supportive. He was practically one of them, and I knew he'd do anything for Graham, Jasper, Knox, Nate, or Sloan.

"That doesn't sound like Pierce."

Jasper seemed to hesitate, and before he could answer, the door to Kai's room opened. I stood, watching as the staff rolled his bed back in. I scanned Kai's form—sleepy but breathing normally. Such a relief.

"I have to go. They just came back with Kai."

"Okay. Tell him hi, and I'll see you both later. I love you."

"Love you too," I said before disconnecting the call. I went over to the bed. "Hey, buddy."

"Mummy?" he whispered, while the nurses monitored his vital signs.

I placed my hand over Kai's. "Yep, baby." I swiped away a tear. "It's me. You feel okay?"

"I'm sleepy." He spoke softly, the words drawn out.

"I know," I said. "You might be for a while. Just rest, okay?"

"Okay."

"You did so well," I said, making sure he had his favorite stuffed dog from Jasper. "So proud of you, baby."

"I wish Dad and Jasper and Rosie were here."

"Me too." I smoothed his hair away from his face. "But Jasper promised to come over as soon as we get home. Sound good?"

"Mm-hmm." His eyes closed once more. "I really like him. I'm glad he's our friend."

"Me too," I said, smiling. Jasper was a lot more than just my friend, but now wasn't the time to tell Kai that. Even so, I had a feeling that when we did finally break the news to Kai, he'd be happy about it.

Kai was quiet for a while, waking up slowly. Finally, he said, "Mummy?"

"Yeah?"

"Are you and Jasper going to get married?"

My eyes darted to Kai's face, my heart stopping at the unexpected question. It had come out of the blue.

"I, uh—" I cleared my throat. "Why would you ask that?"

I braced myself for his response. I expected something like, because he's always over. Or, I saw the two of you kissing. Who knew?

"Because he's nice," Kai said. "And I love Rosie. And I want to keep her."

I laughed. "Ah, okay. So this is really about wanting a dog."

He frowned. "Not just any dog. Rosie."

"She's pretty great, isn't she?" He smiled, so I continued. "And I know how much you love her."

"But what's going to happen when we move out of the hotel?" he asked.

Kai had come into my room the other morning when I'd been looking at house listings from Alexis. He'd joined me on the bed, giving his opinions about the various homes. We'd talked about moving, but I hadn't realized how much he'd been thinking about it.

He sniffled. "I love seeing Rosie every day. I'm going to miss her so much. If you and Jasper got married, she'd be part of our family too."

"She is part of our family, baby. And I'm sure Jasper will still be happy to let you visit."

Tears poured down his face. "But it won't be the same."

"Maybe not," I said, thinking of how the move might impact my ability to see Jasper. Our rare moments together would likely become even more limited. "But that doesn't mean it won't still be good."

"I don't want to move," he cried.

He seemed more emotional, and I chalked it up to adrenaline and anesthesia. Even so, I knew this transition would be difficult for him. Not because he'd grown accustomed to living in a luxury hotel, but because he'd gotten used to seeing Jasper and Rosie every day.

I wasn't sure what I was going to do about it, but I knew one thing. We couldn't keep living at the Huxley Grand LA. Yes, it was convenient—for many reasons. But it wasn't a home. And while Sloan had convinced the board to extend our accommodations for the maximum period allowed, I was running out of time to find something more permanent or risk paying an exorbitant amount to continue staying in our suite. It was time to get serious about finding a place to call home.

CHAPTER TWENTY-FOUR

JASPER

"We should do this more often." I glided my fingers along Halle's spine, tracing patterns on her bare skin.

"Have sex?" she teased. "Because I'm not sure my body can take much more. Three orgasms in the last hour."

"Want to go for round four before we have to head back to the office?" I teased. Well, half teased. If she was game, I was.

She snuggled deeper into my side. "I would, but I found the perfect spot and now I don't want to move."

We were ensconced in her bed, enjoying our lunch break away from the office. An hour alone felt like sheer decadence. A luxury we so rarely got to indulge in. Slow sex. In a bed. Time alone to talk. To cuddle.

"Me either," I admitted. "Maybe we should just spend the rest of the day in bed."

"Right. Because that wouldn't look questionable at all." She laughed. "It might be Friday, but there are still enough people at the office to notice."

Sometimes, it seemed ridiculous that we were continuing

to keep our relationship a secret. Lately, I felt as if I were bending over backward just to make sure no one knew about the most important person in my life.

"Come on." She pushed up, patting my chest. Her hair cascaded down her shoulder, over her breast. She was stunning. "We promised this wouldn't affect our work."

The trouble was, it already was. Even if she didn't realize it. Even if neither of us wanted to admit it.

Pierce's earlier comments rang in my ears, his ultimatum to tell my family, tell the board about our relationship. I didn't want to pressure Halle, but the longer we waited to disclose it, the more suspicious our actions would seem. The last thing I wanted was for the board to lose faith in Halle or me. As Pierce had so bluntly stated, it was all about politics and perception.

I'd waited for Kai to get better. And now that Kai had bounced back from his endoscopy, and he had a diagnosis and a path forward, I finally felt like the time was right to broach the topic with Halle once more.

"You and Kai are coming to the Leatherbacks' home game next weekend, right?" Knox had invited the family to enjoy the game from the owner's suite, and I was looking forward to it.

Kai seemed to be feeling better overall now that he was following a gluten-free diet. That wasn't necessarily surprising, especially now that we knew he had celiac disease. Halle had been upset but also relieved. And since then, we'd researched celiac and felt more confident with how best to support Kai.

"I was planning on it." She pulled on her underwear. "If that's okay with you."

"Of course it is," I said. "I always want you and Kai with me."

She smiled, bending forward to kiss me. I cupped the

back of her neck, holding her close. Our tongues danced and sparred as the kiss turned heated.

I pulled her onto my lap, and she moaned as she rocked against my erection. "Jasper."

"Halle." I squeezed her breasts, her hips, her ass, each one met with an answering sound of pleasure. "Come with me."

She pulled back ever so slightly, her palms pressed to my chest, a smirk playing at her lips. "I didn't realize you were already so close."

"No. Well, yes, that too. Later. But come with me to the game." I took a deep breath. "As my girlfriend." Girlfriend sounded so juvenile, but nothing else seemed quite right either. "It's the perfect opportunity to soft launch our relationship to my family."

"I—" She paused, and I couldn't gauge what she was thinking. The fact that she was hesitating gave me hope that maybe she was actually considering it. "I want to say yes, but there's just so much going on...." She hedged. "Now's not a good time. Sloan's not even back from her maternity leave."

I tried to tamp down my frustration. To remind myself that this was progress. Maybe Halle just needed to talk it through so she'd feel ready. "There's always a lot going on. There will never be a perfect time."

An alarm chimed, and she reached over, grabbing her phone from the nightstand. Halle started grabbing her clothes from the floor. She pulled on her skirt and zipped it up.

"Halle." I wasn't ready to let this go. I understood why she was scared, and I didn't want to let Pierce's negativity impact my thoughts, but I needed some type of assurance that we were still working toward telling my family. Some kind of plan.

"You won't always feel ready to take the next step," I said, taking her hand in mine. "I didn't feel ready when I had to step up to become CEO. Just as I think you also felt some hesitation when you were going to become the SVP. But now that we're in these roles, we're thriving. And I think once we tell my family and the board, we'll feel so much lighter. Please just…think about it. Pierce—" I stopped myself before I could say more, say too much.

"What about Pierce?" she asked, assessing me. Her eyes widened. "Does Pierce know about us?"

I pressed the heels of my hands to my eyes, wishing I'd kept my mouth shut.

"Jasper?"

Fuck.

"He knows I'm seeing someone. He guessed it was you."

She squeezed her eyes shut, and I could sense the fear radiating from her. Where was the strong, confident woman who commanded meetings? Where was the badass who negotiated seven-figure art deals without breaking a sweat?

"He won't say anything," I added. At least not in the short-term. "I'm sorry. I know you didn't want anyone to know about us, but I was trying to protect us. Protect the company. Protect *you*. And the best way to do this is by telling my family and the board."

My phone chimed, reminding me that we had to get back to the office.

"Can we discuss it more later?" She slid into her heels, sans shirt.

I splayed my hands on my thighs, stretching then relaxing them in an attempt to stem my frustration. I didn't want to add even more pressure to an already stressful situation. And I didn't want Halle to think that I was trying to manipulate her into a decision she wasn't comfortable with. But I couldn't keep living like this.

The longer we waited to tell everyone, the worse this would be. My conversation with Pierce had confirmed that.

"Sure," I said, hating the sullen tone to my voice. "How about tonight?" I pressed.

She raced to button up her shirt, not meeting my eyes. "We can't. You have your date. And my mom's coming into town."

Right. *My date.*

I had no idea what the woman from the charity auction was expecting from our evening together, but she'd paid a lot of money for the pleasure of my company. I'd been so preoccupied, I'd nearly forgotten that it was coming up.

"How about tomorrow?" I asked, unwilling to let it go. Not without some resolution. "I have dinner with Sloan, but I could come over before that."

Halle shook her head. "I'm meeting Alexis to look at a few houses."

Wait. What?

"Is that what you and Alexis have been doing when you get together?"

She lifted a shoulder. "Sometimes. Other times, we're just hanging out."

I supposed deep down I should've realized that. Halle's contract stipulated that the company would only expense her housing for so long. With time running out, she didn't want to stay at the Huxley Grand forever; she wanted a home for Kai. But I guessed I'd somewhat foolishly assumed I'd factor into her decision.

Wherever she moved, it was going to affect both of us. It was going to reduce our already limited time together because we would no longer be able to sneak away to her suite midday. And depending on where the house was, commute time and traffic would be an issue.

There was only one solution in my mind. Something that would help with her money concerns, our desire to be together, and the need to keep our relationship secret—for now.

"Move in with me," I blurted.

Yes, there were practical reasons for suggesting it, but they weren't my primary motivation.

"What?" Halle dropped her hand and took a step back.

"Move in with me," I said again, smiling at the idea of it.

She wouldn't let me help her pay for her dad's care, even though I knew she was stressed about it. But maybe she'd let me help with this. It probably seemed impulsive—asking her to move in together. But I'd been thinking about it for a while.

I was so excited about the prospect that I kept talking. "I've been wanting to buy a house. Something in a good school district for Kai. Something close to the office. I'd keep the penthouse anyway for convenience, but we could all move somewhere new—you, Kai, Rosie, and me. A fresh start."

"It's too much, too fast. We haven't told your family or Kai. And then I'd be having him not only move again, but also asking him to accept our relationship." She shook her head.

I sighed, my shoulders drooping. I knew Halle had to do what was best for her son, but it felt as if she was using him as an excuse. Halle said she was all in, but when it came down to it, I didn't like that I had to question if she was.

"Halle—" I dragged a hand through my hair, my agitation growing. "Fuck. Are we ever going to be a normal couple?"

"A *normal* couple?" She frowned.

"Are we ever going to do the normal things that couples do? Are you ever going to tell your friends or family about us? Am I ever going to be allowed to tell mine?" I was trying to remain calm, but it was a struggle.

She crossed her arms over her chest. "I invited you to come to dinner with my mom."

"Does she even know we're together?" The words came out harsher than I'd intended.

"My mom is already dealing with so much. I don't want her to worry about my job or my ability to pay for my dad's care, especially when the price is about to go up."

"I get that, but it's not just about your mom. Will we ever go out on a date in public? Will Kai ever think we're more than friends? Will we ever live together? Spend holidays together? Take a vacation together? Do you even want those things?" My chest was heaving by the end of it, and it felt as if someone were digging around in there with a knife.

"Of course I want those things. Of course I want a life with you, but this is about so much more than us. This decision doesn't just impact me. If I lose my job, it impacts my parents, my son, my future. I can't give up everything I built for a man."

Her words were a punch to the gut. A reality check I hadn't expected.

She opened her mouth as if to walk back her admission, but it was too late. So that was how she really felt. Unfortunately, I couldn't unhear that painful jab, as much as I might want to.

Her eyes glittered with unshed tears. "Jasper…"

"Silly me," I scoffed, feeling like a fool. "I thought we were building a life together."

JACKSON OPENED THE DOOR, EVIE IN HIS ARMS. "JASPER. GOOD to see you." We hugged, and then he stepped aside. "Come in."

It was Saturday. The day after my date with the winner

from the bachelorx auction. The day after my fight with Halle. And I was a mess. But the sight of my youngest niece made everything seem a little better.

"May I?" I held out my arms for Evie.

He placed her in my arms. "Remember to—"

"Support her head. Yes." I laughed, peering down at the precious little bundle in my arms. "Your daddy loves you very much. But dating is going to be no fun."

"Do not utter that word in front of my daughter," Jackson said in a stern tone.

"What? Dating?" I taunted.

He narrowed his eyes at me. "Okay. Time's up."

I laughed, gently spinning away. "Nice try. She's mine for now."

He continued to grumble as I followed him into the kitchen, where Sloan was standing at the stove. I'd visited their house a number of times since they'd had the baby, but I'd never been hit with such a pang of longing as I was now.

The smell of a home-cooked meal filled the air. The sound of Evie gurgling made me ache for a home. Family. Halle and Kai. Because that's what they were to me—my family.

"You okay?" Sloan asked.

"Yeah. Yeah." I tried to clear away those thoughts. "How are you?"

"Good. Sleeping a little more, which is nice. Evie's been smiling more too."

I peered down at my niece. "Have you?" I rubbed my finger along her downy-soft cheek. "Have you been smiling, sweet girl? Are you going to smile for your uncle J?"

"Dinner's almost ready," Sloan said.

"You didn't have to cook for me," I said, giving my niece my finger to play with. No smile yet, but I couldn't wait to see one.

"I know, but I wanted to. It's relaxing."

She turned off the stove, and we carried the dishes over to the table to eat family-style. By that point, Evie had fallen asleep, and I followed Sloan to the nursery. I gently set Evie in her crib, in awe of this new life my sister had created.

"She's precious," I said, peering down at Evie's button nose, her lashes fanning out over her cheeks.

Sloan smiled, hand resting on the railing. "She really is." She turned to me. "I've never asked, but do you want children?"

My thoughts immediately went to Kai, and I tried not to get choked up. I kept my attention on Evie, nodding.

"How's it going with Halle?" Sloan asked.

I froze. "Halle?"

"My chief of staff? The temporary SVP?" Sloan joked. "Ring any bells?"

"Right." I laughed, though it sounded forced. "Halle, yes." Sloan was asking how it was going professionally. "It's going well."

Personally, it was a bit of a shitshow at the moment.

I hadn't spoken to Halle since our argument yesterday. I'd spent the rest of the afternoon working from home. I knew I'd pushed too hard, but I was also sick of hiding how I felt about her.

I hoped it was a fight, but deep down, I worried it was the end.

I wasn't sure where we stood or even where we went from here. Not after Halle had made it clear that she wasn't ready—might never be ready—to tell my family about us. I didn't know how to assuage her fears. I didn't know what more I could do to show her that I was here for her and Kai. Sometimes it felt as if no matter what I did, it would never be enough.

I thought about Halle and how she'd been touring houses.

Planning a future for herself and Kai—without me. It felt as if someone had shoved a dagger between my ribs.

Sloan placed her hand on my shoulder. "You sure you're okay?"

"Yeah. Of course."

"I'm sure the past four months without Graham and me haven't been easy on you, but I'm proud of you."

"Thanks." I rubbed the back of my neck. Sloan's praise was a relief, and I knew she wouldn't have said it unless she'd meant it.

"And I hope that having Halle by your side helped."

"I, uh—" I swallowed hard, eager to change topics. "It did."

We joined Jackson at the table, plating the food. He served my sister first before checking the video monitor resting on the table. I tried not to laugh because I understood what it was like to love a child. To worry about a child. To worry about Kai.

I accepted one of the dishes from Jackson. "This looks amazing. Thank you."

"Absolutely," Sloan said. "So…how was your date?"

My knife grated against the plate, and I cringed. "Date?"

"From the charity auction?" she asked.

"Oh, right." I laughed, though there was an edge to it. So much had happened in the past twenty-four hours, I'd almost forgotten all about my date with the woman from the charity auction. "It was fine."

"Any potential for something…more?"

I shoved a bite of food into my mouth and shook my head.

"Why not?" Sloan asked.

"*Hayati,*" Jackson chided. "Let the man enjoy his dinner in peace."

"Yes. Thank you, Jackson." I took a sip of my wine and gave my sister a pointed look.

"For all we know," Jackson said, "Jasper might have his eye on someone else." When he met my gaze, I tried not to squirm in my chair.

I cleared my throat, trying not to sweat. *Jesus.* The man was a damn Navy SEAL. *Former* Navy SEAL, but still. I certainly felt like I was being interrogated. I needed to change the subject—and fast.

"Think you'll make it to the Leatherbacks game?" I asked.

"We're hoping to," Sloan said.

We talked about the Leatherbacks' season, and I updated them on what had been going on at the company. After we'd cleared the dishes, I'd offered to help clean up, but Jackson insisted on doing it.

"I thought I was coming over to help," I teased Sloan. "You're the new parents, and you're feeding me. Taking care of everything."

"We're just happy to spend time with you. And we're fortunate enough that we can hire help when we need it. Having a night nurse has been a godsend."

My sister had a supportive partner and a night nurse. Who had been there for Halle when Kai woke up in the night? Who had she been able to rely on the past few years since her divorce? *Herself.*

She'd rebuilt her life. She'd supported herself and Kai. Raised Kai practically on her own. And was now financially responsible for her dad's care. There was no one else.

I knew what that was like—to have people relying on you. I had my family, the company, all our employees. But it wasn't all on me. I had support, resources, options.

Even if I was removed from my position as CEO by the board, I'd still have more than enough money to live on. When my family or I needed something, there was no question that we could afford it. But Halle was juggling...so much. All on her own. And she had been for a while now. I could imagine the pressure she felt from all of it.

And while I wished she'd let me help her, I respected her desire to do it on her own. Her independence and self-reliance. I'd never had to worry that I wouldn't have the money or the care I'd need for myself or my loved ones. And it was something she had to consider every day.

"Jasper?" Sloan asked, and I realized she'd been speaking.

"Sorry." I shook my head as if to clear it. "What was that?"

"You seem distracted tonight. Something's clearly bothering you."

I lifted a shoulder, hoping it came off as nonchalant.

"Come on, Jas." She gripped my shoulder, giving it a shake. "Talk to me."

I debated brushing off her concern, but I found myself wanting to talk about it. About Halle. I wouldn't use her name, of course. Especially not now, when I didn't even know where we stood. But I had to hold out hope that Halle would come around to the idea of telling my family. And that maybe this would lay the groundwork for eventually having that conversation with Sloan.

"I was seeing someone, and now…" I took a deep breath. "Now, I'm not sure where we stand."

She lit up. "You were?" I nodded, but then her expression sobered. "I'm sorry to hear that," Sloan said. "Sounds like it was serious."

"It was. *Is.*" I wasn't sure, but I didn't like the idea of talking about my relationship with Halle in the past tense.

I downed the rest of my glass of wine before pouring another.

For not the first time, I wondered how Sloan would react if she knew about my relationship with Halle. Would she feel betrayed? Or would she support our relationship when it came to the board?

Sloan cared about Halle. They were close friends. And I hated the idea of coming between them. I didn't want my relationship with Halle to affect her relationship with my sister or Halle's role in the company.

"I didn't even realize you were dating anyone, let alone that it was that serious. You're not going to pull a Graham on me and suddenly announce that you're married, right?"

I knew Sloan was teasing, but the idea of marriage to Halle was appealing. Continuing to keep our relationship a secret was not.

"Jasper?" Sloan's tone was weighted. "Seriously?"

"You know I enjoy a party too much to elope." I was teasing, mostly.

She laughed. "True. But…well, do you see the potential for that with this woman?"

I scrubbed a hand over my face, groaning. I wasn't even sure that was what Halle wanted. Let alone if it was in the cards for us, especially not after yesterday.

"Okay. I'm getting the sense that you don't want to talk about it," Sloan said. "But if you change your mind, I'm here."

I gave her hand a squeeze, appreciating her support. "Thank you."

"Of course." She squeezed my hand back, giving me a smile.

Evie cried but then resettled.

"Hey." She glanced over her shoulder. "Can we talk about work?"

I laughed. "Of course." I leaned in, lowering my voice. "Why are you being so secretive?"

"Because as much as I've loved being home with Evie, I am ready to get back to the office next week. Also, I know I haven't been as plugged in at the office lately, but it seems like the past few months have gone well," Sloan said.

I nodded. "They have. Things have run smoothly."

"That's a relief." She leaned forward. "What would you think about bringing Halle on permanently as SVP?"

I didn't have to even consider it. "I can't think of a person more qualified or deserving of the position than Halle. She's worked her ass off these past four months, and she's exceeded all expectations for the role."

"I'm not surprised. The potential has always been there, and now it's finally her time to shine."

I nodded. "I couldn't agree more."

I'd promised not to let my feelings for her affect her position with the company, and regardless of what happened between the two of us, she would make a great SVP. She deserved the position, and the company could benefit from her experience. I just didn't know what this would mean for us.

CHAPTER TWENTY-FIVE

HALLE

"So," Alexis said as we entered the backyard of a cute bungalow just as the sun was setting. "What do you think?"

We'd spent the day house hunting, and this one met all my criteria. It was in my price range. It was located in a good school district. And it didn't need too many repairs. On paper, it was a perfect fit. Yet something felt off.

I knew it wasn't the house but me. After my argument with Jasper, I couldn't stop thinking about the things he'd said.

Move in with me.

I thought we were building a life together.

All night, his words, the hurt in his eyes, had played through my mind on a loop. I toyed with my dragonfly necklace, my thoughts on him. On the things I'd said to him. I felt awful about it, especially after everything he'd done to love and support me.

"Halle?" Alexis asked. "Are you okay?"

"I—" I sank down on one of the outdoor lawn chairs to steady myself. "I—" I shook my head.

I hadn't slept well. I'd barely eaten all day. And I didn't know what to think or where Jasper and I went from here.

I didn't know how to fix this. And I desperately wanted to fix it.

Every time I closed my eyes, I pictured Jasper's face. The hurt when I'd blurted the stupidest words I could've said. *I can't give up everything I built for a man.*

I wished I could take it back. It wasn't how I felt.

Jasper wasn't asking me to give up everything. Deep down, I knew that. I knew that he'd been nothing but loving and supportive and patient.

God, had the man been patient. And I'd been so focused on our problems and my fears that I'd continually shut down his solutions. Worst of all, I'd hurt him. I'd made him feel as if I didn't want the same things as him, when I did.

I wanted to share a life together—holidays, families, all of it. But I'd freaked out. I'd said the worst possible thing. And now, I couldn't take back the words I'd said, even though I knew they were wrong. They didn't reflect how I felt about him or our relationship.

"Come on," Alexis said. "You look like you could use a drink, and there's a cute wine bar just down the street." She indicated that direction.

I nodded.

She held out her hand. I placed my hand in hers and stood.

"I don't want to keep you from your family," I said as she locked up.

"Sophia is spending the night at Brooklyn's. And Blair, Cecilia, and Preston are having a dadurday."

"Dadurday?" I laughed. "What's that?"

"Daddy-daughter Saturday," she said.

"Sounds fun. He seems like a really involved dad."

"He is." She smiled. "He always wanted to be a dad."

"My ex *thought* he always wanted to be a dad. But he really just wanted to say he was a father. He didn't want to do the work of being a parent. At least, not until more recently."

"Mm." She nodded. "Sounds a lot like my ex, Sophia's father. Though he's still not very involved."

"Oh. I didn't realize Preston wasn't…"

"He's been a father to Sophia in every way that matters," she said, running a hand through her hair. "But no. He's not her biological father. For many years, I was a single working mom like you. I thought I had to do it all, be it all. I loved my job, and I loved my daughter. But I was exhausted."

"Yes." I dropped my shoulders, feeling relief and acceptance. "I am exhausted."

And part of it was my own damn fault. Keeping this secret was exhausting.

She opened the door to the wine bar, and we headed inside, grabbing a table.

After we'd placed our orders, she leaned her arms on the table. "So…do you want to talk about it?"

I crossed and uncrossed my legs. I hadn't known Alexis very long, but I felt a kinship with her. Maybe it was the fact that we'd both been divorced single moms or that we were career-focused executives, but I'd always found it easy to talk to her.

Even so, I knew I had to tread very carefully. I trusted Alexis, but she was good friends with Jasper's cousin Nate. Emerson too.

"The short answer? I was scared, and I screwed up." I swiped away a tear, angry that I was crying in a restaurant.

Jasper and I loved each other, and the idea of not being with him was excruciating. But the idea of going public with our relationship was terrifying.

"It's hard to accept love again, especially after a toxic ex."

She'd told me a little about her ex in the past, so I knew she got it.

I nodded, raising my glass to toast. We clinked our glasses together.

"How did you get past your fears?" I asked, thinking she seemed so happy with Preston.

"I realized that Preston was worth the risk. I realized that my life was so much better with him, that I was so much happier and my daughter was too."

I nodded. "Kai adores the man I'm dating."

"That's a good sign," Alexis said. "Think about what you want, not just now, but in five years', ten years' time," Alexis said. "Do you picture a future with this man?"

I didn't even have to consider it. "Yes."

"But something's holding you back?" Alexis offered as the waiter delivered our food.

"Exactly." I nodded, relieved that she seemed to get me.

She leaned back in her chair. "And that something relates to what you think you screwed up?" When I nodded again, she asked, "Do you think it can be fixed?"

All this time, I'd felt as if I had to choose between my career and love. Between the life I'd built and the security I'd reclaimed and a relationship with an incredible man. But maybe I was looking at it all wrong.

"I—" I hesitated, utensils poised over my plate. "I mean, yes. I know what needs to be done, but I'm scared to take that next step." For my job. For Kai. For my heart. "When Craig and I divorced, I felt as if I were starting over from scratch. I rebuilt myself and my life, and I…" I shook my head. "I can't go through that again. I can't put Kai through that again." But it would be even worse this time.

If I'd grieved anything after my divorce, it was the loss of the future I'd expected. Not a future with Craig. Just…my future as I'd imagined it. But with Jasper, well, I'd be grieving the loss of him. Because I couldn't imagine my life—Kai's life —without him in it.

Jasper had been there for us—both of us—over and over. I couldn't imagine a better partner for me or a better influence for Kai. Was I really willing to give that up because I was scared about how our relationship would impact my job, not to mention his role in the company?

"Just because your first marriage ended doesn't mean this relationship will too."

She was right, but I'd already known that.

I thought about my relationship with Jasper and all the ways he'd shown up for Kai and me. He'd researched celiac disease and gluten-free diets, educating himself so he could be an advocate for Kai. But it was so much more than even that. It was the way he treated us. The way he was there for us—not just when life was fun and easy, but when it was difficult too.

He'd offer to help, but he also respected my boundaries. He stood at my side while I did things for myself. He was my rock.

It wasn't so much that I feared that I might have to give up my role at Huxley—though that was certainly a huge risk. But even if I kept my job, I worried that I'd lose people's respect. People would no longer see me for my own accomplishments; they might think I'd slept my way to the top. I cringed, but I also knew that I couldn't live my life for other people's approval.

My dad's diagnosis, all the things we'd dealt with since, was a stark reminder of that. There was nothing more important than time with loved ones. I saw how it pained my mom, watching the man she loved slip away. Jasper was here, and we could be together. Why would I let anything stand in the way of that?

Alexis placed her hand over mine, her rich brown eyes

swirling with compassion. "Having to start over isn't easy. It's especially terrifying for someone who values financial stability. That said, some of the best things in my life have come out of having to start over. And it's given me skills and confidence that I wouldn't have had otherwise."

Alexis made a good point. Starting over after my divorce had forced me to reevaluate what was important. It had made me realize that I could rely on myself. That I was strong and capable. I'd reinvented myself before, and I should remember that. I should let it instill me with strength instead of fear.

My divorce had been the end of that relationship but the beginning of my new life. A better life. One where I was true to myself.

I ran my dragonfly pendant along the chain. After Jasper had given it to me, I'd researched dragonflies and their meanings. Some cultures said that if a dragonfly landed on you, it meant *Don't resist change.* Or even, *welcome good fortune and embrace new beginnings.*

Technically, a dragonfly had landed on me and stayed with me. Maybe it was time for me to embrace a new beginning. A new mind-set, where I didn't dwell in fear but moved confidently in the direction of my dreams.

I knocked on the door to Jasper's penthouse, nervous energy coursing through me. I'd spent all night brainstorming different scenarios and solutions, rehearsing this conversation in my mind. Fortunately, my mom was still in town, and I was glad she and Kai were getting to spend some time together. Which meant I could fully devote myself to Jasper and the conversation we needed to have.

The door swung open, and Jasper stood there, as handsome as ever. His smile was hesitant and a little uncertain. We'd only been apart for less than forty-eight hours, and yet it felt like so much longer.

"Hey," Jasper said. "Come in."

Rosie's nails clicked against the floor, and I picked her up. I held her close, needing a little comfort and reassurance. "Thanks."

He closed the door behind me, but he didn't try to hug or kiss me. And his lack of affection made me nervous. Maybe he was holding back until he knew where we stood? Or maybe he really was ready to end things. I didn't want to believe that was the case, but he was certainly closed off.

"Can I get you something to drink?" he asked.

"Maybe just some water," I said, my anxiety growing with every passing second. "Thanks."

He went over to the kitchen and poured us each a glass of water. It all felt so formal, almost businesslike. He wasn't acting at all like himself, and I hated that I'd done this to us. That I'd made him question his role in my life and how important he was to me.

"I'm sorry," I blurted, hating that it wasn't more eloquent.

He straightened but said nothing.

"I'm sorry for what I said. It's not how I feel." I went over to him. "I need you to believe that. I need you to know that I love you, and I hate that I made you question how I feel about us."

"I'm not going to lie, Halle. I've had to question it for a while."

"I know." His honesty was like a punch to the gut, and I hated that I'd made him feel that way. "I do. And I'm sorry for that too."

Even though it was painful, I kept my gaze focused on his. Because I wanted him to know that I was sincere.

"I'm not used to being able to rely on anyone but myself.

Craig was never there for me in the way that I needed him, especially not when it came to Kai. For a long time—until you—my job has been the one thing I could count on. I've worked hard, and my career accomplishments are something I'm incredibly proud of."

"As you should be," he said.

"Thank you." I smiled, always appreciating his support. "But instead of letting my achievements give me confidence, I was more afraid of losing it all. Which is ridiculous. Because I am damn good at my job."

His smile was fond and full of love. "Yes, you are." And I knew he wasn't just saying that. He might be biased, but Jasper respected competence and excellence.

"I understand why you're scared," he said. "I get that you have your parents relying on you. Kai relying on you."

"I know you do. And that's a big part of why I love you." I'd needed to say it. Needed him to hear it. To feel it. "And while my love life should have no bearing on my job, I'm not naïve enough to believe that our relationship won't have an impact. But I'm willing to fight for both—for my job and for us. Because I earned my position, and I refuse to sacrifice it or the man I love."

"Fuck yes. There she is." He cupped my cheeks, his eyes swimming with pride. "That's my Halle." He swallowed roughly.

I smiled, full of love, appreciation, and relief. Jasper was my partner, my equal, in every sense of the word. I loved him, and I hated that he'd ever doubted that. But I promised myself that I would never let him question it again.

"I am yours," I said. "And I want everyone to know it."

"Damn right." He grinned. And then he kissed me—a homecoming, a promise. I wanted to get lost in him, to forget the past two days, to charge forward toward our future. A future filled with love and trust and hope.

But he pulled back, ending the kiss all too soon. "As happy as that makes me, I have to tell you something."

"Okay." I furrowed my brow.

He took a deep breath and smoothed a hand down his shirt. *Oh god.* I tried to brace myself for whatever he was going to say. Because I got the impression it wasn't good.

"Sloan wants to offer you the position of SVP permanently."

"What?" My knees wobbled.

"Congratulations, Halle." Jasper smiled, but it was tinged with sadness. We both knew this made our situation even more complicated. "You deserve the promotion, and it has my full support."

"Thank you," I said, my gears turning. I wanted to celebrate, but I was too focused on trying to formulate a new game plan. If anything, the promotion was further proof of the value I added to the company. So instead of being scared it would be taken away, I tried to focus on using it to prove our case to the board.

"I know I've been advocating to tell the board, but that was before the promotion came into play. Even if our relationship ultimately would have no impact on the board's decision, I don't like the perception of it. I don't want to give anyone a reason to question why you were promoted."

I knew Jasper was only trying to protect me, but all this time, all along, he'd put me first. It was time for me to put our relationship first.

"Neither do I. But my record speaks for itself. I earned this promotion." And I wasn't going to let anything stand in the way of my job or my relationship with Jasper. All along, he'd been willing to take the hit—to his reputation, to the company—despite how much was at stake for him as well. This wasn't just about me and my role in the company; our relationship affected Jasper too.

"We need to tell them," I said. "Before the vote." Because I'd hate for the board—or his family—to feel like we lied to them. Misled them. To lose faith in him as CEO. Or for this secret to impact his relationship with his family.

"You're sure about this?" he asked, searching my eyes.

"Certain," I said. There was no doubt in my mind. I draped my arms around his neck and kissed him. I loved this man, and I couldn't wait for everyone to know it.

CHAPTER TWENTY-SIX

JASPER

The Leatherbacks' stadium was buzzing with activity. The game was about to start, and Knox had packed the owner's suite with friends and family. All my siblings, minus Graham, were here. Their families. And some family friends like Alexis Black and Emerson's twin, Astrid.

Halle was deep in conversation with Emerson, and Kai had been hanging out with me. "I'm hungry."

"Let's grab some food." I placed my hand on his shoulder and steered him through the room toward the buffet.

"Can I have this?" He pointed at some sandwiches.

I skimmed the label. "See this." I pointed out the wheat symbol, indicating there was gluten. "This means it has gluten. So not this one."

He frowned. "But it looks *so* good."

"I know, bud. But you don't want to feel sick, do you?"

He shook his head vehemently. "No way. Nuh-uh."

"Okay." I ushered him farther down the table. "Let's see what we can find. It's important to always read the labels—"

"But I can't always read those long words."

"I know." I tried not to laugh. "But one day, you will. Until then, always ask for help. 'Kay?" After he nodded, I asked, "How about some tortilla chips?" I pointed to the sign. "No wheat symbol. And I think you'd like the queso."

"It's not spicy, is it?" He scrunched up his face. *Adorable.* God, I loved this kid.

"Tell you what." I put some chips and queso on my plate. "I'll try it first." I took a bite and confirmed it wasn't spicy.

We grabbed a few more items for his plate, then searched for empty seats to enjoy our food while we watched the game. Sloan waved us over, and we joined her and Nate.

The match started, and everyone's attention was glued to the field. The Leatherbacks were playing well, but the score was close. Come halftime, the Leatherbacks were in the lead, but they'd have to work to maintain it.

Kai yawned, leaned his head against me, and I was grateful Sloan was distracted by the action on the field.

"Can we have another sleepover tonight?" Kai asked, and I swear to god, my heart stopped.

I could feel Sloan's shock. It reverberated through me like a slap. But Nate was smirking, almost as if he'd known. I tried my best to ignore their reactions. Right now, Kai was my priority. Then, minimizing the fallout, if possible.

"Another sleepover?" I asked, keeping my voice low.

"Yeah. Like the night you slept on the couch when I was sick."

Oh. That. I let out the breath I'd been holding. Still not ideal, but definitely better than if Kai had seen me sneaking out of his mom's room as I did nearly every night.

"Probably not," I said, though I wanted to spend the night at Halle's more than anything. *One day. Soon.*

"When can we fly in your helicopter again?"

Jesus. This kid was going to be the death of me.

"You got to fly in Jasper's helicopter?" Sloan asked. Her tone might be casual, but I could sense the underlying tension in her words. *Fuck fucking fuck.* So much for mini-mizing the fallout.

"Yeah." Kai perked up. "Jasper took Mum and me to Legoland for my birthday."

"Wow," Nate said, eyes pinging between Sloan and Kai and me. "That was really nice of him."

"It was the best day ever!" Kai was growing more animated. "He got me a stuffed dog that looks just like Rosie. And we flew in the helicopter, and we rode on all the best rides."

My mind was spinning with how to do damage control. Nate continued to engage with Kai, but Sloan was eerily silent, watching me. Finally, Alexis's daughter Blair asked Kai if he wanted to play a game with her. He ran off, leaving me alone with Sloan and Nate.

"So…" I scanned the room, seeking an out. "I, uh—" I was at a loss for words. Because anything I would say was only going to make this worse.

Nate grinned. "Fucking finally."

I jerked my head back. "What?"

Sloan's attention whipped to him. "What does that mean? You knew?"

He lifted a shoulder. "Suspected."

I trusted that Pierce wouldn't tell anyone, but damn. Had Halle and I really been that obvious? Or was Nate just that perceptive? And if he'd suspected my relationship with Halle, had anyone else?

Sloan was deathly still, and I was bracing myself for her reaction. The suite erupted into cheers, and she blinked a few times as if only just remembering where we were.

She stood. "Come with me. Both of you. And where's Knox?"

Nate met my eyes and cringed. "I'll get Knox. We'll meet you in his office."

"And Halle," I said, trying to steel myself for the discussion ahead. "She needs to be a part of this conversation."

"I'll ask Em to keep an eye on Kai," Nate said before rushing off.

Sloan and I headed down the hall to Knox's office, the sounds of the game quieting the farther we got from the field. I couldn't get a read on her. Was she mad? Disappointed? Probably a bit of both.

I kept my gaze trained on the floor, a tight ball forming in my stomach. I hated it. Hated that I'd let her down. I was only reaffirming what everyone had always thought of me—I'd never be as good of a CEO as Graham. He'd always put the company first. And here I was, yet again, putting my desires before anything else.

"I'm sorry," I said, the words thick in my throat. My thoughts were spiraling, and I had to do something, say something, to dispel the growing tension. The last thing I'd wanted was to hurt Sloan. "I know you're friends with her—"

Sloan sliced a hand through the air. "I don't care about that."

I frowned. "You don't?"

"No." She laughed. "Actually, I think the two of you would be good together. And if it weren't for the fact that she works for Huxley, I'd be thrilled." I blinked a few times, and she dragged a hand through her hair. "But another scandal is the last thing we need."

I ducked my head. "I know."

I was relieved my sister wasn't upset about the fact that I was dating her friend. Sloan was more concerned about how this would impact the company.

"Ugh." Sloan shoved my shoulder as we entered Knox's office. "Why her? You know how hard it's been to find an SVP, and Halle's perfect for the role."

"She's *still* perfect for the role," I gritted out. I would not let our relationship jeopardize what Halle deserved. "And everyone knows it."

"Right, but…" Sloan's expression was sympathetic. "You can see how this might reflect poorly on both of you. Not to mention the company."

My gut twisted with guilt. "I know, and I'm sorry."

While we waited for the others to join us, she grabbed her phone and tapped on the screen.

I furrowed my brow. "What are you doing?"

"Calling Graham."

What? No.

I grabbed her phone, switching it off before she could connect the call. "Hey!"

I started pacing, Sloan's phone clutched firmly in my fist. I could only imagine what Graham would think when he found out. I tugged at my hair, imagining his disappointment. Or maybe…worse still. Maybe he wouldn't even be surprised. Maybe he'd expected something like this all along. Maybe everyone had.

Sloan placed her hand on my shoulder, and I flinched. "Jasper?" Her tone was soft, concerned.

I shook my head. "I'm not asking Graham to bail us out of a mess *I* made."

"Is that what you think?" Sloan asked, meeting my gaze. When I lifted my shoulder, she stepped closer. "Jasper," she chided, though there was no bite to her tone. "I'm not calling him for help. I'm calling to inform him. He needs to know, so we can present a united front to the board and in public. I know you can handle this, but we're a family. And you don't have to do it alone."

"I know," I said, toeing the carpet.

"Do you?" She arched one brow. "Because lately, it seems as if you've not only taken on Graham's former position within the company but also his determination to do every-thing yourself."

I opened my mouth to protest, to remind her that I hadn't had a choice—not with Graham leaving and her out on leave. But then the door swung open and Nate strode in. Halle was behind him, and I met her eyes, trying to reassure her. This wasn't what we'd planned, but it wasn't as bad as it could have been. Pierce came in next, then Knox, closing the door behind him.

Halle came to stand beside me, and I linked my pinkie with hers. I leaned in, our shoulders brushing, setting me at ease. "You okay?" I asked, keeping my voice low.

She nodded, whispering, "Are you?"

"Yes."

When I lifted my head, everyone was looking at us. Nate and Knox were wearing matching bemused smiles. Pierce's hands were in his pockets, his expression blank. And Sloan was studying us with a mixture of surprise, curiosity, and concern.

Halle took a deep breath and straightened. "I just wanted to say that I'm sorry. To all of you, but mostly—" she turned to my sister "—to Sloan."

Sloan shook her head. "You have nothing to apologize for. You have become an indispensable part of the company and a great friend to me. I think almost everyone in this room knows what it's like to fall for someone you shouldn't. And personally, I'm thrilled that Jasper's found happiness with you."

Halle released my pinkie and went over to Sloan. "Thank you."

They hugged, and something in my chest eased. I should've known that Sloan would be supportive, despite the less-than-ideal circumstances. She'd said as much. But seeing her now, with Halle, confirmed it.

Sloan was right; Graham should be a part of this conversation. What was decided would affect him as well.

I handed Sloan her phone. "Call him."

"Who?" Halle asked.

"Graham," I said.

Sloan's gaze met mine and held. A silent question. I inclined my head—a response. She tapped on the screen, and then the sound of a phone ringing pierced the air. After three rings, I'd resigned myself to the fact that we'd have to leave a message. But then Graham answered.

"Hello? Sloan?" he rasped, his voice deep from sleep. "Is everything okay?"

"Sorry to wake you," Sloan said. "But we have a bit of a situation here."

There was some shifting, and then next time he spoke, he sounded much more alert. "What kind of situation?"

"Jasper." Sloan turned to me. "Would you care to explain? Also, Graham, you're on speakerphone with…everyone."

"Who's everyone?" he asked in a gruff tone, so I listed off all our names.

Then I explained everything. How I was dating Halle. Why we needed to tell the board. The plan to promote her to SVP permanently. When I was done, everyone was silent.

"So what's your plan?" Graham finally asked.

I glanced around, wondering who would answer. Only to realize that everyone was looking to me. Waiting for me.

"Jasper?" Graham was the one to speak. "You're the head of the company. What's your plan?"

I blinked a few times, stunned. I'd expected Graham to start barking out orders, telling us exactly what was going to happen like he would've in the past. Instead, he was deferring to me. Not because it was my problem to solve, though that was certainly part of it. But because I was in charge, and my family was looking to me for solutions.

Sloan gave my arm a squeeze. When I looked at her, she mouthed, "You've got this."

Nate nodded. "You do. You always come up with creative and elegant solutions."

"We're here for you," Knox said. "Both of you." He looked at Halle.

All along, I'd doubted myself. I'd questioned whether I was fit to be the CEO. I'd convinced myself that I only held the position by default. That everyone was comparing me to Graham. But my family clearly believed in me. They had faith that I was up to the task.

Maybe I needed to stop second-guessing myself. I needed to stop focusing on the past and start looking toward the future. It was time to step up and be the leader that the company needed.

"You're sure you want to do this?" I asked Halle, rubbing my hands up and down her arms. I wasn't sure if I was doing it more to soothe her or myself. My chest felt tight, and none of my breathing exercises were doing a damn thing.

It was Sunday, the day after the Leatherbacks game, and I'd summoned the board for an emergency meeting. The other members would be filling the conference room, but Halle and I were cloistered in my office, soaking up these last few minutes before we disclosed our relationship to the board.

She placed her hands on my lapels, smoothing them down my suit. "I'm certain."

I let out a shaky exhale, my insides quivering. "How are you so calm right now?"

It felt as if everything was on the line. Her future. Our

future. That of the company. I had no idea how this would all play out, and that terrified me.

She lifted a shoulder. "Because as long as we're together, I know that everything will be okay."

"True," I said, letting that calm me.

"Plus—" She grinned, though it didn't quite reach her eyes. "We have your family's approval."

"Approval." I chuckled, tucking her hair behind her ear. "That's putting it mildly. You know they're thrilled, right?"

My family, Sloan, was already planning the next time we could all be together. I wouldn't have been surprised if they were planning our wedding. And I couldn't wait—for either event.

Halle and I hadn't discussed it, but I wanted to marry her. I knew she might have complicated feelings about marriage because of her divorce, but I was willing to wait. As long as we were together, that was all that mattered.

Halle smiled, a real smile this time. And I could see both relief and happiness reflected back at me. "Kai is too."

She'd told him yesterday, and he'd been ecstatic. He was currently hanging out with Brooklyn and Emerson, and I was sure he was having a blast.

Halle had also broken the news to Craig, and she'd said he'd been surprisingly supportive. Now, the only people we had left to convince were the board members. Somehow, I didn't think they'd be as overjoyed by the news.

I didn't even realize I'd started breathing more quickly until Halle placed her hand over my heart. I took a slow, deep, cleansing breath.

"What's one thing you hear?" she asked, and I smiled, reminded of that moment all those months ago when we'd been trapped in the stairwell. It felt like a lifetime ago.

I steadied my breathing and listened. Since it was a Sunday afternoon, the office was pretty quiet. "A helicopter." I smiled, eager to take Halle and Kai out for another adventure. After today, there would be no more sneaking around. We would no longer have to hide our relationship.

"What's one thing you smell?"

I dipped my head, inhaling her perfume. "Sunshine. *Home.*"

When I pulled back, she was smiling. She cupped my cheek. "What's one thing you feel?"

I leaned into her hand, comforted by her as always. "The warmth of your touch."

"What's one thing you taste?"

My eyes darted to her lips. Without hesitation, I leaned in and kissed her. "Your salted-caramel lip gloss."

She laughed, using her thumb to wipe at my mouth to remove the tinted gloss. "If we want them to take us seriously, you probably shouldn't show up to the meeting with my lipstick on your mouth."

I hated that I had to put Halle through this. I didn't give a fuck what the board thought about me, but I cared how it impacted her.

"Mm. What if my lips glistened for another reason?" I gathered her skirt in my hands, bunching up the fabric.

She shook her head, batting away my hands. "Absolutely not. We are not having sex right now."

"Why not?" I teased. "It wouldn't be the first time we had sex in my office. Plus, we're not likely to be caught."

She smoothed down her skirt. "Yeah, but now that we're going to come clean about our relationship, I don't want everyone thinking that's *all* we do in your office."

"Wait. So you're telling me that after today, we can't have office sex anymore?"

She planted her hands on her hips. "Of course not."

I wrapped my arms around her waist. "We'll see."

She rolled her eyes, but she was smiling the entire time. "No. We won't."

I chuckled, swaying with her in my arms. I loved this woman. I'd do anything for her.

"Are you going to finish the fifth sense?" I asked.

"I don't know. Are you calmer now?"

I gave my cock a pointed glance. "Does that look calm to you?"

"Jasper," she chided. I gave her a look, encouraging her to continue. "Fine," she huffed. I nearly laughed at her expression, but I knew better. "What's one thing you see?"

"The woman I love. The woman I want to spend my life with. Hopefully—" I gripped her hips, nerves coursing through me "—my future wife. If that's what you want," I added.

"I—" She swallowed, and I braced myself. I hadn't meant to tell her that now, but the words had slipped out unbidden. Even so, I couldn't say I regretted them. "Yes," she whispered.

"Yes?" I rested my forehead against hers. "That's a yes?"

No fucking way.

She nodded. "Yes, Jasper. Yes to everything with you."

I smiled, filled with hope and happiness. I couldn't believe it. I was still trying to wrap my head around it when my phone chimed, alerting me that the meeting was about to start.

"It's time."

CHAPTER TWENTY-SEVEN

HALLE

Jasper's words played through my head as we walked down the hall to the conference room. And even though I felt as if I were marching toward a firing squad, my heart was alight with happiness.

The woman I love. The woman I want to spend my life with.

That's what mattered—us, the future. Things might seem difficult or uncertain right now when it came to our jobs, but our relationship was solid. And that was what I had to hold in my heart when I felt nervous. Because I was definitely nervous about this meeting. What happened today would forever define our careers—his future, mine, that of the entire Huxley brand.

Stay calm.

I greeted a few of the board members as we entered, and then Jasper pulled out a chair for me. We were about to start when the door opened, and Graham strode into the room. I wasn't surprised Graham had shown up. And while, yes, he'd come to show a united front to the board, I also knew he'd really come all this way to support his brother.

There was a rustle of interest through the room as Jasper went over to hug him. The CEO didn't call a last-minute emergency meeting on a Sunday unless something big was going down. Graham's presence was further proof of that.

"Thank you all for coming, especially on such short notice," Jasper said, standing in the center of the room. He looked every bit the CEO that he was. And I knew he finally believed that.

Nervous energy coursed through me, though I tried to maintain a composed façade. This was it. There was no going back—not that I'd want to. We'd kept our relationship a secret for long enough. Too long.

"Taking over as CEO has not been an easy task, but I'm incredibly proud of the progress we've made these past months. We are a family company, and that's one of the things that's always set us apart in the luxury hotel industry. Yes, we deliver excellent service and unparalleled luxury, but at our heart, we are family owned and operated."

Jasper shifted on his feet. He'd spent all weekend working on his speech, wanting to get it just right. I observed the room, trying to gauge the temperature of everyone as Jasper continued speaking.

"My grandparents had a long and successful marriage and a thriving business. It's something I've always admired. Something I've always wanted for myself—a partner who was as invested in the success of this company as I am. Someone who complemented my skills but was a strong leader in her own right."

I inhaled slowly and let it out even more slowly. I knew what was coming next, and I was finally ready to face it.

Jasper turned to me, his smile warm. Encouraging. Full of love and trust. He was checking in with me. Giving me one last chance to back out, and I loved him even more for it.

I returned his smile, confident in our relationship but also in my own worth. I could see the pride radiating from him. It helped steady me, calm me.

"I've found that person," Jasper said, returning his attention to the room. "A partner in every sense of the word. A woman who is resilient and intelligent and so incredible. She adds so much to my life and to this company. Which is why I hope you'll continue to recognize her accomplishments just as you did when the board unanimously voted to temporarily promote her to SVP." He turned and held out his hand. "Halle."

There was a ripple of surprise at his announcement. I stood, my shoulders back, head lifted as I walked over to join Jasper. Standing by his side felt right, all the pieces of the puzzle clicking into place.

"Isn't that a violation of company policy?" someone asked, and I tried not to react visibly.

"Technically speaking," Leith said, "no. Though it is a potential conflict of interest. As the board, we will have to consider the implications for the brand and how it might reflect on the company."

"Halle and I are very aware of the potential ramifications," Jasper continued. "But we see this as an opportunity to remind the public of the fact that Huxley Grand is a family business. And we will always be a family business."

"No disrespect to your relationship," Leith said. "But, technically, Halle's not family. Not legally speaking. You aren't married."

"Not yet," Jasper said, smirking at the shock on his siblings' faces. He slid his hand into mine, his touch warm and reassuring. "I don't believe marriage or even blood makes a family, but Halle and I do want to marry in the future."

There was a murmur of agreement from the room, and I tried not to let myself be too hopeful.

"How is this going to look to our employees? To the public?" someone else asked.

"It all depends on how we spin it," Nate said. "You know that."

I could feel Jasper's excitement vibrating through him. *What was that about?*

"What if…" He looked at me when he spoke. "When we announced our relationship, we also announced a sweepstakes. One lucky couple would win the wedding of their dreams, hosted by the Huxley Grand. Second prize could be a honeymoon at one of our resorts. And third could be a night in the bridal suite."

I nodded, loving the idea. It reminded me of the bachelorx auction, and if the sweepstakes went half as well as that, it would definitely distract from news of our relationship. And as an added bonus, it would garner a lot of positive press.

Everyone seemed to perk up, and when I looked at Sloan, she was grinning. Nate gave Jasper a thumbs-up. Graham surveyed the room with a cool, detached stare. That was nothing new. Even so, the fact that he was here said everything. It was the first board meeting he'd attended in person since moving to France. And he was showing everyone—Jasper included—that he had faith in his brother.

"It could generate a lot of positive buzz," someone on the board said.

"While also downplaying the more problematic aspects of their relationship," said someone else.

I squeezed Jasper's hand, and I tried not to get too excited. Maybe this was actually going to work.

"It sounds like the board has a lot to consider," Leith said, and everyone quieted down. "Jasper, you will have to recuse yourself from any vote relating to this matter." We'd expected as much. "But before any decision is made, we will need more information."

I braced myself. I didn't want to answer questions about my personal life, about my relationship with Jasper. But I also wasn't surprised. I certainly would've had questions if I were on the board.

"You speak of marriage," Leith said to Jasper. "Which leads me to believe this relationship has been going on for a while."

Jasper and I, along with Pierce, had discussed this in depth. We didn't want to lie, but we also didn't want to give the board more reasons to distrust either of us.

"Halle and I have known each other for a while, and we've always enjoyed working together. We didn't want to bring this matter to the board until we were certain of our relationship."

"And are you?" Leith asked. "Certain?"

Jasper looked to me, and I said, "We are."

"It's easy to say that now, at the beginning of a relationship. But what if you break up?" another board member asked. "We've seen how messy divorces can be." She was referring to Knox and Nate, even if she didn't specifically mention them by name. "We don't want that disruption for the company."

"Neither do we," Jasper said.

"But you can't guarantee that your relationship won't have an impact on the company."

"No," I said. "But I think we've shown that we can successfully work together, regardless of our personal relationship."

Leith's expression was impassive, but then he turned to Jasper. "Were you in a relationship when you voted for Halle's temporary promotion to SVP?"

He shook his head. "No."

Leith leaned forward, resting his elbows on the table. "So the relationship began sometime after she transferred to LA?"

Jasper looked at me, and I sensed his hesitation. The fact that we'd been together before my move could both help and hinder our argument. Ultimately, I thought it was best to just put it all out there. Maybe the board would see it as an advantage.

Jasper shifted on his feet. "Not technically speaking, no."

"Technically speaking?" Leith frowned. "What does that mean?"

"We were…" Jasper cleared his throat, and I knew he was contemplating whether to even say the words.

"Intimate previously," I finished for him. I knew Leith was just trying to do his job, but it felt beyond invasive. "Before I moved to LA."

Leith arched one eyebrow. "Is that why you voted in support of Halle's transfer to LA?"

"No." Jasper's voice was strong, clear. "I voted for the transfer because Halle's excellent at her job."

"Right, but—" Leith steepled his fingers "—you can see why we might question your impartiality, considering your personal relationship, can't you?"

Jasper released my hand and stepped forward, fists clenched. "I would not let a personal relationship compromise what's best for the company. Not with my siblings. Nor with a romantic partner."

"Mm." Leith seemed skeptical, as did several other board members. Jasper's family was silent, unemotional but supportive.

"So explain the timeline to us," Leith said. "Because it sounds to me like this relationship has been going on longer than you initially let on. And…more concerning, you broke up at some point."

I tried to resist fiddling with my necklace. We'd been hoping to avoid this, but that now seemed impossible. Pierce had suggested that the board might be more sympathetic if some of the backstory came from me. He wanted to make sure that they saw me as a willing participant, not someone coerced into an affair with a superior.

"Last summer, when Jasper was in London during Sloan's annual sailing trip, we spent a lot of time together. I was going through a difficult time, and he was there for me." I swallowed hard at the memory. They didn't get to hear about my dad. "Things developed from there, but considering the distance and our positions, we decided to end things when he went home to LA."

This wasn't easy, but I could tell that Jasper was beyond proud of me. We were partners.

"When I transferred to LA—" I turned to look at Sloan "—I chose to do so because I love my job. Because I wanted to continue to support Sloan. But I also wanted to be closer to my parents, who live on the West Coast."

The board turned to Sloan. "Did you know about this?" Leith asked.

She shook her head. "I only found out about their relationship earlier this weekend. And I can attest to the fact that it has not negatively impacted their working relationship or the company."

"But you were out on maternity leave," someone said. "How would you even know?"

Sloan squared her shoulders. *Oh boy. She was pissed now.* I tried not to laugh because that board member had clearly underestimated Sloan.

"I may not have been in the office, but I kept a close eye on things. The numbers for the past quarter will show you that the company is doing better than ever. But even more than that, I can see how Jasper and the company have thrived, even in my absence. Not to mention the fact that he took on this new role without a second SVP and while Graham was developing the new Fleur-de-lis line."

There were murmurs of agreement. But I knew this was far from over.

"I think it would be best if we speak to each of you alone," Leith said, addressing Jasper and me. "Jasper, could you please leave us?"

Jasper looked to me, seeking confirmation that I was okay. Only after I nodded did he head for the door. He lingered at the threshold, and I could only imagine how strange it was for him to walk out of a meeting that impacted him and his company.

"Halle," Leith said once the door was closed. "First of all, I want to make sure you're comfortable. I know this isn't an easy topic to discuss, and as much as we respect your privacy, there are certain questions I am required to ask."

I nodded. While I appreciated the sentiment, I was filled with unease. I wasn't sure there was any way to make this conversation *less* comfortable. Pierce had spoken with me over the weekend, coaching me on what might be asked and how I might answer. But it still hadn't prepared me for the reality of talking about my love life in a room full of people I worked for or answered to. Not to mention the fact that Jasper's family was present. *Oh god.*

"I think it would be best to start by asking the family to choose one representative to remain."

I shook my head. "It's fine."

"We don't want you to feel intimidated by their presence."

"I'm not." Besides, they already knew pretty much everything. That conversation had been uncomfortable but necessary. Much like I anticipated this would be.

"Then, if everyone is in agreement—" Leith glanced around the room, confirming everyone's position "—I will proceed."

Since no one dissented, it was time to begin.

"Halle, Jasper is your superior at work. It is understandable that you might feel a power imbalance. Did he ever pressure you to do something you weren't comfortable with?"

"No." I stated it firmly, clearly. "If anything, I am the one who instigated our relationship."

They pressed me on that, and god, was it embarrassing to admit what had happened in front of everyone. Especially my boss, Jasper's sister, and his entire family. But Leith kept pressing, digging into the timeline, the circumstances. How we'd gotten together. How we'd ended things. *Why* we'd ended things.

And then what had happened since. The timeline of events since I'd relocated. If I'd relocated with the intent of resuming my relationship with Jasper. On and on it went. It was exhausting, but I tried to remain calm and cool throughout.

"Have you ever sought to use your influence over him to advance your career?" Leith asked.

"No," I said again. "I know it may not seem like it, considering the reason for this meeting, but professionalism matters to me. This job and this company matter to me. And I would never intentionally do anything to compromise that."

There were some muffled whispers, and I tried to ignore them. Ignore the doubters. The haters. I knew the truth of what had happened, and I tried to keep my head held high. I had nothing to be ashamed of.

"Do you feel that your relationship with Jasper played a role in your temporary promotion?"

Sloan opened her mouth, as if to object, but then

stopped when Graham placed a hand on her arm. I appreci-ated that she wanted to defend me, even if it was unnecessary.

"I'd like to think that my temporary promotion was a recognition of the value I bring to this company and everyone's faith in me to perform the role. I've been with the company for five years," I continued. "And in that time, I've successfully driven strategic initiatives, cross-functional collaboration, and enhanced executive effectiveness. During my time as SVP, I've been able to leverage those skills to provide even more value to the brand. So, no, I don't think my relationship with Jasper played a role in my temporary promotion. And I believe my success as a temporary SVP shows that."

"Why did you not come forward sooner to declare your relationship?"

"Because I was scared."

"Of Jasper?"

I nearly laughed aloud at the suggestion. "Of how it would be perceived. How it would impact the company."

"Not to mention how it might impact your job."

"That too." There was no point denying it. "I've worked hard to get to where I am. And I don't think I should be punished for falling in love."

"Can you think of a time that your professional integrity was compromised by your personal relationship with Jasper?"

I rolled my lips between my teeth. I could think of a few times that we'd been reckless. Sex in Jasper's office, to name one. But not when it came to making decisions that affected the company.

If I disagreed with Jasper, I let him know. And he respected me for it. He encouraged it.

"No. If anything, I feel more invested than ever in the

Huxley brand. I know how passionate and dedicated Jasper is to the company, and he inspires me on a daily basis."

Sloan stood. "And that is exactly why I'd like to move that Halle be promoted to SVP permanently. She handled the role with ease while I was out on maternity leave, and she's been ready for this position for even longer. She deserves to be recognized for her contributions to the company. And we need someone in the role we can count on. Halle is that person."

I... Wow. I was honored that she thought I was ready to take on such a big role in the company permanently. And it was reassuring that she still felt so strongly about it, despite the fact that I'd been dating her brother—the CEO—in secret for all these months.

"Seconded," Graham said.

Leith cleared his throat, his eyebrows twitching. "First, the board needs to vote on whether there was a conflict of interest. And if so, what action should be taken. Then we can approach any other matters, based on the outcome."

Sloan inclined her head, and my stomach lurched, threatening to expel my meager breakfast.

Leith turned back to me. "Were you aware that you were being considered for a permanent promotion as SVP?"

"Not until more recently," I said. "Though it makes sense that Sloan would use the temporary promotion as a trial run."

"You've given us a lot to consider," Leith said. "Halle, could you please step out while we deliberate?"

I excused myself, heading back down the hall toward Jasper's office. The door was open, and I knocked on the frame. "Hey."

"Hey." He glanced up from his desk. "How'd it go?"

I shut the door behind me. "About as well as expected."

I gave him a quick rundown. All morning, I'd tried to

remain calm. But I was officially freaking out. I stood and started pacing along the windows in Jasper's office.

"Halle," Jasper said, coming over to me. "It's going to be okay, love."

"Is it?" I felt incredibly exposed and vulnerable now that the truth of our relationship was out there. It was freeing in a way, but I also felt as if I was in a free fall. I wasn't sure where I'd land or if I'd even survive the drop.

"Give me your hand," he said, and I placed my hand in his. He rubbed the bare spot on my left ring finger, and I knew he was thinking about marriage. About our future.

No matter what happened today, our relationship would survive. And I had faith that, together, we could overcome any obstacle.

He slid his fingers down to my wrist, clasping it lightly as he tilted my hand so my fingers were pointed toward the ceiling. "Breathe in." He traced the outside of my pinkie finger, and I couldn't help but smile.

"Good," he coaxed in a soothing tone. "Now, breathe out," he said after cresting the tip of my pinkie finger.

"In." He traced up the side of my ring finger, and I could feel some of the tension easing from my body. "Then out."

He continued the exercise until he'd finished tracing all the fingers of my left hand. Finally, slowly, he lifted my hand to his mouth to kiss each and every one of my fingertips. The entire time, his eyes remained locked on mine. In that moment, I forgot about everything else. It was just the two of us.

"I love you."

He smiled. "I love you, Halle."

He pulled me to his chest, holding me close. I wrapped my arms around Jasper and just let him hold me. I listened to the beat of his heart, steady and reassuring. Even when everything else felt out of control, he was always there—a calm, solid presence.

When he pulled back, it was only to cup my cheeks. His hazel eyes were filled with such love and tenderness that it stole my breath. He leaned in to kiss me, and just as our lips were about to meet, there was a knock at the door.

I jolted, springing back from him as if I'd been shocked. He chuckled, going over to the door to answer it. One of the board members was standing in the hallway.

"The board would like for you to return." *So formal.*

Apparently, I wasn't the only one on edge. And now that their decision seemed imminent, any small bit of calmness I'd had vanished.

Jasper held open the door and turned back to me. "Halle?"

I nodded, brushing past him as I walked through the doorway. He placed his hand on my lower back, and we didn't speak as we headed back to the conference room.

When we entered the room, I couldn't get a read on anyone. The air was charged with unspoken tension, and it felt as if we were witnessing the aftermath of an intense thunderstorm.

"Please," Leith said. "Take a seat."

Jasper held out a chair for me before sitting next to me. If he was nervous, he was doing a damn good job of not showing it. I straightened, lifting my chin and trying to let his confidence infuse me with courage I didn't feel.

Leith shuffled some papers on the table, and my blood pressure ratcheted up a notch.

"Thank you for coming forward with this matter. This is a big decision and not something we take lightly. With that in mind, the board would like more time to determine whether your relationship is a conflict of interest. For now, we are tabling the question of promoting Halle to SVP permanently.

And we think it would be best if Halle takes a leave of absence."

What? My vision spun, and I gripped the table for support.

Jasper jolted upright. "No. Absolutely not."

I tugged on his wrist, knowing that we needed to keep a clear head. Getting emotional wasn't going to help the argument that we were professional and impartial. Nor would it improve relations with the board.

"Does this proposed leave of absence relate in any way to my performance, or is it purely for optics?" I asked.

"What do you think?" Jasper asked, clearly annoyed, though I knew his ire wasn't directed at me. "It's a punishment. But if they're going to punish you, they should also punish me."

Leith peered at him over the top of his glasses. "Would you prefer that we put you on a leave of absence?"

"I'd like to see you try. This is bullshit, and you know it," Jasper said, growing more agitated.

"What's bullshit," Leith said, a bite to his tone, "is that you had an inappropriate relationship with an employee and now you want to promote her to the second-highest position in the company."

"No," Jasper gritted out, his anger scarcely contained. "Everyone knows the chief of staff position is a springboard, intentionally designed to be temporary. The temporary promotion showed what we already knew—Halle is ready to transition to an executive leadership role. Besides, I'm not the one who advocated for her temporary or permanent promotion. That was Halle's direct supervisor—the person best positioned to know Halle's skills and the role that would suit her."

"Semantics," Leith bit back. "Halle's direct supervisor is your sister. It's not a good look."

Jasper shook his head, his nostrils flaring. "We are a family company. Of course my siblings are going to weigh in. That's why my grandparents put us in charge."

"It's also why they created a board of directors," Leith countered. "To settle any disputes. To keep things running smoothly."

As much as I wanted to jump in and speak, I knew I needed to sit back and let Jasper handle this. If I butted in, I risked looking like I controlled him or was trying to control the company through him.

Jasper huffed. "Putting Halle on a leave of absence makes it look like she did something wrong."

"It's a paid leave of absence," Leith said. "To give the board time to deliberate."

"She might as well leave the company if you're going to do that. It would be better for her future career prospects."

"She's free to do that if she so chooses."

Well, that was disappointing. Were they really willing to let me go so easily?

Jasper shook his head. "This is wrong, and you know it. It's an insult to Halle and everything she's done for the brand. And it's the opposite of what the company needs."

"You're not the only one responsible for deciding what the company needs. And it wasn't until the past year or so that you actually seemed to give a damn about anything more than partying and having fun."

I cringed.

Jasper's fist landed on the table. "I have always cared about the brand. Its employees. Its standards. Our guests. I haven't been CEO for long, but the Huxley is in my blood. My grandparents founded this company, and I am positive they would not agree with what you're suggesting."

"They elected to have a board of directors for a reason. And this scenario definitely qualifies as one of those reasons.

Even if you wanted to override the board—which I would not advise—you lack the necessary votes."

"I wouldn't be so sure about that," Jasper said.

I was silently cheering him on, while also filled with a growing sense of unease. We'd hoped the board would be supportive, but I worried how far Jasper would take this. I worried the board might become resentful or cause trouble in the future based on how this situation was handled.

But I also knew that Jasper needed to stand his ground with the board. Relations so far had been cordial, but he was right to assert his dominance. It was time for Jasper to become the leader he was always meant to be.

Leith was halfway standing out of his chair. "You cannot simply ignore the board's decisions because you don't like them."

Jasper looked to Pierce. What was going on?

Pierce spoke next. "In the event that a member of the family who is on the board is recused from voting, they can designate someone to vote by proxy for them."

"Yes." Leith's tone conveyed boredom. Impatience. I'd never had a problem with him until now. "But the proxy also has to be a blood relative of the founders. And no single blood relative can vote for more than their individual share." Meaning Knox, Nate, Sloan, and Graham were ineligible.

"I'd like to designate my proxy," Jasper said, undaunted.

"Who? Nate's daughter, Brooklyn?" Leith's tone was incredulous. "She's not old enough. Even if she were, she's not your direct descendant. Jude is also ineligible for that reason. Since you have no children, it has to be someone at your level or above."

"Correct. And I have someone who qualifies," Jasper said.

There were murmurs around the room. We hadn't discussed this, and I was racking my brain, trying to figure out who could serve as Jasper's proxy, considering the stipulations. His parents were deceased. He had no children. And all his siblings were present and not allowed to vote beyond their shares.

The door swung open, and I blinked a few times, surprised to see the person standing there.

"Members of the board." Jasper grinned. "I'd like to introduce my sister. Well, if you want to get technical about it, she's my half sister." He went over to her, giving her a hug. "Tabitha."

CHAPTER TWENTY-EIGHT

HALLE

"To Tabitha," Jasper said that evening, raising his glass for a toast.

Jasper's surprise sibling dipped her head. I studied Tabitha again, thinking of all the times she'd served us on the private jet. Now that I knew she was Jasper's half sister, I had so many questions. Had she known she was their half sibling all along? When had Jasper and the others found out? And how? *Gah!*

Now wasn't the time. It was a time for celebration. For family.

After the board meeting, we'd all come up to Jasper's penthouse to celebrate. Everyone was there—Graham and his wife, Lily. Nate, Emerson, and Brooklyn. Knox, Kendall, and Leo. Jackson, Sloan, and Evie. Jasper, Kai, Rosie, and me.

Jasper held up his champagne flute again. "And to Pierce, of course. Thank you both for saving the day."

Pierce seemed unfazed. But Tabitha was clearly still adjusting to her new role within the family. I could relate. Like Tabitha, I'd been employed by their family. Well, fortunately, I was still their employee. But now, I was also part of the family. They'd welcomed me with open arms, even Graham, which had surprised me. He'd always come off as so…brooding and grumpy. But he was actually quite warm once you got to know him.

Sloan came over to me, knocking her shoulder against mine. "I just wanted to say how happy I am everything worked out like it should've."

I nodded, unable to hold back my smile. "Thank you. And thank you for believing in me."

"I always knew you were meant for bigger things. I'm excited we'll get to work together as SVPs."

"Me too," I said, though I knew we'd still have some logistics to sort out. Like who would be my supervisor—not Jasper, obviously. But also, what specifically I'd oversee. "I just hope you won't get sick of me now that we'll not only be working together, but I'm also dating your brother."

She laughed, giving me a side hug. "I'm pretty sure that'll never happen. And I'm thrilled you and Jasper are together. I've never seen him as happy as he is now."

I glanced over to where Jasper was standing with Knox and Graham. Sloan was right. Jasper seemed lighter than he had in months. He was exactly where he was meant to be.

Nate and Tabitha headed over to join them, Sloan going by some unspoken agreement. I hung back, letting them have their moment. I couldn't imagine what it was like to suddenly discover you had a sibling. I assumed everyone had a lot of questions, a lot of catching up to do.

They talked for a while, and when Jackson walked over to Sloan with Evie for a feeding, I went to stand with Jasper.

"Good job today," Graham said, hugging Jasper. I knew Graham didn't say those words lightly, and it meant a lot to Jasper.

"Good job making enemies on the board?" Jasper joked.

"You did what you had to for the company," Graham said.

"Sometimes that means doing the wrong thing for the right reasons." He and Lily shared a secret smile. "And sometimes, making enemies is part of the job."

"Like Moretti," Lily said in a teasing tone.

Graham gnashed his teeth at the mention of the industry rival. And then he wrapped his arm around Lily and whispered something in her ear. She blushed, and I wondered what that was about.

"You did what needed to be done," Knox said, clinking his glass against Jasper's. "And you showed them you won't back down from a fight."

"Brilliant idea with the sweepstakes," Nate said, joining us.

"Thanks," Jasper said, and I could tell he wasn't used to receiving praise for his accomplishments instead of attention for his alleged escapades. It was nice to see that his family was recognizing his hard work and the fact that he'd changed.

After that, conversation turned to other matters. We celebrated until long after the sun had set. It didn't matter that we had work tomorrow; it wasn't often that Jasper's family was all together these days. And we all had a lot to be grateful for.

I'd been named as SVP permanently. With Tabitha acting as Jasper's proxy, the family had been able to secure the necessary majority to force a vote on the matter. A number of the non-family board members had admitted that they were more concerned about the perception of bias based on my relationship with Jasper rather than an actual belief that my SVP promotion was unwarranted. Ultimately, most of them had voted in favor. And we were moving forward with the sweepstakes. But most importantly, Jasper and I no longer had to hide our relationship.

"Well, that was wild," I said to Jasper when we climbed into bed later that night.

Kai had been so wound up that it had been hard to get him to go to sleep. It was late, and I didn't want to think about how tired he was going to be in the morning when I had to get him up for school.

Jasper slid between the sheets. "All's well that ends well."

"I suppose so," I said, joining him.

He immediately pulled me into his arms. "I hope you're okay with how things went down. I'd never want you to question whether you deserve to be SVP."

"Honestly…" I smoothed my hand over his chest, his warmth soaking into me. "I don't. I know I earned that role, and I'm pretty sure everyone knows it. Not just the board, but the employees too."

"They do." Jasper brushed my hair away from my face, smoothing it down over my shoulder. "The board wanted to punish us, punish me, and what they tried to do by putting you on leave was wrong." His body was tense, so I snuggled in closer. "There might be some drama in the short-term, but everyone will forget about it."

"I'm not sure the board will so easily forget about it," I said. "Pretty sure no one saw the secret sister coming. Even me."

A low chuckle rumbled through his chest. "I'm sorry for not warning you about Tabitha. I'm still reeling from the fact that she's my half sister."

"How long have you known?"

"I found out yesterday when Pierce mentioned the idea of using her as my proxy as a sort of Hail Mary. But I wasn't sure if we could even pull it off. Honestly, I was hoping we wouldn't have to."

"Wait." I pushed up so I could see his face. "You didn't

know you had a half sister until yesterday?" Jasper shook his head. "Did anyone know?"

"Pierce."

"None of your siblings, though?"

He shook his head. "Pretty unbelievable, right? We've had this secret half sibling all along, and none of us had any idea."

"She's younger than you, right?" I asked.

"Younger than Sloan too."

I shook my head, still trying to make sense of it all. "So how did Pierce know Tabitha was related to you? And how long has Tabitha known?"

"Apparently, Tabitha's dad needed a kidney transplant last year. She didn't know that he wasn't her biological dad, so when she offered to be tested for a match, the truth came out. Tabitha's mom told her that she'd had an affair with my dad before she'd met the man who'd raised Tabitha. And eventually, Tabitha confessed the truth to Pierce."

"Why Pierce?" I asked.

"That part wasn't clear to me, but I guess maybe because she knew he was our lawyer?"

"Wow. So she's probably just as surprised as all of you were." After he nodded, I asked, "What about you? How do you feel about it?"

"I think we're all a bit stunned. I'm definitely still processing everything, but on the whole, I'm happy. I could be upset that my dad had an affair, but he's been gone for so long. And when you've lost so many people you love, it seems like a blessing to find out that there are more of us."

I smiled, brushing my lips against his. "You are incredible."

He slid his hand around the back of my neck so he was cupping my skin. "So are you."

And then he kissed me again, deeply and full of passion. When he pulled me on top of him, I groaned. He felt so good, and as we writhed against each other, shedding clothes and whispering promises of love, the future had never seemed brighter.

∾

Several Months Later

JASPER AND I GRABBED SOME DRINKS AND HEADED OUT TO enjoy a quiet evening on our back patio as we so often did. It was one of my favorite things about our new home. A tiled patio, large grassy lawn, and a pool that had already been the source of so many fun memories.

Jasper settled on the lounge chair first, then I sat in front of him, leaning back so I was resting against his chest. My birthday was coming up, but I already had everything I could ever want.

We chatted about recent events, about life. It was one of my favorite parts of my day—this ritual we'd developed in the evening. It was nice to wind down and reconnect.

I heard a buzzing noise, and I frowned. "Do you hear that?"

"Hear what?" Jasper whispered against the shell of my ear. I shivered.

I sat up, straightening. "It sounds like..." I looked to the sky, but I couldn't see anything. "It sounds like a bunch of bees."

The sound was faint but distinctive. I stood, trying to determine the source. But then the sky lit up with colorful dots, and I realized it was a flock of drones.

They hovered above us and moved into a series of elaborate formations that were both impressive and beautiful. *What on earth?*

I glanced back at Jasper, but he didn't seem surprised. If anything, he was watching me intently. What was he up to?

The drones moved again, spelling out my name. *Halle.*

They were choreographed to transform into a heart that cycled through a number of colors. It was beautiful and mesmerizing, like looking into a kaleidoscope. And then in a scripty font, the words, "Will you marry me?" appeared. This time when I turned to Jasper, he was kneeling. My eyes widened.

"Halle." He could barely speak, his voice was clogged with emotion. "I love you and Kai, and I want to spend the rest of my life with you. I know we don't need a ring or a certificate to make us a family, but I want to be your husband. Please say yes. Say you'll marry me."

I didn't even have to think about it. "Yes! Absolutely. I love you, and I want that too."

He removed a box from his pocket and held up a ring. It was a gorgeous sapphire-and-diamond cluster ring that had to be vintage. It was unique, and I absolutely loved it. But I loved the man holding it even more.

"This was my grandmother's ring." He slid the ring onto my finger, and it was a perfect fit. "She left it to me with a note. She told me that I would know when I met the right woman to wear it. And she was right. Because the only person I could ever imagine wearing it is you."

I swiped away a tear. "You—" I cupped his cheeks "—are everything I never knew I wanted. I didn't think I'd ever want to get married again, and yet, I can't wait to be your wife. I see how much you love Kai, and it makes me fall even more in love with you."

He tilted his head, a tear tracing its way down his cheek. I swiped it away with my thumb. "I love you, and I'm so grateful you were brave enough to give us a chance."

"Was there ever any other choice?" I teased, and now I

was crying. I was full of so much love and gratitude and hope. This man and the life we were building together was… everything. And I couldn't wait to see what the future held.

The next morning, I was exhausted but satisfied. More than satisfied. Jasper always made sure I came first and often, and last night had been no exception. But there was something about being engaged that seemed to bring out the primal caveman in him. My fiancé had been ravenous. *Fiancé.* I stared down at my ring with a smile.

I'd arrived at the private airport just in time for the family jet to land. Jasper had asked if I could pick up Graham and Lily from the airport. It seemed like a strange request since they usually preferred to have their bodyguard drive them when they were in town, but I didn't question it.

When the door of the plane opened, the first person to descend the stars wasn't Lily or Graham. It was Zara.

Wait. What?

I shielded my eyes from the sun. "Oh my god. Zara?"

Zara had been talking about visiting for a while, but I'd had no idea she was flying in for my birthday. I wondered how long she and Jasper had been planning this surprise.

Zara practically ran down the steps from the airplane to where I was waiting on the tarmac. We hugged, and it felt like it had been so much longer than eight months since we'd last seen each other. I'd missed her. Texting and phone calls weren't enough, but I was glad she was here now.

"How was your flight?" I asked, still shocked by her appearance. "I can't believe you're actually here. I thought you had a work conference."

She smirked. "I would never miss my best friend's birthday, but Jasper and I wanted it to be a surprise. So, I had to come up with something to throw you off."

"Oh no." I groaned, though we both knew it was in jest.

"The two of you working against me. Should I be scared?" And how had he even gotten her number?

I was too happy to even care. I lifted my hand to swipe away a happy tear when Zara stilled. "Also, congratulations." She gestured to my engagement ring.

"Why do you not sound surprised?" I asked.

"Jasper *may* have asked for my opinion on engagement rings." She grabbed my left hand, holding it out to admire my ring. "Damn, babes. This is even more gorgeous in person than any of the pictures he sent."

"He sent pictures?" How long had he been planning this?

"Of this and a few, more modern rings. He thought you'd like the history and significance of wearing his grandmother's ring, and I agreed."

The light caught the facets, making the diamond sparkle even more. I couldn't imagine loving a ring more. "You were right."

"When did he propose?"

I bit back a smile, thinking back to the magical evening he'd created. "Last night."

"I'm so excited for you." She hugged me again. "I want to hear all about it on the way back to the house."

The rest of the crew descended the steps of the plane, including the new flight attendant the Hartwell Agency had sent over since Tabitha was no longer in the position. Jasper had invited her to join the family business and learn more about the Huxley Grand empire.

"Did you fly with Graham and Lily?"

She shook her head. "Just me."

I laughed. "Very sneaky."

We put her luggage in the trunk and then climbed into the car. During the drive back to the house, I told her the story of the engagement. She thought the drones were both cute and unique, and I couldn't agree more.

"Does Kai know?" she asked.

"Not yet. Jasper's family doesn't either, but we're planning to tell everyone at my birthday party."

"How do you think Kai will take the news?"

I smiled, imagining his reaction. "He'll be thrilled."

"Good. I'm so glad Kai is doing well with the move and everything," she said. "I know you were worried about it, but everything really seems to have worked out for the best."

"It does," I said. "He loves Jasper, and Craig's house is less than twenty minutes away."

She checked her makeup in the mirror, reapplying her lipstick. "I still can't believe Craig moved here."

"I know. Sometimes I can't believe it either, but he loves it. He's totally embraced the LA lifestyle."

She furrowed her brow. "Meaning…"

I laughed. "You'll have to see for yourself. He's coming to the party."

I could feel her eyes on me. "So you guys are friends now?"

"Yeah." I smiled, turning on my indicator. "We kind of are. And I can't wait for you to meet the rest of Jasper's family. You're going to love Kendall and Emerson. And my LA friends—Alexis, Lauren, and Juliana. She planned the party, and she has an amazing menu that's entirely gluten-free. The cake is to die for."

Life was so much better now that we knew Kai had celiac disease. While some people might dread such a diagnosis, I was grateful. Because it had finally given me answers. More than that, Kai felt so much better. He was like a completely different kid.

"I'm looking forward to it. You've told me so much about them, I feel as if I already know them. When does your mom fly in?" Zara asked.

"Tomorrow night."

"That's right. And your dad? It sounded like your last visit went well."

I nodded. "He still has good days and bad days, but I'm always grateful to spend time with him. Jasper has made sure that we see them at least once a month, if not more."

She sighed. "Ah. The perks of dating a billionaire."

I laughed. "Something like that."

"And you're sure all his brothers are happily married?" she teased, though she already knew the answer. "He doesn't have a secret half brother somewhere, does he?"

"No, but they have a good friend who's practically a brother," I said, thinking of Pierce.

"Is he single?" she asked. When I nodded, she added, "Is he a billionaire too?"

"No. Well…" I hedged. Pierce might not be a billionaire, but I got the feeling he had money. "Anyway, I'm kind of wondering if there's something going on between him and Tabitha."

"Ooh, really? Why do you think that?" Zara asked.

I lifted my shoulder as we turned onto our street. "I don't know. Just a feeling."

I couldn't put my finger on the reason, but I'd seen the way they reacted to each other at the past few family gatherings. I sensed there was some tension between them.

"Mm." She hummed. "Interesting."

I pressed the button on the remote, waving to our security guard, Tim, as the gate swung open to reveal the tree-lined drive. It was a view that would never get old. It didn't matter how many months we'd lived here; I was still in awe that this was my home. The limestone façade struck the perfect balance of modern and traditional, with the clay tile roof giving a nod to its Californian roots. But it was the inside that I loved most because it felt like home. Cozy and chic and effortless. Alexis had nailed it.

"Blimey, babes," Zara said as we pulled up to the house. "Is that guy always at the gate?"

"Usually. But if not Tim, then someone else." Jasper had insisted on hiring Hudson Security. If it gave him peace of mind, who was I to disagree?

"This place is even more gorgeous in person," Zara said.

"Thanks." We got out of the car, and I grabbed her suitcase from the trunk. "Come on. Kai can't wait to see you."

She marveled at the entryway. "This is incredible. All the artwork." Zara shook her head, holding a hand to her mouth. "Halle."

"I know." I smiled.

"Did you pick all of these?"

I bit back a smile. "Perks of dating a billionaire," I joked.

Unfortunately, the painting I'd loved all those months ago when Jasper and I had gone to view Dimitri's collection was gone. Sold. I hoped whoever had purchased it appreciated it.

Zara nudged me. "That's what did it, huh? He got you with that unlimited art budget?"

"No, but he does spoil me." And not just with material things. Jasper spoiled me with affection and attention. He was my biggest cheerleader and champion, and he was amazing with Kai. He'd been exactly what we'd both needed.

"Good." Zara wrapped her arm around my waist and gave me a hug. "You deserve to be spoiled. How's work?"

"Good," I said. "The sweepstakes ends soon, and I can't wait to see the winners' reactions."

The sweepstakes had been a huge hit. Everyone was buzzing about it. We'd even hired a production company to film the winners and the prizes.

Thanks to the popularity of the competition, the board had been much more amenable when it came to Jasper's ideas since then. And I'd been enjoying my new role as SVP more than I'd even expected. Running the company with

Sloan and Jasper was a dream come true. Graham chimed in when necessary, but he seemed to be more than happy to take a supporting role to the three of us.

"Come on," I said. "Kai's probably out in the pool with Jasper."

After grabbing some drinks, we headed out to the backyard. Where, as I'd guessed, we found Kai and Jasper splashing around, playing in the water. Rosie was curled up on a nearby lounge chair, snoozing beneath an umbrella.

"Zara!" Kai shouted, climbing out of the pool.

Rosie lifted her head, and then she ran over, sniffing at my ankles until I picked her up for a cuddle.

Jasper turned, and when he spotted me, he lit up. He climbed the stairs to greet us, and Zara cleared her throat, averting her gaze as if she couldn't quite believe her eyes. Hell, I didn't blame her. The man was hot.

His skin was bronzed from the sun, and he looked relaxed and happy. Water sluiced down the planes of his chest before disappearing into his swim trunks. I wanted to lick him.

Kai ran up to Zara, arms outstretched. Before I could even tell him to stop, Jasper called out, "Wait a second."

But Zara laughed, saying, "It's fine."

Kai wrapped his arms around Zara. She laughed, not caring that he was soaking wet. "I missed you too."

I rolled my eyes, laughing. And then my smile softened as Jasper leaned in to kiss my temple. "Hey, love."

"Hi. Having fun?"

"Always. Though…" He lowered his voice. While Kai and Zara were still catching up, he rasped in my ear, "We didn't get to finish what we started earlier."

"You mean the two times before that weren't enough?" I teased.

"With you, it's never enough."

"Later," I mouthed as we followed Kai and Zara into the house.

Some of the heat dialed down in his eyes, going from scorching to a simmer. It was still there, just…not as all-consuming.

Jasper and Kai showered off, and then we all headed back out to the patio where our new chef, Melanie, had set the table for dinner.

"This is delicious," Zara said, swirling some more pasta onto her fork. "And it's gluten free?"

"I know, right? Melanie is a wizard with gluten-free food, especially pasta."

When Jasper had initially suggested hiring a private chef, I'd been opposed. I wanted homemade meals and family time together. But I'd quickly realized I didn't have time to cook every night. Between our commute, school, the demands of my new position, it was too much. Now, we were eating healthy, delicious food that met Kai's dietary needs. And we enjoyed our meals as a family, and that was what was most important.

That night, as I fell asleep in Jasper's arms, I couldn't think of a time I'd been happier. I had a fulfilling job. A loving partner. And Kai was thriving. My birthday might be tomorrow, but I didn't need to blow out a candle to know that my every wish had already been granted.

CHAPTER TWENTY-NINE

JASPER

When Halle stirred, I pulled her even closer into my arms. "Happy birthday, love." I pressed my lips to her neck. The bare skin of her shoulder. Lower still.

"Mm," she hummed. She was still half asleep, but I sensed that her body was waking up.

I ran my hand up her stomach, over her breasts. Teasing her nipples as she started to writhe against me. Her ass was pressed against my hard-on, and I groaned.

"Again?" she teased.

Last night, we'd made love after Kai had gone to bed. Then again in the middle of the night. And now. I couldn't get enough of her, of my beautiful fiancée.

I took her hand in mine and held it up so I could see the ring on her finger. It was perfect, and it suited Halle.

"We'll have to be quick. Kai could come in at any minute," she whispered, reaching behind her to pull my mouth to hers for a kiss.

"I can do fast." I shifted, making sure she was lying on her back as I slid beneath the sheets. "But I'd rather take my time with you."

She pulled the sheets over her head so we were both cocooned beneath the covers. It was cozy and intimate, and with the sunlight just peeking through the window, it bathed her skin in this beautiful warmth, turning her curls more bronze. I took a moment to just admire her.

Her smile was soft, her eyes pinging between mine. "What?"

"You're beautiful." I kissed her hip. "Absolutely." Another kiss, this time on her stomach. "Beautiful."

She threaded her fingers through my hair. "I love you, Jasper."

"I love you too," I said. Sometimes I still couldn't believe that she was mine. That this was our life. "Now, spread those legs for me, love." I gave her thigh a little tap.

She hesitated a moment. "I'm a little sore."

"Let me kiss it better," I said, nudging her legs apart. "I'll be gentle."

She opened for me, letting me see her. "That's it, love. You're so good. Following my instructions." I kissed her mound, my cock growing painfully hard. "Trusting me to take care of you."

I kissed her clit, taking my time even as I ached to speed up.

"Always," she said on a sigh.

My dick was pressed against the mattress, providing some friction, but it wasn't enough. If anything, it was a tease. But I was determined to keep the focus on Halle. Making her feel good was my only goal at the moment.

"Mm." I lapped at her, and she reached down to link our fingers together. That was what I craved more than anything —the connection. "Feeling any better?"

"A little." Her breath was shaky.

"Should I keep going?" I asked, mostly in jest. There was no way I wanted to stop, not unless she asked me to. And based on her body's reaction, I didn't think that was going to be an issue.

She swallowed hard, loud enough for me to hear in the quiet of the morning. "Yes," she whispered.

"Yes, what?" I asked, her folds glistening with desire that also coated my mouth. *Fucking delicious.*

"Yes, please." It was practically a whine.

I chuckled, low and deep. This woman did something to me. I fisted my cock, giving it a few pumps. *Fuuuck.*

"Since you asked so nicely…" I ducked my head, licking and sucking, slowly taking her to the edge over and over.

When she writhed against the sheets, I banded my arm across her stomach, forcing her to stay still. I lapped at her, determined to get her off using only my mouth. She was close, so close. And I was patient. Determined. When it came to Halle, I could wait as long as it took.

She let out a hiss, her back arching off the bed. "Oh god. Right there. Yes."

She was gorgeous.

After that, she let out a string of unintelligible words as her body convulsed with pleasure. I kept at it until she started giggling.

"Okay." She placed her hands on my head. "Okay. Stop." She laughed. "You have to stop."

"Are you sure?" I arched a brow.

"Yes." She flopped onto the mattress, her limbs languid and body relaxed. "I can't take any more."

"I think you're wrong, but we'll stop…for now." I climbed up, brushing my lips against hers briefly before pushing out of bed.

"Mm. Wait." She grabbed my wrist, her eyes lingering on my naked form. "I think I changed my mind."

I chuckled. "Is that so?"

Before she could answer, she caught sight of the surprise I'd left on her nightstand.

"What's this?" Halle asked. It was a rectangular shape, wrapped in brown paper.

I crossed my arms over my chest and leaned against the wall. I was about to tell her to open it and find out, but *holy fuck.* The sheet slid down, baring her breasts to me.

"God. You are gorgeous," I said, forgetting she'd asked a question. "I am the luckiest man alive."

I went to her, crawling up the bed over her. She was taunting me with that gorgeous body of hers. I cupped her breasts. "Damn."

She laughed but then winced slightly.

"You okay?" I thought I'd been gentle, but maybe she was still tender from earlier.

"Probably just pre-period tenderness," she said, though she didn't sound convinced.

I frowned. "I thought you were supposed to get your period last week."

She'd had her IUD removed about six weeks ago, but it seemed way too soon to get pregnant. Though...with the number of times we'd had sex lately, maybe it wasn't that farfetched.

"I..." Her eyes widened, and she grabbed her phone from the nightstand, tapping frantically on the screen.

"Halle?" I asked.

"I, um..." She wouldn't look at me. "Think you can run to the drugstore before Kai wakes up?"

I pulled out my phone and placed an order for delivery. There was no way I was leaving her alone right now. "It'll be here in twenty minutes."

"Thank you." She sighed, sinking down on the edge of the bed.

"You okay?" I asked again, though this time, I was referring to her mental state.

We'd discussed this. We'd agreed that we wanted to expand our family. And while it had been tempting to wait until things felt more settled both at home and at the office, I hadn't wanted to. And Halle had agreed. That said, I was worried she might feel differently now that it might actually be happening.

Work was going well. I might not have been my grandparents' pick for CEO all those years ago, but I no longer questioned if I was up to the job. The board seemed to respect me more now that I'd taken charge. They might not like me as much, but I was done pretending this was a popularity contest. I was done trying to be my older brother or anyone else, because I was more than enough.

Halle had shown me that. Sumner had helped, as had Darla and my family—especially Sloan. I wasn't CEO by default; I was more than capable of effecting positive change in the company in this role. And even though I was no longer an SVP, it was important to still find ways to nurture my creative side, my desire to improve the guest experience.

Halle was rocking it as the new SVP, and the data proved it. More than that, employees loved her. She was perfect for the job, just as we'd all already known.

Kai was thriving at his new school, settling in and making friends. Adding a new baby to the mix would definitely be a challenge—for all of us. Even so, if Halle was pregnant, I would be ecstatic. But only if that's what she wanted too. Right now, I wasn't so sure.

"I'm—" She shook her head, unwilling to say more.

I went over and knelt before her, my heart aching for her. "Halle, love. Tell me what you're feeling."

"I'm…" She swallowed hard then glanced up at me with tears in her eyes. "Scared."

Fuck.

I cupped her cheek, realizing how vulnerable she seemed in that moment. "Why?"

"What if the test is negative?" she asked, and something in my chest eased. She wasn't scared of the idea that she might be pregnant. She *wanted* to be pregnant, and she was scared to get her hopes up.

"If it is—" I took her hand in mine, rubbing my thumb across the back "—then we'll just have to keep trying." I waggled my eyebrows.

She laughed, rolling her eyes. It might be silly, but it had had its intended effect.

"Either way—" I kissed her forehead "—it's all good, right?"

She considered it a moment then nodded. "It's all good."

I sat beside her on the bed, pulling her into my arms. "If we have more kids, great. If not, I'm perfectly happy with our family as it is now."

"I know," she said. "I just know how much you'd love to be a dad."

"I'm already a dad," I said, and I meant it. Kai might not be my biological child, but he was my son. And I felt honored to be a part of his life.

"I didn't..." She blew out a breath. "I'm sorry. That came out all wrong."

I brought her hand to my mouth for a kiss. "I know what you meant. Sometimes I hate that I missed out on so much of Kai's life, and I'd love to experience everything with you."

She nodded, and my phone pinged with an alert from the delivery driver. They'd arrive in five minutes, so I texted Tim from Hudson Security to let him know to expect it.

"Do you want to open your gift?" I asked, determined to ground us in the present instead of spinning out with thoughts of the future.

Right now, we were together, and that was enough. More than enough.

Besides, today was supposed to be about Halle. We were celebrating her birthday, and I'd wanted to give Halle her present while it was still just the two of us.

"You've already given me so much." Halle's lips were a tender caress against my jawline.

"I love to spoil you."

She reached for the gift, carefully tearing away the brown wrapping paper. When she saw what was inside, she gasped.

"Oh my god, Jasper." Her attention bounced to me, then back to it. "Seriously?"

I nodded, smiling the entire time. I loved seeing how she lit up as she opened it.

She peeled off the rest of the paper, revealing the painting in its entirety. "How? Dimitri told me it had sold." She ran her fingers along the edge of the frame, her expression full of longing and awe.

"It did." I grinned, knowing how disappointed she'd been when she'd tried to purchase it for our home. "To me."

"What?" she gasped. "When?"

"I purchased it the day we went art shopping for the Golden Key Penthouse and the presidential suite."

She blinked a few times. "Are you serious? All this time, you had it?"

"You want to see the receipt?" I teased, though there was no way in hell I was letting her see how much I'd paid. She'd try to return it.

She shook her head. "I'm not sure I want to think about how much it cost."

"Then don't." I wrapped my arm around her shoulder. "It's a gift. It's meant to be enjoyed."

"Oh, I will definitely enjoy it," she said, holding it in her lap. "Thank you." She turned to kiss me. "I love it."

"I'm glad," I said, just as my phone pinged again. "I'll be right back."

I kissed her temple and then dashed down the stairs to grab the tests from Tim. When I returned to our bedroom, Halle was still sitting on the edge of the bed where I'd left her.

I held up the paper bag, grateful for the discreet packaging. "You ready to do this?"

She nodded. "I need to know."

I'd figured as much, and it was a relief. But still... I couldn't deny that I was nervous. What if it was negative? What if it was positive? My heart started racing at the possibilities.

I leaned my hip against the sink, reading the instructions while she took the test. She returned and placed it on the counter before washing her hands. I set a timer, and then I pulled her into my arms while we waited.

I rested my chin on the top of Halle's head, and we just... fit. My eyes fluttered closed, and the longer we stood there, the more settled I felt. The more aware I became of her body. The feel of her chest pressed to mine, our hips kissing. The way it felt to hold her in my arms—with tenderness and reverence. The sense of peace that washed over me.

When the timer went off a few minutes later, she jolted. I tried to remind myself that either way, the result didn't matter. If we were pregnant, I'd be thrilled. And if it hadn't happened this time, we'd try again. There were no downsides.

"Do you want to look?" I asked.

She peered up at me. "Can you?"

I laughed. "Together?"

She nodded.

"Okay." I took a deep breath. "No matter what, you know I love you, right?"

"Yes." She grinned. "Of course I do."

"One. Two." We turned together. "Three."

When I stared down at the test sitting on the counter, I still couldn't believe the result. I looked at Halle, trying to temper my reaction. I wanted her to feel supported and loved, regardless of the outcome.

She threw herself into my arms, and it was only then that I allowed myself to feel everything I'd been holding back. Joy. Excitement. Hope. And, most of all, love.

As I held Halle, our child growing inside her, I felt like the luckiest man alive. It wasn't about running my grandparents' company or the new house. It was about us. About Kai and Rosie. About this new life we'd created—together. Family traditions and rituals.

My gran had always said that family was the greatest blessing you could receive. And she'd been right, of course. Finding someone who saw me for who I really was, who loved me for me, was the greatest gift of all. And for the first time since my grandparents' deaths, I felt whole again, content. Not because I'd needed someone to fill the hole they'd left, but because I knew what it meant to love and be loved in return. This life, this family, was everything I'd always wanted.

Acknowledgements

I think one of the biggest compliments a reader paid me about this series was when she told me that she didn't normally like the billionaire trope, but she loved my billionaires because they had heart.

Of all the characters in the Tempt Series, Jasper might be the one with the biggest, most tender heart. And it was fun to explore his challenges and his aspirations. He was such a sweetheart, and I loved spending time with him and Halle.

And Halle—the single mom who will do everything for her son. I loved seeing her let down her guard to let Jasper in. To realize that she deserved a partner who valued her worth and adored her son.

Sometimes we have to be with the wrong people to find the right one. And while heartbreak isn't fun, we shouldn't harden our hearts to love.

This could be the end of the Tempt Series, though obviously, I've left the door open for another book. I just loved the idea of a secret sibling that no one saw coming.

I'm sad to leave this family behind (at least, for now), but I'm also SUPER excited about my next series which is based around the Hollywood Hawks—LA's pro hockey team.

Thank you for going on this journey with me. I've been blown away by the response to the entire Tempt Series. And I am so so happy that so many of you love these characters as much as I do!

A HUGE thank you to all the readers who share your love for my stories. I could not do this without you.

Nor could I do this without my incredible team. Thank

you to Angela for always being encouraging and supportive. For helping me with all the details, so I can focus on the big picture.

A huge thank you to my beta readers. Thank you for making me a stronger writer, for offering your unique insight and advice. You each bring something different to the table, and I'm always amazed and impressed by your suggestions. I'm so incredibly honored to have you on my team!

Thank you, Jade. You make me a stronger writer, and you challenge me on pacing. You are so clever and always provide great insight. I'm so grateful for your friendship, and our long chats! This story wouldn't be the same without you. Thank you for reading a million different versions of this story and always providing such valuable suggestions.

A huge thank you to Kristen for being such an amazing friend. I value your judgment and honesty, and I so appreciate your support. We've been through so much together, and I treasure your friendship and advice. Seriously, I cannot thank you enough for all that you do. You are my "hype girl." You always pump me up and make me feel fabulous.

Beth, thank you so much for your encouragement and support. I'm so delighted that we reconnected after all these years! And I always have so much fun with you. I'm not sure I've ever had a friend who makes me laugh as much as you do.

Thank you to Ellen, as always. Thank you for sharing your incredible eye for detail. Your comments are always priceless, and this book was no exception! I couldn't do it without you. And gah, your edit is STUNNING.

To my editor, Lisa with Silently Correcting Your Grammar. I so appreciate your attention to detail, and your patience with my questions. You always go above and beyond and this time was no exception.

A huge shout out to all my fellow authors. Sometimes this job can feel so solitary, but I know you're all out there. And we're all cheering each other on.

A big thank you to the Hartley's Hustlers and my Sweetharts. You rock! I cannot possibly tell you how much your support means to me! I appreciate everything you do to promote my books and to encourage me throughout my writing journey.

Thank you to my husband for always encouraging me. For always supporting my dreams and believing in me. You are better than any book boyfriend I could ever imagine. You constantly build me up, and I couldn't ask for a better partner.

And to my daughter, for always putting a smile on my face. You are spirited and independent, and I wouldn't have it any other way. Dream big, my darling.

Thank you to my parents for always being so encouraging. For reading my books. For being my biggest fans!

And to my mother-in-law, who is always cheering me on and lending a willing ear to listen to my writing adventures.

Dear reader, if this list of people shows you anything, it's that dreams are often the effort of many. I'm grateful to have such an awesome team. And I'm honored that you've taken the time to read my words.

ABOUT THE AUTHOR

Jenna Hartley is *USA Today* bestselling author who writes feel-good forbidden romance, much like her own real-life love story. She's known for writing strong women and swoon-worthy men, as well as blending panty-melting and heart-warming moments.

When she's not reading or writing romance, Jenna can be found tending to her growing indoor plant collection (pun intended), organizing, and hiking. She lives in Texas with her family and loves nothing more than a good book and good chocolate, except a dance party with her daughter.

www.authorjennahartley.com

<u>Love in LA Series</u>
Inevitable
Unexpected
Irresistible
Undeniable
Unpredictable
Irreplaceable

<u>Alondra Valley Series</u>
Feels Like Love
Love Like No Other
A Love Like That

<u>Tempt Series</u>
Temptation
Reputation
Redemption
The Exception
Discretion

<u>Hawks Series</u>
A hockey series coming 2026!

For the most current list of Jenna's titles, please visit her website www.authorjennahartley.com.

Or scan the QR code on the following page to be taken to her author page on Amazon.com